A PIRATE'S SONG

†

Chane van der Walt

1

Dedication

This book is dedicated to the love of my life, Marco Barbosa, who has always supported and encouraged me to follow my dreams.

"When I saw you
I fell in love
and you smiled
because you knew"

WILLIAM SHAKESPEARE

Prologue
Evangeline

I sat beneath the light of the full moon. The night was eerie as a thick fog rolled into the coast, coating the town in a layer of white.   I pressed my knees tightly against my chest and looked down at the water that lapped at the rocks beneath me. My bare feet brushed over the coral and shells that stuck to the surface of the ragged boulders as I hummed along to an old tune. Drunken people stumbled out of a bar nearby. Their voices were slurred. Glass shattered and laughter rumbled in the air.

The water below seemed to call to me when I stared into its depths. I stopped humming and crept closer to the edge of the rocks. I stuck my foot out to dip my toes into the calm lap of water. I gasped as the cold liquid caressed my warm foot and tightened my grip on the boulders.

My foot began to shimmer a slight silver and my breath caught in my throat as I scurried away from the edge while wrenching my foot out of the water. Silver scales clad the flesh on my foot and I watched as they slowly began to disappear until only soft, pale skin remained.

My hand instinctively shot up to grip the piece of metal that dangled around my throat. It was a charm made of silver. It was delicate and small. The shape was that of an anchor and seemed innocent enough. I glanced down at the charm that could never be removed from my neck before I got up in a hurry and turned my back on the sea.

A harsh gust of wind whipped past me and I froze. I turned to look back at the black waters of the night. A shadow was creeping into the coast and from the looks of it, it was a ship with black sails.

One of the drunken men from the bar, looked out onto the ocean and squinted. He took a swig of his whiskey and stumbled down to the docks to get a closer look while I stood frozen in place. At the edge of the docks he paused. He loosened his grip on the bottle causing it to shatter at his feet. He sobered up quickly.

"Pirates" he muttered under his breath as he stared at the approaching ship in horror then turned to make a run for it.

"Pirates!" he cried out and bells began ringing from the towers above. I gripped at the material of my white gown with sweaty palms and took a shaky step back as a black pirate's flag came into view.

The town's people began to gather at the edge of the water behind me with pitch forks and torches. The ship pierced the fog and I could see a man standing on its bow. The man wore an old brown coat and had a black pirate's hat on top of his head. His eyes roamed over the shore and eventually landed on me. The moment our eyes locked, a chill shot down my spine. His gold gaze was enough to see straight into my soul as it trapped me in place.

"Captain, cannons a yonder!" someone onboard the ship bellowed and the man turned his attention away from me long enough for me to slip away. I hurriedly turned on my heels and maneuvered my way back across the rocks.

The Captain noticed me retreating and yelled at his crew "Dock the ship!"

I forced my way through the crowd and ran in the opposite direction. I headed for the edge of the beach where the buildings began.

"Tonight, we pillage and feast for tomorrow we sail for the Nest!" the men onboard the ship cheered and laughed at their Captain's words and I glanced back towards the water. The ship had docked and men were jumping down from its deck to slaughter the town's people with rusty old, swords. The Captain met my eyes and I struggled to catch my breath before turning to run down the cobble stone street. I didn't dare loosen my grip on my dress for fear of falling as I raced for an escape.

A man who was carrying a torch slammed into me and I stumbled over my feet as he disappeared down the street. I gasped and dared to look back when the sound of a man crying out in agony pierced the air. The Captain was right behind me and had cut down the man who ran into me. His eyes scared me. They cut deep into my very being as he stalked down the street. He was hunting me like I was his prey.

I hurriedly glanced from left to right and noticed a small alleyway off to one side. I scraped the material of my dress together and ran for the alley. I ducked into it and scurried past a few people until I reached a backdoor that led to an inn.

I hurried into it but not before looking back to see if the man was still following me. A trail of blood seemed to follow him as he move but his eyes were locked solely on my form. I hurried past the bar where a waitress was shuffling scared women and children into a room hidden beneath the bar through a trap door.

I frantically ran up the stairs and to the third floor while tripping every few steps.

"There be no point in running" his voice was gruff and husky. It was deep but strained as it spoke from a floor beneath me. I panted as I took a sharp left and scurried down the hall to an open door near the end of it. I slammed the door shut behind me and locked it, searching desperately for a way out. In my frantic state I'd managed to climb three floors, trapping myself high above the town. There was a balcony opposite the door and a bed was sat next to it with the white curtains fluttering in the sea breeze.

For a moment, I forgot what was happening as I watched the ocean stretch out onto the horizon but I was brought back to reality by the handle on the door rattling behind me. I turned sharply to face the door and started slowly backing away from it.

"Why must ye be so difficult?" the man asked through the door after giving off a long sigh. Everything went silent. The door stopped rattling and I thought he'd given up when suddenly the door burst open to reveal the man with his foot raised. I sucked in a breath of air and turned to make a run for the balcony but stopped at the railing to grasp it. I looked down at the town in chaos but there was something oddly calming about the discord.

I contemplated jumping and raised my foot but a warm chest pressed up against my back stopped me dead in my tracks as a strong arm snaked its way around my waist.

"Don't be rash, love" his voice whispered in my ear causing goosebumps to form on my exposed arms. I gripped the railing tighter and expected him to drag me back to the bed. I expected him to rape me as I squeezed my eyes shut and swallowed hard in anticipation of what was to come. His lips brushed over the shell of my ear and sent tingles down the back of my spine.

"Sing to me" he uttered and my eyes shot open. They were wide as I stared out onto the ocean. He unwrapped his arm from around me and started slowly backing away. His boots thudded against the floor as he left me standing on the balcony. The sound of a chair scraping across the wood reached my ears and I dared to turn my head to look back at him.

He used it to jam the door shut then shrugged off his jacket and started unbuttoning his brown coat, leaving him in a white shirt that he quickly tugged over his head to reveal his naked torso.

He wasn't big but he wasn't exactly skinny either.

He tugged off his boots. He wore a pair of black trousers as he slumped down on the edge of the bed and rubbed at the stubble covering his jaw.

My feet began to move on their own accord as I stepped back into the room. I watched him lay down among the white pillows and sheets. He closed his eyes and folded his hands over his stomach while I paused.

"Well? I be waiting" he said when I didn't start singing and turned onto his side so that his back was to me. I glanced around the room for a second chair but there was none so I decided to sit down on the foot of the bed. I faced him to make sure that he didn't try anything.

I was still in shock as I watched him. His chest slowly rose and fell as he breathed. There he was, a pirate Captain with all the power in the world to do what he wished and yet his only requested was that I sing to him. I opened my mouth but my voice caught in my throat as I tried to think of a song that he might like. He cracked open his eyes to look at me. His gold orbs peered into my mismatched ones as he expectantly waited.

"W-Where can we go with the black jack jailor?" I began but at a much slower pace than the original and in a much smaller voice than usual. The corner of his lips twitched and for a moment, I could've swore that I saw the hint of a smile but as soon as it was there, it was gone. He closed his eyes and listened to my tune as I looked towards the mirror that was mounted on the wall opposite me.

My reflection stared back at me. It was the reflection of a nineteen-year-old girl with long, ivory hair that was as white as snow and two different color eyes. One eye was crystal blue while the other was a stormy gray. I Kept singing, repeating the song as I gripped my necklace in hand. I listening to the screams of men and women outside the inn as they mixed together with my song.

I finished the tune and looked down at the sleeping pirate in the bed beside me then looked towards the door where the chair held it tightly shut. I glanced at his coat where a dagger and sword were placed on top of it. My hand twitched and I contemplated using them to kill him in his sleep but when my gaze fell onto him, I found that he was harmless.

I stood from the bed and he stirred slightly as I picked his shirt up from the ground. It smelt of sea salt and sweat. I folded it and placed it down beside his coat and weapons before returning to the bed. This time, I laid down beside him on the mattress. I faced him but laid a fair distance away as I glanced at his face.

He had long, brown hair that was tied up into a messy bun as a deadly scar ran down the left side of his face and gold hung from his ears. Dangling around his neck was a shark tooth necklace and decorating his fingers were various rings that were made of silver and gold. I remembered thinking that his face was something pleasant to look at before I drifted off to sleep.

Chapter One

I stirred as the morning light crept into the room and shone onto my face. I squeezed my eyes tightly shut and tried to roll over to escape the sharp rays but instead I collided with something solid.

My eyes shot open and I found the face of the pirate staring back at me.

His arm was snaked around my waist when I tried to escape, preventing me from falling off the bed.

"Calm down, love. I won't hurt ye" he reassured me and slowly let go of my waist to roll over onto his back. He sat up on the edge of the bed so that his back was to me and stretched out his aching muscles.

His skin was dark. It was burnt from the sun and his back was covered in markings. I wanted to reach out and touch them but I restrained myself and sat up on the bed. He looked back at me from over his shoulder and for a moment the sun reflected off his golden eyes which made it seem as if they were glowing.

He stood and started getting dressed. He began with his boots then tugged his shirt over his head. He buttoned up his coat and strapped his weapons to his belt before he stuck his Captain's hat on top of his head.

"It be time to go" he announced and started heading for the door. I followed his movements with my gaze and watched as he dragged the chair that was jamming the door aside. He opened it then turned to me expectantly. I looked down at myself. I was wearing a thin, sheer dress that would look like a sleeping gown to most women of much higher status. It dipped low in between my breasts and was fastened around the waist with two strips of thin material.

"My crew be waiting" he said and it was then that I realized what he meant. He wanted me to go with them. My mouth dried and my eyes widened as I looked up at him. The inn was empty and all was silent as he waited for my response.

"You wish for me to go with you?" I questioned after a moment's pause. I wanted to protest but I didn't want to test his patience so I decided to play it safe and tread a much lighter path of conversation. He shifted his stands. He moved his weight from one leg to the other "I be in need of a singer and ye shall do" with that he turned on his heels and disappeared down the hall. I looked at the balcony beside the bed and glanced at my reflection in the mirror.

My hair was a tangled mess and my face was free of makeup. I looked tired and drained but I decided to follow the man nonetheless. I knew that if I didn't then he'd most likely hunt me down and not be so generous next time. I hurried down the hall and to his side.

"Me? But Sir, I'm sure there are other more beautiful women to take" the pirate did little in response to my words and thudded his way down the stairs. The boots he tugged on earlier sounded like heavy stomps on the thin wood as he moved. I clutched my dress skirt in hand and scurried after him, out the door we entered the night before and past the corpses of various men.

"There's a brothel just up ahead. The men speak of a woman with gold hair who knows how to properly please a man" I tried again to get him to reconsider. At the end of the alleyway he sharply turned causing me to stumble into his hard chest before he spoke up in a stern tone.

"I don't want a whore" he said. He bit out the word *whore* and grabbed hold of my wrist to steady me. His grip tightened when I looked up into his golden gaze "I want *you*" for any woman it would've made quite the romantic moment but for me it had the opposite effect.

He let go of my wrist and stormed off. He shifted his Captain's hat as he walked. I glanced in the opposite direction. I once again contemplated whether it would benefit me to run but I knew he would find me eventually and when he did, it wouldn't be pretty. I followed him. We headed for the docks as the sun rose up above the horizon and the streets were coated in a layer of morning dew.

"If I may ask, Sir, why?" I was curious about his intentions and what attracted him to me. *Perhaps it was because I was on the rocks the night before or because of my attire? Was it my exposed breasts?* I stepped around a man who was lying in a pool of blood and felt the warm liquid stain my feet.

"It's because of the way ye look" was his reply. I glanced down at my breasts and nodded but he noticed. He once again turned towards me with a sharp and deadly look in his eyes "Not ye body, love. Ye eyes" his eyes pierced mine and I felt my heart stop in my chest for a moment as I watched his features change from calm to irritated at the sound of laughter and an approaching voice that yelled out above the rest.

"That's where Captain went. Found himself a woman for the night!" his head turned in the direction of the voice and I began to fear for the man who's spoken. I trailed after the pirate Captain until we reached the docks where a total of fifteen men were waiting for us, including one who wore a similar hat to the Captain.

"Is she ready?" the Captain asked the man in the hat and he nodded. He reached out to place his palm flat against the ship's side as if brushing a horse's neck "Aye Captain, that she is" the Captain didn't say a word as he boarded the ship and shot a look at the man who I assumed to be the second in command.

The man instantly knew what his Captain wished for him to do and before I knew it, I was being thrown over his shoulder.

"Up ye go, lass" he said in a thick Irish accent as I screeched and grabbed hold of the fabric of his shirt. The first mate with the brown hat grabbed onto a piece of rope from the ship and began scaling its side.

"Don't look down, miss" just as he said it, I looked down at the smiling and grinning faces of his crewmates.

I yelped when I was thrown onto the ship's deck and landed in a thud. I groaned and shot a glare at the second in command from my place on the deck "Sorry about that, lassie" I could tell it wasn't a sincere apology but I let it go and tried standing, only for the man to toss me back over his shoulder like a ragdoll.

"Let me go!" I demanded as the rest of the crew crawled their way onto the ship's deck. The Captain stood at the head of it. He watched as I kicked and thrashed in the man's grasp.

"I said, let go!" I snapped to the amusement of a few crew members. They laughed and one even nudged his friend to say, "She's a feisty one" his friend snickered and nodded in agreement "Aye, she be the Captain's type" I shot a glare in the snickering pair's direction as the man carrying me turned to face his Captain which meant that he was giving him a full view of my rear.

"What will it be, Captain? The cells?" he asked. He was expecting to hear the same thing he'd heard many times before but instead of that, the Captain turned his back to us and said in a low tone "Take her to my chambers" the crew went silent in response to the Captain's orders. None of them were expecting to hear that and froze

11

for a minute until the Captain shot them a look and the man carrying me nodded.

"As ye wish, Captain" he then turned and started towards the door that led down to the Captain's quarters at the back of the ship. I stared at the Captain's back as we thudded down the stairs and into the room below. I hit my head on the door and the man carrying me chuckled lowly as if it brought him joy.

"Let me go right now or I swear, I'll cut off your fingers and feed them to the fish!" I bit out just as I was flung onto a large mattress. I gasped and hurried to sit up as the man grinned down at me.

He raised his hand, wiggled his fingers and shot me a crazed look "Ye can go ahead and try, lassie" I crawled back onto the mattress until my back was pressed against the wall behind me and the man burst out laughing. He then turned and proceeded to head above deck. I tilted my head to look up at the wooden floorboards as a pair of heavy feet moved across them followed by a familiar voice.

"Ready the sails!" the Captain called and the men cheered. I waited until I felt the ship jerk and the wind start to catch in the sails before relaxing and taking in the room around me.

There was a small nightside table beside the bed and a desk pressed up against the opposite wall with a map of the world above it. There was a red Persian rug in the middle of the room with an armchair pushed into the far corner beside a dresser. A bathroom sat off to the side. I noticed something on the nightstand and started crawling towards it. It was a book with a brown cover that read 'A map of the seven treasures' I reached out to trace my fingers across the words but retracted my hand due to a sudden voice.

"Can ye read?" I turned to face the Captain and questioned whether it would be a good idea to answer truthfully or not. I decided that I needed to stay useful to him in order to survive.

"Yes" I said as I followed the Captain's movements. He strode over to his dresser and opened the top drawer. He pulled a red dress from it and placed it on the desk chair beside the dresser.

"Get dressed" he ordered while taking a seat in the armchair. I looked at the fabric then at him and wondered whether he was going to give me some privacy but he didn't move.

I got up from the bed and made my way to the dress. I untied mine and allowed it to drop down to the floor so that I was stood naked with my back to the Captain. It was a short red dress with a

12

brown corset middle. I tugged the material over my head and tried tying the corset but I couldn't reach it.

The sound of a chair shifting caused my back to stiffen as he started tying the corset for me. His breath tickled my neck and his hands worked quickly. They worked skillfully as if he'd tied and loosened many corsets in his days.

"I need ye help" he began in a much gentler tone than before when he spoke to his crew. He let out a long, exaggerated breath and finished tying the corset.

"I need ye to read that book for me so that I can find them treasures" he explained. He nodded in the direction of the book that I'd taken an interest in earlier. I turned to look at it and the dress moved along with me. I started towards the book, picked it up and turned it over and over again in my grasp.

"Is this why you took me?" I asked. I was referring to the novel as being the reason why I was onboard the ship in the first place. The Captain stayed silent for a few moments until I looked up at him and found him striding across the room towards me. He reached out to take the book from my hands as his eyes locked onto mine.

"Ney" he began. He blinked then looked down at the book in his hands. He flicked through it and stopped on a page that had a hand drawn map scribble onto the paper. He slowly traced his index finger along the lines but paused to look up at me.

"I took ye for me" he slammed the book shut and tossed it onto the nightside table with a loud thud that made me jump. He closed the distance between us until he was standing a hair's width away. I staggered back on instinct but met with the side of the bed that trapped me in place.

He reached a hand out and ran the back of his knuckles along my cheek bone. Tingles shot through my skin at the gentle contact and my eyes began to droop in response to his touch. His large palm cupped the side of my face and I instinctively leaned into it as his eyes trailed over my features from my small button nose to my plump, pink lips.

"Ye better start reading" he suddenly said while dropping his hand back to his side. His relaxed posture shifted to that of a tense one and he backed away from me. He then thudded his way back towards the stairs and disappeared onto the main deck. He left me standing there breathless and alone.

I glanced down at the book and slumped down onto the edge of the bed. My legs felt like jelly and my stomach fluttered as I struggled to catch my breath.

After a while, I reached for the book and started reading. I eventually fell asleep among the pillows and bed sheets.

Something heavy slammed down on the nightside table beside me and I jerked awake from the sudden sound which was followed by a loud, bellowing laughter. The book I was reading tumbled to the floor as my chest rose and fell in rapid sync.

"Didn't mean to startle ye, lass" a familiar Irish accent said from beside me and I instantly knew who it was.

I turned to look up at the man wearing a brown pirate's hat. He chuckled and held onto his stomach until he eventually stopped and acknowledged my glare.

"Captain said to bring ye dinner" he explained and motioned to the nightstand where a wooden tray sat. On top of it was a piece of bread and what looked like a stew of vegetables that didn't appear at all appetizing. He breathed a laugh and turned to leave but paused to glance back at me.

"Oh and Captain wants to see ye above deck" with that he was gone and I noticed that candles were lit inside the room to give off some form of light.

I threw my legs over the side of the bed and reached for the book. I closed it and neatly placed it on the bed beside me before I reached for the tray. The bread was stale and the stew was disgusting but I was starving from not having eaten anything in a long time so I hurriedly and unattractively scarfed it down. I gulped down a cup of water and ran the back of my hand across my lips.

I stood up from the edge of the bed and headed for the stairs where a skinny man with rotten teeth and an eye patch jumped up out of nowhere, scaring me. I shrieked and shrunk back. I nearly tumbled down the stairs as a chorus of laughter echoed throughout the night. Another pirate stepped up and grabbed the one-eyed man by the shoulder.

"Come, Snaggletooth. Leave the lady alone" they staggered off and I reached up to grip my chest as a few men nearby chugged down cups of rum and wine. I tentatively stepped out onto the deck and had to do a turn to survey my surroundings. I was trapped in the middle of the ocean with nothing but the open sea on all sides. The water stretched out onto the horizon.

My body quivered and I felt my legs weaken as I looked upon the ocean. It called to me like an enchanting curse. My feet started moving on their own accord. They carried me towards the bow where the figurehead was placed. My mind went blank with nothing but the water in mind as I ascended the steps and reached out to grip the ship's railing. My leg raised as I tried to step out onto the figurehead but a strong hand grabbed hold of my shoulder and pulled me back. It pulled me out of my daze.

I looked up at my savior to find a young man who was dressed in dirty, brown clothes. He was taller than me but he was around my age with blonde curls and a crooked nose "The Captain is that way, miss" he directed while jerking his head in the opposite direction as the to where two men were placed high above the rest of the ship. They were hunched over something and they were arguing. I looked at the man and swallowed hard.

"R-Right" I said as I headed towards the stern but paused to look back at him "Thank you" with that I descended the steps and shook my head as an attempt to clear my mind. I tried my best not to look at the water as I climbed the ladder that led to the ship's stern. I reached the highest deck and approached the two men.

"You wanted to see me?" I asked in a small tone that caught the attention of the Captain and his first mate. They looked up at me simultaneously and I instantly felt a pressure in my chest as I took a small step back. The Captain looked at his second in command and jerked his head as a signal for the man to leave. He left without a word, leaving the Captain and I alone beneath the stars.

"What did ye find?" he questioned me. He placed his palms down on the surface of a table that looked to be connected to the ship. There was a large map on it and a compass that sat close to the Captain's hands.

I knew that he was talking about the book and the seven treasures so I swallowed hard and threw my head back to look up at the small lights in the black sky. I followed them until I turned a hundred-and-eighty degrees and looked towards the horizon.

"The first treasure, lies towards the East where two mouths meet and a light is cast upon it" I repeated the words from the book

15

and turned to look back at the Captain. His facial expression didn't change as he watched me then suddenly turned to face the crew.

"Change course, East!" he snapped and the crew sprang to life. Men climbed up the sides of the sails and some loosened ropes "Aye, aye, Captain!" they bellowed and the ship jerked. I stumbled as it changed course and I found myself falling into the Captain's arms.

He managed to catch me as the ship steadied itself and pressed my back flat against his chest. I stiffened in response to his touch and gripped his arms through the material of his coat.

"Captain Caleb, Sir" the second in command said as he reappeared on the stern. I wrenched myself from Caleb's arms and scurried off to the side to place some distance between us. A murderous look flashed in his golden eyes as he turned to his right-hand man.

"What?" he demanded and the man shrank back in fear. Caleb waited impatiently for him to speak up and when he finally did, his Captain's nostrils flared in anger "Why have we changed course?" Caleb glanced over the man then started towards him with a slow and threatening stride. He resembled a panther stalking its prey as he moved. I watched his posture relax slightly when he reached the man wearing a brown pirate's hat and glanced at the thing on top of his head.

"Ye hat" the Captain began, motioning to it. The pirate tilted his head back and reached for his hat. He placed his palm flat against the top of it "What about it, Captain?" Caleb straightened out his shoulders and dropped his arm back to his side before turning to look back at me.

"Give it to her" the man's breath caught in his throat and the crew went dead silent as everyone placed their attention on the conversation between their Captain and his first mate. The man who for some reason enjoyed torturing me glanced at me then back at his Captain who was returning to the map.

"But Captain-." he tried to argue but Caleb left little room for argument. He rounded on his first mate and snapped in a loud tone that held a hidden roar beneath its surface "Now!" I stood frozen in place as the second in command scurried across the deck towards me and placed the hat on top of my head. I half expected him to toss me overboard from the anger in his eyes but he didn't. Once the hat was on top of my head, he left the stern and the crew went back to their sniveling.

"Why-?" I began but was cut off by Caleb who didn't bother looking up from the map "Ye are of more use to me" I reached for the hat and pressed down on the top of it to get it to more comfortably fit my head. The worn out and dark material of it stood out against my white hair.

I allowed my feet to glide across the wooden flooring until I was stood at the very back of the ship, looking out onto the horizon with the wind whipping through my hair. I raised my hand to grip the necklace that dangling around my neck.

In just a few days my life had gone from being an orphan to somehow becoming the first mate of a pirate Captain and sailing the across the seas to find seven treasures.

Chapter Two

I was ordered back below deck and there I sat reading as much as I possibly could about the first treasure until Caleb came down the stairs. He started stripping once his feet hit the floor of the room. He threw his clothes in every direction with little care in the world.

He was drunk and reeked of rum as he stumbled across the floor to the nightside table. He forced open the top drawer and grabbed a silver heart locket in his hand. He curled his fist tightly around it and collapsed on the bed beside me.

I lowered the book and placed it on the sheets next to me "Sing" came the word in a low grumble. It was followed by heavy breathing as he blinked up at the ceiling. I put some more distance between us and leaned back against the wall. I tilted my head to look up at the cracks between the floor boards where the stars were glistening in the sky.

"Up and down the shore again, let the waters foam, Pat Long we've ventured on the open sea. Now we're safe at home, Pat" I sang while thinking back to the various songs I'd heard over the years that I spent waiting at the bar where sailors used to drink to the early hours in the morning.

Caleb closed his eyes and listened to me sing well into the night until he finally fell asleep. I stayed up most of the night reading as much as I could and a few hours before dawn I was just about to fall asleep with the book in my lap when Caleb stirred beside me.

"M-Mary" he muttered in his sleep and began thrashing. I jolted upright and looked down at the struggling man. It looked like he was trying to get free of something. His head rolled from side to side as he continued to repeat the name that so desperately clung to his lips.

"Mary!" he yelled and started thrashing more violently. I made a split-second decision and threw one leg over him so that I was straddling his waist. I reached for his shoulders and pinned him down on the mattress.

"Caleb!" I called out to him but it was no use. He tried shoving me back but I grabbed hold of his arms and tried desperately to pin them down beside him.

"Caleb, wake up!" I cried while cupping his face in my hands and his eyes shot open to look up at me. His entire body stiffened at my close proximity.

My face was mere inches away from his.

His arms fell limp at his sides and his breathing deepened as he tried to catch his breath. I slowly began to sit back on top of him. I let my hands slide down to grip his shoulders as his hand unclenched around the silver necklace that he'd been clinging to. The metal cluttered to the floor and caught my attention.

It was a locket but a familiar heart shaped one with fine detailing. It sprang open when it came in contact with the floor to reveal a set of gears and mechanisms inside. A tune began playing. It was a soft and gentle tune but it stopped half way as the gears began to jam.

"That song" I whispered. I remembered it from somewhere but I couldn't place my finger on it. I leaned down and reached for the locket but Caleb shoved me off him and got up. He stuffed the locket into the pocket of his pants as I fell back onto the soft material of the bed and gasped from the sudden movement.

"Where did you get that locket?" I breathlessly asked while staring at his back as he sat perched on the edge of the bed. I pushed myself up onto my elbows while I waited for his response. There was something odd about the locket and the way he acted about it. He didn't respond and instead ran a hand across his features. I shot up to grab hold of his shoulder.

"Answer me" I demanded but he wrenched his shoulder out of my grasp and stood up from the bed. He reached for his boots and tugged them on one by one. I stood causing the book of treasures to fall to the floor. I glanced down at it as Caleb shrugged his coat on over his shoulders and started towards the stairs.

"Wait!" I called and he froze but refused to look back at me as he waited for me to speak. I took a step towards him and mustered up enough courage to speak.

"You can either tell me what that locket means to you or I'll refuse to help you find the seven treasures" Caleb's back muscles shifted through the material of his coat and his boots thudded when he slowly turned to face me. His jaw was set and his hands balled into fists at his sides. There was no going back so I straightened my shoulders and held my head high. He crossed the room in a few steps and took a stand in front of me.

"Ye really want to know?" he asked. His eyes searching mine for a trace of uncertainty but he found none as I slowly nodded in response. He dug his hand into the pocket of his trousers and pulled out the locket. He held it up between us for me to see.

"This trinket used to belong to the woman I loved before she was taken from me by the sea" he said while he turned the locket in his hand before he crushed it in his fist and stuffed it back into the pocket of his black pants. He then turned and stalked his way above deck. I was left alone to maul over what he told me.

I found myself contemplating whether it was possible for a pirate to love something but from the crazed look in his eyes when he spoke about her, it was very clear that they could.

I noticed a pair of woman's boots that were placed off to the side. They were made of brown leather and matched my dress with a white trim on them. I went over and tried to tug them onto my feet. They were a size too big but I managed to walk in them as I made the bed and tossed the book on top of it.

I noticed the sun rising through a porthole in the side of the ship and reached for my pirate's hat before I decided to head above deck. The crew were hard at work. Some were scrubbing the deck while others manned the sails.

They bowed their heads in respect as I passed them on my way to the back of the ship where Captain Caleb was perched. He looked out onto the sea while steering his vessel. I Climbed the stairs and gripped the railings tightly as the ship rocked from the waves. I kept my head down for fear of seeing and being drawn to the open ocean.

My feet moved once the ship stilled and carried me over to the map that was fastened to the table on the ship's stern. I placed my palms flat against the wood and studied the map but there was nothing but random lines. I turned to face Caleb.

"Where are we?" I asked but got no reply as he brooded and tapped his fingertips against the helm. Rolling my eyes, I made my way around the helm to stand in front of him so that we were stood face to face yet he still refused to even look at me. My earlier courage had given me a new sense of power when it came to the Captain.

"Caleb-." I began to which he slammed his fist against the helm and leaned towards me. His lips parted to reveal a set of pearl white teeth.

"Don't ye ever call me by me name" he snarled. His breath fanned my face and smelled of sea food. I shrank back slightly but caught myself. The ship rocked again and I stumbled while I watched the man lean back and once again place his gaze on the horizon.

"Well then, *Captain*-." I spat the word "I believe I asked you a question" Snaggletooth choked on a chicken bone as the rest of the crew went silent. They were waiting for their Captain's response.

Caleb looked down at me and turned to face the map behind him. He retrieved a compass from the belt around his waist and slammed it onto the table.

He used an odd device that had a needle on each end and walked it across the paper as he calculated where we were.

"Thirty-five degrees North of South America" he replied as he tossed the device and his compass down onto the map before he turned back to the helm. I examined the map. Curiosity drove me as I tried to determine how he figured that out.

"The Caribbean?" I questioned to the Captain's annoyance. He sighed heavily with his arm resting on the helm. He attempted to ignore me. When he didn't reply, I picked up the compass and started toying with it. I watched the needle point in a random direction that was supposed to be North.

"Teach me" I insisted. I turned to face Caleb's back with the compass in hand. His body tensed and the crew grew dead silent yet again.

"Teach ye what?" Caleb bit out in question. I walked around the helm for the second time in order to face him head on and raised the compass.

"Teach me how to navigate" the crew burst out laughing except for one man who sat brooding in the corner. He lowered his head and scoffed which caught the attention of everyone onboard. I looked back at him from over my shoulder.

"Ye first mate can't navigate, Captain" the previous second in command highlighted as he glared up at us from beneath his black bandanna.

I lowered the compass just as Caleb shoved his way past me. He jumped down the stairs and stomped his way over to the jealous man. He grabbed him by the collar of his shirt and leaned him over the side of the ship.

21

"What did ye say?" Caleb demanded as he leaned into the man's face. The man struggled against him while looking down at the raging sea below. The crew watched with fear in their eyes as the man struggled against their Captain.

I dropped the compass and hurried after Caleb as soon as I noticed that the man was in danger.

"She can barely read a map, yet ye decide to make her ye first mate!" the man yelled in a frantic hurry.

I reached the pair and grabbed hold of Caleb's arm. I tried to pull him away from the Irishman. The young man from the day before who'd saved me from diving into the sea, hurried to my side. He wrapped his arms around my waist as he tried to peal me away from the two pirates.

"Let go!" I cried while struggling against the young man as he dragged me away from the pair. Caleb didn't bother paying me any attention as he snapped.

"But she can read, can ye?" he demanded of the man as he stuck his arm further out which caused the former second in command to lean further back until he was barely onboard the ship.

"N-No, Sir!" he quickly answered. His hands clawed at Caleb's one that was wrapped around the fabric of his stained and dirty shirt.

"Then ye are of no use to me" Caleb said before he set the man back down on his feet and tossed him off to the side. The Irishman slid across the ship's deck. The Captain then stalked his way back to the helm. He ascended the steps that lead to it with a growl in his throat. The man was gasping for air on the ground as the one holding me loosened his grip on my waist but I was frozen in place.

"Around here, fights are common" the young man explained. His lips grazed the shell of my ear when he spoke and snapped me out of my daze. I turned my head to glance back at him from over my shoulder to find that his eyes staring at my lips.

"What is your name?" I questioned, deciding that I wanted to know. He loosened his arms from around me and settled for firmly placing his hands on my hips.

"Ben" he answered. His eyes searched my features as his grip tightened on my hips. I grabbed hold of his forearms and I felt something inside me stir.

The former first mate staggered to his feet and spat in my direction "Ye're nothing but a woman!" he threw at me then stumbled off to go down a bottle of rum.

I pried Ben's arms away from my hips and turned to face him with hopeful eyes. He instantly let go of my waist but didn't move as I turned.

"Will you teach me?" I questioned as I searched his brown gaze and took in the sight of his blond curls. He was rather handsome with a toned jaw and tan skin. He wore simple clothes and still had manners unlike the rest of the crew.

"Teach you?" he asked. He wasn't sure what I was referring to. I motioned towards the stern where Caleb was stood watching and explained.

"How to navigate?" Ben shot a glance in Caleb's direction but the Captain did very little. He only stared straight ahead at the sea so Ben nodded his head and agreed.

He showed me to a room next to the Captain's chambers where meetings were usually held and the kitchen was located. He sat me down with a few maps and various devices including a compass and began to teach me. I struggled to even begin to understand how to navigate and eventually found myself exasperated.

"Enough already" I complained to which Ben chuckled and started rolling up one of the many maps. I was lying on my arms with my face buried in them as I listened to him tidy up the room.

"You were the one who wanted to learn how to navigate" he reminded me and I groaned. I raised my head to look at him. He was stood near a desk and he was stuffing the maps into one of its drawers as he waited for my sarcastic response but before I could cleverly retort, Caleb's voice pierced the air.

"Port Gull!" Ben tilted his head back and looked up at the ceiling to where Caleb was most likely positioned near the helm.

"It looks like we'll be making port" Ben announced as I rose from my seat and glanced towards the deck. I stepped out onto it to find that the sun was starting to set over the horizon. A small town sat in the distance. It was made up of wooden houses and much smaller boats. Ben followed me out onto the deck and gripped my shoulder.

"We'll continue your studies tomorrow" I groaned at the thought of having to repeat the process. I was never one who liked learning new things and sometimes even despised it. I used to procrastinate a lot but something told me that Ben wouldn't allow it.

"Dock the ship!" Caleb's voice bellowed and the crew, including Ben began to scale the sails. They rolled them up and tied them down as the ship sailed into the bay.

It jerked and I stumbled as a few crewmen helped to lower the anchor and hopped off the ship's side, onto land. Most of the crew were already on the docks when a loud thudding of feet approached me from behind. A pair of strong arms scooped me up into the air.

"What are you-?" I demanded as the man held me over the side of the ship.

"Catch" Caleb's voice demanded which was followed by him dropping me. I screamed as I fell through the air and into a pair of equally as strong arms. Ben chuckled as he placed me onto my feet. I huffed and brushed out my dress skirt as I watched Caleb throw himself overboard.

He landed in a crouch beside me and I yelped in surprise. The entire crew burst out laughing in response to my shock. I glared at them but they just stumbled off towards the nearest bar. They left me alone with the Ben and the Captain.

My eyes caught sight of the horizon that was starting to turn a bright orange and that same voice that called out to me, once again began beckoning me out to sea.

"I want to go swimming" I announced. Caleb shot me a look then left for the bar without even bothering to care whether I decided to go swimming or not. Ben on the other hand decided to be much nicer than the Captain.

"There are a few lagoons up this way" he informed and started leading me in that direction. We stepped off the docks and onto sand. I instantly untied my boots and carried them in my hands as we walked along the beach. Ben didn't care much for the sand and kept his shoes on.

"Don't you enjoy the sea?" I asked while looking back in the direction of the bar. A few of the crewmembers were seated on the beach with no shoes or coats as they sipped on a few bottles of wine and rum. They laughed and sang yet Ben refused to remove his shoes.

"I never liked the ocean" he responded with his hands held behind his back as he walked. He looked down at the sand and tensed every time the water would get too close.

"But you're a pirate" I argued which drew a chuckle from Ben as he stopped walking and motioned towards a set of rocks. There were holes in them further down that people could swim in.

"Just because I'm a pirate, it doesn't mean I like the sea" he said and then started towards the bar.

I began climbing the rocks and made my way to the farthest lagoon where I sat my shoes down and started untying my dress. It was a pain to remove the corset but eventually I managed to loosen it enough for me to slip through. Next was the dress which was a breeze to remove compared to the corset. I stood naked on the rocks and stepped down into the water.

The lagoon was deep and clear as an orange hue was cast onto it from the setting sun. I stepped onto a rock in the water and sunk down to sit on it. My legs up to my knees were consumed by the water as I reached for my necklace. I unclasped it and took a deep breath in before I set it aside.

It wasn't long before my legs began to shimmer like silver in the water as I kicked them back and forth. They merged into one and I gasped when scales started to appear on them. A fin formed at the base of my feet and soon it was swishing in the water.

I glanced back in the direction of the bar to make sure that it was safe then leaped into the water. My eyes grew accustomed to the salt and the rest of my lower body took on the form of a Mermaid's tail as I moved through the water. I breathed in through the gills that formed on my neck and swam down to the bottom of the lagoon.

A crab was walking along the sand but froze when I approached it. I watched as fish swam past me and an octopus retracted itself into the cracks of the lagoon wall. I glanced towards the surface of the water where the sun's rays danced along it and closed my eyes to listen. A whale cried out into the water nearby, a dolphin clicked and the movement of fins could be heard through the liquid.

Minutes turned into hours that I swam along the walls of the lagoon. I longed to break free of its cage but I knew that if I was to escape into the sea that all hope would be lost. I breeched the surface a few hours later and heaved myself up onto the edge of the lagoon.

I glanced down at my tail that shimmered in the moonlight. It was a pale silver color that sometimes appeared violet. It matched my pale skin and snow-white hair perfectly. I reached for my necklace and clasped it back on. This caused the scales to disappear from the waist down but stopped where my feet were still dangling in the water. I heaved them out and placed them on the rocks where they once again turned into feet instead of a fin.

I stood and began dressing. I decided to carry the corset and boots in hand as I walked back to the ship. My legs gleamed and glistened but by the time I reached the rest of the crew they were back to normal.

"Ye enjoy ye swim, girl?" a random crewmember asked when I approached them. I brushed it off and went over to where Caleb was lounging underneath a tree. He was looking out onto the sea.

A half-finished bottle of wine was planted in the sand beside him and most of his clothes were discarded. He only wore his pants and hat. I dropped my corset and boots onto the pile he'd made with his clothes and joined him.

"What do ye want?" he asked without bothering to even look at me. I reached for his bottle of wine and took a swig of it. This caught his attention and got him to look up at me from beneath the brim of his hat.

"What do I want?" I repeated. I set the bottle down and looked out onto the ocean. The waves beckoned to me. They called my name in an enticing whisper. I tucked my legs underneath me and buried my hands into the still warm sand.

"I want to be free" Caleb rolled his eyes and turned his head to the side so that he could look down the length of the beach to where the former first mate was yelling curses at the ocean while waving an empty bottle around.

"Don't we all?" the Captain muttered under his breath. The furious man tried taking a swig of his empty bottle but there was nothing so he threw the bottle into the sea and fell onto the sand.

"Sing" Caleb demanded while turning his attention back to the sky above. He crossed his arms beneath his head and tipped his hat forward to hide his face as he tried to fall asleep. I looked up at the stars and began to sing the first song that came to mind.

"The queen and her court sent the king to his death and tied him in his grave. The waters are hers and by the curse where she be is he" a few crew members nearby heard me singing and listened intently to my song. I continued to sing until the song was done and the members were snoring around a bonfire that they'd started earlier.

Caleb rolled onto his side and caused the locket from before to tumble out of his clenched fist. I reached for it. I picked it up off the sand and held it in the palm of my hand.

It was then that my breath caught in my throat and an image clouded my vision.

I was stood beneath a waterfall. I was dressed in nothing but a sheer white shirt and I ran my fingers through my hair. I laughed and looked back onto the rocks where a younger version of Caleb sat watching me. He smiled. It was something I never dreamed of seeing. He got up to join me in the water and I turned as he stepped towards me. I stood up on the tips of my toes to press my lips to his.

I threw the locket down on the sand and shot up off the ground. I looked at it as I blinked my eyes a few times and tried to clear my thoughts. I shook my head and glanced down the length of the beach. The sun was starting to rise over the horizon and I furrowed my brows as I wondered where the time had gone.

Caleb stirred beside me and sat up in a groggy blur. He blinked down at himself then started to panic. He searched the sand around him until he found the locket and reached for it but his eyes caught sight of my feet. He looked up at me with fear in his eyes.

"What did ye see?" he asked which terrified me even more since he knew that I saw something. I began backing away from him. I took slow and messy steps. He got up on his knees and stuffed the locket into the pocket of his pants.

"Mary" he started and a chill ran down my spine. My name wasn't Mary; it was Evangeline but he didn't know that. I turned on my heels as he reached out to me and started running in the opposite direction. I tripped over one of the sleeping crewmembers and he muttered something in his sleep as I struggled to get to my feet. I ran and I climbed the hill that led to a forest. I disappeared into it and ran until I couldn't run anymore. I toppled over and fell to my knees in between the leaves and dirt as I thought back to the vision.

The woman had blond hair instead of white but other than that she looked exactly like me. Her eyes were mismatched and her figure was the same as mine. Her skin tone was a bit darker but she was still the spitting image of me.

I glanced at the forest ahead and took a few deep breaths before I shot back up off the ground and continued running. My bare

27

feet carried me until I was lost in the forest of the port. I ran for what felt like forever when a familiar voice pierced the air behind me.

"Mary!" I turned to look back at the man chasing me. He was gaining on me and when I turned my attention back ahead, I came to a sudden halt. I broke through the forest and found myself on the edge of a cliff. I stumbled back a few steps and gripped at my dress skirts as I gasped for air.

My back hit solid rock and I tensed when strong arms wrapped around me. They turned me to face the man who was in charge of them. Caleb stared down at me with wild eyes. He still wore his hat and his pants but his chest was left bare as he gripped my shoulders to force me to look at him.

"Mary, listen to me-." I cut him off as I tore myself free of his grasp and took a small step back.

"My name's not Mary. My name is Evangeline!" my voice was shaking, along with my body as tears began to fill my eyes. I felt threatened for some reason like there was something going on that I didn't know about. Caleb stiffened in response to my words and had to pause before he reached for me again.

"Evangeline, ye need to listen to me" he said in a calm tone but I shook my head and took yet another step back. I felt the earth start to crumble out from beneath me. I turned my head to stare down at the raging waters below. I contemplated jumping and dragged my feet back a few inches.

Caleb shot forward when I began to fall back and grabbed onto the material of my dress. He yanked me onto my feet and into his chest where he wrapped his arms around me before he took a large step back, away from the edge of the cliff.

"Ye be the reincarnation of my love" he said into my hair as one hand tangled itself into the white strands. He pressed my face into his chest as his other hand tightened its hold on my waist. I had to take a few moments to process his words as he leaned back against a nearby tree.

I pulled away from him to look up at his face. The scar hadn't been there in my vision and his hair wasn't as long. He looked to be at least a decade or so older than me and I understood.

"Mary" I whispered. I placed my palms flat against his chest and pushed him away from me as I took a few steps back. I needed to breath while I thought about what I'd seen and heard.

"The locket" I muttered since my brain was only able to process little pieces of information at once.

"That's why you took me" I concluded while looking up at him and he nodded. I searched his features and turned on my heels. I headed back in the direction of the ship and its crew. Caleb called out to me and hurried to follow as I stormed my way through the forest.

He only wanted me because I looked like his previous lover.

"Evangeline!" he called as I broke through the tree line and onto the beach. The crew stood nearby. They watched as their Captain ran after me. One of the crewmen shook his head.

"Our Captain be losing it over a woman" he muttered when I stepped onto the docks. Caleb reached for my wrist and turned me to face him. I was ready to slap him but froze when I noticed the way his aura seemed to change.

"I don't care if ye're angry. Ye will get me to those treasures and ye will not speak a word of this to the rest of the crew" I shrunk back at his harsh tone and whimpered when his grip became bone crushing around my wrist. Ben appeared on the deck of the ship and looked down on us in question.

"Captain?" he asked which forced Caleb to let go of my wrist. I rubbed at the sensitive skin and looked up at the angry man before me. Caleb turned towards the beach and yelled out in a snarl.

"Bring me, me things!" the crew instantly snapped into motion. They hurried over to the tree where Caleb had been sleeping to scooped our clothes up off the sand along with what remained of the bottle of wine. The Captain shot me a look before he climbed up the side of the ship and barked for Ben to get me onboard so that we could set sail.

When Ben finally got me onboard the ship, he asked me if I was alright but I ignored him and headed straight for the Captain's quarters where I collapsed on the bed with my face buried in the pillows and sheets.

I eventually fell into a deep sleep.

Chapter Three

"Land ho!" someone bellowed and awoke me from my sleep. I pushed myself into a sitting position and glanced around to find that I was alone in the Captain's quarters. The book was placed on the nightside table beside me along with a piece of bread and a cup of water. I reached for the bread and devoured it then proceeded to down the water.

I placed the cup beside the book and decided to head to the deck in order to take in where we were but as soon as I exited, I noticed that the entire crew were gathered on the right side of the main deck. They were staring at something on the horizon.

I ran the back of my hand across my lips and followed their gazes to find what looked like two rock towers that stretched high above the sea's surface. Caleb stood near the helm. H was also looking out onto the same spectacle.

"The first treasure lies between two mouths where a light is cast upon it" I repeated while looking towards the sky where the sun was starting to set in between the twin towers. I rushed past Caleb and pointed towards them.

"There! We will find the first treasure there!" I announced and Caleb harshly spun the helm. The crew went flying as the ship turned and I had to tighten my grip on the railing to prevent myself from falling overboard.

"Set course due East!" Caleb yelled and the crew jumped to their feet. They began to readjust the sails in order to accommodate the ship's course. As soon as the wind caught in the sails, the ship jerked and sped up. I watched as the two towers crept ever closer until we were sailing right in between them.

I stared up at the flat, rock walls on either side of us and felt my mouth drop at the sheer height of them. The sun was setting faster than before and we only had a little light left to help guide us to the treasure.

"Anything else ye like to add?" Caleb asked as he looked back at me from where he was steering the ship. I tried remembering what I'd read about the first treasure and looked up at the sky where seagulls were circling.

"Not above" I muttered while looking at the clear, blue waters beneath us "Not below" I repeated the words that were written in the book "Follow your eyes" I looked towards the setting sun, in the direction that we were heading and something caught my attention from out of the corner of my eye. I look towards it and found something gold shimmering in the light of the setting sun.

"There!" I cried out as I pointed at the glowing shard that was imbedded into one of the towers. Caleb steered the ship in its direction. He was careful not to hit the sides of the structures that rose up and out of the water on either side of us.

"Lower the anchor!" Caleb demanded when we reached the glowing speck. The anchor dropped and with a loud thud beneath the water caught onto something. It steadied the ship.

"Fetch the hooks!" Caleb's voice yelled out as I stared up at the source of the speck which was in the mouth of a small cave. Ben, appeared beside me on the stern with a hook and rope in hand. He stared up at our objective.

"Quickly, before the sun sets!" I hastened and they hurried. A few of the crew members appeared and they tossed their hooks at the mouth of the cave. They then scaled the side of the tower as darkness began to fall and the sun disappeared beneath the horizon. My breath caught in my throat as I watched them climbing but they quickly returned to the ship, shaking their heads from side to side.

"The hole be too small, Captain" they argued and Caleb slammed his fist on the table behind the helm. I looked back up at the cave and began to unbutton the front of my dress.

"Give me your shirt" I insisted as I glanced at Caleb before turning my back on the crew. Wolf whistles and cat calls filled the air when my dress dropped down to the deck. Caleb appeared behind me. He shielded me from view as he shrugged off his coat and tugged his shirt over his head, handing it to me. I pulled it onto my form and expected it to go down to mid-thigh from the vision I had where my prior reincarnation was wearing a similar shirt of his. The less restricting article of clothing would aid me in my endeavor. I stepped up onto the ship's railing and reached for one of the dangling ropes.

"This is madness" Ben argued but I shook my head and looked back up at the cavity above.

"I'm the smallest person here. I might just fit" I argued and tightened my grip on the rope. I stepped off the railing and swung until my feet collided with the rocky surface of the tower. I glanced down at the water below then turned my head to look back at Caleb.

"Anything specific that I need to find?" I asked as his jaw tightened. Ben looked at me like I'd lost my mind but I wanted to get to the first treasure and find the others. In my mind, the quicker I could find the treasures, the quicker I could go home.

"Find me a gem" I nodded and started climbing. I used all of my strength to get to the cavern. It took me twice as long to reach it as it had the crew but it was because my arms were much weaker. I heard Ben yelling when I was high enough for the crew to see up the bottom of my shirt and figured that he was telling them to avert their eyes.

When I reached the cave, I dragged myself up onto its floor and sat there while I panted heavily. I looked down at the ship to find Caleb watching me with a worried gaze but as soon as it was there, it was gone, replaced with an impatient scowl.

I forced myself up onto my feet and started towards the back of the cave where a crack had been made in the rock. It was a narrow fit but I managed to squeeze through and into what looked like a sea of gold. My feet were met by a few inches of water and above that was enough gold to fill an entire room. The gold was spread out along the bottom of the cave.

I had to remind myself that I was searching for a gem and raised my head to find a pile of gold that sat on the opposite side of the cave. Moonlight was starting to spill into the cave which reflected off the gold but my eyes noticed a gleam of red. I trudged through the water and gold to get to a gem that was perfectly placed on top of a golden tray.

I picked it up and twisted it back and forth in my grasp. I inspected it before the cave started shaking. I looked at the ceiling in fear as bits of it started to crumble. The towers were collapsing and I knew that I had to get out as quickly as I could. I ran for the crack in the wall and squeezed through it but when I reached the other side, I realized that there wouldn't be any time for me to climb back down to the ship. I glanced towards the water then looked at the ship where the crew were struggling to raise the anchor.

"Evangeline!" Caleb called up to me as the walls beside me started crumbling. I was breathing hard as I desperately searched for an escape. My eyes landed on the water which looked too enticing for comfort.

"Catch!" I yelled and tossed the gem into the air. It twisted and fell until it landed in Caleb's clenched fist. I glanced back at the cave behind me and reached for my necklace.

"Go!" I insisted and the ship began to sail for the opposite end of the towers.

"No!" Ben protested as he climbed to the far back of the ship to look up at me in fear and worry. He was frantic as he searched for a way to get to me. I gripped the edge of the cavern and waited for the ship to exit the towers before I tore my necklace from my neck and leaped into the air.

I dove into the water just as the towers came crashing down on top of me. My legs morphed into one single unit that was tipped with a fin and I swam down towards a coral reef. I tucked myself underneath it's structure and prayed to the gods that the pieces of the towers wouldn't crush me beneath their weight.

After a few minutes of trembling, the waters went silent and I opened my eyes as I slowly began to swim out from underneath the reef. There was a large chunk of the towers resting on top of it. I heard a crash in the water and looked up to find that Ben had jumped into the sea in an attempt to try and find me but he was sputtering about on the surface for a moment until he finally decided to dive down in search of me. He dove and swam further down until he lost all air and sucked water into his lungs.

I swam towards him and wrapped my arms around his torso as I dragged him to the surface. Once we breached, I pretended to gasp and cried out a frantic "Help!"

The ship was nearby and the crew quickly spotted us. Caleb ordered them to lower the rowboat and I threw Ben into it before I tied my necklace back around my neck.

I heaved myself up onto the side of the boat so that my lower half was out of the water and paused to allow my thighs to separate properly. I then sat up and tucked my legs beneath the side of the boat in order to hide them. Water dripped down my fin which casted a violet glow that I prayed only I could see. Once my feet were fully separated and we were hoisted onto the ship, I turned to Ben. I tried feeling for a pulse.

"He's not breathing" I announced as the crew dragged him out of the boat and onto the ship's deck. I fell to my knees beside him and tilted his head back. I placed both hands on his chest and started pressing down hard. I repeated the action until my hands started to cramp.

"Wake up!" I yelled at him as I slammed my fists into his chest but he didn't move. I looked up at Caleb who stood nearby and my I pinched Ben's nose shut with my fingers before I delved in. I pressed my lips to his cold ones and breathed out. Ben instantly started coughing and vomited water. I hurriedly turned him onto his side and hugged him to my chest while patting his back as he gasped for air.

"It's alright. You're alright" I reassured him as the crew cheered and Caleb shot me a look before heading back towards the helm where he began to steer us away from where the twin towers used to be. I could've sworn that I saw a glint of jealousy in his eyes but I shrugged it off and grabbed Ben's face in between the palms of my hands. I forced him to look at me.

"That was incredibly idiotic" I scolded him as if he was a child. He managed to calm down enough to look me in the eyes with a relieved and grateful gleam in his.

"You're okay" he breathed out. His eyes moved to glance down at my slightly parted lips. I cleared my throat and stood up, to which I felt the cool breeze hit my nude form and I realized that the white shirt I was wearing was soaked through. I quickly raised my arms to cover my breasts and nodded.

"Yes, I'm fine" I announced then hurried off to the Captain's quarters where I stripped out of Caleb's shirt and tossed it off to the side as I searched for something else to wear. I dug through his dresser and found a similar shirt in navy blue. I tugged it onto my body followed by my boots.

As I sat on the edge of the bed while doing up my laces, I could hear music and singing coming from the deck. I stepped out onto it and found that the crew were dancing and drinking. They cheered and they laughed at the simplest of things. One of the men stumbled over to me. He placed his arm around my shoulder and offered me a sip of his rum.

"Tonight we celebrate" he announced then stumbled off to join the rest of the crew after I politely rejected his drink. Ben was sat on the stairs beside me with a cup in hand.

"Want a drink?" he asked as he held his cup out to me. I took it and sniffed the content. It was strong and had a sweet smell to it. I took a swig of the wine and handed the cup back to him.

"Loosen up a bit" Ben said when he noticed how tense I was.

He downed the rest of his drink and got up to go fill it with some more wine near a large barrel. He then handed the cup to me and found another one for himself. He filled it up and turned to me.

"Cheers" he cheered and clanked his cup against mine before downing his drink again. I threw my head back to follow his example but I stumbled and nearly fell as I finished it.

"Now you're getting the hang of it" Ben pipped while reaching for my cup to refilled it. He then stuffed it back into my hands. A couple of drinks and a few hours later, I was dancing around the deck with Ben. I sang along to a song that I didn't know the words to and cheering with the best of them. Snaggletooth snapped his teeth and the man beside him nodded.

"Ye said it, mate!" he agreed and burst out laughing. I raised my cup.

"Here, here!" I bellowed and laughed as I threw my head back to chug the rest of my drink but a man grabbed my cup and held it out of reach.

"That be enough" Caleb said while reaching for my upper arm with his free hand. I hiccupped and tried to reach for my cup as I said in a drunken slur "Gimme that" but he refused and handed my cup to the closest pirate before dragging me off. I nearly fell on the way to his chambers.

"Ye need sleep" he insisted as he motioned towards the bed. I closed my eyes and swaying back and forth on my jelly legs as every few second a hiccup escaped my lips.

"Why?" I asked. I didn't move as Caleb watched me with an annoyed scowl. I opened my eyes and leaned forward while waiting for him to respond "Because ye need to read, not get drunk with a few dirty pirates" I raised my hand and pointed a finger at him with a pout on my lips.

"Hey, you're a dirty pirate too" I stated. I didn't care about the consequences of my actions or words. Caleb's golden gaze narrowed into an intense glare as he watched me sway.

"And besides, I already know where the next treasure is" I babbled as I raised my arms and shrug my shoulders when another fit of hiccups escaped me. Caleb's eyes lit up at my words and he quickly proceeded to ask "Where?" I placed a finger on my chin and looked up at the ceiling in thought. I tapped my foot against the floorboards beneath me as I tried to remember the exact words.

35

"*The cold is next, in a crow's nest near a white sea,* or was it a white plain? I can't remember. It was something or the other" I sang the riddle instead of saying it but the rest was all babble which added to Caleb's annoyance. Judging from the look on his face, it was clear that he didn't understand a word of it and was waiting for me to explain.

"The cold?" I tried to give him a hint but he just kept staring at me so I threw my hands up in the air and stalked over to the bed. I fell down onto it with boots and all.

"North, we head North" I muttered while throwing my arm over my eyes as I tried to get the room to stop spinning by placing one foot on the ground. Caleb grumbled and began to strip out of his coat and boots. He placed his hat and weapons aside so that he could climb onto the bed beside me. I felt the mattress dip and groaned when a sudden jolt of nausea hit me.

"Please stop" I begged but there was no reply. There was only silence as Caleb fell asleep and I finally dozed off.

Chapter Four

I groaned when someone grabbed hold of my foot causing me to stir in my sleep. I tried blinking to get my eyes to adjust to the light that poured into the room. When I could finally see, I found Caleb at the foot of the bed. He was untying my boots before slipping them off my feet. I grouched and turned onto my side as I tore my foot out of his grasp. I buried my face into the pillows.

"Five more minutes" I sleepily mumbled to which Caleb roughly gripped my foot and slipped my second boot off. He then shoved my foot aside which caused my body to jerk and a heaving sound to escape my lips when the contents of my stomach swished around in sync with the motion.

"I need a course" he announced and I turned my head to look at him through a curtain of pearl white hair. I huffed, blowing some of the strands out of my face so that I could see him from where I was lying on my stomach.

"North. Head North" I grumbled. I tried to close my eyes and hoped to fall back asleep but Caleb wouldn't have it. He tore the covers off me and left me exposed, in nothing but one of his old shirts. I huffed in annoyance and pushed myself up onto my hands and knees.

"What?" I demanded as I looked back at him from over my shoulder.

He shot me a glare for my tone but I ignored it and sat back on my knees. I stretched my arms out high above my head which caused the shirt to slightly slip off my shoulders.

"What exactly are we looking for?" he questioned and I scratched at the back of my head. I yawned into my sleeve and smacked my lips at the end of it.

"We're looking for a ship" I stated while blinking tiredly up at Caleb as he stepped around the side of the bed so that he could look directly at me.

"Pirates?" he questioned. His eyes filled with worry at the thought of the second treasure being in the grasp of other pirates. I shrugged my shoulders.

"I don't know" I muttered, falling onto my back and straightening out my legs as I blinked up at the floorboards above.

Caleb slammed his fist onto the nightside table.

"What do ye mean, ye don't know?" he demanded and I yelped at the sudden, loud noise. I shot him a glare and pushed myself up onto my elbows as I tried my best to make him understand "The book doesn't give specific descriptions of what awaits us. It only gives us a few detailed words to guide us" Caleb glanced at the book on the bed side table then at me as I rolled over onto my side so that my back was to him. I curled in on myself and closed my eyes as I snuggled into the bedsheets.

"Set course for North!" Caleb yelled at the top of his lungs then thudded his way back above deck. I groaned in response to his loud voice and tried falling back asleep. After an hour of rolling around and trying fall sleep, I eventually gave up.

I threw the covers off and huffed as I looked up at the floorboards overhead. There was movement as someone walked onto the stern above Caleb's chambers and I watched as the figure moved across the floor. I heard him speaking to himself and stood up on the bed to get as close to the ceiling as possible to try and decipher what he was mumbling on about.

"Sea folk" he muttered under his breath while pacing the length of the stern. He moved back and forth "Sea folk are coming" I peeked through the crack in the boards to find one of the crewmen there. His eyes were wide and sweat was forming on his brow. He looked nervous and paranoid. I reached up to place my hands against the wood just as the ship jerked and it send me tumbling off the side of the bed onto the floor.

I hit my head on the nightside table and blacked out before coming too sometime later. I blinked my eyes and turned my head this way and that to take in my surroundings. Everything was blurry at first and a sharp pain shot through the back of my head. I reached for it. I pressed my fingers to my head and felt something wet and warm coating my fingertips. I looked at my fingers and found that there was blood on them.

Groaning, I pushed myself up onto all fours and eventually onto my legs. The ship rocked again and I stumbled. I had to catch myself on the nearest furniture. I blinked to try and clear my vision enough to find the stairs that led to the deck.

My feet dragged as I climbed them and my hands gripped the walls in desperation until I reached the deck. There were dark clouds hovering overhead and the crew were yelling. They ran around the ship as a means to try and get us out of harm's way. Rain poured down and lightning sounded. I shrank back below deck and gasped to try and catch my breath. I glanced down at my body, at the necklace dangling around my neck and at my exposed legs.

"Fasten the sails!" Caleb's voice pierced through the storm and I looked up to find a few crew members climbing the sails with little to no fear.

"Tie down those boats!" the rest of the crew ran to the boats that were onboard the ship. A nearby boat was starting to lift off the deck and it threatened to fly overboard. I glanced around at the crew but everyone was too busy to notice the boat so I made a split-second decision and ran out onto the deck. I grabbed the ropes that were flailing around the boat and tugged them down. I tried to securely tie them to the deck.

"Prepare yeselves!" Caleb's voice called just as a wave struck us from the side. I tightened my grip on the ropes as water poured onto the deck and pooled around me. I gasped and kept my head down. I fell to one knee in the water. My legs were starting to shimmer silver as I held onto the side of the boat.

"No, no, no" I repeated to myself just as another wave hit us. It drenched me once again. I glanced up to where Caleb was near the helm and noticed that he wasn't paying any attention to me which was a good thing. I looked at the rest of the crew and found that they were too busy trying to save the ship to pay me any mind.

A wave struck the back of the ship and Caleb fell into the railing from the force. This caused the red gem to tumble out of his coat pocket. The jewel fell onto the deck "Get me that gem!" I glanced from the boat to the jewel then I glanced at my legs before diving for the scarlet stone. I slid across the deck with my hand reaching out to snatch it just as a huge wave nearly capsized the entire ship. It sent me overboard.

"Evangeline!" Caleb's voice pierced the air and was soon drowned out by the sound of swirling sea water. I swallowed some of the water and tried reaching for my necklace but it was tangled in my hair. I dangled beneath the water. I was unable to let go of the gem and unable to tear the necklace from my throat which me oxygen deprived as I struggled to reach the surface. I looked up in what I assumed was the direction of the ship and then down to the jewel in my hand.

39

I stuffed the gem into my mouth and began to swim in an upward direction as fast as I could. Near the surface, I felt something in front of me and latched onto it. I allowed the crew to pull me out of the water and back onto the ship. The object was a net and as soon as my body struck the deck, I spat out the gem and started coughing violently. Caleb ran for the jewel and picked it up. He then stuffed it back into the coat pocket as Ben dropped to his knees beside me.

"Are you alright?" he yelled above the storm as I vomited up salt water and tried to push myself up onto all fours. I raised my head and looked at Caleb who wasn't paying any attention to me. He was trying to get the crew to tend to the ship. It was then that I realized that I was nothing to him. I was only a means for him to retrieve the treasures and nothing more.

"I-I'm fine" I reassured Ben as another wave struck the boat and soaked us in cold water. I looked back at my legs and felt bile rise in my throat at the sight of faint scales that were starting to form on my skin. I grabbed onto Ben's shoulder and met his gaze with a pleading stare "Take me below deck" I said. I was becoming weaker the longer I stayed on all fours.

My body started leaning towards the deck and Ben had to catch me. He scooped me into his arms and carried me to the Captain's quarters. Halfway down the steps he paused when his eyes locked onto my legs. They caught the light from a nearby lamp that allowed them to start shimmering silver. I reached a hand out towards the armchair.

"Please" I breathed and Ben snapped out of it. He walked me over to the chair and gently eased me onto it. I tugged at the shirt that I was wearing and motioned to the dresser. Ben caught on quickly and hurried over to it. He retrieved a random cream-colored shirt before he returned to my side. I coughed while I reached for the hem of my soaked shirt and tugged it upward but I was too weak to lift it over my head.

"Let me help" Ben whispered as a crack of thunder sounded and the ship continued to rock from side to side. I fell back against the armchair and looked at him with pleading eyes. He reached for the hem of the navy shirt and slowly started lifting it over my head until I was left naked in front of him. My breasts and torso were covered in silver scales which gave me some form of dignity as he pulled the dry shirt over my head.

I closed my eyes and leaned back into the chair as Ben knelt beside it. I felt fingers running along my leg and opened my eyes to find Ben staring at the scales that were slowly starting to disappear. I shivered and moaned at the sensitive sensation his touch sent through my skin and up my spine.

The sound caught Ben's attention and he looked up at me with curiosity and desire in his chocolate brown eyes.

"You're a *Mermaid*" the word sent fear coursing through my veins as I tried sitting up straighter and I reached for him.

"Please" I repeated as my hand snaked up to grip the anchor pendant that dangled from my neck.

"Don't tell anyone" I begged and Ben glanced towards the deck as if contemplating telling Caleb but then he met my tired eyes and nodded. He stood up, scooped me into his arms and carried me over to the bed to lay me down beneath the sheets. He then sat beside me on the edge of the bed and reached for my hand.

"Your secret's safe with me" he reassured me while giving my hand a small squeeze as I dozed off to sleep. He sat there long after I fell asleep. He ran his thumb over my knuckles and made sure that I was safe during the remainder of the storm. It was then that I realized that the only person I could trust onboard the Sunken Soul was Ben and that if Caleb was to ever find out about my secret, that he'd have them harvest my scales and sell them to the highest bidder.

Mermaid scales were said to possess incredible foreseeing capabilities which meant that they were highly valuable.

Chapter Five

By the time I woke up the storm had passed and the sun was starting to set, signaling that it was past noon. I sat up on the bed to find that I was alone with a tray of food waiting for me on the nightside table. I threw my legs over the side of the bed and placed the tray in my lap. To my surprise there was a piece of descent meat waiting for me which I quickly finished and moved on to the bread and water.

A loud thud caught my attention and I looked in the direction of the stairs to find Caleb making his way below deck. I quickly averted my eyes and tried to ignore his presence.

"How're ye feeling?" he asked and I accidentally dropped my cup on the floor. He was stood near the foot of the bed as he expectantly waited for my reply.

"What do you care?" I asked while bending down to pick up my cup and place it back onto the tray. Caleb stiffened from beside me and stomped his way around the bed so that he was stood directly in front of me.

"Excuse me?" he asked and I sighed heavily. I placed my tray on the nightside table before getting up off the bed to meet Caleb's heated gaze "You don't care about me-." I began as I reached for the book that was lying on the bed. I held it up for him to see.

"All you care about is this" I placed emphasis on the word 'this' and shook the book before lowering it again.

"As long as I can still read then you don't care about what happens to me" it felt like I was taking a stand. I was just a small pixie standing up to a giant or rather a terrifying cyclops. Caleb's eyes grew darker as they looked me over and his aura grew blacker. He took a threatening step towards me and I backed away into the side of the bed.

"Watch ye tone, girl" he said in a domineering tone. I refused to back down and stood up on the tips of my toes to make myself look bigger against his height and build.

"I refuse. Just like I refuse to help you find the rest of those treasures" as soon as the words were out, I regretted saying them. Caleb's hand shot out to tighten itself around my throat. The book slipped out of my hold and cluttered to the floor by our feet as my hands shot up to grip his wrist. I tried desperately to pry his hand away.

"Ye will lead me to them treasures or I'll make ye walk the plank" he barked in my face as he tightened his grip with every word. I gasped and tried talking but no words would come out. Only strangled gurgles escaped me.

"Don't think that just because ye look like Mary, that I care about ye" with that, he let go of my throat and I fell to my knees on the floor. I grabbed and clawed at my neck as I began to cough violently. Caleb took a step back to give me some room but his eyes continued to glare holes into my skull. I gripped the edge of the bed and looked up at the man before me.

"I 'm *not* Mary-." I began as I forced myself onto my feet. I took a stand in front of him as I bit out the word *'not'* as if to spit it in his face. Caleb shifted from one foot to the other but kept his eyes locked on mine.

"I'm not stupid enough to fall in love with a monster like you!" I shoved his chest which sent him staggering back a step and I tried to get away but Caleb reached out to grab my upper arm. He turned me around to face him. His face was mere inches away from mine when he spoke the words in a deadly tone.

"Don't ye ever speak about Mary again" he then shoved my arm away which sent me falling back onto the bed. There was blood on the pillow beside me from when I'd hit my head and Caleb seemed to notice it for the first time. He turned his attention to the pillow and picked it up. He inspected the large stain before he looked back at me.

"Ye're hurt" he stated while he tossed the pillow aside and reached for me but I backed away. I crawled to the corner of the bed that was the farthest away from him.

"Evangeline" he said in a threatening drawl like a father scolding his daughter. I shrunk further into the corner with my hands gripping the walls on either side of me. He climbed onto the edge of the bed and I suddenly felt trapped like a caged animal.

"Don't touch me!" I snapped when he reached his hand out towards me. He paused at my tone but continued to take hold of a few strands of my hair that framed my face. He held them out in front of me and I noticed that they were covered in fresh blood.

My hand shot to the back of my head and I felt a warm liquid start to coat my skelp. My fingers began trembling as I realized that our argument had caused the wound to start bleeding again. Caleb reached for me once more but I started thrashing as he tugged me across the bed and towards him.

"Let go of me!" I yelled. I kicked and screamed as he tried to pin me down long enough to see the back of my head but he couldn't since I was moving around too much.

"B-Ben!" I screeched and Caleb released me instantly as if the name escaping my lips had somehow stung him. In a matter of seconds, Ben came running. He looked at me and Caleb with furrowed brows. I quickly shrank back into the corner when Caleb released me.

"She's hurt" Caleb explained then got up and left, leaving me alone with Ben. Ben hurried to my side and sat down on the edge of the bed.

"Let me see" he insisted and after a few moments' hesitation, I began to make my way towards him. I held my bloody hand out to him as if trying to show him that something was wrong and touched my soaked hair to indicate where it was hurting. Ben gently turned me so that my back was to him and started picking apart my hair to get to the wound.

"You shouldn't've slept after hitting your head" he scolded me as he got up off the bed to go get a bucket of water and a cloth. He then started dabbing the wet cloth to the back of my head as an attempt to clean the wound so that he could more clearly see the extent of the damage. I flinched whenever the cloth touched the wound which gained me a few muttered apologies from Ben.

"It could've caused more harm" Ben explained as he finished cleaning my wound and used his fingers to spread the injury apart.

"It doesn't look too serious" he announced then got up to start cleaning the mess he'd made. I followed him around the room with my eyes until he came to a stop near the foot of the bed beside me.

"Thank you" I muttered. My eyes softened at the sight of him. His gaze roamed over my body, from my legs to my shoulders which were exposed due to the shirt being too big for me.

"How is it possible for you to have legs?" Ben surprised me by asking. I looked at my legs and ran my hands along my thighs before meeting Ben's confused gaze. I reached up to grip my necklace. I held the anchor out for him to see.

"This necklace was given to me by my mother before she died" I began, thinking back to the few memories I had of her before I was orphaned and spent the rest of my younger years at an orphanage "She told me that it was blessed by a Witch to give me legs as long as I wore it" I never knew the Witch who blessed it but she was a good friend of my mother's. I twisted the anchor back and forth between my fingers as Ben took a seat on the bed.

"That's how you survived the jump" he muttered and I realized that he was talking about the dive I took at the sight of the first treasure. I dropped my necklace causing the metal to thud against my chest and glanced at Ben.

"Yes" was all I said as I looked away and to the pillows at the head of the bed. Ben looked like he wanted to ask something else but he was cut off by Caleb's voice yelling "Land ho!" Ben turned to look at the stairs that led above deck and I got up from the bed. I tugged the boots I had onto my feet as Ben made his way towards the stairs.

I followed him and stepped out onto the deck to find the burning light of the sun waiting for me. I raised my hand to shield my eyes from the sharp rays and looked out onto the open sea.

There was an island in the distance that looked abandoned and empty but then I noticed something. I stepped towards the edge of the ship and leaned over the railing to get a closer look at the figure waving and yelling for us to help her.

She wore a ripped, white under dress and had fiery red hair that burnt brightly in the sunlight.

Ben stood beside me and tried to make out what was going on as I pushed myself away from the ships railing and rushed up the steps that led to the stern where Caleb was stood. He was staring emotionless at the desperate woman on the horizon.

"We need to help her" I declared as I reached him. He turned his head to look down at me with a hard gaze then opened his mouth to hiss out a single word.

"No" I listened to the woman yelling in a thick English accent for a few seconds then tried again.

"She needs our help" I tried to reason with him but he turned his back to me and looked at the map on the table behind the helm "She's not our problem" I looked at the small island then at the crew. Some of the men were whistling at the woman and yelling perverted things while Ben looked away and blushed slightly at the sight of her in her under dress.

45

"Fine then" I declared and reached down to tug my boots off my feet. I threw them at Caleb. One hit him on the back which caused him to turn and glare at me.

"Evangeline!" he snarled but it was too late. I stepped up onto the ship's railing and dove off its side, into the water. Ben quickly rushed to the side of the ship to check on me as I broke through the surface and started swimming in the direction of the island.

"Damn that woman!" Caleb's voice yelled in frustration from somewhere behind me before it was followed by a much louder.

"Get me to that island!" the crew scurried and began to adjust the ship's course as I swam through the water and allowed the waves to carry me to the shore. When I reached the sand, I stood up and started trudging through the water. I gripped the hem of my soaked shirt as I approached the yelling woman but as soon as I got close enough for her to see my face, she froze. Her eyes went wide and her mouth fell open in shock.

"Mary?" she asked in bewilderment and allowed her eyes to roam over my form. I stopped in between the waves and was about to protest when she interrupted me.

"I thought you were dead, Caleb said-." she stayed rooted in place and her guard went up when I didn't say anything.

"What's wrong?" she asked just as the ship sailed into the sand beside us. A heavy thudding of feet reached our ears and both the woman and I looked up to find Caleb looming overhead.

"Rebecca" Caleb greeted the woman with a jerk of his head as a few of the crewmembers threw ropes overboard for us to be able to climb onto the ship. The woman placed her hands on her hips and turned to face the Captain.

"You have some nerve Caleb Campbell" she began. Her accent shone through as she began scolding him. Caleb sighed heavily and looked away as she grabbed hold of my arm and pulled me closer to her.

"I thought she was dead!" she screeched which seemed to annoy Caleb even more. He glanced down at the two of us.

"That's not Mary" he argued then pushed away from the edge of the ship to thud his way back towards the helm. Rebecca looked at me and let go of my arm, long enough for her to realize that there was something not right about my appearance according to her mental image of Mary.

46

"Wasn't Mary blond?" she randomly called out to Caleb and made her way to the rope. She then started climbing and scaling the side of the ship until she reached the deck. Ben was shoved out of her way as she tried to follow Caleb around.

"What the bloody hell is going on here?" she questioned as I huffed and started towards the rope. Ben helped to lift me onto the ship and handed me the shirt off his back to dry myself with as I sat on a barrel and watched Rebecca stalk her way up the stairs to the stern.

"She's Mary's reincarnation" Caleb explained as the redhead neared him. Ben was listening in on the conversation while the rest of the crew couldn't shake the sight of her breasts peeling out of her white corset and her skirt sticking to her legs from the sea water.

"So she's not Mary" Rebecca concluded. She turned to look back at me as I sat with Caleb's cream shirt sticking to my body and my wet hair clinging to the sides of my face.

"No, she only looks like her" Caleb agreed as he leaned forward on the helm with his arms as he watched Rebecca study me.

"But she has Mary's soul" Rebecca argued as she looked back at Caleb. I froze at the thought of having someone else's soul trapped inside my body and chose to listen intently to what they were saying.

"And her aggression" Caleb muttered to which Rebecca threw her head back laughing. She walked across the stern to the map and took a long look at it.

"As feisty as ever then" she replied as she ran her fingers along the map until they came to a sudden halt and she turned on her heels to look at Caleb with wide eyes.

"You're going after the seven treasures" she declared to which Caleb stiffened and shot a quick glance in my direction. Rebecca stepped around the helm to face him.

"You don't honestly believe that it's going to work, do you?" she questioned to which Caleb grew silent. He stood up straight with his hands clenching and unclenching at his sides. His eyes went to Ben and he barked out in a demanding tone.

"Take her below deck!" Ben instantly grabbed hold of my upper arm and started to gently guide me below deck through a trap door. The small beds on either side of the narrow passage we found ourselves in, smelt of mold and salt. A few lamps hung from nails that'd been hammered into the wooden support beams. They gave us enough light to find our way to the end of the passage where a door stood slightly ajar.

Ben let go of my arm to open it, revealing a small room that had a bed pushed up against the far wall and rope littering the floor apart from a table on which various maps were spread out.

"You can take a seat" Ben urged with his hand held out towards the bed as I entered the small, pocket sized room. The door squealed shut behind me which was followed by Ben dragging a chair from the corner towards the bed. I sank down onto the edge of the mattress as he took a seat in the chair. He was too much of a gentleman to want to sit beside me on what I assumed was his bed.

"What was that about?" he suddenly questioned which made my back muscles stiffen as I looked up at him. His brows were furrowed up in confusion. I could hear faint yelling coming from the deck but I couldn't make out what they were arguing about. I sighed.

"I'm the reincarnation of Mary" I explained. I spoke the words that I so hated. I wasn't her. I didn't want to be linked to her like I was. There was a loud bang that caught Ben's attention and made me jump.

He glanced towards the deck as he spoke "Who's Mary?" my hand clenched and unclenched against the fabric of his bed sheets as I contemplated the question. *She was Caleb's dead lover? Rebecca's friend? Who was she really? What kind of person was Mary?*

"She's Caleb's deceased lover" I decided to say which had Ben's head hurriedly turning to look at me. In his mind, it meant that there was something between Caleb and I.

"B-But there's nothing between us" I quickly went to object before he got the wrong idea. I turned my head to look at the dirty old mirror that hung on the wall above the bed.

"I just look like her" my voice whispered as I reached up to touch the side of my face. I pushed the hair back and out of the way to reveal small patches of silver scales that were almost unnoticeable.

The ship rocked violently and water came in from the sides. It spilled across my feet and Ben's boots. I steadied myself as I felt Ben's intense stare on me and I gasped while watching my feet.

"They're beautiful" I froze at his words. My hands gripped the side of the bed while the scales that appeared on my feet reflected the light of the candles around us. They created small specks of light that stuck to the walls and furniture.

The chair scrapped across the floor as Ben stood and I silently watched him move across the room to a small barrel where he filled a wooden cup with water. I was unsure of how I felt about his words. *Did he find them beautiful because they could fetch him a pretty penny or, did he honestly just find them beautiful?*

"May I?" he politely asked when he came to a stop in front of me. He towered over my form with the cup raised above my head. I glanced from the cup to him and nodded.

The cold liquid first met my already damp hair then trailed down my forehead, over my nose and cheeks to my lips where it dripped down my chin. It followed the curve of my neck to the dip between my breasts.

The air escaped his lungs at the sight of me and the cup fell into the water at our feet. My hair gained a silver gleam as many scales appeared on my cheeks, forehead, neck, chest and chin where the water had touched. My eyes glowed s bright gray and blue as gills began forming on my neck which making it slightly harder for me to breathe. My round pupils became slits but as soon as I blinked my eyes they were back to normal and my scales began to fade. My hair went back to its usual ivory color.

"*You're* beautiful" my lips slightly parted to reveal the small fangs that were retracting. His words were a confirmation that he didn't just think my scales were beautiful because of their worth but because they were mine, but because they were a part of me.

"Ben-." his name left my lips in a voice that sounded like that of a Siren's song. It had him completely entranced. He moved closer to me as if I'd summoned him.

He placed one knee on the mattress in between my legs and loomed closer. His hand snaked around the back of my neck and tilted my head up so that he could lean down. He paused only to glance at my rapidly rising and falling chest through my shirt. I could feel his warm breath against my parted lips and my eyes drooped at the thought of tasting his.

My hands slid up his chest and over the material of his tattered shirt to feel everything that lay underneath before coming to a stop at his shoulders. I gripped them. He attempted to close the gap between our lips but was snapped out of his trance when the door to his chambers flew open.

49

I turned to glance in the direction to find the silhouette of an angry man.

Ben quickly scurried off me. He moved to stand with his back pressed up against the far wall "C-Captain" was all he could get out as I lowered my leg from where it had been rubbing up against Ben's thigh only moments before.

Caleb's nostrils flared as he looked from me to Ben. His feet stomped their way over to the younger man and he grabbing hold of his shirt's collar to shove him further into the wall. The look in Caleb's eyes was almost feral as Ben struggled against him.

"Ben!" I shot up from my place on the edge of the bed, no longer lost in the moment as I reached for Caleb's arm. I tried to get him to let go but it was no use. He was stronger and he ignored me as his eyes burned into Ben's skull while contemplating murder. I got in between them so that my back was pressed up against Ben's chest while my chest brushed against Caleb's.

"Stop it!" I yelled. My hands moved to grip the material of the Captain's undershirt and coat. He stared past me as if I didn't exist, as if I was invisible to his glaring golden eyes.

"He didn't do anything wrong!" I tried again while shoving at him. I banged my fists into his chest as I heard Ben gasp for air behind me. Caleb's hand was wrapped around his throat, lifting him slightly off the ground. I glanced back at Ben with fear in my eyes.

"It was me!" I frantically cried "I seduced him!" Caleb's eyes began to grow gentler. They grew sadder as they met mine and there was a hint of pain that reflected in their depths before it was replaced by the stone cold glare he always wore. His hand released Ben, who slid down the wall while coughing and clutching at his throat. I knew my words would give Caleb the wrong impression but I was desperate to stop him from killing Ben.

"So ye fancy the boy" he began as he took a step back so that we weren't as close. I glanced down at a confused Ben who moments before had been trapped in my spell and wasn't sure how he got on top of me in the first place. I had no response, no words to speak since they caught in my throat. Caleb shifted his weight.

"Fine then, if ye want to whore around with the boy then have at it!" he snarled in my face. His eyes were wild and his fists clenched at his sides. His knuckles were starting to turn white as if he wanted to punch something.

He turned to storm off but paused in the doorway to glare back at me from over his shoulder "Just get me them treasures" he slammed the door shut which caused the walls to tremble and then he was gone.

I stayed rooted in place as a pang surged in my chest in response to his insult and how he didn't care what I did as long as I got him the treasures. There was a loud fit of coughing and I was snapped out of my thoughts. I turned and fell to my knees in front of Ben. My hand moved to caress the side of his face.

"I'm so sorry" I apologized to which he furrowed his brows and ran the back of his hand over his lips where saliva had trickled down to his chin from the deprivation of air and the force of Caleb's grip on his jugular.

"W-What just happened?" he stumbled over his words. His eyes met mine in the dim light of the candles. I could tell that there was a gap in his memory and felt guilty for something I couldn't control. I let my hand slip away from his face to brace itself against the floorboards. The small layer of water washed over my fingers and knuckles.

"I didn't mean to compel you; I was just-." I began to hurriedly explain but he cut me off as the color returned to his features and he reached for the wall behind him.

"Compel?" he stood, leaning back against the wall as I mimicked his movements. I stood and caught him in my arms when he staggered forward, falling into me with most of his weight. I felt the air leave my lungs from the force but helped him over to the bed where he sank down onto it.

"Mermaids have lured drunken sailors into the water for years" I tried answering his question as I took a seat in the chair opposite him. He rubbed at his throat and his eyes filled with understanding when he looked at me.

"To feed on their souls" I averted my gaze. I stared down at the floorboards. Mermaids were mythical creatures, said to prey on the souls of men who dared to venture out onto the open sea. My lips parted when the tense silence grew uncomfortable.

"In order to do so they would compel them to enter the water" my head nodded as I thought of how it must've made me look. A woman who preyed on the souls of human men, tempting them then devouring them. Ben was the only person onboard the Sunken Soul who treated me as an equal and I didn't want him to fear me or see me as some type of monster.

51

"But we can only compel men if we're attracted to them" I quickly added as my head turned to meet Ben's eyes. He watched me with eyes that gave away nothing, no fear, no confusion only a blank stare while he processed all of it.

"I see" he eventually uttered and relaxed his shoulders. I didn't want to lose the only person I could trust and spoke before I could even process the words while they rushed out.

"I didn't mean to compel you, sometimes I can't control it when-." I was cut off by him standing up from the mattress and placing his hand on the top of my head as if to tell me to stop talking. My voice trailed off as I watched him leave my side and head for his cupboard.

"I understand, now let's get you into something dry" his subject change took me by surprise and left me speechless as he rummaged through his closet in search of something decent for me to wear.

Chapter Six

I stepped out onto the deck. My arms and torso were covered by an old brown shirt that I tied around the waist with a piece of rope.

My shoulders were bare and the shirt had slits that ran up the sides to my hips. Ben decided to stay behind and rest after what happened.

The sun had already set and lamps were lit, providing light for the crew as they drank their ale and chugged their wine.

Caleb sat on a chair in the center of the deck. He watched Rebecca dance. She moved her hips in a way that could entice any man while a member of the crew played some music for her. It was upbeat. It forced her to twist and turn much like a gypsy would.

Caleb's eyes flickered in my direction when I fumbled to tighten the rope around my waist. He took a large swig of the wine in his cup then went back to watching Rebecca. His body tensed and his jaw muscles tightened while his hand constricted around his cup.

"Enough!" he barked out when I headed for his chambers. The music stopped, Rebecca stilled and the world fell silent. I too froze from the command in his voice and waited for him to speak.

He downed the rest of his wine and threw the cup across the deck causing it to clutter loudly. My head shot in the direction of the noise as the Captain ran the back of his hand across his lips. He sloppily leaned forward in his seat.

"Did ye enjoy yeself?" he bluntly asked in a drunken slur. There were a few whistles, some calls and laughter from around us but they died down as soon as Caleb's hand jerked up to silence them. I slowly turned to face him. The orange light casting shadows across his features.

"You're drunk" I simply stated. I was about to turn back around when his hand slapped down onto the arm of his chair, hard enough to cause the wood to groan.

"And ye're a whore" the sting from his words made me flinch which Rebecca noticed. Her hands were still at her sides as she quietly observed from afar. I felt my shoulders straighten. I was about to snap at him but I caught myself "I refuse to entertain your childish ways" with that I was once again heading for the stairs. My hips swayed as I walked with a fiery fury. I was at the top step when his voice reached out to me for a second time.

"Sing to me" my hand gripped the doorframe with one-foot placed lower on the stairs than the other. I breathed in through my nose and let it out in a long, exasperated sigh that was followed by a sudden calmness. He was drunk and an idiot so I chose to ignore his earlier comments. I made my way over to where Rebecca had been dancing. She took a seat on a barrel off to the side and watched intently.

"Oh, they are searching for you, there are five sailors on the waters. Oh, they are coming for you, there are five sailors on the waters-." I sang, my voice calling out over the sea and holding the eyes of the crew. It was like a haunting melody that rang like the echo of a music box. My voice was small yet bewitching.

Once I was done, Caleb's eyes went back to their emotionless state. The dangerous gleam resurfaced in them as if my song had only suppressed it for as long as I continued to sing.

"She sounds just like her" Rebecca whispered. She was bewildered as Caleb rose from his seat and staggered his way towards me. My instinct was to run but something kept me rooted in place as I watched him reach his hand out to trace my cheek with his fingertips. I winced at the contact and expected him to hit me but instead his palm caressed the side of my face. He tenderly ran his thumb along my cheekbone until it dipped down to my bottom lip. His thumb across my lip then flicked it as his eyes roamed over my facial features. They were clouded over by his drunken state and the image of Mary.

"Beautiful" the single word escaped his lips in a low, almost nonexistent breath that caused my eyes to widen as I stared up at him. It was the second time that a man had referred to me as beautiful but what made it even more shocking was the fact that he was a true pirate. He was a man of the sea and to a pirate there was nothing more beautiful than the ocean.

His hand dropped back to his side and he pushed past me, heading towards his chambers. I stared after him, wondering how a man could change so suddenly as to insult me then tell me that I'm beautiful almost in the same breath.

Rebecca appeared at my side as she untied the sash that was slung around her hips.

"Go to him" she whispered in my ear then was gone, in search of something to drink. I didn't recall why but I felt the need to do as she said. My feet carried me down the steps that led to his room where he'd stripped out of his shirt, coat, boots and hat. He was splayed out across the surface of the bed with the locket resting on his chest. It played a haunting tune that was so familiar yet so foreign.

"Please" his voice spoke when I neared the edge of the bed, looming over him. He was drunk but at the same time when he turned his head to look at me there was awareness in his eyes.

"I know ye're not her-." he moved to sit up, the locket cluttering to the floor but he didn't seem to care like he would've hours before. I could see desperation in his golden orbs when he pleaded with me.

"But at least pretend to be my Mary, just for tonight" I could hear the desperation in his tone, a vulnerability that I had yet to see in Caleb. It made me curious as to who the man was that my past self, had fallen in love with.

I nodded slowly only to have him stand and cup both sides of my face in his much larger hands. I closed my eyes, waiting for him to take me, to do as he pleased but instead, I felt something warm press against my forehead. My eyes shot open to find that he had placed a gentle kiss there, one that seemed to linger long after he had pulled away to embrace me, pressing me into his form with his arms wrapped tightly around my shoulders and waist. He buried his face in my hair, breathing in then began to sob.

My eyes widened, starring up at the ceiling with the locket's tune playing in the background. He cried like a child who had been torn away from their mother's embrace, weeping like a little boy.

Where had the fierce pirate Captain gone? Where was the monster that I'd grown so accustomed to seeing?

My arms trembled when I raised them, wrapping them around his form, pressing my face into the side of his neck as one hand tangled into his long dark hair.

"Forgive me, I couldn't save ye, Mary, please forgive me" he repeated over and over again to which I had no response.

I closed my eyes for a brief moment but when I opened them again, I was no longer on the ship, no longer in Caleb's arms but floating aimlessly through the water, starring up at the light of the moon illuminating the surface above.

I wore a light blue gown made of silk that danced around me, strands of golden hair moving past my vision as my hand reached for something. I was desperate to get to the surface, unable to breathe as a man leapt into the water. A younger Caleb swam further and further down towards me only to retreat back to the surface for air.

He too was desperate as he tried time and time again to reach me. His voice calling out to me when he would breach to gasp for air.

'*Mary!*' the call was haunting as my eyes began to droop, my vision becoming blurry. I then chose to accept the embrace of the ocean, not afraid of that which I loved.

A figure appeared in front of me, a woman made of water that had eyes of glowing sapphire. She had legs but her hands and feet were webbed as a tail swished in the water behind her.

'*A heart of the sea*' she spoke in a language that wasn't English but that I somehow could understand. She reached for my hands, taking them in hers as we sank further and further down towards the sea bed.

'*Return to me*' her lips touched mine, breathing air into my lungs as her crystal blue hair moved around us, enveloping us in its cocoon. A bright light tore free from my chest when she pulled away, her hands letting go and pushing me further down while she remained floating in place, watching me.

My eyes shot open to find that I was back on the ship, Caleb sobbing into my hair and shoulder, whispering to Mary. I could only take him in for a few moments before my legs gave in and I fell unconscious, the song from the locket echoing in my ears.

"Evangeline!" Caleb's voice reached out to me but by then it was too late, the darkness was too comforting, too welcoming for me to dare try and fight it.

Chapter Seven

I was standing on a sandy beach, the sun long since set having with only the light of the moon reflecting off the black surface before me. I could hear it, the sound of a whale calling out to its pod, the crashing of the waves around me as the water soaked my feet, the swishing of fins against the water and the power that the moon had over it, pushing and pulling.

The tattered gray gown that hung to below my knees clung to me as the wind swept across the ocean, whipping my white strands back and out of my face.

Why was I there? I went to bed hours before at the orphanage. Why did it all seem so familiar?

'Mary' the call was but a whisper carried by the wind, beckoning me into the vast body of water ahead. I recognized the voice. It was a familiar sound that made the lure of its call that much harder to resist.

I stepped deeper into the water, my foot sinking into the sand as the waves were pulled back, white foam splashing against my calves. I felt a weighing need to find something, to fill the void that had grown inside my chest and the water promised me that, persuading me, seducing me.

'Mary' the voice spoke again, the voice of a man but this time louder, clearer. My body moved on its own accord. One step followed by another and another until the hem of my nightgown was soaked in saltwater.

My eyes began to glow, one a bright, vibrant blue, the other a silvery white. I had no recollection of finding my way to the shore but the only thought I had as I continued to head deeper into the water was the echoing whimper of *'I have to find it'*

'Mary!' louder it rang this time, coming ever closer.

Who is Mary? Why does the voice seem so familiar? Why is it reaching out to me?

I pushed the urgent tone of it aside and felt a strong wave crash into my thighs, forcing me back a step only to pull me further in. I felt mindless, as though I had no control over my body or actions, driven only by the need inside me, a need for something that I couldn't identify.

'Mary!' the voice came from right behind me, snapping me out of my daze, my eyes returning to normal, the need to find something fading as if I had finally found it.

I turned sharply in the water to find a man standing there in only a pair of pants. He looked worried as he watched me, his long hair tied at the back of his head as he leaned closer to where I was.

My eyebrows furrowed up in confusion at the sight of him but also at the sight of the setting sun that moved across his exposed torso. *Hadn't the sun already set hours before?*

I glanced down at myself, finding that my gray gown was now a silk pink dress that I had hiked up at the skirt. The hair that hung down my shoulders was blonde instead of white and my skin was tanner than it had been.

'Ye shouldn't venture off on ye own' the man scolded, moving closer to me. A feeling of love washed over me, enveloping my chest in a warmth that I had yet to feel beforehand. I smiled at the sight of his panicked state, my lips parting to release a small fit of laughter as I moved to meet him halfway, letting go of my skirt to place my palm flat against his cheek, caressing his features as my eyes searched his.

'Isn't it beautiful?' I asked, letting go of him to turn and gaze out onto the sea where the sky overhead was painted a mixture of orange, pink, purple and blue. His arms wound themselves around my waist, his chest pressing flush against my back as he leaned down.

'Not even the sea could compare to yer beauty' he argued, nuzzling his face into my hair and breathing in deeply. I turned my head to look up at him, his eyes flickering to my parted lips that he so wanted to taste.

He leaned down to do just that, the light of the sun catching between us before the scene changed.

I was under water, drifting down to the ocean floor with my hand outstretched towards the surface. I began to panic when my lungs started to burn, my body begging for a breath of air. I tried to swim upward but the water kept dragging me down until I gasped it in, filling my lungs with liquid.

I was drowning, I was going to die. I had to get to the surface. *I had to breathe!*

I shot straight up on a feather mattress, gasping and panting as my hands gripped the sheets on either side of my body. Sweat trickling from my forehead and my heart racing, the frantic beating ringing in my ears like the beating of a drum.

I stared straight ahead, eyes wide and filled with panic until I managed to process that I was still alive, still breathing. My chest began to slow its rise and fall as I blinked, taking in the view of the wall, the white sheets beneath me, the brown shirt that I wore, tied at the waist with rope. I took in the room, eyes moving from the book on the night table to the chair on the other side of the room where a drunken man was snoring, fast asleep with a locket clutched in his right hand, the heart shaped pendant reaching for the floorboards below as he slept.

'Caleb' I thought as I threw my legs over the side of the bed, causing my head to spin. I gritted my teeth and placed my palm flat against my forehead when the memory of him holding me, crying came flashing back.

I remember seeing something in that moment but all that came to me was the image of water followed by me passing out and him calling for me. I tried remembering my dream but I could only see bits and pieces in my memory, the ocean at night, Caleb stood across from me, the water.

I bit out a cry when the pain intensified, as if forcing me to stop trying to remember. The more I would attempt to think back on it the worse the pain would get.

I stopped, breathing in sharp, short pants as my head dropped forward and into the palm of my hand. I squeezed my eyes shut only to stare down at the floor between my fingers when I had the strength to move again.

It was still dark, the room cast in the light of the moon. I got up from the bed, my hand dropping back to my side while I moved to where Caleb was resting, his hair a mess with strands dangling across his face, light stubble coating his jaw. Something was different inside me, perhaps it was the way he had wept like a child before or maybe how he looked when he slept with his muscles relaxed but whatever it was, I didn't like the feeling it created. A mixture of caring compassion and adoration.

I forced them down and turned to head for the deck when something stopped me, the locket that caught the light also managed to catch my eyes, the tune coming back to me, so familiar, so haunting. I could feel myself wanting to touch it, fingertips twitching with a need to hold the heart in my palms but something tore me away from it and onto the deck where I sat on top of the figure head, watching the sun slowly start to rise over the horizon.

My mind would wonder back to my vision and dream but whenever it would, tears would start to run down the sides of my face in a mixture of agony and frustration.

Chapter Eight

We neared a small port town a few hours later with Caleb stood near the helm, completely ignoring me and the fact that I existed. Rebecca was stationed on the stern alongside him, wearing a skimpy coat that barely covered her chest and thighs.

They argued over the map as the former first mate napped on the deck, Snaggletooth snapping his teeth at the rest of the crew as an attempt to say something.

I watched him, wondering if he used a specific sequence of snaps to talk similar to morse code.

"Dock the ship!" Caleb ordered, startling the crew into action. Someone shoved the former second in command who groaned but got up to scale the ship's sails, lowering them.

Ben was among them, his arms bare from where he had rolled up the sleeves of his shirt, exposing what looked like a scar on one of his forearms. I watched him move, tightening ropes and shouting to the others until Caleb caught my eyes.

He was staring down at me as Rebecca tried to convince him of something, speaking to a wall. He glanced from me to Ben then turned to address the fiery haired woman, snarling a response as if to get her off his back.

One of the crewmen moved to lower the anchor near where I was perched, legs dangling off the side of the ship.

"Where are we?" I asked him, my head turning to take in the view before me of mostly men scurrying about the pier, carrying large crates while a few pirate hats stood out among the crowd. There were other ships in the dock, most looked similar to the one I found myself on, flags of crossbones dancing in the sea breeze.

The man lowered the anchor, causing the ship to jerk. I grabbed hold of the figurehead with one hand in an attempt to steady myself.

"Welcome to the Pirate's Nest, sweetheart" he answered, chuckling before he disappeared, leaving me with furrowed brows as I watched the pier. The heavy clanking of feet met my ears and I looked back to see Caleb addressing his crew.

"We set sail at dawn!" the men cheered and flung themselves overboard, some using roped to descend while others preferred to use the water as a net. These men were mad and probably the most maddening of them all was their Captain.

Rebecca appeared at his side, her own boots thudding almost in synch with his.

"You know she wouldn't want this-." she rushed out, moving around him to block his path. He glared down at her, eyes contemplating whether he wanted to shove her overboard or stuff a piece of rope down her throat in an effort to stop her from talking.

"Think about how she would feel!" she tried again but he remained silent, face set in stone before he stepped past her, his shoulder bumping into hers. She stumbled but quickly recovered and hurried after him. His hand gripped the railing of the ship, about to hoist himself over when she frantically spoke "Think about Mary!"

His muscles stiffened, body tensing, his eyes staring at the men moving along the pier. There were a few women but they seemed to be in the market for something other than piracy, their bodies almost completely nude as they brushed up against the men, asking them for money in exchange for a *good time*

"Get off me ship" Caleb growled in a low tone like a warning to the red head before he leapt from the ship and was gone. I watched him weave through the crowd until I couldn't see him anymore.

"Damn that stubborn bastard of a Campbell!" Rebecca cursed, stomping her foot against the floorboards. I tore my eyes from the peer to look at her as she stalked her way over to the trap door that led below deck. She paused for a brief moment, her eyes locking onto mine before she huffed and was gone, the trap door slamming shut behind her.

Ben took a seat beside me, his back towards the peer as he gripped the railing, looking to where Rebecca had disappeared off to.

"You're awfully quiet" he stated, turning to look at me. I watched as crates filled with exotic animals, weapons and rare jewels were being tossed around.

"What is this place?" I found myself asking, hoping that he could give me a better answer than the man I had asked before.

He frowned at the pier, his eyes growing hard at the sight as if they reminded him of everything he hated.

"The Pirate's Nest-." he began, his gaze moving from the people and buildings, bars and brothels to me, his brown eyes boring into mine as he slowly continued, taking care not to cause me any panic "It's a place where Pirates come to trade in the black market or to seek information"

The words 'black market' reached me, sticking to me like a threat. My eyes darted down to my legs that were currently dry, hiding my scales within the flesh of my human form.

Ben knew what I was thinking and reached for my hand, cupping it with his.

"We'll stay on the ship, away from the water until Caleb returns" all my doubts about him wanting to turn me in for a profit seeped away, replaced by a sense of security as I searched his eyes. He knew my secret and despite the gold it may fetch him, he remained silent to protect me.

My eyes landed on his lips that were tugged up into a small, reassuring smile before I quickly looked away and changed the subject "Information?"

His hand slipped away from mine as he leaned further back on the railing, his eyes staring up at the sky where seagulls circled overhead, smoke rising into the blue, gray canvas.

"Regarding treasures, mythical creatures, old legends-." he trailed off, knowing exactly what I had meant. I nodded my head slowly, understanding why we had stopped at the Nest in the first place.

Caleb most likely wanted confirmation that I was leading him in the right direction or wanted to find something out regarding the seven treasures.

They were all he cared about, that and the ghost of Mary. "Well as long as we're here, we might as well go over what I taught you" he didn't have to elaborate, he didn't need to add the word 'navigation' for me to groan loudly, not wanting to feel such a headache or think as hard ever again.

He pushed off the railing and chuckled, reaching for my arm to lightly tug me onto the ship's deck. I stumbled down the steps when Ben let go of my arm to disappear into the Captain's quarters. He came back with my first mate's hat, popping it on top of my head before turning to motion towards the Stern.

"What course will we sail for next, Captain?" he mockingly said, pretending that I was his Captain. I couldn't help but giggle at the sight of his dramatic movements.

I straightened my shoulders and raised my head up high as if I were imitating Caleb. I hurried up the steps and over to the map, glancing at the compass that was placed there.

"We head South West" I pointed in the direction of the docks which had Ben faking confusion as if he was looking for water.

"Will we be sailing through land then, Captain?" he placed a hand over his eyes to shield them from the sun, narrowing his gaze at the shore as if planning our rout. I shook my head, acting as if I knew exactly what I was talking about.

I turned in that direction when I spoke "First we head South till we round the island" he nodded, moving over to the map to take in the sight of the continents and islands that were scribbled onto it.
When he met my eyes, I could tell that there was a sinister glint hidden within their depths.

"How far will we be travelin until we reach them treasures, Capin?" he spoke, over exaggerating the pirate accent as if mocking the rest of the crew.

I couldn't help but laugh at how ridiculous he sounded. The only people onboard the ship who could speak proper English were, Ben, Rebecca and myself but I had never heard the men speak as poorly as Ben had in that moment.

I caught myself and headed over to the map, once again playing the part of Captain. I grabbed the metal device that had pointed tips on each end and walked it along the map.

"We be traveling sixty miles South, first mate Ben" my accent made me snicker but he kept a straight face, moving towards the stern's steps as if he was about to set sail.

"Arg, aye, aye Capin" his added response while he nodded his head was too much for me. I placed a hand over my mouth to stifle my laughter that instantly died down when he paused to look back at me in all seriousness, saying in his usual accent.

"Watching you try to navigate is like watching a fish attempt to fly" I lowered my hand, my mouth hanging open at being compared to a fish out of water, spluttering around but not going anywhere.

I moved to shove his shoulder with my hand, barely getting him to stumble as he chuckled at the sight of my pouting bottom lip.

"But the accent wasn't too bad" he continued to which we both shared a laugh. I knew it was terrible, I knew he only wanted to be nice but even I could admit that my impression of a pirate was terrible.

"What kind of pirate say's, Arg?" I teased, never having heard any of the crew use the expression before. Ben grinned at my attempt to taunt him and shot back.

"What kind of Captain sets course against the current?" I hadn't even considered the current before he had brought it up and I realized my mistake. I placed my palm flat against my face and sighed heavily.

"I'm never going to get the hang of it" Ben laughed at my defeated self, shoulders hung and face hidden in embarrassment. He placed his palm on the curve of my back and pressed lightly, steering me in the direction of the steps.

"Looks like we're back to square one" I tried to protest but before I knew it, I was seated in front of a table with maps splayed out across it, books pilling up on one side, a compass in front of me and my hat dangling from a hook on the wall as I listened to Ben go on and on about the currents and how they would change at specific times during the day and year.

I was bored out of my mind but tried my best to listen and understand since I didn't want to steer Caleb in the wrong direction for fear of him making me walk the plank.

Chapter Nine

Once the sun had set, Ben left to go help stock the ship with barrels of wine and rum along with crates of bread and vegetables.

He told me to examine a map and determine how long it would take to sail from point A, that he circled in black ink, to point B, by the time he got back.

The candle he had lit was flickering beside me on the table as I pondered over the flow of the current, wondering what time of the year we would sail such a length and feeling frustrated since he'd left me with little to go off of.

There was a bang and my head shot up in the direction of the navigation room's glass doors. They were flung open and Rebecca was slumped against the doorframe, a bottle of rum in hand. She was certainly a force to be reckoned with, a lady with a dirty mouth who drank rum straight from the bottle was never one to risk upsetting.

"Rebecca?" I greeted though it came out as more of a question as she pushed off the door and moved towards me.

She licked her bottom lip where a few drops of rum threatened to trickle down her chin and stopped on the other side of the desk.

"Becca, call me Becca" she placed her free palm flat against the table's surface and leaned in closer. Her vibrant emerald gaze narrowing as they searched my features, taking in my button nose, my mismatched eyes, my long white hair and plump, pink lips.

"It's like staring at a ghost" she muttered, raising the bottle to her lips and throwing her head back to take a long swig of the liquid.

I knew she was referring to how much I looked like Mary and wished that they would stop comparing me to a woman I barely knew. Naturally I wanted to know more about her but asking Caleb would only anger him and since Rebecca was the only other person on the ship who had personally known Mary, I decided to take my chances.

"What kind of a person was Mary?" Rebecca pulled out a chair and slumped into it, her shoulders slouched and her arms dangling at her sides, causing the bottle to scrape across the floorboards below. She huffed as if the question was too hard for her to answer, eyebrows furrowing up as she tried thinking back. She was drunk and thinking was a difficult task for anyone when drunk.

"Mary-." she breathed the name, her eyes darkening, a sadness filling them when she remembered what we were talking about. There was an unsettling silence that followed and I began to squirm, wondering if I had made a mistake by asking.

Just as I was about to change the subject she spoke "She was a noble woman from the South, raised rich and isolated from the world" Rebecca paused to take another swig of her rum, as if trying to drink away the memories that she was calling forth.

I listened intently, wanting to know as much about Mary as possible. *A noble woman and a pirate Captain? How had it come to that? How could she possibly have fallen in love with such a beast of a man?*

"She was obsessed with the ocean and its mysteries but being locked away in that stuffy mansion meant that she could only stare at it, sometimes for hours on end" my head throbbed and I squeezed my eyes shut when an image of a mourning Mary standing on a balcony, wearing a laced up ball gown flickered across my eyes.

"She heard rumors of pirates venturing towards the South and snuck out one night to meet them" I could see Mary in a black cloak, glancing around a cobble stone corner to see if there was anyone there before she scurried along the narrow streets, her head held low and her hand gripping at the cloak to shield her from the eyes of commoners.

"She always envied the life of a pirate, free to do as they please, come and go as they desired but the thing she was most jealous of was their intimate connection to the sea" my hand slipped from the table to grip the side of my head, my mouth gaping at the sharp, intense pain that came along with the images.

I could see Mary staring at the old oil painting that hung above her father's fireplace in the study of their mansion. It was of two ships battling on a stormy night. One was a pirate's ship and the other a fleet vessel. Her eyes looked haunted, empty as she stared at the crossbones on the flag of the pirate ship, dreaming, longing for such a life.

"She met with the Captain that night, Captain Caleb Campbell, the bloody moron, and he agreed to take her out to sea" Rebecca uttered the insult, taking another swig of her rum.

I tried opening my eyes to look at her but everything was a blur, clouded by the image of a blonde haired woman pleading with a golden eyed pirate to take her out to sea only if it were to be for just a few simple minutes.

"He took her places she could only dream of, showed her the beauty of the water and somewhere in between their months together they both fell in love" the first vision I'd ever seen of them in a pool of water near a waterfall flashed past my eyes, the sight of them kissing with her dressed in only his shirt.

There were thousands of images, one by one filling my mind at a speed so rapid that I couldn't keep up, a small cry escaping my lips as I tried to force them away. I wanted to tell Rebecca to stop talking but at the same time I had to know what happened to Mary, how she had died.

"Their relationship was to be kept a secret because of her status as a noble, quite the cliché romance if you ask me" the sound of rum swishing inside the bottle met my ears followed by a loud gulp.

Mary and Caleb meeting at an old abandoned church outside the city came to the surface, sharing a passionate kiss as they met at around midnight, their acts forbidden but made worth it by the smiles they both wore.

"But as his love for her grew, her love for the sea grew even greater. It grew so strong that she sacrificed herself to become one with it" Mary stepped up onto the railing of the Sunken Soul, staring down at the water below before she took the leap, diving under the water only to sink further and further down as Caleb's voice frantically called out to her.

"They were out on the water one night and she dove in. She was never taught how to swim. She began to sink and Caleb tried his best to save her but, in the end, she got what she wanted. She drowned herself to forever be with the greatest love of her life"

A calming look came over Mary's features as she watched Caleb struggle on the surface. Her eyes closing when she felt the water enter her lungs, causing her chest to burn but despite it she was happy, she was smiling.

"The sea" I gasped, my hands gripping the table in front of me when the images finally stopped and I could breathe. Rebecca barely even noticed my struggle, too drunk to process the world around her.

"That's the story, I guess" she muttered, shrugging her shoulders and tipping her empty bottle upside down, shaking it, as if expecting more rum to come flowing from its neck.

She abruptly stood and nearly fell forward onto her face but managed to catch herself.

"I'm going to get some more rum" with that she left, leaving me staring at the ground with wide eyes, my body trembling and chest aching from the emotions I had just experienced.

Footsteps neared the room I was in just as my hands lost their grip on the table and I tumbled to the side, about to hit the floor but strong arms scooped me up against a solid chest before I could hit my head.

"Evangeline?" a frantic voice called and I knew from the familiarity of it that it belonged to Ben.

Maps were strewn across the floor and he had dropped a trey of food in his haste to catch me. My eyes began to droop, my arms dangling at my sides, too weak to move.

"Caleb" I whispered the name, feeling the person beneath me stiffen as I once again passed out, an image of the Captain's face smiling down at me dancing in my mind, such a beautiful image, the image of a man in love.

When I woke up, I was back in the Captain quarters. The ship was moving again and I was alone. Shouting came from above deck and the sun's rays spilled into the room through the porthole.

It was growing colder the further we ventured North and judging from the way my breath would condense I gathered that we were closing in on the location of the second treasure.

I threw my exposed legs over the side of the bed and could barely feel the chilly air nipping at them. As a Mermaid I couldn't really feel the cold.

I reached for my boots near the foot of the bed and tugged them onto my feet, one by one followed by a thin jacket that I had found in one of Caleb's drawers. It hugged my arms and torso, making it seem as if I was trying to keep warm when really, I didn't need it.

I snatched my hat from the nightside table and headed above deck to find slabs of ice drifting in the waters around the ship. Fields of white stretched out into the distance as far as the eye could see.

The crew were awestruck by the sight as Caleb guided the ship further into the biting frost.

I hurried to the stern where Rebecca was fast asleep, perched on a barrel near the helm, a blanket draped over her shoulders as her head rested on the ship's railing.

"We're here" I announced, appearing beside Caleb who looked at me with furrowed brows that eventually faded into a stern, annoyed scowl. I looked ahead to what awaited us. Two large ice shelves sat on either side of us.

"Slow her down!" Caleb snapped, causing Rebecca to stir from her slumber and the crew to do as they were told, tying the sails so that the ship slowly crept into the narrow space between the shelves. I could hear them groaning, the sound echoing through the water beneath us almost as if they were annoyed by our presence.

The redhead blinked up at us, her eyes adjusting to their surroundings.

"Evangeline?" she questioned but I ignored her when the sight of a shipwreck came into view. I rushed past Caleb, my hands gripping the railing as I shouted "There!"

The Captain nodded, his teeth gritting when he ordered for his crew to lower the anchor. The ship jerked and I grunted when my hip struck it's railing due to the sudden movement.

I gazed down at the ice waters and the pieces of ice that floated across it before, hurrying down the stern's steps to scale down the side of the ship until I was stood on one of the ice slabs.

"Evangeline!" Ben called after me while I leapt across the ice to where the ship had been wrecked on some rocks. I climbed up onto one of them and was able to get onboard the ship without much struggle.

"Lower the boats!" Caleb yelled from somewhere behind me followed by the sound of heavy objects colliding with the water's surface.

I tentatively stepped onto the floorboards, hearing them creek beneath my weight, groaning as I slowly made my way across them to the rope ladder that led to the ship's lookout point.

"In the crow's nest" I repeated, my memory going back to the book and its words. I started climbing up the ladder, my hands burning and legs trembling as I scaled ever higher.

I glanced down to find two rowboats traveling towards the wreck; Caleb was at the head of one while the Irishman, the former first mate was at the head of the second. Ben and Rebecca stayed behind to guard the ship.

"Get me, me gem!" Caleb snarled at me when he noticed that I had stopped climbing. I nodded and hurried to the top, dragging myself into the nest. I was heaving, muscles aching from the climb.

There was something odd about the way I felt. I was weaker, dizzier than usual. It felt as though I hadn't slept in days when in fact I'd just woken up from a long night's rest.

I could hear heavy boots thudding onto the deck below while my eyes searched for something in between the straw, empty bottles and snow that had gathered in the crow's nest. I fell to my knees when I noticed a sapphire stone catching the light of the sun and scooped it up. It was identical to the first with the only difference being its color. I stared at the jewel and furrowed my brows in confusion.

"It's too easy" I breathed when realization struck. I jumped to my feet and peered over the edge of the lookout point to find that most of the crewmen were staring at the water below, including Caleb who unsheathed his sword.

My eyes landed on a figure that was as pale as the snow but had hair made out of the arctic water. She was leaning towards one of the crewmembers. Her soulless black eyes peering at her unsuspecting prey. Her webbed fingers were decorated in sharp talons.

"Sirens" I uttered, watching her lunge and grab the man, dragging him into the water that quickly turned red as it was stained with blood.

"Sirens!" I yelled when more of them began to surface. Caleb turned decapitating one of the creatures as it lunged at him. My eyes followed him as he moved, cutting down a few more until one managed to pop up right in front of him, baring her fangs.

I searched for something, anything, eyes landing on one of the glass bottles which I hurriedly grabbed and threw directly at the Siren, the glass shattering against the side of her head. She hissed, her eyes narrowing onto me before Caleb's sword slid down the length of her back causing black blood to splatter across the floorboards.

I heard a loud, high pitched screech and looked down at the ladder that led to the crow's nest. One of the Sirens were making their way towards me. Her albino form stood out against the dark wood. I stumbled away from the railing only to find that a second Siren was scaling the opposite side of the pole upon which the nest was perched.

"Evangeline!" Caleb's voice called out to me, drawing my eyes to him in the crowd below as men fought against the soul devouring creatures. My chest rose and fell as I frantically searched for a route to take, my eyes landing on the water then on the gem. I stuffed it into the pocket of my coat then hurriedly stripped out of it.

"Caleb!" I yelled as I threw the coat at him, he caught it in confusion as I kicked my boots off and stepped up onto the side of the crow's nest. One of the Sirens reached me, reaching out to claw at my leg.

I cried out in pain when she pierced my skin and leaped from my perch, tearing the necklace from my neck as I dove into the arctic waters. Blood pooled around me as a few Sirens dragged some of the crewmembers down into the dark oceanic depths to feast.

My legs twisted into one, a fin decorated in silver scales as my eyes began to glow and my fangs extended, hands webbing while more scales decorated my chest, face, torso and arms. My ivory hair danced around me in the water, skin as pale as moonlight.

I found myself watching the Sirens, wondering how I was any different from them. I called Caleb a monster but in truth, I was the real monster.

I looked to the surface where I could hear the voices of men shouting and heavy swords being swung. My lips parted and I began to sing, a sound that resembled that of a whale's call, low and haunting. The Sirens halted, clutching at their ears and shrieking, some fleeing at the sound of my voice, a voice that could cause an eardrum to burst from how high pitched it was. Humans couldn't hear it which meant that they had no idea why the Sirens were retreating, thrashing in the water until they were out of sight. I stopped singing, taking a deep breath in through my gills before clasping the necklace back around my neck.

My tail parted into two limbs, my eyes no longer glowing, webs fading as I returned to my naked, human self, dangling in the water with no air to breathe until I was sure I could return to the surface.

I kicked violently against the current and broke through the water, gasping for air, breathing hard as I clung to the side of one of the rowboats.

Caleb sheathed his sword and rushed over to where I was, my coat in hand as he leapt into the boat, reaching for my arm to pull me from the water, pressing me firmly up against his chest as he wrapped the coat around me in an attempt to warm me up.

I was trembling from the cold but not as much as I would've if I had been human. I would most likely have had hypothermia by then if that were the case.

"Return to the ship!" Caleb ordered, tightening his hold on me as his men hurried back to the rowboats. They began to row us back to the Sunken Soul before the Sirens could return. I knew they wouldn't but remained silent, my hands gripping at the material of Caleb's jacket and shirt.

They hoisted the rowboats back onto the ship while Caleb scooped me up into his arms, causing me to cry out in agony. He glanced down at my right calve where I had a set of four claw marks running across the ivory flesh, dripping crimson blood onto the deck.

My eyes landed on Ben among the crew. He looked like he was about to rush to my side but Rebecca grabbed hold of his shoulder and shook her head, motioning towards the boats. Caleb carried me below deck, to his chambers where he sat me down in the armchair that he had previously been sleeping in.

"It hurts" I whined, gritting my teeth and clutching at the wound with my hand to try and stop the bleeding. The warm liquid pooled past the gaps in between my fingers and spilled onto the rug and wood, staining them.

Caleb didn't move, his face stern and his eyes searching my features. I looked to him with pleading eyes and I realized why he wasn't helping me. It was because of how I reacted when he'd tried to clean my head wound earlier. I was shaking, exhausted and terrified because of what I had seen. Men being torn apart in black water by creatures similar to me.

"Help me" I squeaked out. My vision became blurry with unshed tears due to the pain. I gritted my teeth and squeezed my eyes shut as I cried "Please!" the word was frantic, strangled like the whine of a wounded, dying animal.

Caleb hurried to get everything he needed. A needle and thread, a bucket with some fresh water, rum, a cloth and bandages. I let go of my leg when he took hold of it and gripped the arm of the chair that I was seated in. Caleb turned my leg to examine the wound then grabbed the bottle of rum, removing the cork with his teeth.

"This'll hurt" he warned but before I could protest, a sharp sting shot through me. I threw my head back, mouth gaping as I screamed, my back arching and muscles tensing in response to the pain.

73

The coat I wore had slid down my shoulders, leaving me naked to his eyes but neither of us seemed to care. I was too blinded by the pain and he was too focused on disinfecting my wound.

He poured more rum onto the wound then set the bottle aside as my nostrils flared and my breathing came in short, quick pants.

"Breathe" he instructed, his eyes flickering up to my face. I was staring at him but could hardly process what was happening. He wet the cloth in fresh water and began dabbing at my leg, it didn't hurt as much as before and it gave me time to calm my breathing.

My eyes had drooped shut and I was about to fall unconscious when something pierced my skin. I shot back up, eyes wide and mouth gaping, a shriek piercing the air. He dug the disinfected needle into my skin again, repeating the action as I wept and screamed and pleaded for him to stop, to stop the pain.

"No, no, stop, please stop, please! Please, stop!" He ignored me and went from one gash to the next until all four were stitched up with thread. He tied off the last stitch and tossed the needle aside to once more dab at my wounds with the wet cloth.

Sweat coated my forehead, my body shaking and my mind spinning. I felt him bandage my leg, gently folding the fabric around and around until it could be tied in a knot below my knee.

My arms dropped to my sides, knuckles scrapping across the floor as my head fell limp onto my shoulder.

"I'm sorry" his arms wound themselves around me, moving me so that my head was resting on his shoulder. He was still kneeling on the ground between my parted legs. His breath was warm as he whispered the words, his hand running through my hair as if to try and comfort me.

"T-Thank-." I coughed, my body shaking from the sudden fit. My voice was raspy from the screams and scratching at my throat whenever I would speak.

"You-u" I felt like I was dying, like my body was going to give in at any moment but before it did, I had to give him the jewel. I tried moving my arm but it only made things worse, using up the little amount of strength I had left.

The jacket slipped down my arm and cluttered to the floor, the blue rock tumbling out of its pocket and onto the floorboards. Caleb stared down at it for a while, in silence.

"We head…S-South-East" I managed to get out before I slipped from his shoulder, his arms catching me when I was once again thrown forcefully into a deep slumber, wondering why I was willing to do so much for a man I barely even knew.

Chapter Ten

For the first time in what felt like forever, I didn't dream about Mary. I could sleep, regain my strength and when I finally woke back up, I found Ben seated on a chair beside the bed in the Captain's quarters. He was staring down at the book of the seven treasures, unable to read but looked to be interested in the letters.

"Be-n" I managed to get out, wanting to move my arm but all I could do was twitch my index finger. I was frail and weak. I was starving and my throat felt dry.

He looked up at me with wide eyes and rushed to get me a cup of water, supporting the back of my head as he pressed the cup to my lips. I gulped down most of it before I started coughing. He set the cup aside, easing me down onto the mess of pillows and blankets.

"You're awake" he stated, clearly shocked. Slumping down into his chair, hand gripping the arm of it as if to steady himself.

My eyebrows furrowed up in confusion as to why he sounded so baffled, his eyes filled with relief as he ran a shaky hand through his blonde curls.

"Why do you...look-?" I began, needing to stop to take a deep breath before I could finish my sentence "So sur-prised?" my voice was raspy and almost nonexistent with a few letters barely coming out and others coming out as too high pitched.

He looked at me laying there with my hair knotted and my eyes drooping, my leg bandaged and my voice all but gone.

"Evangeline, when we left the Pirate's Nest you were asleep for three days, this time it was five" my muscles stiffened at his words. Was *I really asleep for so long?* It didn't feel like it, it only felt like a couple of hours.

The ship wasn't moving which meant that we were docked somewhere or were currently stationed in the middle of the ocean with the anchor lowered.

"What?" I questioned and tried to sit up, gritting my teeth as I pushed myself into a seated position. Ben was up on his feet again, easing me into the pillows instead of helping me onto my feet like I wanted him to.

"The...trea-sures" I protested, fighting to throw my legs over the side of the bed. He sighed at my persistence and watched when I flinched when my wounded leg scrapped across the mattress.

I could hardly keep myself upright, one leg almost useless while the other steadied me. My hands gripped the sides of the mattress as tightly as possible.

"Forget the treasures. You need to rest" he argued, coming to a stand in front of me. I was panting when I looked up into his concerned eyes.

He had most likely been sitting at my side for days on end, hoping that I would finally wake up and there I was, awake but determined to get back on my feet as quickly as possible.

"At least eat something" he reached for the trey on the nightside table and took a seat next to me with it in his lap. My stomach growled and I realized that I was hungry. I nodded, allowing him to feed me the cold vegetable soup that tasted terrible but went down quickly. Any food was better than no food at all. I ate like a starved animal until every last bite was gone and I felt like I had at least regained some strength.

I tried to stand, Ben having to catch me when pain shot through my right leg "Take it easy" I breathed hard, using him to support my weight then pushed off, hobbling towards the stairs.

My hands slapped against the wall beside the steps that headed above deck and I looked up to find my first mate's hat dangling there on a hook. I took it, placing it on the top of my head before forcing myself to climb up the steps. Taking them one at a time.

"Evangeline!" Ben yelled and rushed after me, standing behind me in case I was to fall backwards. I got to the deck and everything fell silent. Snaggletooth, the Irishman, whose name I still didn't know, and the rest of the crew all went still at the sight of me.

I ignored their reaction and turned, my hands gripping the railing as I ascended the steps to the stern. Rebecca's voice went quiet as soon as she noticed me, her eyes wide and her mouth slightly agape while the open sea stretched onto the horizon for miles behind her.

The foot of my wounded leg slipped on one of the steps and I bit out a cry as Ben caught me.

"Be careful" he scolded, steadying me. I rolled my eyes at him for worrying too much and continued on until a familiar back came into view. Caleb's back clad in a red coat was turned to me and somehow made me feel safe. I opened my mouth, my hands clinging to the railing for dear life.

"A m-move-." I flinched when I accidentally placed too much weight on my injured leg "Moving island" I got out which caught Caleb's attention.

He turned to look down at me, his eyes filling with a mixture of relief and worry only to be replaced by anger.

He moved towards me, Ben sinking back and away from the predatory man that was on top of me within seconds.

"Why are ye out of bed?" he demanded, his eyes glaring down at me like they usually did. I could feel my temper start to get the better of me. There I was trying to help him and all he could do was yell at me in response.

"I thought I told ye to make sure she stays in bed!" Caleb snapped at Ben who kept one hand on my waist in case I were to stumble and fall. I looked at Ben who had fear in his eyes then to Rebecca who was just as concerned about the situation and finally to Caleb.

"If I knew that ye couldn't even follow a simple order, I-." I cut him off "Shut up!" I yelled, wincing when my throat ached in response to my sudden outburst.

Rebecca looked shocked at first then raised her hand to cover her mouth, the other clutching her stomach as she stared at us with tears in her eyes. She was trying her best to stifle her laughter due to the look on Caleb's face. He fell silent and was staring at me in disbelief while the rest of the crew merely gaped.

"I can take care of myself" my words weren't as delayed anymore but they still sounded like I was having trouble speaking, sometimes going too high or going too low and it hurt to talk like that but I was past my breaking point. I was exhausted, wounded, confused and frustrated and Caleb's attitude wasn't helping.

"Chair! Now!" I snapped at the crew below and they immediately shot to their feet. A chair was placed near the map on the table behind the helm and I stumbled towards it, slumping down onto it as Rebecca leaned against the railing, hand still clasped over her mouth. I looked at Caleb.

"Head South-East and use your eyes instead of your mouth to look for a moving island" Rebecca lost it, throwing her head back as a rumbling laughter escaped her. She clutched her stomach and gripped the railing with her free hand, sinking down onto her knees from the laughter.

Ben was horrified, looking at me as if he didn't recognize me while Caleb looked like he had been slapped clear across the face.

"Oh no, stop, please, it's too much!" Rebecca kept laughing, wheezing in between her fits. Caleb turned and moved towards me, a feeling of slight fear overcoming me but I suppressed it, glaring back at him just as he was glaring at me.

Rebecca glanced at us, wiping at the tears that streamed down the side of her face when she finally regained her composure. She was sat on the floorboards, breathing heavily with a few breaths of laughter in between. Caleb grabbed the ship's wheel.

"Set course, South-East!" he barked, the crew, including Ben scurrying off to do as he said before one of them got struck by the fist that was meant for me.

The ship jerked and my chair scraped across the wood but I managed to stabilized it with my left leg. I grunted, knowing that he'd turned the wheel more forcefully than was necessary on purpose. I shot him a narrow eyed look that he ignored and glanced over the map, trying to remember what Ben had taught me.

We'd been sailing for a few hours and I'd asked Ben to bring me the book of the seven treasures along with a quill and some paper. He sat on a chair beside me at the table as I tried teaching him how to read in exchange for him teaching me how to navigate.

He had been so interested in the letters when I awoke that I decided to help him understand them.

"You're getting your 'd' and your 'b' mixed up again" I said, glancing down at the chicken scratch that he had scribbled onto the piece of paper in an attempt to write the word 'rod'

He grumbled to himself in frustration, glancing back at the sheet where I had written down the entire alphabet both in capitals and non-capital letters. I'd sung the song the orphanage had imprinted into our heads about a million times but he somehow still managed to confuse some of the letters.

"Try writing the word 'oar'" I urged, motioning to the oars of the rowboats that were fastened to the deck below.

Rebecca was looming over us, her head tilted to the side with interest. I took it that she too couldn't read and found it just as difficult to understand as Ben. She plucked the quill from Ben's hand and tried copying my handwriting, first writing an 'o' then an 'r'. She stood upright with a triumphant smirk plastered across her lips.

"There, easy" I could see Ben gaping at her like she was the fastest learner alive, envy in his eyes at thinking that she was right. I held my hand out to her, palm facing upwards. Silently asking for the quill.

"You forgot the 'a'" I rewrote the word 'oar' on the paper in more than half the time that it took her to copy the letters. Her face went blank and Ben's eyebrows furrowed up in confusion as to why there was an 'a'

"Or when written with just an 'o' and 'r' is the or that you use when you say, for example 'please bring me some wine or rum'" I had the two looking at me with blank stares, trying to take in everything I was saying while at the same time attempting to understand what language I was speaking.

"And oar with an 'a' is the oar you use to row with" Rebecca nodded her head, pretending to understand while Ben remained silent, clearly not understanding what I had just said. I sighed heavily, holding the quill out for him to take.

"Try writing your name. Start with a capital" he nodded, his eyes studying the alphabet for a few seconds, lips moving as if he was trying to pronounce the word and hear the letters.

He slowly scribbled a capital 'b' across the paper but it wasn't in cursive. If I had to teach them how to write in cursive it would most likely drive me insane. He wrote an 'e' which had me leaning forward in anticipation as he started on the last letter which was the 'n'. Once done he looked up at me as if to seek my approval.

"Well done" I praised. He glanced down at the paper and seemed proud for a second, his name escaping his lips in a low whisper. I felt proud and was about to give him something else to write when he locked eyes with me and said in a very blunt tone.

"I wish you could learn to navigate this quickly" my mouth dropped open and Rebecca threw her head back laughing. Ben grinned tauntingly at me as I snatched the quill from his hand and stuck the feather in his face.

"Don't get cocky, you only managed to write one word today" he fell silent, his grin fading into a fearful look which had Rebecca laughing even more loudly in the background. I looked at her, my eyes narrowing onto her figure.

"And you learned absolutely nothing" her laughter caught in her throat as she looked back at me, Ben once again grinning at her like a little boy as if to say 'I won'. She placed her hands on her hips and moved closer to look down at the piece of paper she had scribbled the word 'or' onto.

"Not true, I learned how to write that one" she pointed at it and I could feel myself wanting to laugh from her lack of memory. She couldn't say the word nor could she tell me what it meant or how it was used in the English language. I shook my head and tossed the quill onto the table.

"That's enough for one day" I announced to which Ben sighed in relief and started cleaning up the table, returning the things to where he had found them except for the book that I decided to keep on my person at all times. Becca crossed her arms over her chest after Ben left and spoke with a confident smile.

"Well since you're teaching me how to read, how about I teach you how to drink like a pirate?" I glanced up at her. Caleb still stood by the helm, having been silent since that afternoon, not bothering to care about my reading and writing lessons as he manned the ship but it was then that he looked in our direction.

"What a useful thing to be taught" I sarcastically responded. She grabbed two cups from on top of the barrel she had been sleeping on when we were in the Northern waters and filled each of them with wine.

"You're a pirate, are ye not?" she mockingly used the word 'ye' to which Caleb shot her a glare. She held a cup out for me to take as I pondered over her words.

Was I a pirate? I could feel my hat as it weighed down on my head. I was a first mate. *Didn't that technically make me a pirate?* I took the cup and held it in between my palms, starring down at the sweet liquid which Ben had also offered me before.

"If I get drunk enough, will you teach me how to dance?" I asked. She set her cup down on the table, fingers gripping the rim as she laughed.

"If you get drunk enough not to feel the pain in your leg then yes" she replied, smiling down at me with daring eyes, silently challenging me to drink as much as I possibly could. I nodded, about to take my first sip when she grabbed hold of my wrist, stopping me. The physical contact between us caused Caleb to stiffen from behind the ship's wheel.

"The rules are that whenever I take a sip, you have to do the same" *only bad things can come of this*. Is what I told myself but I nodded and raised my cup, still bound to my chair where I had been sitting for hours on end.

I wanted more than anything to walk, to dance or swim but I couldn't and just sitting there would be the death of me by the end of the night. The light from the setting sun caught her hair, making it look as though her curls were on fire.

"I accept your challenge" she let go of me, laughing as she leaned back against the table and took a swig of her wine. I did the same, mimicking her actions.

The sweet liquid ran down my throat, hot and strong, making the irritated skin inside feel better somehow. My voice still sounded off but with time it got a little better.

Ben came back a few moments later when I was on my sixth sip and noticed that I had a cup in my hands.

"I'm glad to see that you've finally started to let go a bit" he said, referring back to the first time I drank with him when he told me to let go and to relax. He joined us, drinking at his own pace as Caleb brooded in silence.

Challenging Rebecca would be a mistake I would come to regret but most lessons in life are best learned through making mistakes.

Chapter Eleven

Rebecca was barely drunk, sat on her barrel and watching me with smiling eyes as Ben too enjoyed the conversation.

"Tell me a secret" Becca urged, swirling the liquid in her cup as she leaned her head against her palm supporting the weight with her elbow propped up onto the railing of the ship.

Caleb had taken a seat on the steps that led down to the deck, his own cup in hand as he listened in on our exchange of words. I looked at my fifth cup of wine and hummed.

"I've never been with a man before" I stated to which Rebecca nearly chocked on her wine and Ben grew awkwardly silent. Caleb glanced back at me from over his shoulder, eyes emotionless as he watched me. I turned to face him, slamming my cup down on the table.

"But despite that fact, I am still a whore" yes, drunk me was still slightly upset about his prior comments.

Rebecca erupted into a fit of laughter, finding it all amusing and wanting to throw some wood onto the fire. She evilly twisted her cup back and forth in her hand and tilted her head to the side, faking curiosity.

"Oh? How so?" she asked, causing Ben to clear his throat loudly, turning so that he was gazing out onto the black sea, not wanting to be part of our conversation. I furrowed my eyebrows up in question, mauling over my response.

Why haven't I been with a man before?

"I guess it's because I've never been in love" everyone fell silent, Ben shooting me a glance as Caleb watched me with stern features. I stared at the table in front of me then gazed at the liquid in my cup.

The crew began playing an upbeat tune that made me want to dance for some reason and before I knew what I was doing I was up on my feet, hobbling over to the steps. I pushed past Caleb who bit out his annoyance, thinking that I was going to head to the deck but I stopped on the steps, grabbing hold of his hand with both of mine.

"Let's dance" I insisted to which Becca snorted into her cup and Ben's jaw began to drop. Caleb tore his hand out of my grasp, causing me to sway back and forth, having to grip the railing to prevent myself from falling.

"Go dance with the boy" he shot at me, his head jerking in Ben's direction. I pouted, bottom lip sticking out as I leaned in so that our faces were only inches apart. His golden orbs seemed almost glowing or maybe it was because of the amount of alcohol causing my head to spin but they were more beautiful than I remembered as they glared at me.

"But I want to dance with you" I whined like some child, the act only seeming to amuse everyone around us. He breathed in, taking in the smell of alcohol lacing my breath then turned his head away, not bothering to reply to my ridiculous request.

"Please" I urged, my hand moving to brace myself on the step between his legs as I stared up at him with big mismatched eyes.

He slanted back when I leaned towards him as if trying to avoid me but I could see his eyes flickering down to my pouting lips then to my chest that was left slightly exposed to his gaze.

He only watched me so I threw my hat aside, letting it land on the deck below as I snatched his from the top of his head and stuck it on top of mine.

He instantly got up like I had hoped he would and rushed after me. I ran across the deck, barely able to feel the pain in my leg anymore as I laughed.

Strong arms wrapped themselves around my waist and scooped me up into the air. I shrieked and kicked, my toes pointing in the air while the crew around us laughed at the sight. The music had stopped playing and the laughter grew deaf to my ears as Caleb pressed me up against his chest with one arm and used the other to retrieve his hat.

Everything happened in slow motion, my smiling features, his arm winding around my waist in a familiar way, the way he placed his hat back onto his head. Then an image filled my mind of a smiling Mary with her feet in the sand, watching the sea. She had her back pressed up against his chest. Similar to how we were positioned.

I turned my head to look up at him, the rim of his hat hiding our faces from the rest of the crew as I met his gaze.

Time stood still, Mary's emotions fluttering around in my chest, the emotions from her memories tangling in between mine in that moment. I stood on the tips of my toes and felt his breath tickling my lips before they touched his for a brief moment, a tender, sweet kiss that lasted seconds but felt like a lifetime.

84

I saw her, Mary, wrapped only in bed sheets and lying across his bare chest, her hair a mess and their bodies covered in a layer of sweat, breathing hard from what they had been doing. It was her first time; I could tell from the emotions that the scene induced within me.

She had given herself to him, she had loved him so much that she was willing to give him all she had to offer. She was happy, the happiest she had ever been in that moment, listening to his heartbeat thundering in her ears as they lay on the bed in his chambers, wound together.

I lightly pulled away from him to find that he was looking at me in both confusion and need which faded the moment I tore his arm away from me and hobbled off, uttering a quick "Sorry" as I headed to his quarters, slumping down into the armchair that sat in the far corner of the room, my mind filled with memories, scenes from the past that weren't my own, emotions that were starting to cloud mine.

I was drunk, sad, frustrated and angry. I felt tears stream down the side of my face as I tried to understand how something like that could happen to me.

I wasn't falling in love with Caleb, I was merely feeling the love that a woman from the past had felt for him. I fiercely wiped at my tears, questioning why I was having these unwanted visions, these unwanted emotions but I forced it all aside to curl in on myself, not wanting to use the bed because of what I'd seen so I pressed my head against the back of the chair and closed my eyes, feeling the dizziness start to fade into a deep sleep.

I awoke hours later to the sound of voices yelling, one of which I knew exactly who it belonged to.

I groaned, gripping the side of my head when the prior evening's events resurfaced in the back of my mind. Caleb's shock and confusion, the taste of wine on his lips, those soft lips.

I grunted loudly, leaning forward with my face in my hands. There was a sharp pain and I flinched, running my fingers through my messy curls as I glanced down at my leg. I felt like an idiot for running around like I had with a wounded leg and for challenging Rebecca in the first place.

There were red stains soaking through the bandages but they were small, not enough for my stitches to have torn so I pushed myself onto my feet and limped across the rug to the steps where I used the railing to pull myself onto the deck.

There was a barrel of water stood beside the door that I dipped my hands into, splashing the water on my face and running my palms over my features as if to wash them.

"She's alive" a feminine voice called out when I gripped the edges of the barrel and stared at my own reflection in the water. I tilted my head back to look at Rebecca, stood on the stern and grinning down at me.

My head spun from the sudden movement and I groaned, clutching it in between the palms of my hands. The ship rocked "Make it stop" I muttered, my legs dancing beneath me to steady myself. Rebecca's laughter pierced the air, an all too familiar sound. The sky was gray and gloomy, portraying how I felt.

"A hungover pirate-." she began, shaking her head from side to side as heavy boots approached me "That's a first"

I looked up at the person nearing me to find Ben, dressed as plainly as ever in a white shirt and brown trousers. He wore leather boots that were a few shades darker than the rest of his attire.

"We all had to start somewhere" he defended, gazing up at the redhead with his thumbs hooked onto his beltloops. She dramatically rolled her eyes, leaning against the railing as she swiped her hand in the air, brushing him off.

"Details, she's a horrible drinker" Ben's lip twitched up into a smile that I didn't notice since I was too busy staring at myself in the water.

My hair was down in wavy curls, my skin burnt a few shades darker from life on the sea and my cheeks were still red from the previous night's drinking.

"Not to mention a terrible navigator" Ben added to which I shot him a glare, dipping my hand into the water to flick it at him. He dodged, chuckling when I quickly gripped the sides of the barrel again. My stomach began to do flips when the ship rocked for a second time.

"But when it comes to a first mate, I'd say she's doing a pretty fine job" Rebecca finished, shooting me a brilliant smile.

My lip twitched but as soon as it did, I had to squeeze my eyes shut and tightened my hold on the barrel, trying to fight the wave of nausea that overcame me. Ben agreed, coming to my rescue when he realized that I wasn't going to go anywhere on my own.

"One-." he began, bending down to place one arm behind my knees and the other underneath my arms.

"Two, three" he scooped me up, the quick motion causing me to groan, my hand clamping down over my mouth as if to stop whatever wanted to crawl up my throat from escaping my lips.

He laughed, heading up the steps to the stern with little regard for my hungover state. I was placed onto a chair, the arms of which I grabbed hold of, teeth clenching as I tried to regain my composure.

When I could finally open my eyes again, I noticed Caleb behind the ship's helm, his eyes locked onto the horizon, heading South-East with features set in stone. He was angry, I could tell from the way he cursed when a strong wave took us by surprise "Damned wind!"

I jumped at the harshness of his tone but noticed that he didn't blame the sea. Pirates worshipped the waters and to him, insulting the sea would be like placing a bad omen on the Sunken Soul.

"Steady them sails!" he snapped at his crew, his voice growling as they rushed to do as they were told. Ben was above me within minutes, untying the sails and adjusting others.

Watching him climb was like watching a Mermaid swim. It seemed to be almost second nature to him.

The calls of men faded into the distance when I looked back down at the ocean, my gaze landing on an island that appeared to pop out of the water in front of my very eyes. My lips parted, eyes growing wide as the trees penetrated the surface followed by jagged rocks and a shore of white sand.

"Gigas" I muttered under my breath, getting up onto my feet as I stared at the gigantic structure moving alongside us. A large wave struck the side of the ship when the island had surfaced, forcing me to grab onto the helm and table to steady myself.

"Gigas" I repeated, my hand moving to grab hold of Caleb's upper arm. He looked down at my grip on his red coat, eyes filled with irritation. His lips parted, about to snap at me when my free hand moved to point at the island that only I had seemed to notice "A moving island"

His golden gaze followed my extended arm until it landed on the island that hadn't been there before. My hand dropped away from his arm when he moved to bark more orders, demanding that the rowboats be lowered, handing the wheel over to Rebecca who steered us closer to the island's shore. Ben grabbed onto a piece of rope and used it to slide his way back down onto the ship's stern, landing on the balls of his feet beside me.

"Mermaids, Sirens and now this-." he mumbled more to himself than anyone else around him. I couldn't avert my gaze, having heard many rumors of an island that could disappear and appear as it pleased in various different locations across the seven seas.

"It's Gigas" I found myself breathing, catching not only Ben's attention but that of Rebecca and Caleb as well. The Captain paused on his way to the deck to glance back at me from over his shoulder.

"One of the Guardians of the Sea-." I elaborated to which Caleb and Rebecca shared a look while Ben listened intently "It's said that he is a giant sea turtle that carries an island upon his back"

Rebecca's head whipped around to look at the large scale portion of land, traveling at breakneck speed beside the ship. The palm trees bent against the force of the winds and the sand washed away at the edges to reveal the small portions of brown shell that resided underneath.

"You're telling me that, that is a turtle?" Rebecca questioned, her hand motioning towards the sight as if it was beyond believable. Ben remained silent, his lips slightly parted, knowing that I was right from everything he had witnessed beforehand.

I nodded my head once, sharply and Caleb descended the steps to head for one of the rowboats, leaping over the side of the ship to land with a thud on the wood below. I moved to follow him but Rebecca grabbed hold of my wrist.

"You're hurt" she stated, her eyes flickering from my confused gaze to Ben. She jerked her head in the direction of the rowboats as if to urge him to go with Caleb.

He looked to me then left despite my protests. I tried to pry myself free from Rebecca's grasp but she had an iron grip.

"I have to help him!" I argued to which she simply ignored me, keeping her focus on the helm and steering the ship as close to the edge of the turtle's shell as possible. I clawed at her hand with my free one to no avail.

Caleb was ordering his crew to push off the side of the ship once they got close enough to guide the boats onto the island's beach.

"I have to-." she cut me off, turning her head to look at me with narrowed eyes. She seemed deadly serious, not the usually playful Becca that I had grown used to.

"You have to stay right where you are, Captain's orders!" she shot back over the harsh winds that were whipping our hair in every direction. I had to squint past pieces of ivory hair that struck my face from all sides to make out her stern features.

She turned her head to steer the ship closer, the gray clouds above growing darker, the winds becoming colder.

"Now men!" Caleb ordered and the crew pushed off the side of the ship as hard as they could. I twisted my arm out of Rebecca's grasp and ran towards them, my hands slapping down onto the wooden railing as I leaned over the side, my eyes locking onto clouded golden ones.

"The gem lies at the bottom of an endless pool!" I yelled as loud as I could over the wind.

The boats connected with Gigas's shell, skidding up onto the shore where the crew hopped out to tug them higher onto the layer of sand so that the water wouldn't wash them away. Some of the crew worked to fasten them to nearby palm trees.

Caleb nodded his head in response to my words then commanded for his men to depart into the forest of trees that lay beyond the shore.

They were gone and I glanced up at the sky, praying to the ruler of the seas that the turtle didn't decide to dive back down any time soon. All I could do was watch and wait as seconds ticked into minutes, minutes into hours of Rebecca manning the wheel and I staring at the island, expecting it to go under at any given moment.

I was worried about Ben, worried about Caleb, Snaggletooth, the Irishman despite his anger towards me.

I slammed my hand down onto the railing, the sound catching Becca's attention even past the howling winds.

"That idiot!" I yelled, turning to start hobbling across the stern, going in one direction then the other until it appeared like I was pacing back and forth regardless of the pain in my leg, throat or throbbing head. The redhead watched me in silence.

"He planned this from the start" I concluded, coming to a halt near the table in the middle of the ship's stern.

Caleb had told Rebecca of his plan to leave me behind on the ship and made sure that I fell right into their trap. I grunted in frustration, running a hand through my hair but pausing to tug at a few of the strands.

"He's worried about you" the words were like ice water, causing my entire body to stiffen as I looked to the floor with wide, mismatched eyes. The shock quickly turned to confusion and then annoyance when I concluded that she had to be lying.

Caleb Campbell only cared about finding the seven treasures and to do so I had to be kept alive because of the simple fact that I could read. For a person to be able to read and write was rare and I so regretted the day I'd started to understand the English language.

"He's worried about finding the rest of the treasures" I corrected, shaking my head as I sank down into the chair close to the wheel.

I tried thinking about how mortal men could ever possibly fetch a jewel from the bottom of an endless pool of water.

Did he think he could hold his breath for that long? Did he not stop to ask what this treasure would require him to do?

He was a moron, a reckless idiot.

"You've been passing out a lot lately, sometimes for days on end, you're badly wounded and hungover-." she began, her eyes boring into mine. Her grip on the helm tightened when she looked back in the direction of the island, a mixture of jealousy, understanding and sadness coming from her when she spoke up again to repeat herself once more.

"He's worried about *you*" she placed emphasis on the word 'you' when she said it.

There was something in the way her eyes clouded over, how her hands wrung the wood of the helm which made me believe her but it also made me realize that I knew nothing about the woman who stood before me, nothing from her past, her present or what she desired for her future.

I decided then that if we all survived to see another day, that I would try to get to know her a bit more and get that bloody Irishman's name while I was at it.

Chapter Twelve

I shot up from my seat and hobbled to the deck when the crew pushed off the island's shore and grabbed hold of the net on the side of the ship to steady the boats.

Caleb scaled the ship, landing with a loud thud on its deck, directly in front of me with his nostrils flaring and eyes narrowed. The rest of the crew followed his lead, fastening the boats to the Sunken Soul and climbing onboard, soaked from head to toe.

A drenched Ben stayed behind on one of the rowboats.

"Are ye toying with me?" Caleb questioned, looming dangerously over me, his face just inches away from mine. His breath fanned my features as he snarled the words like some rabid animal.

The Irishman slumped down onto a nearby barrel, a bottle of rum already clutched in hand.

"How exactly do ye expect us to get down there, lass?" he asked, taking a swig of his alcohol. Trying to warm himself.

Snaggletooth looked terrified, snapping his jaw at me with eyes wide and clothes soaked through. He looked like he'd come close to death, trembling in fear.

The rest of the crew apart from Ben continued to complain. Their comments on how deep the pool was, on how they couldn't hold their breath for that long, on how it was out of their reach and impossible to get all danced around me.

"Well? Have ye any ideas?" Caleb asked, his tone sarcastic and laced with annoyance. They were all staring at me, waiting for me to tell them of a secret way to get to the gem, as if the book held all the secrets.

I shoved past Caleb, our shoulders bumping as I limped to the side of the ship.

"I'll get it" I declared, glancing back at Caleb and Rebecca from over my shoulder. I used the netting to climb down to the boat where Ben stood waiting.

Once I was safely onboard the rowboat, he pushed off the side of the ship and sent it skidding up onto Gigas's shore, preventing anyone from following us.

Ben knew that without me the gem would be lost to the crew. He understood that the only way to retrieve the jewel would be through the assistance of a Mermaid or some creature that is able to breathe under water.

I stepped over the side of the boat with Ben's help, using his hand to steady myself so I wouldn't fall.

My eyes narrow onto Caleb's. He was stationed on the ship's stern, his gaze following my every move.

"Show me to the pool" I instructed, turning my attention back onto Ben. He nodded and began walking into the tree line. I followed, hobbling as fast as I could, however he still had to stop to glance back at me, making sure that I was still there, still alright. He slowed his pace to match mine, listening to the heavy sound of my breathing.

"Let me carry you" he offered, able to see the irritation in my features, the anger that I had towards Caleb and his idiocy.

There was a reason I wanted to go along in the first place but he had me stay onboard the ship, wasting everyone's time then accusing me of taking him for a fool.

"I'm fine, my anger is fuel enough to keep me going" was my response, my pace picking up when Caleb's face surfaced in the back of my mind, causing me to grunt in annoyance.

Ben silently watched me, the corner of his lips tugging upward as we reached a large slope of rocks that we had to scale. I came to a sudden halt.

"If he hadn't left me behind, we would've been done with this already" I complained, my hands reaching out to grip the rocks, dragging myself up onto them so that I was crawling up the slope on all fours. Ben stayed close behind me, ready to catch me if I were to slip and fall.

"An idiot!" I snapped when my hand slipped and I skidded back a few paces. I regained my grip and started climbing again, teeth gritting and limbs trembling.

"A bloody moron!" I added when I applied too much weight on my wounded leg, causing me to wince as pain shot through my body.

Ben tried to bite back his laughter at my frustration, watching me as I scaled the remaining few lengths to the top of the slope.

"He's a brainless, clueless, good for nothing pirate-!" my words died down in the back of my throat when I stood upright, eyes landing on the body of water in front of me.

It was as clear as crystal and went down into the turtle's shell like a deep crack. At the bottom of it I could see a flicker of yellow reflecting in the shimmering water.

"Captain" I finished my rant in a low mutter that was barely audible as Ben appeared beside me.

I could see schools of fish swimming in the crystalline waters below, a colorful coral reef that stretched up along its walls, the sight more beautiful than anything I had ever seen before. My body moved on its own accord, entranced by the sight, the water almost glowing when I stepped onto a rock in the pool. The water reached my knees. I tore my eyes away from the enchanting sight to tug my shirt over my head, holding it out for Ben to take.

He averted his eyes, too much of a gentleman to gawk at me like the rest of the crew would.

His hand brushed against mine when he took the shirt from me, eyes only daring to return to my form once my back was turned to him.

My legs started shimmering, silver scales running up along my calves and over my shins, but the scales didn't bind together to form a fin just yet. I knew they wouldn't as long as I wore the necklace that kept me human. I sat down on the rock, the water covering my thighs and lapping at the flesh beneath my breasts when I reached to unclasp the chain from around my neck.

The moment it was pried away from my skin, my legs began to morph together, bandages tearing away to form a silver tail that had white detailing and appeared to shimmer violet when the light struck it. I let it swish back and forth in the water, growing used to the feel of having a tail again.

Although I was born a Mermaid, I'd spent most of my life on land, growing up among humans and barely venturing out into the water for fear of it consuming me, my need to be one with the sea allowing me to get lost in its depths never to find land again.

I turned, holding my necklace out for Ben to take "Don't lose it" I warned when he knelt near me and clutched the chain in his clenched fist.

He was staring at me, my face and tail, my fangs and slit pupils, staring like he had before, in his chambers onboard the ship.

There was something in the way he studied me, how his eyes slowly moved from my hair to my eyes and fell onto my lips that made me forget why I was even there. I reached a webbed hand towards him, cupping his cheek in my palm when a rumbling sound from above snapped me out of my daze.

93

Caleb's golden eyes surfaced in the back of my mind and I reminded myself of what I was there to do. I turned my back to Ben quickly and abruptly, eyes boring down into the water in search of that distinctive yellow gleam from before.

When my sights locked onto it, I dove down, leaping head first into the water as I moved my tail, beating it against the water to swim as far down as I possibly could. A tiger shark swam past me, fish sputtering when I would near them, my arms almost glued to my sides. The pool stretched on for miles, narrowing the closer I got to its floor.

My fin folded beneath me, allowing me sit as if on my knees in the sand when I reached the bottom of the seemingly endless pool. I tilted my head back to gaze up at its surface. Ben stood on the rock I had previously been on, watching me. He was the size of a small sea shell due to the distance between us.

I looked back to the sand, my eyes searching for the source of the yellow glow, moving from rocks to shells to something buried in the sand, a chest that was half open. I swam towards it, my fingers digging into its opening to pry it open. There were gold coins, jewelry, a golden flask inside the chest but what caught my eyes wasn't the gold, it was the gem laying in the center of it all.

My hand wrapped around the yellow stone, lifting it to examine its edges, turning it around and around until I was certain I had found what I was looking for.

A rumble vibrated through the pool walls around me and I hurriedly gazed in every direction to find that nothing was falling. It wasn't like the first treasure when the walls had crumbled. This was different.

My eyes widened when I realized what was happening, my attention darting back to Ben who was being submerged in water. Bubbles tore from his mouth as he struggled, twisting and turning with both the shirt and my necklace in hand. Gigas was diving.

I pushed off the pool's floor and swam upward as fast as I could, my fingers curling around the jewel as I shot past fish and coral, my mind focused on Ben and only Ben.

My left arm caught on some of the rocks, causing me to cry out when a sharp pain tore through me, blood mixing with the water to form a red streak that seemed to follow my movements.

I didn't have time to worry about myself, my tail propelling me out of the pool and into the dark ocean water where Ben was drifting far beneath its surface. I no longer had to worry about the rocks or walls limiting my movements as I darted through the water. Ben had stopped struggling, his grip on the shirt and my necklace loosening when I grabbed hold of his wrist.

Both items began to sink down into the depths below. I watched them go, my eyes moving from the necklace to Ben. The decision wasn't at all difficult to make, Ben came first. I began to drag him towards the surface, his brown eyes staring up at me through the water. He was weak but still conscious.

I swam to the ship that had stopped sailing the moment Gigas began its dive, swimming through the whirlpool that the sinking motion had managed to create and braking through the water at the ship's side.

Ben grabbed hold of the netting, coughing violently as I let go of him, making sure that he had the strength to keep his hold on the net.

"Give this to Caleb" I instructed, handing him the gem before diving once more. My eyes locked onto the necklace, the anchor pendant standing out against the darkness beyond it.

There was movement in the water above me followed by Ben's voice calling out to me "Evangeline!" my name broke through the water and air, reaching my webbed ears as I kept delving deeper.

My arm extended when I got close to the chain, fingers and claws outstretched to capture it. When it was fully in my grasp I came to a sudden halt, my tail beating beneath me as my eyes took in the sight before them.

A giant turtle with an island on its back was descending through the water, its skin a mixture of blue and green with a brown shell that had trees growing from it. It opened its mouth, creating a low, trembling sound that shot through me, speaking to me with the voice of a man.

'A heart of the sea' it whispered in the back of my mind. Something about those words were so familiar, so important but when I tried to remember where I'd heard it before, a sharp pain tore through my skull and arm.

I looked to my shredded arm then upward to where the shirt was still floating its way downward, being much lighter than the necklace which meant that it sunk at a much slower pace. I watched the material dance and made my way towards it, tugging the fabric onto my frame as I ascended, only clasping the necklace back around my neck when I was a few feet from the surface.

I paused, drifting, floating as my fin separated into two limbs, kicking through the salty liquid. My face returned to normal, my hands no longer webbed as they treaded water to push myself upward, closer to the ship.

I broke through with a gasp, feeling a hand grab hold of my wrist, pulling me onto the last remaining rowboat since the other had been taken by Gigas.

I slumped against the side of the ship with my head tilted back while I struggled to catch my breath. Ben fell to his knees in front of me, hands cupping the sides of my face, brushing away wet strands of hair that stuck to the flesh.

"Ben?" I questioned, my eyes adjusting to take in his worried expression and furrowed eyebrows. His chest was rapidly rising and falling as he breathed heavily.

He no longer had the jewel with him and I assumed that he'd managed to give it to Caleb before he jumped back down onto the rowboat in search of me.

"I'm fine, I-." I tried to say when the concern in his eyes only grew, searching my body for any sign of a wound or other medical symptoms like a fever or a cough.

He noticed the cut on my arm but it wasn't as deep as I had expected it to be. It was bleeding but not enough to be a cause for concern.

My words were cut off when he pressed his lips to mine, hungrily, fiercely. My eyes widened in shock and my body stiffened, my hands gripping the netting behind me even tighter than before.

He was the only person who truly cared about me.

My eyes slowly drifted shut, my muscles relaxing as I reached up, one hand gripping his shoulder while the other cupped the side of his neck. I melted into him, my body pressing up against his when he pulled away to catch his breath, his right hand gripping my hip to hold me in place.

We looked at each other, something sparking between us as if to drag us back together again but before he could capture my lips with his for a second time, a voice spoke up from somewhere overhead.

"Raise the boat!" Caleb snarled at his crew. My head turned to glance up at him, his eyes holding a trace of sadness in them when he turned his back to us and stalked his way across the deck.

My hands slipped away from Ben, his also letting go when the crew began to hoist the boat up and onto the deck. We sat in silence as they worked, a sense of guilt overcoming me. I glanced in Ben's direction.

The feelings I had towards him were my own, they weren't forced onto me by a past incarnation like they had been with Caleb.

Feeling guilty because of emotions that weren't mine didn't make sense to me so I suppressed the guilt and focused instead on what I knew for certain were my own emotions.

Once on deck I noticed that blood was trailing down my arm, droplets dripping from my fingertips to stain the wood below. My leg was burning, caused by the salt in the seawater but the stitches were intact and it wasn't bleeding like I had thought it would.

Rebecca was at my side, her hand forcefully grabbing hold of my arm as she dragged me towards the Captain's chambers. Once inside she let go and I turned to address her.

"What are you-?" my words were cut short when a sharp sting radiated from the side of my face, a slapping sound echoing out around us when my head flew to the side, my eyes staring emotionlessly at the ground. Her hand was raised and a fire burnt in her eyes, scorching me.

"Have you ever stopped to think about the effect that your actions would have on him?" she demanded, not having to speak the name for me to know exactly who she was referring to.

I straightened out my shoulders, my hands balling at my sides, one drenched with blood. My eyes turned to meet hers, stern and piercing as I stared into her gaze, challenging her, not backing down like she had been expecting me to.

"I. Am. Not. Mary" I bit out past clenched teeth, sick and tired of the influence the woman who went by the name of 'Mary' had over me and my life. Rebecca's hand lowered back to her side as I took a threatening step towards her.

"My name is Evangeline-." I began, my hands trembling at my sides as I suppressed the need to strike back at her. I was a better person than she was but that didn't mean that I was going to keep my mouth shut.

"And I refuse to let my actions be dictated by a ghost-." she visibly flinched at my use of the word 'ghost' like referring to Mary as being dead had struck a nerve.

Her lips were narrowed in a thin line, silent as I continued "I can kiss who I want, fall in love with whoever I want!" my voice was louder now, piercing the air around us and echoing like her slap had before it.

My eyes were clouded by tears, foggy as I turned to the side, about to head in the direction of the small bathroom when I finished "I didn't choose to have this face, I was born with it and I sure as hell am not some rich noble girl from the South"

I stormed off, slamming the door to the bathroom behind me so that I could strip out of the wet and bloody shirt I was wearing to clean my wounds with some fresh water.

I felt the tears streaming down the side of my face as I worked, repeatedly running the rag over my skin. I sat on my knees on the floor next to a bucket in which I would wrung out my cloth.

The room beyond the door was silent, no footsteps or sighs could be heard and I assumed that Rebecca had gone above deck, leaving me to tend to my cut like a dog lapping at her wounds.

Chapter Thirteen

When I stepped out of the bathroom, nude from head to toe, a figure was seated on the bed in front of me. A woman dressed like a pirate with hair of blazing red fire that shielded her face from my view.

I paused then chose to ignore her, heading over to the dresser where I retrieved a long white gown, tugging the material over my head and onto my body to conceal it from the hungry eyes that I was so used to feeling.

"Why are you still here?" I finally asked, tugging my hair out from the neckline of the dress as I turned to face her. There was a hairclip on top of the dresser that I used to pin my hair up, clasping the strands back and out of my face.

"Let me see your arm" she insisted, getting up from the bed and moving towards me.

I pulled my arm away from her hold as if she had burnt me and took a step back. She reeked of guilt and was obviously looking for any way to make up for her earlier actions.

"Please leave" I tried to get her to go but she stayed rooted in place, her empty features looking down at me since she was a few inches taller than I was.

My mind went back to the promise I had made to myself. A promise to get to know her and I reluctantly held my arm out for her to take. She slowly eased the sleeve of the dress up to examine the cut, her thumb pressing down beside it. I winced and pulled my arm back.

"You should bandage it" she warned, turning to open one of the dresser drawers, revealing a roll of bandages that she unwound to again reach for my arm.

I stayed still as she wrapped it around the wound, using her teeth to tear the fabric and tie it off at the end. She glanced down at my leg and started guiding me towards the bed but I protested instead I sank down into the armchair. I didn't want to go near the bed; I didn't want to lay on the same sheets Mary had shared with Caleb.

Rebecca shot me a curious look, bending down to tenderly bandage my leg.

"How do you know Caleb?" I randomly asked. There was slight hesitation in her actions but she quickly went back to tying off the bandage. She set the remainder of the bandages aside and stood upright.

"We grew up together" was her brief reply. She reached for the chair behind the desk and slid it closer to me. She took a seat in it with her front pressing up against the back of the chair and her legs parted, her dress skirt shielding my eyes from what lay between.

"His mother was a harlot and mine was a bakers' wife" she had a way of telling stories, a way of painting pictures when she spoke but this was different from when she had spoken about Mary, there were no visions, no unwanted images or sharp pains yet I could still see the story unfolding in front of me.

"He had a habit of always getting himself into trouble-." her voice was as captivating as her dancing.

A small smile lit up her face at the thought of a younger version of Caleb, always coming home with cuts, scrapes and bruises from having gotten into fights with the older kids.

"Because he grew up poor, he started stealing-." the smile faded as if that was the turning point where the usual trouble for a boy would take a terrible turn and end in something much worse.

"It started with food then petty change. Finally he began to steal jewels and valuable items" she stared down at the ground, her mind going back to that time many years ago.

"He was thrown into the brig a few times by the Campbell family-." my eyebrows furrowed up in confusion at her words. I remembered that she'd called him 'Caleb Campbell' when we had rescued her from the island.

She noticed my confusion and proceeded to explain "Caleb's father was a nobleman who regularly paid to lie with a harlot. His noble blood was kept a secret for many years, only his parents knew of who he really was"

I found it hard to believe that the brute of a pirate Captain I knew was half noble, he didn't act like it, couldn't read or write and hardly cared about his appearance at all.

"His father wanted nothing to do with him and treated him like just another common street rat" my eyes fell back onto her, finally understanding why he was the way he was.

He was raised as a poor harlot's son and not as a wealthy nobleman's boy. Your blood could be entirely noble but if you were raised by commoners then you are a commoner.

"He got locked away a few times and shortly after he turned seventeen, he caught word of a pirate ship having been spotted near the port-."

My hands gripped the arms of my chair, waiting for her to continue, to shed light on how Caleb had gone from a half noble street rat to a pirate Captain.

"*Where there are pirates, there is gold*' he said before he set out to steal from Captain Solstice" stealing from a pirate was a mistake everyone knew not to make. For Caleb to have considered such a thing he had to be confident in his skills as a thief, so much so that he would risk his life to get his hands on their treasure.

"The Captain caught him in the act and threatened to have him walk the plank" the image of a younger Caleb, poorly dressed with his wrists bound, standing on the edge of a plank with his back to the sea lit up my imagination.

Rebecca breathed a laugh "But Caleb has a way of getting out of things" it wasn't a positive trait but I could tell that she was grateful for it because if he hadn't been able to persuade the pirates to spare him back then, then he would've most likely been killed.

I shifted to a more comfortable position, tucking my legs underneath me as I clasped my hands together in my lap.

"He promised to bring the Captain the Campbell family's most valuable possession in exchange for his release" '*A bargain made with the devil*' I thought but said nothing, too afraid that if I spoke, she'd stop her tale and leave me with more questions than answers.

She pressed her forehead to her folded arms that were draped across the back of the chair she was seated on.

"'*You own the Campbells; you own the city*' he said. It was an offer that a pirate like Solstice couldn't refuse" there was a long pause as she stared down at her skirt.

I felt like I had to say something so I decided to prompt her to keep going, hoping that it wouldn't hinder her story.

"What was their most prized possession?" my voice was small, almost nonexistent, a mere whisper that reached her. She shook her head from side to side and smiled up at me, meeting my eyes with a sad but serious stare.

"Their daughter and Caleb's half-sister" the air escaped my lips in a long released breath. She propped her elbow onto the back of the chair as she pressed her thumb to her lip in thought, eyes searching the corner of the room "Of course, he had no idea that she was his sister at the time"

It made sense that he would've thought that she was just some snobby rich girl who had everything he could only dream of having. She, too him, was just another privileged noble who had nothing to do with him, Rebecca or his mother.

"Once they had her in their grasp, the pirates invaded the city" there was a sense of fear radiating from her as she closed her eyes, almost as if to will away the haunting memories that refused to leave her mind's eye. I knew exactly what she was feeling, desperately wanting for the memories to go away but the difference was that the memories haunting me weren't mine, they were someone else's.

"They pillaged the shops, raped the women, murdered the men and burnt homes to the ground" the fire in her eyes reflected the image only she could see of a city engulfed in flames, the screams of women and children echoing out into the night as the streets ran red with blood.

"Caleb's sister, Claudia, was murdered on this very ship" chills ran down the back of my spine, causing the hair at the nape of my neck to stand on end. Goosebumps rose along my skin while my fingers nervously picked at the material of my dress.

My eyes glanced in the direction of the steps that led to the deck.

"His mother managed to tell him of his noble blood before she was dragged into the streets, stripped naked, raped and killed for being a harlot" I could hear the menacing laughter of pirates in the background as if to mock the woman who had birthed Caleb, as if to scorn him for being the son of a whore.

"Caleb killed Solstice, took control of his crew and the Sunken Soul along with them" the very ship I was currently harbored on was the place where he first became a pirate, the place where he had watched his sister be killed and made a bargain that would end up sentencing hundreds of innocent people to death.

"He buried his mother and Claudia before setting sail. He left me behind to grieve the loss of my family-." I couldn't understand. My brows knitted together as I wondered how she could possibly care about a man who'd caused the death of her parents?

She looked at me, drawn out of her memories and back to the present where I was seated on the edge of my seat hanging on her every word.

"He killed off his entire crew and he managed to replace them over the years" I felt more at ease with the thought of not being surrounded by the pirates who had murdered so many people.

I was sure that the Irishman wasn't innocent but at least I knew that with both Caleb and Ben around, he wouldn't dare try anything.

She was done, her eyes sad and empty from traveling so far back in time but there was a question I had yet to have answered.

"Why do you care so much about him?" her eyes regained their life as she contemplated telling me. She stood, rising from her seat and grabbing hold of the back of it.

"Because-." she began in a whisper, smiling down at the floorboards "I fell in love with him long before he met Solstice" there was a sharp pang in my chest for some reason, my body tensing and my breathing becoming ragged.

She noticed the changes in me when she began to drag the chair over to the desk where she had found it. She looked at the surface of the desk, both hands still gripping the chair.

"But he only ever loved Mary" with that she allowed her hands to slip away from the chair and turned to leave me to my thoughts.

She was jealous of the noble girl, jealous of the effect she had on Caleb, jealous of the fact that I looked like Mary, like the love of his life. I assumed that deep down she was relieved that I was more interested in Ben than Caleb but at the same time she just wanted him to be happy and seeing me with Mary's face giving affection to another man didn't exactly do that.

I could understand why she had reacted the way she did earlier, my hand raising to touch my fingertips to my cheek that no longer stung. There were so many pieces to the puzzle that made up Caleb and his life, so many questions I still had regarding Mary, so many things I still didn't understand.

I closed my eyes and went back to that moment under water, watching Gigas delve deeper into the ocean's depths. The voice that had reached out to me and the words it spoke 'A heart of the sea'

What did that mean and why did it sound so familiar as if I'd heard it somewhere before? When I opened my eyes, they landed on the leather bound book that was resting on the nightside table.

I lowered my feet to the ground and stood, approaching it. I ran my fingers over its binding.

Something inside of me believed that once we would collect all seven treasures, I would finally understand what I had been seeing, what it all meant.

I took the book in hand and sunk down onto the floor, leaning back against the side of the bed to continue reading, picking up where I left off at the location of the fourth treasure.

Chapter Fourteen
Twelve Years Ago
Caleb

I peered through the bakery's window, crouching down on the roof of the building next door to get a good look at the redhead inside. She was working late into the night kneading bread and baking sweets for the people of the city.

I opened the window when I noticed that she was alone and crawled through, using my arms to lower myself onto one of the cleared tables below, landing with a not so graceful thud.

The girl barely seemed phased by the noise. She continued to work, not even bothering to look at me or spare a glance in my direction "What do you want, Caleb?"

I leaned back on the table, placing my hands palm down against the wood to support my weight while I took in my surroundings, parted legs kicking back and forth.

The girl in question was fifteen-year-old Rebecca, the baker's daughter who was rumored to be as skilled with her hands as she was with her hips.

"Someone's in a foul mood" I teased, eyes locking onto the baked goods that sat across from me on the table separating us. Rebecca reached for the rag that hung from her shoulder and stared wiping her hands. I slowly leaned forward. My hand outstretched towards the cookies being careful not to be caught. She picked up the trey she had been prepping and turned to pop it into the oven. I shot back abruptly for fear of being caught stealing one of her famous sugar cookies.

"I hate baking" she said, bending to check if the oven's coals were still to her liking, warm enough to bake the dough without burning it. I attempted to reach for a cookie when her back was to me.

"So why do it then?" I questioned, hoping that the casual conversation would play in my favor, preventing her from realizing that I was up to something.

She sighed heavily, turning to face me. I shot up, the table rattling beneath me from the sudden movement. I glanced from the table to her, hoping that she hadn't noticed.

"Not everyone has a choice" she muttered, heading over to the shelf beside the table I was seated on, grabbing another trey that was made of polished silver to start on yet another batch. I relaxed when she didn't seem to acknowledge my stealthy attempts at stealing one of her treats.

"Some of us are born into responsibility" she began, talking in her 'high born' ways again. She was raised to speak proper English, was bought nice things while growing up and would one day inherit the bakery.

I heard the speech a thousand times, about how she hated to bake and loved to dance at the tavern down the street every other night. If Rebecca had it her way, she would trade her apron for a stage any day.

"Born into it or forced into it?" I asked, clasping my hands together as my eyes followed her around the room. She stacked some dough onto the trey, grabbed a fistful flour and a clean knife then went back to where she had previously been standing, prepping her next batch for the oven.

"Is there really a difference?" she questioned, glancing at me before she turned to knead the dough and cut it into little squares. I eyed her back, every now and then shooting a quick glance in the direction of the cookies.

"No, so why are you letting yourself be forced into it?" I replied, leaning forward again, my fingers brushing over the counter in front of me, just too short to reach one of the baked, brown shapes.

Rebecca looked up at the window in front of her, pausing as she contemplated my words. Being born into something made it sound like a privilege whereas being forced into something made it sound like a burden when in reality they were the exact same thing.

"Because...if my parents-." she tried to argue, pausing to count her words as she spoke.

I sighed when my arm dropped back to my side and I was left glaring at the cookies in frustration. I contemplated getting up and taking one but she was smart, she knew that I hated moving when it didn't really benefit me so obviously there would be a reason for my movements.

I interrupted her "And what if they found out about you working at the bar?" it wasn't uncommon for girls her age to start waiting at taverns or work at whore houses but Rebecca was different, she wasn't poor or in need of money, she just loved dancing. The only reason she did it was to feel free after being cooped up inside the bakery for most of her life.

She hurriedly turned to look at me from across the room "Why would they-?" I could hear the end of her sentence before she even spoke it *'Why would they find out?'*

She was nervous and terrified of the thought, her hand gripping the edge of the table she had been working on. Again I cut her off when I realized that she didn't understand what I was implying.

"If it would make them mad then why are you doing it?" I tried rephrasing my question. She bit at the inside of her cheek, something she did whenever she was nervous or distraught.

I watched her, silently willing her to turn back around so that I could start my fourth attempt at stealing one of her treats but she didn't. Her eyes were glued to the baked batches in front of her, lost in her own thought.

"Because I love it" came her simple reply. She shrugged her shoulders as if it was obvious. I propped my elbows onto my knees and leaned slightly forward, half wanting to see the realization in her eyes, half wanting to taste something sweet.

"But you hate baking" I stated.

She glanced at the oven in the corner then quickly turned back around to start folding the dough into small, delicate shapes. My eyes narrowed, knowing fairly well that she was catching on to my argument and wanted to avoid it.

"If you love dancing but have to keep it a secret then are you really taking full responsibility for the bakery or are you just pretending?" her movements began to slow, her hands stilling in front of her as she silently gazed down at the folded pieces.

I slowly crept forward, my arm extending once more as I slid closer to the edge, fingertips brushing against one of the treats that were within my grasp.

"Because if that's what you're doing then isn't your life just one big act?" I added, glancing in her direction to make sure that she didn't turn around or notice me.

My hand moved to curl around the biscuit but I froze when a knife flew past my head and imbedded itself into the wall behind me. I looked up at Rebecca who was glaring at me, fiercely wiping her hands on the same cloth from before.

"Nice try" she complimented, moving around the counter towards me. I shot upright on the table and looked down at her when she came to a stop directly in front of me. Her eyes were blazing dangerously but they soon softened as a small smile crept onto her lips.

"You know, sometimes I regret teaching you how to speak proper English-." she informed me, pausing to turn and pluck the cookie I had been after up from its trey to examine it as if it was some sort of rare gem.

"You have a way of toying with people's minds" she added, her hand moving to take hold of mine, turning it so that the palm was facing up and placing the treat in the center of it. She let go of my hand to retrieve the knife from the wall then went back to cutting and kneading the dough.

I wasn't sure if her words were meant to be taken as a compliment or if she was scolding me but she didn't seem to want to elaborate so I resorted to changing the subject "I heard there are pirates in the bay"

The knife cluttered onto the floor following my words, having slipped from her grasp. I stuck the cookie into my mouth and chewed, the familiar sweet and cinnamon taste filling my senses but before I could swallow, Rebecca turned, shooting me a terrifying glare.

I froze "No" she abruptly stated, leaving no room for argument. I slowly started chewing again then swallowed with a loud gulp. She looked as though she was going to erupt at any moment.

"I know what you're thinking-." she started, raising her hand to point a stern finger at me from across the room. The candlelight highlighted her angry eyes, making her seem much older "And there is no way that I am letting you go through with it"

It was safe to say that she knew me better than anyone else and her assumption wasn't wrong. The worry hidden behind her anger wasn't without reason. I sighed, hopping down from the table to move around the room and over to where she stood. Her hand lowered back to her side as she watched me.

"I'm not going through with anything" I lied, bending to scoop the knife up off the floor, mostly because I was afraid that she would chuck it at my head again and I felt safer with it in my possession. She studied me, eyes looking for any telltale sign of a lie.

"You're lying" she finally stated. I pressed the tip of the knife against the tip of my index finger, twisting it around a few times as if I were going to prick the skin but didn't apply enough pressure to do so.

"Me? Lie? Never" I sarcastically said, turning to lean against the table with one elbow propped up onto it. I shot her my most dazzling smile but she didn't seem to find it entertaining in the slightest. I tightened my grip on the knife to make sure she didn't snatch it from me.

She had a tendency to chase people with sharp objects.

"I'm being serious, Caleb" my smile faded and I huffed in response to her words, turning my head to look at the streets beyond the bakery's window. They were empty, cobblestone roads that were lit with orange lights which radiated out from the many street lamps.

"So am I" my tone was empty, almost sad which Rebecca quickly noted. She shoved my shoulder, hard, sending me staggering back a few steps, the knife cluttering out of my hand and to the floor near my bare feet. I didn't have any shoes, not even a shirt to cover my back. All the money I stole went to my mother, to give her everything she had to sacrifice so that I could eat, so that I could live.

"Don't be an idiot!" she yelled at me, the flames from the candles flickering around us and making her look angrier than she really was. My hands clenched at my sides, not sure how to respond to her so I waited for her to continue.

"What exactly are you planning to steal? Crossbones? Rum?" she demanded, throwing her arms up in exasperation as she stalked closer to me, hiking up the skirts of her dress so that she didn't step on them in her haste. I leaned back but stayed where I was.

"Where there are pirates, there is gold" I informed her, staying calm as her nostrils flared and she glared up at me, ready to throw a punch at any given moment. She snorted loudly, her hands tightening on the material of her dress.

"You're going to get yourself killed" she said, her voice serious but not as loud as it previously was. She stood upright, her shoulders square and her head shaking from side to side as she stared down at the floor.

"I won't let you leave here" she declared, her eyes meeting mine once more to show how determined she was to keep me captive in that bakery for as long as it took for the pirates to leave the city.

I smiled down at her, a sad smile that was interrupted when the smell of something burning tickled our noses.

"The cookies!" she exclaimed and rushed to retrieve them, grabbing a cloth from the counter and wrapping it around her hand as to not burn herself when she took the trey out of the oven. She hurriedly tossed the trey onto one of the nearby tables when it started to burn through the fabric.

"Ow! Dammit!" she cursed, dropping the cloth and shaking her hand, blowing on her burnt fingers as she rushed over to a bucket of fresh water. She dipped her hand in the water to calm the stinging.

By the time she turned to face me, her hand gripping the wrist of her wounded one, it was already too late.

She realized that in her frantic search for something to calm the burning, I had slipped away into the night.

The tavern was filled with laughing men, singing women, the scent of alcohol and a thick layer of smoke when I entered through the door. My eyes scanned over the many faces, most of which were the faces of men.

There was a group that stood out among the rest, pushed into the far corner as they looked to be debating something. I took a seat a few tables down from theirs, listening in on their conversation that grew louder the more they drank.

The man in charge wore a black Captain's hat and a red coat, his gray beard decorated in feathers and colorful beads.

"We be sailing at dawn for the first treasure" he announced, holding his bottle of rum out towards the rest of his men. They clanked their cups against the bottle and cheered in response before downing the rest of their drinks.

My ears perked up at the mention of treasure, eyes glancing towards the leather bound book that sat on top of the table. If they were to leave at dawn, then that meant that there was very little time for me to steal their loot right out from under their noses.

"Can I get you anything?" I was snapped out of my train of thought by a woman who placed her palm flat against the surface of my table, leaning closer with an annoyed scowl plastered across her stained red lips. She was a waitress judging from her apron and the trey that she balanced on one hand.

I knew that if I said something sarcastic or rude that it would attract too much attention. I didn't want the pirates to notice me so I nodded and spoke up politely.

"Some ale, if you please" she glared at me, her eyes trailing down to my stolen shirt, torn trousers and warn boots. I had gotten them from a man who'd been passed out in the stables outside the tavern but she didn't need to know that. It would've been even more suspicious if I hadn't been wearing any shoes or a shirt.

"Coming right up" she finally said after examining me. I shot her a forced smile when she turned to leave, her voice calling out across the bar to where a man was serving drinks.

Once she was out of sight, I shot up, my hand grabbing the hat off the top of a nearby man's head and placing it on top of mine, hiding my face as I left. The drunken man didn't even notice his hat being stolen.

I tossed the hat across the street when I exited the tavern, glancing in the direction of the docks, the sound of the waves in the distance reaching my ears along with the smell of sea salt. I stuffed my hands into the pockets of my torn trousers and headed in that direction, whistling occasionally when I would get bored from the long walk. The black body of water came into view long before the ships did, seeming to stretch on forever onto the horizon.

I pressed my back against the wall of the post office when a watchman walked past, his boots thudding loudly against the cobble stone.

My eyes landed on my newfound boots and I huffed when I had to pull them off, setting them aside since they would make too much noise.

When the guard disappeared into the distance, I strode around the corner, searching the ships for anything that struck me as unusual or odd. I froze when my eyes landed on a large ship with black sails and a woman figurehead. One flag in particular stood out from the rest, the crossbones that were painted on black fabric dancing in the sea breeze.

I searched for a way onboard and to my luck, my eyes landed on the netting that went up, onto the side of it. My head turned to see where the watchman was, not finding a trace of him as I strode onto the docks. There was something painted on the side of the ship in big black letters but because I couldn't read, I shrugged it off and took it as being the ship's name.

I bent my knees and reached out when I leapt from the dock, hands and fingers tangling in the ship's netting to hoist me up higher so that my feet could find leverage. My body had struck the side of the ship, sending a loud thud into the night that caught the attention of the watchman.

I heard the sound of a dog barking in the distance along with the handle of a lamp squeaking as it violently swayed back and forth. My body began to move on its own accord, quickly scaling the side of the ship until I could heave myself over its railing and onto its deck. I hunched low when the sound of feet nearing the ship, alerting me of someone's presence. The orange light from the lamp was raised as if to inspect the ship and after some time it faded back into the distance.

I released the breath I had been holding and stood upright, eyes scanning the deck only to find crates, row boats and barrels strewn across it. The stern harbored nothing special either. I noticed a door close to where I was and moved towards it, hand grabbing onto the handle to see if it was unlocked. To my surprise, it was. I descended down the steps into what looked to be the Captain's quarters. The room had a large bed, a desk, nightstand, dresser and armchair but nothing of immense value. I opened the dresser's drawers but only found clothes.

I searched the cluttered desk but there was nothing but maps, maps that I couldn't read. There was nothing, no treasure, no gold, no jewels, only the essentials. I was about to turn and leave when the door to the Captain's chambers slammed shut, catching me off guard.

"What do we have here?" the Captain's voice from earlier reached my ears. My head turned to meet with the sight of the man in a red coat. Two more pirates stood on either side of him. The Captain grinned at me, gold teeth catching the moonlight that pooled in through the porthole.

"A street rat, looking for something to steal" my eyes roamed from one pirate to the other. *Why hadn't I heard them coming? Why were they back so quickly?* The Captain noticed my confusion and chuckled, his chest rumbling and head thrown back.

"Ye take me for a fool, boy?" he asked once he stopped laughing, his hand motioning towards the shirt I wore. It was an old brown shirt with leather sleeves, something I hadn't noticed at the time but leather sleeves were rare.

"Ye shirt belongs to a very kind gentleman who helped me read this" he pulled the book from before out of his pocket and held it up for my eyes to see. There were gold and silver rings littering his fingers and I kicked myself for not bothering to steal them instead, it would've been better than to waste my time with the ship since there was nothing of value to be found onboard.

"Of course, this was before he left and ye stole his clothes" I stayed silent, eyes scanning the room for any form of an exit but there was none, only the small porthole and the door that they were blocking. I cursed my idiocy, making a mental note that if I was to ever go unnoticed in a bar again, that I stole clothes from a man who hadn't been at that bar before I was. He stuffed the book back into his coat pocket and turned to his men.

"Get him" the two short forward, ambushing me. I tried to fight, getting a few punches in before my hands were bound in front of me and I was dragged onto the deck. The Captain paced impatiently back and forth with his hands folded behind his back as the rest of his crew gathered around us. They were watching me, cheering and laughing, some even spat insults in my direction. The Captain paused to rushed forward to grab hold of the hair at the scruff of my neck, tugging on it and forcing my head back so that I was staring into his almost obsidian, dark gray glare.

"Tell me, boy, do ye know what happens to thieves onboard a pirate's ship?" he asked, his breath smelling strongly of alcohol and blood. I tried struggling but when I did, he tightened his grasp on my neck, prompting me to answer him.

"N-Not quiet" was my sarcastic response. He searched my face, eyes going to the corner of my lips that tilted upward from the pain that shot through my neck and head. His nose scrunched up in disgust and he shoved me aside, towards the ship's railing.

"Make him walk the plank!" his crew erupted into cheers of excitement. Two of the crewmen grabbed hold of my arms while a third slid the plank into place, making sure that it wasn't stationed near the shore or docks. I could easily swim to land if need be but if both my wrists and ankles were tied, how could I? Anyone could drown in shallow water if the ropes were tight enough. I was lifted into the air, kicking as one of the men tied some more rope around my legs and feet to hold them in place. I stood on the plank with my back to the pirates, the tips of their swords digging into my back through the material of my stolen shirt.

"Jump, street rat!" one of the men bit out, a slight chuckle to his tone. I glanced down at the water below, dark and cold judging from the breeze that dug into my skin. Rebecca's words echoed through my thoughts 'You have a way of toying with people's minds'

I slowly turned to face the men, their eyes brimming with bloodlust and excitement as they stared at me. The Captain was sat on a chair behind the rest, silently observing from afar as his men chanted for me to jump.

"As much as I would like to get off this ship-." I began, the crew falling silent when I spoke. I looked at the water beneath me and sighed heavily. It wasn't the time to panic, I had to be smart, use my words to cheat my way out of death "I'm afraid this method just isn't doing it for me" the Captain shot up from his seat, storming his way to the plank. He drew his sword to point it at me, its tip tilting my head back and threatening to cut my throat.

"Ye think this be some joke, boy?" he questioned, his lips pulling back as if to snarl at me. It would be a lie to say that I wasn't terrified, but my better judgement told me to suppress the fear since fear was what all pirates preyed on. I tilted my head to the side to avoid his blade and raised my bound hands to push its edge aside.

"Not at all, I'm merely suggesting that we find another way for me to vacate this ship" like many, the Captain only stared, confused and not catching on to what I was implying. I tried giving hints, hoping that at least he could put two and two together.

"I'm a thief, a decent one, or at least that's what I would like to believe-." I continued, wanting to punch myself for making a simple mistake which had gotten me into the mess I was in. The crew chuckled at my words, finding it funny that I saw myself as a skilled thief even after having been caught.

"I'm particularly good at stealing things, valuable things from rich, noble people" at the use of the word 'noble' an intrigued gleam flickered in their eyes. The crew shared looks and muttered under their breaths as the Captain pulled his sword back to relieve me of the blades pressure.

"The Campbell's?" he questioned, a sinister glint lighting up his eyes but as soon as it was there, it was gone, replaced by curiosity and confusion. He again stuck his sword out towards me, letting the tip press into my left shoulder.

"And what could they possibly have that would be of any value to me?" he allowed for the tip of his blade to dig into my flesh. I gritted my teeth, fighting the urge to scream when he twisted it as if attempting to torture the answer out of me. My upper lip twitched and my muscles tensed throughout my entire body in response to the ongoing pain. Eventually I cried out.

"Their daughter, their most prized possession is their daughter!" the Captain stopped his torment once my desperate response filled the air and pulled his sword back once more. I breathed heavily, the warm red liquid soaking through the fabric of my stolen shirt as I glared at the pirate on the other side of the plank. He enjoyed seeing me squirm, feasting off the pain of others like the cruel and unforgiving man that he was.

"Their daughter? What do ye expect me to do with a girl? Sell her for a bottle of rum?" he demanded unable to picture the endless possibilities that lay before him due to how narrow minded he was. He was fierce and brutal but he wasn't smart which was most likely why he had no treasure, no gold or jewels because they were all he could think about. I breathed a laugh.

"She's leverage" I bluntly stated, the laughter in my eyes replaced by an irritated glare that I shot in his direction. The Captain sheathed his sword, the familiar sound of metal scraping against metal meeting my ears. The blade reflected the orange light that the lamps provided.

"Leverage for what exactly?" I couldn't contain the anger that shot through me. He was older but certainly not wiser, bigger and stronger but he didn't have the wit in order to properly use his strength to his advantage. If I hadn't been bound and placed on the edge of a plank, I would've easily been able to outsmart him, escaping though, with thirteen other men onboard the ship wouldn't have been possible either way.

"What are you? An idiot?" I snapped, the crew falling silent around us. The Captain shot me a dangerous stare, his hand tightening on the hilt of his sword as if fighting the urge to cut me down to size. I quickly calmed myself and added.

"With the girl in your grasp you own the Campbell's and if you own the noble family, you own this entire city" he quickly halted his

115

actions, pausing to maul over my words for a moment. I wasn't offering him a rare stone or gold; I was offering him a city which was more than what any pirate had ever owned. He could rule over it, gain all the gold he desired, have all the jewels he could ever dream of. He could live a life of luxury in exchange for my life, of course.

He nodded "Untie him" the Captain ordered to which his crew dragged me back onto the ship. They unbound my legs and wrists then tossed me aside. I landed with a loud thud onto the deck which managed to knock the air out of my lungs. I gasped when a pair of boots came into view beside my head followed by the Captain bending down so that we were face to face.

"Ye bring me that girl or I shall have ye head" he threatened, eyes haunting as they bored into the depths of my soul. I nodded hastily, pushing myself up and onto my feet.

"Toss him overboard!" came the snarl and my feet were once again lifted off the ground only to be tossed over the side of the ship and into the sea. I resurfaced, gasping and coughing from having swallowed some of the water. The Captain came into view above, leaning across the railing to peer down at me.

"Ye have one day before I send my men to find ye" the warning was followed by his laughter, his crew cheering as they returned to their tasks, drinking and dancing, singing and cursing. I swam for the shore, dragging myself onto the sand and feeling a sharp sting radiating from my shoulder which caused me to vomit into the shallow waves around me.

When I could finally rethink the terms of the bargain I had struck, it was already too late to go back on my word, I had to find the Campbell's daughter and bring her to them or else I would die an agonizing death. If I were to flee the city, they would attack, killing the people, killing Rebecca, my mother.

I shook my head to try and clear it as I forced myself onto my feet. I had to go through with it, for the sake of everyone I cared about.

Chapter Fifteen
Leyland Manor
1739
Caleb

Claudia Campbell was a rich noble girl around Rebecca's age. She was known throughout the city for her beauty and grace that could captivate any man. Her hair was said to be as black as a raven's feather and her eyes could see straight through a man, burning as brightly as the sun.

As a thief, I had heard many rumors, always keeping up with the gossip of men and women alike in case I would ever need to make use of the information. Only a handful of people had ever laid eyes on her since she was rarely ever seen outside of the Leyland manor.

I crouched low on top of the bell tower that was positioned near the manor, allowing myself to get a bird's eye view of the place. I studied the structure, taking in every window, every door, every balcony and every guard that passed by the front gates.

I discarded the shirt that I'd stolen and was once again left only in a pair of trousers. The cold breeze hardly doing anything in comparison to my wounded shoulder.

The blood had stained my skin and trickled its way down my left arm. I began formulating a plan, contemplating each and every way for me to get inside the manor's gates.

My eyes locked onto the ocean behind me, its waves sending a chill through my spine as I slowly stood upright on the edge of the bell tower. There was just something about the water that I hated, something I couldn't explain no matter how long I would ponder over the possibilities or reasons. I glared at the water then began my decent from the tower, using my arms and feet to scale down its side until I could leap from my perch and land with my knees bent, absorbing the impact.

There were very few people who wondered the streets at that time of night which made it easier for me to move around without being detected. I headed in the direction of the manor, my mind repainting the image of the windows, the doors and balconies in exact detail as I planned the route that I would take.

My feet came to a stop outside the old black gates of the manor. They were closed to the public. I found myself staring up at the sigil of a lion that had been infused into the metal. It was their family crest, symbolizing the Campbell bloodline and for some reason it intrigued me as I stood there, almost mesmerized by its roaring face, canines bared and eyes glaring dangerously at me.

I was pulled from my thoughts by the sound of a heavy door slamming and a woman screaming in frustration.

My eyes darted towards the double doors of the manor where a young girl was hurriedly descending the front steps, clutching the skirts of her emerald green dress that appeared black against her tan skin tone.

I quickly hid behind some nearby bushes, watching her as she stormed off in the direction of the garden, muttering things under her breath.

As I followed her movements, I took notice of a tree that stood close to the fence and crept towards it making sure to keep my eyes glued onto her petite frame for fear of losing sight of her.

She entered the rose garden and stopped at the center of it, surrounded by thousands of red, yellow, white and pink flowers.

I ducked behind the tree then began to scale it, hoisting myself up onto one of the highest branches and creeping along it until I could jump down onto the manor's grounds. She didn't realize that I was there, too furious and distracted by her own rambling to see me approaching, slowly moving closer like a lion would when stalking its prey.

The guards didn't petrol the gardens which provided me with the perfect opportunity to attack.

I was just about to grab her from behind when she abruptly turned, nostrils flaring as she glared up at me with fierce, golden eyes, eyes that reminded me of my own.

"Can I help you?" her voice was delicate but strong, feminine but held the authority of a highborn woman.

I halted, my eyes scanning her features, taking in the sight of a very beautiful young maiden. Her black curls were braided in an intricate up do on the top of her head with some of the strands framing her face while others had already broken away from their woven

118

bounds. Her nose was small and her lips were plump with high cheekbones. To me she looked like a painting, a flawless masterpiece that was close to perfection. There was no doubt in my mind that the girl who stood before me was the Campbell family's most prized possession, Lady Claudia Campbell.

She hardly seemed phased by the sight of my wound or the blood that stained my skin.

"Well?" she pressed, her voice laced with irritation, the kind of annoyance and impatience that I recognized in myself.

I didn't really care for anyone other than my mother or Rebecca but something inside of me drew me to the girl that stood a few feet across from me, her chest rising and falling with every breath that she took.

"Well?" she repeated, her eyes narrowing onto me, not afraid, not unsure but instead they were angry and frightening. I had assumed that I was the predator and she the prey but her blunt response and calm demeanor made me realize that it was in fact the other way around. She was the predator and I was her helpless prey.

"Is it gold that you seek? Silver? Jewels?" she demanded, her one hand letting go of her dress's skirts to reach for the necklace that dangled around her neck. It was made of gold and had emeralds imbedded into it.

To me it would've meant buying nice clothes, food for a month, a beautiful dress for my mother and some more of Rebecca's cookies but to her it meant nothing.

"Then take it" she tore the thing from her neck and tossed it onto the gravel near my feet. I had to take a step back when she threw it, her aggressive movements catching me off guard as my eyes landed on the jewelry piece below.

"It is not like I care for any of it" my eyes flickered up to look at her. She had turned so that her shoulder was to me, eyes scanning over the flowers, statues and hedges that made up the garden. I could tell that much like Rebecca, she hated the life she was born into, hated the pampering, the lessons in proper etiquette, the strict schedules and proposals. She was just an ordinary girl like any other despite what I had heard, she just wanted to be free.

I felt a pang in my chest when I began moving towards her, the gravel digging into the soles of my feet as I neared, my hand reaching out to grab hold of her forearm.

119

"What are you-?" she cut herself off when a strangled cry escaped her lips. I twisted her arm behind her back and bent her over the garden table, pressing her into the cold concrete. She turned her head to glare back at me, not afraid but enraged.

"You will let go of me at once!" she yelled, her eyes scorching and dangerous. She could easily bring a man to his knees with those eyes, eyes that made me pause for a moment as if to reconsider what I was doing.

I shook my head, an image of a woman dressed in red silks flickering past my eyes, the image of my mother's smiling face clouding my better judgement.

I leaned most of my weight onto her, forcing her further down.

"Forgive me" I whispered then struck her in the back of the head with a stone pot that had been resting on top of the table as decoration, causing her to fall unconscious, her muscles relaxing and her eyes growing empty.

At first, I thought I'd killed her, stumbling back a few paces, the pot slipping from my fingers and falling with a loud thud onto the gravel.

There was blood on my fingertips, blood that wasn't my own and I raised my hand to stare at the crimson liquid in horror, my body trembling in response to the realization of what I'd done.

Claudia didn't move. Her arm slipped from her back where I'd pinned it in place and dangled limply at her side. Her dark hair was wet with blood that seeped from the gash on the back of her head.

I looked towards the manor then around the garden before moving closer, placing my hand close to her nose. A sense of relief filled me when her warm breath struck my skin. She was still breathing.

I heaved her onto my shoulder and started heading for the fence, planning my escape now that I had a woman in tow. I paused in front of the fence, eyes searching for a way to hoist her over it when my eyes landed on what looked to be rust. The bars were old, the iron most likely eaten through by the damp ocean air.

I laid her down onto the grass, my hands moving from one bar to the next until I found one that was loose. I bent it just enough so that I could crawl through and slip Claudia's unconscious body underneath it. I tucked my hands beneath her arms and dragged her over to the tree I had previously climbed, trying to think of a way to not seem suspicious for carrying an unconscious girl through the city's streets.

I knelt beside her and started untying the laces of her dress, tearing the heavy thing from her body, leaving her in only a white under gown. I tossed her shoes aside and tore her dress to tie some the excess material around her head like a sash to cover the gasp and absorb most of the blood.

I heaved her onto my back like I would a sleeping woman and began my walk, sticking to the back alleys as I made my way towards the docks.

I was wounded, covered in blood while carrying a girl who I'd kidnapped in order to hand her over to a band of pirates. For once in my life, I found myself wishing that I had listened to Rebecca and stayed away from the pirates instead of finding myself in that situation.

I reached the docks a few hours later, tired and warn out from the long walk and the wound I had endured. I staggered over to the ship where a plank was placed, acting as a makeshift ramp.

I climbed it, the crew acknowledging my arrival. They called out to their Captain as I fell to my knees on the ship's deck, moving the girl so that I could take a look at the back of her head. The wound was no longer bleeding, to my surprise and a relieved sigh escaped my lips.

"Well, would ye look at that-." the Captain's voice reached my ears, followed by the thudding of his boots. His crew parted around me, allowing him through. He glanced from my hunched form to Claudia then back to me with a sinister grin plastered across his face.

"The boy held true to his word" I glared up at him, the light of the lamps illuminating the side of my face. The man in front of me was a pirate and all pirates were monsters in my eyes. He looked at Claudia, his eyes scanning her, taking in every inch of her body.

"She's the Campbell's daughter, is she not?" he questioned, not quite sure if he could believe me. I tossed the piece of torn and bloody emerald material to him and he caught it. He studied the fabric, pure silk embroidered with gold thread. He gave a satisfied hum then threw the bloody rag aside as he turned to address his men.

"Take the city!" the crew erupted into cheers, drawing their swords as they flung themselves overboard, cutting down anyone that stood in their path including the watchman. I could only watch as he bled out near the water, arm dangling from the docks as one of the crewmen lit a torch, grinning wildly. I moved to stop him from jumping over the side of the ship but the Captain clamped his hand down onto my injured shoulder, forcing me to my knees as he dug his fingers into my wound.

"Watch boy, watch ye city burn" he instructed me, chuckling at the sight of terror in my eyes.

Two of the crewmen stayed behind on the ship to guard their Captain and I knew I would be no match against them, not in the state that I was in.

My eyes landed on the post office as orange fire consumed it, a fire that began to spread deeper into the city.

"No" I breathed, my thoughts going to my mother and to Rebecca.

"No!" I yelled. I tried to stand but was forced back down by the Captain's iron grip on my shoulder.

Claudia began to stir behind me, her eyes fluttering open as a painful groan left her lips. I turned my head to glance back at her, her fierce gaze signaling me out once she was able to register what was going on around her. She tried to push herself onto her hands and knees.

"You-." she was cut off by the two crewmen dragging her onto her feet and towards one of the ship's poles, tying her to it to prevent her from escaping. She glared at one of the men then turned her heated stare onto the other, her teeth gritting.

"You will pay for this!" she snapped at them before her gold eyes locked onto mine seething with hatred as her chest rose and fell in rapid sync with her anger. She looked to the Captain with no fear and not a trace of uncertainty in her voice when she spoke "All of *you*" her threat rang through my ears, followed by the sound of women screaming and children crying in the distance. Men were laughing while others yelled for reinforcements.

The Captain stood up, letting go of my shoulder to draw his sword, aiming it directly at her throat but to his surprise she didn't so much as flinch.

"Ye best keep ye mouth shut if ye want to live, girly" he warned, pretending to be at least half as brave as she was. I could finally move, my eyes scanning the deck for any sign of a weapon but before I could find one and help her, she spoke. The words would be scorched into my memory forever.

"I'd rather die than live to see this chaos" her statement was followed by the sound of a sword cutting through the air, a cry of agony and fabric ripping as blood splattered across the deck. I watched in horror as she was cut open, her eyes still glowing with anger as she met my gaze.

"Y-Your faul-t" it was a low whisper before her head fell forward and blood trickled from her parted lips, those wild eyes growing empty. I had never seen so much blood and the sight of it made me almost frantic. She was dead, Claudia was dead and it was my fault, the city was being burned to the ground and it was my fault.

The Captain's laughter snapped me out of it. I had to get away. I had to get to Rebecca and my mother. I shot up from the deck and threw myself over the side of the ship, landing on the dock below. I had to roll in order to catch myself before I broke out into a sprint.

"Bring him to me!" I heard the Captain's voice order but I didn't dare look back as I raced through the chaos. Everything was burning, bodies littered the streets, blood flowed like a river against my feet. Women were being raped, men cut down like they were nothing and children were being killed.

My heart hammered in my chest and I grew sick with the realization that I had caused it, all of it.

I stopped in the middle of the chaos, my eyes staring down at my blood stained hands when two faces illuminated the darkness that I had found myself lost in. They were enough to prompt me to start running again, rushing towards the whore house first. The bakery had a hidden room built into its foundation and I knew that Rebecca would be well hidden there. My mother however didn't have anywhere to hide.

The door to the brothel hung on its hinges, the cries of women coming from within. I shot through the door, ignoring the pirates below and headed for our room, the room at the very top of the building where my mother and I would stay when she was not busy working.

The door hit the wall when I stormed through only to find my mother stood near the window, watching with fear in her aged eyes as the city fell into ruin before her.

"Mother, we have to go!" I hurried, reaching to grab hold of her arm. I began dragging her towards the door but she stopped me with her hand moving to cup mine as if the world wasn't ending and she gave me a faint, sad smile.

"There is something that I must tell you" she insisted, removing my hand from her arm as she held something out towards me. She'd been clutching it in her other hand. I looked down at the object resting in her palm and found that it was a pendant of a roaring lion. It was the Campbell's sigil.

My eyebrows furrowed up in confusion, not understanding why she had it or what it even meant.

"A long time ago a man came to me in search of my talents-." she began, her thoughts travelling back to the past as she traced her thumb across the pendant.

I could hear the pirates creeping ever closer. Their heavy boots thudding up the first flight of stairs. I reached for my mother's arm again but I froze when she interrupted my movements "He left this behind" her hand trembled when she spoke of the crest, my eyes staring at it.

What did that mean? That Vincent Campbell, Claudia's father had visited the brothel and paid my mother to be able to bed her? Why was it even important? She'd been with many men over the years, all to provide for me, what did one more man matter?

"And-." she breathed, her eyes filling to the brim with tears. Those tears, coming from those gentle, warm eyes made me forget about what was going on around us. I didn't want her to cry.

"A-And nine months later, you were born" her voice broke when she said those words. It was like someone had dowsed me in ice water, the color draining from my face as I stared at her in both a mixture of shock and sheer horror.

Vincent Campbell was my father; Claudia was my half-sister. My bottom lip began to tremble, my eyes starting to well up with unwanted tears as I realized what I had done. I not only kidnapped and killed a nobleman's daughter but my own sister, I sentenced my sister to death.

There was a loud bang and my mother shoved the crest into my hands, moving to push me into the cupboard, locking it so that I wouldn't get out and endanger myself. I was frozen, unable to move, unable to breathe as time slowed around me, my eyes wide while the men broke into the room, grabbed my mother by the hair and began dragging her down the stairs.

I could hear her screaming but I couldn't do anything no matter how badly I wanted to. Not even my thoughts screaming at me to help her could get me to move, I was too dead inside to react. I stayed there for what felt like an eternity, weeping, screaming and thrashing until all I could do was just exist. I was consumed by anger, my thoughts blinded by a need to kill, to seek revenge.

I finally kicked open the doors to the cupboard I'd been locked in and made my way outside. The sight of my mother's body, left bare and lifeless in the street only fueled my anger, my hand grabbing for the first weapon I saw laying on the ground which happened to be an abandoned kitchen knife.

I didn't stop moving, nothing seeming to matter to me as I retraced my steps back to the ship. I had to avenge them, I had to do something, I had to stop the growing need and hatred inside of me from spreading even farther than it already had.

The Captain was alone this, busy drinking and singing an old pirate's tune. He sat on the ship's deck with his back to me, feet kicked up on the railing. He didn't notice me until the knife's blade was firmly being pressed to his throat.

"I figured ye'd return" he calmly said, lowering his bottle of rum as he stared out onto the ocean. There was a deep affection in his eyes as he admired the sight. One he had seen countless times before yet it still amazed him as if he had only ever seen it once.

"I couldn't have asked for a more beautiful sight" I tore the blade back, fast and without hesitation, slitting his throat and causing him to slump over in his seat. My eyes landed on the bloody knife that I held in my no longer trembling hand. They then focused onto the girl beyond it who had been left tied up against one of the poles even though she was dead.

I tossed the knife aside and began to dress in the Captain's clothing, his hat, his red coat, his boots, then threw his body onto the deck for his crew to see when they would return.

My hand gripped the back of the chair he had been seated on, turning it so that I could face the opposite end of the deck.

There I sat as the sun rose behind me, waiting patiently for the crew to return and when they did, they didn't just find a boy waiting for them, they found a pirate. One by one each of them slowly went down onto one knee, bowing their heads to show their devotion to their new Captain.

Rebecca

I could remembered the day as if it was just yesterday. The day my hometown was under siege by pirates. I could still hear the screams of women and the wailing of children as men were being they cut down in the streets.

My father came rushing down the stairs with my mother in tow "Open the cellar door!" he ordered and I did as I was told. I abandoned my freshly baked batch of cookies and reached for the trapdoor. I quickly opened it. We usually stored ingredients in the cellar.

My parents were halfway down the stairs when my mother paused.

"The coins!" she exclaimed while wrenching her hand out of my father's grasp. She rushed back up the stairs as I stood waiting near the trapdoor. It was our only hope. It was a place where the pirates wouldn't be able to find us.

"Claire!" my father called after my mother. The screams were getting louder and the smell of smoke hung thick in the air. I glanced at the bakery's window and I could see pirates approaching.

"They're coming" I fearfully stated. I knew that Caleb had something to do with the mass destruction and chaos. My mother appeared at the top of the stairs with a leather pouch in hand. It jingled when she hastily rushed down the stairs and grabbed hold of my father's hand. He guided her towards the trapdoor but it was already too late. There was a loud bang on the bakery's door.

"Get in" my father ushered me down into the cellar and tried to urge my mother forward but she had other plans. She threw the pouch into the cellar then closed the door behind me, locking it. She knew that there wouldn't be enough time for them to join me.

"Claire, what are you doing?" my father demanded but the woman ignored him.

"Mother? Father?" I called out to them as I banged my fist against the trapdoor in an attempt to open it but it wouldn't budge. It was locked from the outside. I froze when the bakery's door was kicked down. My father rushed forward to prevent them from entering but was stabbed in the abdomen. He stumbled back and gripped at the sword as blood trickled from his lips.

The pirates laughed in amusement and forced their way inside as my father collapsed onto the floor.

"Thomas!" my mother cried out as she hurried towards him but before she could reach her husband, the pirate who'd stabbed my father grabbed hold of her arm. He pinned her up against the wall with a knife pressed against her throat.

I couldn't scream. I couldn't do anything other than watch. I was trapped beneath the floorboards and if I made so much as a single sound then the pirates would find me and my mother's sacrifice would've been for nothing.

I sat down on the cellar's steps with my hands clutching my mouth to help suppress my sobs. Tears streamed down my face when the pirate spoke.

"Don't ye fret deary, ye'll be joining him soon enough" it was then that a loud thud came from overhead that caused me to flinch. Blood seeped through the floorboards. Droplets trickled down onto my legs and stained my dress. I had to sop the gasp that threatened to escape me when I looked up.

My mother's face was staring down at me through the cracks in the floorboards. Her lifeless eyes were wide with fear and her throat was slit. A few droplets of blood dripped down onto my face. "Claire!" my father shrieked as he struggled to get to her while the pirates merely laughed.

"Bag the goods!" one of the pirates ordered causing the rest of them to start ransacking the bakery and our home. The pirate who'd stabbed my father approached him as he tried to crawl across the bakery's floor and wrenched the sword from his abdomen. My father grunted then screamed when the blade was plunged into his back. The pirates exited the house. The last one to leave the Bakery was the man who stabbed my father and murdered my mother. Even though they were gone, I still couldn't speak. I couldn't do anything but watch as my father crawled his way towards my mother's corpse. He wrapped his arms around her in a loving embrace and looked at me through the floorboards.

"Live" he said while choking on his own blood and causing it to splatter across my face before he fell limp. His eyes grew empty and lifeless.

I remember sobbing. I cried for what felt like days on end while I was trapped in that cellar with the bodies of my parents hovering over me. I barely moved and I refused to eat as I listened to the sound of chaos echoing throughout the town. It wasn't until the world grew silent and birds began to chirp that I finally decided to leave the cellar.

I couldn't leave through the trapdoor. It was locked and the bodied of my parents were on top of it. They blocked my path. There was a small, barred window on the other side of the cellar. I approached it and stepped up onto one of the crates to reach it. The pouch that cost my mother her life was tied to my waist as I tried shaking the bars. I was testing if they were loose enough for me to wiggle them free.

I wanted nothing more than to lay there in that cellar. I wanted to weep and disintegrate but I knew that I couldn't. My father wanted me to live and that gave me enough strength to push forward.

One of the bars broke and I tossed it aside with a clutter before I began working on a second one. I banged my fist against it until it broke with a loud clang. The bars were already rusted through which made it easier for me to escape and when the third one broke, I hoisted myself up. I crawled through the gap and into the bloody street.

I froze at the sight before me. Countless bodies were piled up outside the bakery.

I was shaking and covered in my parents' blood. I staggered onto my feet and navigated through the numerous corpses. I looked at their faces. Some were recognizable while others were unknown to me. They were the faces of men, women and children alike. I kept studying their features since I was afraid that the next lifeless face I'd see would be Caleb's.

My stumble quickened into a jog and finally it turned into a sprint as I rushed towards the brothel. The bodies of harlots littered its entry way and the door hung on its hinges. I rushed up the stairs while I ignored the sight of naked, raped woman with their empty eyes staring up at me and their mouths gaping.

When I reached the top floor, I was filled with a sense of relief. *They weren't there so perhaps they escaped?* The relief was short lived when fear set in.

What if Caleb and his mother were kidnapped by the pirates? I spun around and rushed out of the brothel. I headed in the direction of the docks with adrenaline coursing through my veins.

I reached the docks but the ship had already departed and was growing ever smaller as it disappeared onto the horizon. I stared at it and froze when my eyes locked onto a familiar golden pair.

Caleb was positioned on the ship's stern. He watched me with the Captain's hat placed on top of his head. He looked haunted by the events that transpired. He clearly saw me but chose to turn his back on me and bark orders at his crew.

I was left behind to not only mourn the loss of my parents but to cope with Caleb's abandonment on my own. I fell to my knees on the docks and watched him disappear until all I could see was the setting sun and an ocean that seemed to stretch on forever.

I buried my parents in a field outside of town and burned the bodies of the town's people. I was just a fifteen year old girl at the time. I was orphaned and abandoned by the one person I loved more than anything. It took me months before I eventually decided to track Caleb down. I needed answers. I needed to know what happened that night and so I found myself at the Pirate's Nest where I worked at one of the taverns as a dancer.

Every day I hoped to run into Caleb and every day I was disappointed. Years went by until one day a woman stepped into the tavern. Her brown hair was dreadlocked and one side of her head was shaved. There was a tattoo of a knife on the side of her face and a silver cross earing dangled from her earlobe.

She watched me dance. She studied my movements late into the night and when my performance was done, she followed me outside. "What do you want?" I demanded when I realized that she was following me. The woman didn't make much of an effort to hide herself.

"To make you an offer" she admitted. She wore a red pirate jacket and had her hands stuffed into its pockets.

"Come dance for my Captain and I will give you anything you desire" she tried to strike a deal and I told her that I was looking for someone. She offered to help me find Caleb if I danced for her Captain. It was a deal I should never have made but I did. I later found out that the woman's name was Sonja and that she was the first mate.

We never really got along except when it came to pleasing Captain Darkheart.

I embarked on the Gray Ghost. I danced for Captain Darkheart and the Red Pirates as they sailed from port to port. At first, I thought that they were selling legal goods as we travelled along England's coast but I later discovered that they were selling something else entirely.

I was too focused on my search of Caleb who'd become the Captain of the Black Pirates to realize that they were kidnapping people and selling them as slaves. I tried confronting Sonja about it to which she threatened me and told me that my job was to dance not meddle in their business.

A year went by with no sign of Caleb. I'd nearly given up all hope. It wasn't until we docked in Martin's Port where the Sunken Soul was spotted that I finally found Caleb but he was in love with a noblewoman named Mary.

I confronted him at a bar one night and he told me everything. He told me about his noble blood, about Claudia's death and his deal with Captain Solstice. He told me about Mary and how he fell in love with her.

After so many years of chasing after him and loving him, I learned that he was in love with someone else.

"Nothing good could ever come of you being with her-." I warned him as he nursed his cup of wine. He looked so different. His hair was longer, his face aged and his skin was riddled in tattoos but despite all of the changes he was still the Caleb I knew and loved.

"She's a noblewoman and you're a pirate Captain" I stated and he grew furious as if his love for Mary was all he had left. I met her a few times. It was always a brief encounter but her face would be embedded into my mind forever.

I knew that Caleb's relationship with Mary would end horribly but I didn't think it would end in death. At least not *her* death. The night Mary drowned was the night something inside of Caleb died. I remember watching him as he dragged himself to the shore and began screaming at the ocean. He cursed the water, he cursed Neptune and he cursed the gods for taking the love of his life away from him. He cried like I'd never seen him cry before as he frantically dug through the water. He was looking for her. He was desperate to find her.

I grabbed onto him and dragged him out of the water for fear of him drowning himself in the process of mourning her loss. We fell onto the sand as I hugged him from behind.

"She's gone, Becca" he told me "Mary's gone" all I could do was hold onto him as he wept. He didn't seem to care about anyone or anything after that. He started drinking heavily and rarely left the taverns. He was trying to drown his memories of her in rum and tears. Shortly after that Caleb left Martin's Port and he didn't say goodbye not even after I took care of him on his drunken nights.

I tried following him. I tried convincing Captain Darkheart to pursue Caleb but the Captain refused and when I tried to leave, Sonja took me captive. They branded me as a slave on the back of my neck using the symbol of a knife then tossed me into the brig.

I was only allowed out of my cell when I was forced to dance for the Captain or had to meet his other needs.

I remember being dragged out of my cell in the middle of the night. I was escorted to the Captain's chambers where Darkheart was waiting for me in bed with Sonja laying on his chest. They were both naked and only their lower halves were covered by the blankets.

"Join us" Darkheart insisted on as he motioned towards the bed with a ringed hand. The crewmember who'd fetched me untied my chains and shoved me in the direction of the large bed. It was covered in fur blankets and candles were lit around it.

"I'm sure we don't need her my love" Sonja tried to argue. She pushed herself onto her hands and knees then straddled him. She forced him to look at her. The look in her eyes was one filled with seduction as she licked her lips and bent down to trail kisses across his chest.

She didn't love him. She was merely using him.

"Come" he ordered as he ignored her. When I didn't respond or move towards them, he grew impatient and looked at his crewmate. He gave a single nod which was followed by a sharp pain that coursed through my scalp.

I cried out as the crewmember grabbed a fistful of my hair and forced me onto my knees.

"Ye will do as ye Captain says, whore!" he bit out with his lips close to my ear. I tried clawing at his hand but he shoved me forward and I fell into a heap on the carpet. Sonja sighed as she sat upright on top of Darkheart. She shot a glare in my direction.

"What is it about her that has you so intrigued?" she asked her Captain. He looked up at her then reached out to run his fingers through her dreadlocks. I pushed myself onto my hands and knees then watched as his hand slid its way down her neck, over her shoulder and to her breasts.

"Have ye ever had a redhead?" he asked her as he gave her breast a firm squeeze. She yelped from his grip which caused him to chuckle in amusement. He leaned closer to her then whispered in a sinister tone,

"They taste like fire"

They forced me to sleep with them that night. They didn't take my maidenhead. Someone else had taken it a long time ago but they made me feel dirty and disgusting. I spent hours scrubbing at my skin and days trying to nurse the bruises they'd left. They weren't gentle.

They enjoyed causing pain and seeing others suffer. It happened a few times while I was their prisoner and it was during that dark time that my love for Caleb died.

His abandonment had grown too much for me to overlook and though I still cared about him as a friend and had long since forgiven him for the death of my parents, I still harbored anger towards him for tossing me aside especially when I needed him most.

The only person I knew I could rely on was myself and so I began observing the crew. I took note of the ship's layout and I silently plotted my escape.

On the night that I managed to escape, I was being dragged out of my cell and onto the deck where crewmembers were busy hoisting one of the rowboats back onto the ship. I'd snatched the key to my restraints from the pirate who'd fetched me and when we began ascending the steps to the stern, I freed myself.

I shoved the pirate down the steps and darted past him. I leaped into the rowboat and the men hoisting it up were shocked. They let the boat slip from their grasps causing it to crash down onto the water. I hurriedly pushed off the side of the ship.

"Get her!" Sonja ordered to which the men started readying the second rowboat in order to pursue me but thunder rumbling overhead had the Captain ordering otherwise.

"Leave her! Let the storm deal with her" he told his crew. He was certain that the approaching storm would kill me. The storm was a horrific one. The ocean's waves grew larger by the hour and it became impossible for me to navigate the currents. Rain pelted down onto me and soaked through my clothes.

The boat was capsized by one of the waves and I was thrown into the water. I wondered if I was going to die but just when I was about to drown, the sea spat me out onto an island where I violently coughed and wheezed for air.

It was the island that Caleb's crew found me on after months of being stranded there with very little to eat or drink. The first time I saw Evangeline I thought I was seeing Mary's ghost. She had paler skin and white hair instead of her golden blond curls.

It brought back memories from the night Mary died.

Chapter Sixteen
1751
Present Day
Evangeline

I was floating, drifting aimlessly through the water. My legs were outstretched beneath me and my eyes stared emotionlessly down into the dark depths of the ocean. I couldn't breathe but there was no need to. My lungs didn't beg for air or burn as the water filled them. My eyes began to adjust to the darkness around me and slowly they took in the sight beneath me.

Mary descended towards the bottom, her tranquil gaze staring right through me as her arms floated limply at her sides. She looked so calm, so at peace. Her eyes began to droop, the air escaping her in a cluster of bubbles that moved through my chest in their quest to find the surface as if I wasn't really there. As if I was merely a ghost.

A woman made of water swam up from the ocean's depths, appearing before Mary with eyes of glowing sapphire.

A sea Nymph.

She had a tail that resembled that of a catshark, swaying back and forth behind her with hair that seemed to be never ending, made of sea foam and salt water.

She took in the sight of Mary, from her curly blond hair dancing through the water around her to her slightly darker skin tone and mismatched eyes. One blue, one silver. They were my eyes or was it that my eyes were hers?

'A heart of the sea' the Nymph announced, speaking in an ancient tongue that sounded foreign at first but later registered in the back of my mind.

The words that Gigas had spoken to me, words that felt so familiar yet so foreign.

The woman took both of Mary's hands in her webbed ones and leaned down so that her face was close to Mary's.

'Return to me' the Nymph said moments before her lips gently pressed to Mary's, causing the noblewoman's eyes to widen in a mixture of both shock and a desire to fight, a sudden need to live instead of die.

The Nymph broke away from Mary, shoving her further down into the ocean's depths. A bright light erupted from Mary's chest, her mouth gaping as if she were in immense pain. I tried observing for as long as possible, squinting at the sight but I had to look away when the light grew too intense for my eyes. It was blinding. The sound of someone crashing into the water above reached my ears.

'Mary!' Caleb's voice registered in the back of my mind, but when I looked towards the surface, I was no longer in the water, not staring at a struggling man but instead I was staring up at a starry night sky.

The moon stood out against a black canvas, small lights flickering against its stark background. My eyes lowered onto the sea in front of me and I froze when I was met with the sight of my own reflection.

The woman's eyes were just like mine but her hair was blond instead of white, her skin was a few shades darker and an expensive blue gown hugged her figure. She was stood among the waves that crashed around her, her features calm and her posture relaxed as she moved towards me.

I stayed rooted in place as she approached, every step made with grace and elegance, her toes pointing whenever she would lower her foot into the water and sand.

She gripped the fabric of her dress, moving, acting as a noblewoman would with her head held high and her shoulders rolled back as if she was stepping into a ballroom.

I was naked, my skin littered with silver scales that glistened violet in the moonlight. My hands were webbed, claws forming where nails had once been. My hair seemed almost silver as my fangs probed the inside of my mouth and my eyes studied her movements with slit pupils.

She came to a stop directly in front of me, her height matching mine, her body curved and sculpted like mine down to every last flaw.

She gave a small, sad smile then stepped forward, crashing into me. Her body dissolving into water on impact, the liquid flowing around me. I turned to watch as it evaporated into thin air. An overwhelming feeling of sadness overcame me causing my eyes tear up at the thought of her death. She was gone yet she had been so close to the touch just seconds before. I remember thinking that Caleb must have felt similarly when Mary leapt into the water, when she drowned herself. She was right there yet so far out of his reach.

"Lassie?" the word came as a whisper that I tried to ignore. The sun was starting to rise around me, painting the unknown world that I was trapped in, in beautiful pinks, blues, purples, oranges and yellows.

"Lass!" the voice yelled from behind me and I abruptly turned to find that I was back on the Sunken Soul, the Irishman standing across from me with his hands gripping my shoulders as if he had been shaking me.

It took me a minute to realize what was happening. I'd sleepwalked my way onto the deck and was heading for the ship's railing as if I wanting to jump overboard.

The man in front of me had worry in his drunken eyes. I could smell the alcohol rolling off him in waves and staggered back a few steps to distance myself from him. I didn't like the feel of his touch against my skin even if it was only through the material of my dress.

"Ye be walking in ye sleep" he explained, his arms falling back to his sides as he watched me. My fear of him was greater than the fear I had for Caleb and I readied myself to run in case he tried to throw me overboard.

I stayed silent and he narrowed his eyes onto me.

"Ye're seeing things" he declared, causing the hair on the back of my neck to stand on end.

How could he know about the visions? Did he know that I was seeing Mary?

My eyes searched the deserted deck in case anyone was near to hear his words but found that we were alone and that all was silent. My lips parted.

"H-How do you-?" he shrugged his shoulder, causing the words to die down in the back of my throat.

He was a muscular man, close to Caleb in size with light brown hair and a beard to match. He wore a low cut shirt and trousers that were tucked into his rusty, red leather boots. Around his neck dangled a few gold and silver chains with an earring that hung from his right earlobe.

"Me mum was an Oracle" he casually stated to which I furrowed my eyebrows up in confusion. He brushed it off and stepped past me, heading for the trap door when my hand shot out to grab hold of his wrist, stopping him. He glanced down at my hand as if I'd stung him.

"What-what's an Oracle?" I asked, my eyes searching his features. He looked up at me, his gaze locking onto mine to fine that I was desperate and needed to know more. Something inside of me made me feel like the Irishman knew something that could help explain what I was going through.

"Ye really are just a simple woman" he muttered, shaking his head from side to side and tearing his arm away from me. His lip curled up as he contemplated telling me. After a while he turned his head to the side, staring out onto the open ocean.

"An Oracle is someone who can see things-." he began. His memory took him back in time to a decade or so earlier. The Irishman was older than Caleb by at least five years or so and had wrinkles covering his face but despite that he was still as fierce as someone in their youth.

"Whether it be the past, present or future-." my eyes widened. The visions had to be from the past since Mary had died a long time ago. I eagerly waited for him to continue.

"They often have odd dreams and sleepwalk most nights"

If I was an Oracle then what did that make me? A Mermaid who was able to see the events of the past? I had so many questions but I wasn't sure whether I could ask them or not.

He turned his gaze back onto me, his eyes cold and hollow.

"I suggest ye drink some sea water before bed, me mum used to say that it helped with her visions" with that he turned once more to open the trapdoor so that he could head below deck to where Rebecca, Ben and the rest of the crew were most likely fast asleep. I reached out to him for a second time but this time with my voice.

"Wait!" the single word came out louder than intended. He halted with one foot on the steps and one on the deck. I could tell that he was growing increasingly irritated with my refusal to let him retreat below deck.

I thought back to earlier that day when I was sat on the chair near Rebecca who manned the ship, to when I'd promised myself that I would get the Irishman's name so that I could be able to refer to him as something other than *'the Irishman'* or *'the former first mate'*

"What's your name?" my words came out as a low, unsure whisper that caused him to glance back at me from over his shoulder.

There was confusion in his eyes as if to ask 'Why does this woman care about something like that? Why is she even talking to me to begin with?'

"Nolan" he uttered like it was obvious but to me it could've been anything from Tom to Christopher.

I nodded, feeling an awkward silence fall between us.

"Evangeline" I responded, not knowing what else to say. He shot me a crooked smile and shook his head before he started down the steps. Nolan paused before to muttered an almost nonexistent "Night, lass" then shut the trapdoor behind him, leaving me alone with my thoughts.

Perhaps I was just seeing things that happened in the past because I met Caleb or maybe it was because I was the reincarnation of Mary? Either way, I found comfort in the fact that I wasn't the only person out there having to live with such strange dreams and confusing visions.

I returned to the Captain's quarters, my feet moving from one step to the next until they stilled at the sight of Caleb fast asleep on the feather mattress.

He was facing the room, his bare back directed towards the ceiling with his arms tucked away underneath his pillow. The blankets only covered his lower half and the bed beside him was a mess. The sheets were tossed aside and wrinkled. It looked as though someone had been sleeping there.

Had I been sleeping there?

The book of the seven treasures sat on the table beside the bed and I realized that he'd most likely found me on the floor, fast asleep. He then picked me up and tucked me into bed.

The thought of sleeping on that bed beside him, on the side where Mary used to sleep made me feel like it wasn't my place. That spot wasn't meant for me, it was meant for her and I wasn't her.

I stood beside the bed, hand moving to trace my fingertips along Caleb's cheek, cupping it then letting my hand drop away. Mary's emotions were becoming stronger, growing inside me like a virus that threatened to consume me whole. I could feel myself wanting to kiss him, wanting to lay beside him, to feel the warmth that radiated from his skin but I fought the urge, once again reminding myself that those emotions, those feelings didn't belong to me. They weren't mine.

I wondered through the room, eyes scanning every surface, taking in the carpet, the blood stains my wounded leg had left behind, the dresser that had various different trinkets scattered across the top of it. From a glass dolphin to a gold coin, a picture frame with nothing in it and a bottle that had a replica of a ship in it.

I ran my fingertips along the dresser's surface and over to the desk that was littered with maps, scattered pieces of paper and letters, one of which that caught my eye.

It was a folded white envelope that was sealed with an unbroken seal. The seal was that of a red rose. There was something about the rose that looked so familiar, like I had seen it somewhere before.

An image of Mary, sat behind a desk and melting red wax in the middle of the night surfaced in the back of my mind. She was beautiful, her hair done up in delicate curls, her lips painted a brilliant scarlet.

I blinked and the image was gone. I was back in the Captain's quarters, my eyes staring down at the envelopes. My hand moved on its own accord to pick up the letter, turning it over in my palm. I stiffened when I noticed that the name *'Caleb'* was written across it in black cursive writing, my hand writing. I felt myself growing numb with the thought.

How could one person be so similar to another, almost as if they were an exact copy of someone else?

"Read it to me" my head shot up, my body turning in the direction of the voice to find that Caleb was perched on the edge of the bed, running a hand over his face. He had been watching me.

Did I wake him?

My hand constricted around the envelope when I remembered that it was still sealed because he didn't know how to read, he had spent years not knowing what Mary had written to him in that letter, what she had wanted to say before she died.

I looked at the letter, contemplating whether I wanted to know what stood beyond the thin layer of white paper. I was afraid that it would cause the visions to intensify and the emotions to surge. My eyes flickered over to the letter opener that lay on the desk. I had to know why we were so similar, why she was haunting me, why I could feel her emotions as if they were my own?

My hand moved to pick the letter opener up, cautiously as if it was going to burn me. The light from the candles reflected off its surface when I tore through the seal, expecting to see another vision of Mary but there nothing came.

After my pause, I set the opener down and reached into the envelope. There was a folded piece of paper inside along with a dried red rose and a piece of golden hair that had been cut off and tied at one end with thread.

I held the hair in my palm, the strand so soft and alive as if they were still attached to her head.

Caleb observed me, his muscles tensing when I set the rose and hair aside to unfold the letter. I realized that I was trembling when I noticed that the paper was shaking along with my unsteady hands. My gaze scanned the words and my mouth grew dry, my tongue wetting my lips. I took a deep breath.

"*Caleb-.*" I began, my voice barely audible. The opening line made my heart start to ache in my chest "*Please forgive me-.*" my mind went back to the night he'd held me, sobbing, asking for Mary to forgive him but there she was, asking him to do the same "*I didn't have the heart to tell you myself-.*' I could feel the sadness weighing down on me, Mary's growing pain, her grief and regret filling both my body and mind.

"*I couldn't stand to see your face. Forgive me. I had no choice*" her repetition made me pause to take a deep breath. My hands started shaking even more violently, so much so that Caleb noticed, his eyes locking onto my trembling figure "*My father knows, they all know about us*" a sense of fear overcame me, a great anxiety that left me feeling minute and helpless "*Tonight we will meet and go out onto the sea like we have always done-.*" I knew that she was referring to the night she drowned. She was talking about how they'd meet, venture out onto the sea where she would end up jumping into the water with the intention of drowning herself.

"*I will hold you, kiss you, taste you-.*" my breathing became ragged, my eyes growing foggy as I continued to read her words, her emotions out into the air between Caleb and I "*But it will all be for the last...time*" my voice broke, in between 'last' and 'time'

I couldn't control what was happening to me, couldn't control my actions or feelings "*A life without you in it isn't a life worth living-.*" my eyes flickered up to where he sat, a look of sadness and grief in his gaze as he stared down at the floor, emotionless and quiet.

"*You, to me, are like the sea-.*" I leaned back against the desk when my legs felt like they were going to give way beneath me "*Wonderfully beautiful, dangerous, filled with mystery*"

I sobbed when I read the next sentence, my trembling hand shooting up to cover my lips as a tear slid down the side of my face.

"*A-And my love for you is far greater than its depths*" I continued to read when I managed to compose myself. Caleb looked at me again, his gaze intense, eyebrows furrowed up and hands clasped together with his elbows propped up on his parted knees.

"*Tonight I will take my own life because without you in it, I am just a rose trapped in a glass box*" my eyes glanced at the seal then flickered to the rose on the desk beside me. Mary had been locked away behind stone walls for most of her life and all she ever wanted was to go beyond them. Caleb had taken her there, shown her how to live and she didn't want to go back to what her life was like before she'd met the pirate Captain.

"*I hope you can forgive me*" she said, her voice coming through me, projected through my body as if speaking directly to Caleb herself. I looked up at him, my hands no longer able to hold onto the piece of paper. It fell to the floor by my feet.

"*Yours always, Mary Grace Sillvan*" I couldn't hold back my tears anymore, my eyes closing as I wept. Knowing that Mary didn't jump into the sea because of her love or need for it came as a shock. She'd sacrificed herself because if she couldn't be with Caleb like her heart wanted her to be, she didn't want to go on living. As a noblewoman, her father would've hunted Caleb down, tried to kill him for being with his daughter but instead Mary took her own life, allowing Caleb to live a life of freedom.

I slid down the leg of the desk until I was sat on the floor with my knees pressed up against my chest. My hands clasped over my mouth, my body convulsing with each and every sob.

She was such a noble, brave and caring woman. She was the type of woman that I could only dream to be.

I squeezed my eyes shut when the sound of footsteps approaching me reached my ears.

I could never compare to her beauty and her grace. Her heart was kind and loving. Caleb knelt in front of me, his hand resting on one of my knees to help steady himself. My eyes opened to find him staring at me with a blank expression.

My need to be close to him, to touch him grew even more urgent the longer I stared at him until I finally threw myself at him. My arms wound themselves around his neck as I hid my face in his shoulder. He tensed at first but after a few moments he wrapped his arms securely around my waist. He held me as I cried, one hand tangling into the hair on the back of my head.

I could feel him. I could sense him and the thought of him being therein person. The thought of me not having been torn away from him like the letter suggested served to calm me.

I gasped for air, taking the time to slow my breathing and while doing so a sudden exhaustion overcame me. I collapsed into him, curling up against his chest with my hand moving to grip his as if I was a little girl. I was afraid that if I let go of him that he would disappear. He cradled me, moving to lean back against the dresser and pulling me onto his lap.

I could smell the scent of alcohol, sea salt, leather and sweat coming from him. They mixed together to form his particular scent that was so familiar and comforting to me.

In that moment, in his arms, I felt safe and protected from the harsh world around me.

I couldn't remember who Ben, Nolan or Rebecca were, all I could remember was him, Caleb. He was all that mattered, all that I could think of and despite not knowing where my emotions began and Mary's ended, I felt happy. I gave into her emotions, giving myself permission to fall.

I stepped from the edge of that giant cliff without hesitation. It was in that moment that I started to fall for him, that I began to fall in love with the pirate Captain, Caleb Campbell without really realizing it myself.

Chapter Seventeen

When I awoke, sunlight spilled into the room through the porthole. My hands curled into fists near my face as I lay in the center of the feather mattress.

I stared at the letter that was placed on the bed beside me along with the red rose that had long since been preserved.

I could remember falling asleep surrounded by his warmth. I could still hear his steady heartbeat echoing in my ears and smell his familiar scent.

The words written in the letter came back to me. Mary's devoted love for the ocean that seemed to be stronger than anything turned out to be nothing in comparison to her love for Caleb. It was that very love that danced within my chest due to the fact that I was able to feel her emotions.

I pushed myself into a seated position and tucked my knees away beneath me. My hair fell into my eyes, dangling down my shoulders when my gaze landed on the leather bound book that had been placed on the nightside table. It was then that I realized that I'd neglected to instruct Caleb on where to find the fourth treasure.

I rose from the bed and headed above deck.

There was not a cloud in the sky which meant that the crew were hard at work. They stepped around me, moving barrels and fastening ropes. One man in particular caught my attention. Nolan was carrying a heavy crate and his hands were bound with bandages due to them having been cut and bruised. I wasn't sure how long they'd been moving things around for but it must've been for some time if his hands had gotten that warn down from the work.

"Good morning" a voice greeted from beside me.

I looked up at Ben who was cradling a smaller barrel in his arms. I felt like smiling but at the same time there was something inside of me that told me to avoid him. I decided to ignore the urge and forced a faint smile that barely reached my eyes.

"Morning" I uttered, nodding in hid direction. He noticed that something was off but before he could question it, Nolan snapped at him from across the deck, telling him to stop his flirting and get back to work.

"Got to go" Ben said, shooting me a brilliant smile. I watched him go, feeling awkward due to the new found feelings that were erupting inside my chest. I gave a heavy sigh.

"Well that was awkward" my head snapped back to look up at the stern where Rebecca was grinning down at me with her chin propped up onto her palm. She seemed amused.

I brushed her off and began making my way up the steps, to the stern where Caleb was hunched over the table, examining a map. The ship wasn't moving. My chair was still placed near the table even though my leg seemed to be doing much better. My arm on the other hand, stung whenever I used it.

"What's going on?" I quickly changed the subject when I reached Rebecca, glancing down at the crew. Rebecca leaned back against the railing, her eyes moving from Caleb to me.

"He's looking for a box" was her casual response. Caleb heard her and shot a glare in her direction. The red coat, thick boots, gray shirt and Captain's hat that he wore, made him appear much more frightening than he had been the night before. I quickly averted my eyes to avoid meeting his.

"For the last time, it be a chest not a box" he gritted out.

The sound of his voice caused something inside of me to stir. His dangerous gaze locked onto me but I kept my eyes on the horizon. After a long pause he huffed and went back to his map. Rebecca was watching me with furrowed brows.

"What's inside the box?" I hurriedly questioned. I didn't give her enough time to bring up the noticeable tension between the Captain and I. She narrowed her eyes as if suspecting me of something then shrugged her shoulders, eyes glaring at Caleb's back.

"He won't say" I knew that they had most likely gotten into a fifteen-minute argument concerning the contents of the box before I joined them. Caleb's palm struck the table he was leaning over, causing me to jump.

"Chest! Not box, chest!" he didn't bother looking back at us so he didn't see the annoyed grimace that crawled its way onto Rebecca's face. She turned to look out onto the deck below, propping her chin onto her palm while releasing a long sigh.

"I hope that whatever's inside the *BOX* is worth all of this commotion" Caleb abruptly spun around to glare at her but all he was met with was her back.

I tightly pressed my lips together, trying to suppress the laughter that threatened to escape me. The emphasis that she'd placed on the word *'box'* had made the scene all the more humorous.

"What are ye? Deaf?" Caleb demanded with one hand the table and the other dangling at his side with a compass clutched tightly in its palm. Rebecca made a show of perking up. She turned her head this way then that until she finally locked eyes with me.

"Did ye hear something?" she asked, using the word *'ye'* as a form of mockery. It was like watching two toddlers bicker back and forth when really Rebecca was twenty-seven and Caleb, twenty-nine. Caleb harshly slammed the compass down onto the table.

"Ye be acting like a child" he declared through gritted his teeth. He chose to focus on the map instead of entertaining Rebecca's ways. She seemed to enjoy poking fun at him. Her face scrunched up in mock confusion as she pretended to listen.

"There it was again-." she raised her hand to make a motion with it that involved her four fingers touching her thumb as if to mimic a mouth, opening and closing repeatedly.

"It's like an irritating buzz, ringing in my ears" at this Caleb turned, ready to bite back at her but before he could, I threw my head back laughing. Both of them watched at me as I gripped the railing to prevent myself from falling. I gasped for air, clutching at my stomach with my free hand as Rebecca smiled down at me and Caleb, as usual, glared.

"Y-Ye be fighting like siblings" I managed to get out in between my fits of laughter. I tried making my own attempt at mocking Caleb's way of speaking. His nostrils flared but somehow his angered face didn't seem to bother me anymore. Becca turned to address him, her voice stern when she spoke.

"See? I told you that it's annoying when you talk like that" her serious tone made it that much more comical as I observed them.

He moved his intense stare from me to her but instead of being weary, she simply challenged the glare with a look that screamed *'as a matter of fact'*

"How I talk is none of ye business" the words came through clenched teeth. Rebecca raised her hand, pretending to wipe spit from her face then shook it. She took a deep breath in and let it out through her nose.

"It is, when I'm the one who went through all of that trouble to teaching you how to speak proper English" her statement took me by surprise. I wasn't aware that Caleb could speak three sentences without using the word 'ye' at least once. My lips parted with a need to speak, a need to hear him talk like a proper Englishman and not a pirate but I was cut short by Nolan's voice calling up to the stern from the ship's deck.

"Be this it, Captain?" Caleb pushed his way past Rebecca to gaze down at the Irishman. Both Rebecca and I turned to catch a glimpse of the 'box' we'd been so curious about. To our surprise it was a wooden chest with a golden lock and some delicate hand carved detailing. Becca groaned.

"Finally-." she moved towards the steps to go investigate the chest for herself but Caleb's dominant and demanding tone brought her to a sudden stop.

"Take it to me chambers!" it was clear that he didn't want anyone to know what was inside the chest. Not even a long-time friend that he'd known since he was a child. I couldn't help but be curious as to what it was or why it was being kept such a secret from all of us. Not even the men who'd been searching for it for hours on end were allowed to know what was inside the chest.

"Aye, Captain!" with that, Nolan disappeared from our sights along with the chest. Rebecca and I shared a furrowed eyed glance which Caleb ignored and went back to staring at the map. I pushed the thoughts of the chest aside and moved to where he was. I glanced down at the map and noticed his muscles tensing due to how close I was.

"We head South" I declared, thinking back to what I'd read regarding the location of the fourth treasure. Caleb looked up at me, his eyes briefly flickering down to my lips before he nodded and turned to address the rest of his crew.

"Set course, South!" a series of shouts came in response to the Captain's order as the crewmen began untying the ship's sails.

The fact that he didn't question me proved that he had finally placed his trust in me.

When he returned to the map, I spoke again "The gem lies within a red sea" he paused and Becca looked at me as though I'd gone mad. After everything they had seen, from Sirens to a giant turtle that carried an island on its back, it was the simple red sea that made them

145

that made them question my sanity. I sighed heavily when they didn't understand the metaphoric quote from the book.

"A desert. We're looking for a desert with red sand" at the mention of the word *'desert'* Ben glanced down at me from his perch above. His concern was relevant. I wasn't meant to be on land for long periods of time, let alone wondering a scorching desert where all you had to protect you from the heat were the clothes on your back and maybe an old pirate's hat.

Caleb stepped up behind the ship's helm to man it.

"A desert it be then" he muttered, his eyes gazing out onto the open ocean with his back to me. I was dreading the next location but there was no way around it.

If he wanted the seven treasures, he would have them and maybe I could be left in peace, no longer surrounded by pirates or haunted by vivid visions of a woman I hardly knew.

After a long day of sailing, Caleb decided to dock the ship near a small town where he allowed his men to go drinking or whoring if they so wished. I wanted to stretch my legs and decided that I would join them on land. Ben had already gone ahead, dragged off by a few of the crew and since Caleb didn't really care about what happened to me, I was left alone on the ship. I debated whether it would be easier for me to climb down the ship's side using the netting or whether I should risk jumping.

"Ye in need of a hand, lass?" I turned to find Nolan watching me with an amused look plastered across his rugged face. I opened my mouth to respond but instead gazed down at the docks below contemplating my decisions.

Did I really want his help? Rebecca had gotten down just fine on her own a few moments ago.

"I-I can do this on my own" I denied his help, hiking up the skirt of my white dress to place one foot onto the ship's railing. I climbed up. Nolan tried to suppress his laughter when I nearly fell, a high pitched shriek escaping my lips as I frantically waved my arms about and grabbed hold of some nearby ropes to steady myself.

"Graceful" the word came as a taunt and was followed by a loud gulp as Nolan took a swig of rum from a green glass bottle.

I shot him a glare. My eyes shot down to the dock that seemed so much farther beneath me than it had previously been. I slowly began to lower myself into a kneeling position, sitting so that my legs were

146

dangling down the side of the ship. After attempting to let go of the ropes a few times and shrieking every time I would begin to tip forward,

I managed to grab hold of the railing on either side of me. I could hear footsteps approaching, my eyes going wide when I realized that Nolan was standing directly behind me.

"Any day now, lassie" he chuckled, reaching out as if to shove me. I flinched and slipped off the railing, my hands frantically grabbing onto the ship's netting to catch myself. I squeezed my eyes shut, waiting to feel the impact of my body with the dock but there it never came. When I opened my eyes, I found that I had successfully gotten into position to safely climb down the netting. Nolan watched as I slowly scaled the side, leaning over the railing to watch me while taking regular swigs of his rum.

"Ye look a bit thirsty there-." I could tell that he was joking but when I looked up, the image of Nolan tilting the bottle down towards me made my eyes widen in horror.

"Here, have some rum" he enjoyed toying with me, more so than anyone else on the Sunken Soul. Caleb was just dangerous and deadly, Ben kind and caring, Rebecca fierce and reckless but Nolan was a sadistic man around thirty-six years of age who enjoyed watching me squirm.

"No!" I yelled, my hands accidentally letting go of the netting. I gasped when I fell onto the deck, landing flat on my rear. His rum trickled down to form a puddle in front of me, in between my parted legs.

I groaned as his laughter echoed in my ears and I rubbed at my aching behind. I glared up at the pirate while I stood. Nolan effortlessly flung himself over the ship's side, landing in a low crouch directly in front of me.

I yelped at his sudden appearance and stumbled back a few steps. My hand shot up to grip my chest, making sure that I was still alive after nearly having a heart attack. He stood upright, a grin plastered across his lips and the bottle still clutched in his hand.

"Did I scare ye?" I glared at him then stormed off. I shoved my way past him, feet slapping against the docks. I could hear him chuckling behind me as if my anger made everything that much more entertaining. The light from the lamps that hung along the docks guided me towards the shore. The sound of heavy boots thudding behind me crept closer as I stepped onto the sand, feeling it in between my toes.

"Come now, lass, there be no need to be mad" Nolan said but I refused to acknowledge him. I refused to even spare him a backwards glance.

The tavern was located on the other side of the shoreline and I decided to head in that direction, towards the sound of music and laughter.

"It was a mere joke" he was at my side now, his strides much larger than mine. I ignored him but was quickly made aware of his presence when he blocked my path. I collided with his chest.

"I can see why ye're his type" I gripped the skirt of my dress, hands tightening around the material when he pointed a ringed finger at me only to throw his head back, taking yet another swig of his rum. He was starting to annoy me but something inside of me wanted to know exactly what Caleb's 'type' was.

"Why?" I questioned, my eyes narrowing onto him. He bent down to untie one of his boots, tugging it off to shake the sand the sand out of it.

"Ye're feisty, got a temper and there be that look ye always get around the Captain" he did the same with his other boot then tossed them both aside as if they didn't really matter.

My eyebrows furrowed up in confusion towards his last statement. *What look?* I eyed the half-drunken man.

"What look?" my question was followed by a round of laughter. He ran the back of his hand across his lips and stepped closer to me so that his chest was pressed up against mine. I could smell the rum on his breath and my nose wrinkled up in disgust.

"Ye a whore" his words cut through me like a knife and my face grew emotionless, eyes dimming as they narrowed. I was about to tell him what exactly a whore was when he burst out laughing again, pointing at my face like it was something amusing.

"There it be, that no bullshit, go fuck yeself face that the Captain likes so much" I froze, my face clouded in a mix of confusion and irritation. Nolan was starting to get on my nerves and I was just about ready to step around him when I paused. I thought back to the night when Caleb called me a whore. I'd given him the same look.

"He called me beautiful" I muttered, thinking back to that night. Nolan's ears perked up in response to my words and he nodded, stumbling a bit before he gulped down yet another mouthful of rum.

"Ye think it was because of ye voice?" he questioned, his face clouded with humor and amusement as he turned to head in the direction of the bar.

"No, it be that face, them eyes of yers telling him to go fuck himself that's gets him all riled up" Nolan then left me standing there with so many unanswered questions. *Was that when Caleb first started feeling something for me? Did what happened the night before just add to that attraction or was it because Mary and I shared the same face?*

I shook my head from side to side as an attempt to clear it. *Why did I even care?*

I huffed and started in the direction of the tavern, pushing the conversation with Nolan to the back of my mind along with my seemingly endless train of questions.

Chapter Eighteen

The tavern was filled to the brim with people. I searched for a familiar face among the crowd.

Caleb was seated in the back nursing a cup of wine. Rebecca was positioned close by with her feet kicked up onto the table. Various anklets adorned her ankles. They would jingle whenever she'd walk of dance. Her dress skirt was tucked in between her crossed legs. Ben leaned over the bar, talking to the barman.

The smell of sea food tickled my senses and caused my tongue to tingle with the thought of eating something other than a broth that consisted mostly of vegetables and water. I began making my way over to the table when the barman handed Ben two cups. He started back towards the table but nearly collided with me.

He smiled and held one of the cups out for me to take. The red liquid inside it swished with the quick motion, a few drops spilling onto the tops of my feet causing me to take a quick step back.

"Sorry" Ben rushed out, glancing down at my feet. I was about to stumble into a man seated at the table behind me when Ben's hand shot out. He grabbed hold of my arm and pulled me closer to him.

I glanced back at the table to find that the men looked like giants. Their chests were bare, their faces covered in beards with long and unruly hair. They looked like warriors, their skin littered in tattoos and markings as they laughed among themselves.

"Fights here are common" Ben whispered into my ear, the heat from his breath sending a chill down my spine. I looked up at him, the warning in his tone was evident. It made sense that in a place so stacked full of people that some were bound to get agitated. I wondered how annoyed they'd get if a woman bumped into them. I nodded.

"Right" I made a mental note not to watch where I was going and removed my arm from Ben's grasp. I took the cup he offered and threw my head back to take a large swig of the wine. It burnt its way down my throat, leaving behind a sweet taste.

Ben laughed when I nearly fell over from downing too much of my drink and began steering me in the table's direction. Rebecca tilted her head back, listening to the music with closed eyes while Caleb watched the people around him. He observed them as if he was trying to see right through them.

"She's a pirate alright" Ben announced, taking a seat near Caleb as I finished my drink. I slammed the cup down on the table and ran the back of my hand across my lips, silently hoping that the wine would get rid of the many questions I had.

"You keep drinking like that and we'll have to carry you back to the ship" Rebecca said, one eye opening to peer up at me. I braced my hands on the table, palms flat against the surface as I met her stare. She wasn't the slightest bit drunk but I knew that the cup in her hand had to have been refilled at least three times by then.

"Would that be a problem?" I asked, half-jokingly with my eyebrows knitted together and my head tilted to the side. My hair hung down, almost reaching the table's surface because of how long it was. Instead of the redhead, it was the Captain who answered me.

"No, but it be a pain in the ass to babysit ye all the time" he bit out in irritation. I was agitated myself, particularly at him for being the cause of all of my problems. All the questions I had that were unanswered were about or revolved around him, his past or someone from his past. Before him everything had been so peaceful but then he just had to kidnap me and force me join him on some treasure hunt that I didn't want any part in. My head snapped up in his direction, eyes glaring and nostrils flaring.

"You know who's the real pain in the ass?" I asked to which both Ben and Rebecca looked at me with wide eyes. They knew what was coming next and they knew that it wouldn't end well.

"You and having to lead you to those stupid treasures, so the least you could do is 'babysit' me" I placed emphasis on the word 'babysit' biting it out like it was some shameful scorn that I was placing onto him. Caleb's eyes narrowed, Ben chocked on his wine, coughing loudly from beside me as the Captain leaned back in his seat.

"Ye hit ye head, scrape ye arm, wound ye leg and now ye start drinking like a fish-." he began, going on as if I was some clumsy child that he always had to take care of. My hands balled into fists on the table's surface when he nodded his head in the direction of my empty cup.

"What be next, cursing?" he asked to which I sucked in a deep breath, holding it for a few seconds before I leaned across the table towards him. My teeth were gritted, my eyes narrowed and my tolerance of him was at its limit.

"If it was, it be none of ye damn business" Rebecca tried to keep her composure but even I could see the grin threatening to break out across her lips.

Caleb stayed silent, his eyes roaming over me, moving from my face to my body and back to my face before he took a slow gulp of his drink. His eyes never left me, even when a hand clamped down on my shoulder and I turned to look at its owner, Caleb's eyes still watched me.

"There be that look I was talking about" Nolan whispered, his hand slipping away from me as he made his way around the table. He was drunker than before which led to him slumping down onto the chair beside Rebecca. I looked at him for a few minutes then turned my attention onto Caleb when the Irishman's words registered in the back of my mind.

The look the pirate Captain held was challenging one, a daring one, an aroused one. I quickly sat down beside Ben, attempting to make myself seem as small as possible to the eyes of the lion observing me.

"Drink?" Nolan asked, holding his half empty cup out for me to take. I eyed it then him, eventually deciding that I needed whatever was inside the cup. I quickly downed the brownish liquid that was not as sweet as the wine and twice as bitter. I coughed, sliding the empty cup back across the table. Nolan caught it and eyed the inside of his now empty cup.

"Me rum" he complained, eyebrows scrunching up in confusion as if to ask where it had gone. Rebecca laughed and raised her own cup to take a swig of the red substance.

"You offered" she argued when he blinked at me. I ran a hand over my face as Ben watched me curiously and Caleb remained silent. The Captain slumped back in his seat with his chest exposed due to his red coat being unbuttoned.

An upbeat tune began to play and Rebecca shot up, her cup hastily forced into Nolan's hand as she grabbed hold of mine.

"Let's dance" she insisted while I stumbled onto my feet. I paused, glancing back at the table to where Ben was smiling his caring and Nolan was stealing sips of Rebecca's wine. Caleb's golden gaze locked onto me like that of a hungry predator signaling out his prey. I shook my head in order to clear it and smiled up at Becca.

"Let's" I needed to get my mind off things and her showing me how to dance was one way of doing it. I just hoped that I didn't make a fool of myself.

Our dresses swayed in synch to the rhythm. My hands gripped the skirts of my dress while Rebecca spun me around a few times. She laughed when she showed me how to move my hips in a more seductive way. I didn't give up and tried again until she seemed satisfied then we'd start on our next lesson. Every now and then, she would get lost in the music and forget that I was even there. She twisted and turned, swaying her hips this way and that. Her arms danced above her as the anklets around her ankles jingled in time with her precise movements. Watching her was like listening to a Siren's song. It was mesmerizing, enchanting like that of a Witch's spell. It captivated everyone around her, men and women alike as she did what she loved most.

A few more drinks and enough dancing to last me a lifetime later, we were all located on the tavern's balcony, overlooking the sea beyond. The men were lounging in the chairs. Rebecca was perched on top of a table while I climbed onto the balcony's railing.

"Careful" Ben quickly rushed out, moving to grab hold of the arm that was closest to him since he was the one who constantly made sure that I was alright. I pulled my arm away from his grasp and stuck my tongue out at him.

"I can balance on my own" I stated proudly. Ben breathed a laugh, shaking his head as he watched me walk along the railing, placing one foot in front of the other until I lost my balance and had to swing my arms around wildly in order to catch myself. Rebecca and Nolan shared a laugh at the sight of me. I was a tipsy mess.

"So, Eva-." Rebecca began, leaning back on the table as she kicked her legs back and forth. She hardly felt a buzz, much like Caleb who sat observing me with glaring eyes. He was most likely contemplating whether I had a death wish due to where I was standing. I paused at the sound of the nickname, my head turning to look at the redhead.

"Yes?" I questioned, tilting my head to the side like a curious puppy. *Was she going to ask me about Caleb? About Mary? Had I given myself away somehow? Did she know that I was a Mermaid? Did she know about my visions?* My paranoia seemed to be nothing more than a fragment of my own imagination.

153

"Well since you know so much about us-." she paused, motioning to both her and Caleb. I knew she was referring to the night she'd told me their backstory and how Caleb fell in love with Mary.

"I think it's fair that we get to know something about you" I could feel Ben's eyes on me. He knew the most about me but even he didn't know about my past, about my upbringing and adventures. I tilted my head back to look up at the stars, pressing an index finger against my chin in thought.

"Let's see-." I muttered under my breath as a light breeze danced through the material of my dress, allowing it to tangle in between my legs. I lowered my finger and turned to face them with little care whether I fell or not. Ben flinched, ready to catch me incase anything happened.

"I was raised an orphan with around sixteen little brothers and sisters-." my mind traveled back to my days at the orphanage. They were days of gray that were mainly spent scrubbing floors, making beds, cooking and taking care of the younger children. I had to squint as I tried to remember the highlights.

"I took care of them, fed them and played with them. I also taught them how to read and write" I used to have strange dreams about the ocean and I sleepwalked often. When that would happen, I would find myself on the shore, always facing the water.

"Because I was the oldest, I never got adopted-." a thick silence followed my words but I stared straight ahead with eyes lost in thought. I never knew what it was like to have a mother or a father since I was just a little girl when my mother abandoned me to the orphanage.

"People want children to raise not another house maid to take care of" my siblings would come and go as the days turned into years.

My shoulders slumped slightly at the thought but it quickly faded when I remembered something that was a lighter shade of gray compared to all the rest.

"There was this boy, Douglas that lived rather far away from the orphanage-." I giggled, moving to sit down on the railing that I was still balancing on. It was a clumsy motion that nearly had me tumbling over backwards. I gripped the railing and steadied myself when Ben shot forward but I brushed him off, going back to my story.

"He would always steal one of his mother's yellow roses and leave it on my bed for me to find" Douglas was a few years younger

154

than me and it hadn't been anything but a boy's crush. He outgrew his flirtations later on.

"I remember running into Douglas when I went down to the docks to buy some fish. He and his older brother were about to go out on their family boat" I looked up, kicking my feet back and forth. I could feel the cool breeze in between my toes as I squeezed my eyes shut, lost in the memory of the two noble brothers.

"The brother's name was Deacon. I don't believe I've ever seen such a finely dressed man before-." Ben stilled beside me while Caleb remained silent with his hand clenched on the table in front of him. Nolan was laying on his arms, half asleep while Rebecca leaned forward, her eyes wide with curiosity.

"He was handsome and I must've done something right, maybe it was the way I did my hair that day or maybe it was because his little brother liked me so much-." I pondered out loud.

The image of the tall man dressed in tailored clothing with chestnut brown hair and light freckles resurfaced in my memory. He had a strong jaw line and dangerous green eyes that were much like that of a snake.

"Or maybe it's because I always manage to attract the dangerous ones?" Rebecca laughed as she shot a glance in Caleb's direction. I nodded, deciding to myself that the latter was the reason why and continued telling my story.

"Deacon took a liking to me. He bought me gifts and jewels and dressed me up in fancy dresses but it was all-." I trailed off, my mind going back to that moment when I realized what he was doing.

I, the orphan girl, stood in the tailor's shop, wearing a gown that wasn't meant for the likes of me. The words Deacon had whispered were like cold ice being thrown over me 'You'll make a beautiful noblewoman' I wasn't a noblewoman, I wasn't meant to have riches or a large mansion, I was meant to be me. I was meant to be free.

"It was all just a ploy. He manipulated me into acting more like a noblewoman and less like myself. I was a puppet on a string and he was the puppeteer-." I wiggled my fingers to mimic the puppeteer's movements. There was a long pause as I looked between the members of my audience.

Rebecca was the first to speak, her chin propped up onto her palm as she imagined what it would've been like to be spoiled by a handsome nobleman with all the money in the world.

155

"What did you do?" I thought back to that tailor's shop and grabbed the cloth that sat on the table directly in front of me. I hopped down from the railing and wrapped the fabric around Ben's neck, pulling him down so that he was at eye level with me.

"I said *'I am not a noblewoman, I do not want jewels and fancy dresses, I want to be free to be myself'*" I spoke all this to Ben who was slightly confused. It hadn't happened exactly as I'd said in that moment. I turned, tugging the fabric away from Ben's neck only to throw it at him before I curtsied with the material of my skirt clutched in each hand. Ben fumbled to catch the cloth.

"Now I bid thee farewell, kind Sir" Rebecca laughed at my dramatic antics, her smile unable to be contained as I stepped up onto the table before me, one foot on the chair and the other on the tabletop.

"I stormed out of the tailor's shop in only my nickers, but I'll be damned if I don't say that I did it with dignity" I stood up straight, my chin held high and my shoulders square.

Rebecca burst out laughing along with Ben who had slightly tinted red cheeks. Caleb looked up at me with furrowed brows as if questioning my sanity. My eyes moved from the people around me to the open waters beyond, realizing something that I hadn't been able to since I first left that small town.

My world was no longer just mixtures of gray but colorful, painted with pinks and purples, blues and reds.

I fell to my knees on the table, the thoughts of where I'd been raised bringing forth a newfound appreciation for where I'd found myself, for the pirate Captain that kidnapped me.

This was more of a home to me. Ben, Nolan, Rebecca and Caleb were more like family than any family I'd ever known. I smiled faintly and without thinking the words left me in a faint whisper, carried off by the breeze.

"I'm home" even if it was just a small realization of something I'd already known deep within myself, it still made me feel like I had someplace I belonged.

I was no longer a kidnapped girl onboard a pirate's ship but instead I was a member of the crew, sailing the open seas, witnessing things I'd only dreamed of before then.

Once we'd find all seven treasures, I hoped that Caleb would allow me to remain on his ship and not just abandon me to the waves when I'd done exactly what I was taken to do.

Chapter Nineteen

We returned to the ship sometime close to dawn. Ben and Rebecca dragged a passed out Nolan below deck, leaving me alone with Caleb who'd been silently brooding all night. It was as if he'd been contemplating something over and over again in the back of his mind.

I headed to the Captain's quarters, rubbing at my aching neck muscles as I descended the steps only to pause at the bottom of them. A dress had been perfectly laid out on the bed.

My feet carried me towards it, the gold and yellow silk material standing out against the orange light of the candles. I stopped directly in front of it. My hand reached out to caress the delicate beading, the pearls that decorated the bodice and the tulle that formed ruffles along the sweetheart neckline.

It was beautiful, beyond anything I'd ever seen before, beyond anything Deacon had ever dressed me in.

Caleb stilled on the steps, watching me, his eyes moving from my figure to my outstretched arm and finally coming to a rest on the dress.

"I had it made for Mary-." I quickly pulled my hand back at the mention of her name. I didn't want to taint what was meant to be hers with my hands.

I looked at him, studying his every move. He'd noticed my sudden retreat and allowed his gaze to roam over me before he came to stand beside me. His eyes landed on the gown. There was a pause as he reached for it, scooping it up into one hand.

"I want ye to have it" he held the dress out for me to take. I took a staggered step back, not sure if he really wanted me to take it. Our eyes met, neither of us drunk, neither irritated or angry but instead calm. We were gentle towards one another.

His golden depths all but pleaded with me to take it and after remembering the effort he'd put into finding it for me by instructing his entire crew to search for the chest it was stored in, I gently took the gown from his hands. I held the dress up in front of me.

"It's beautiful" I imagined the dress being something Mary would've married him in, a gown grand enough for a queen that must've cost him everything he had just to make. My fingers danced through the silk as I marveled at the sight of it.

"Try it on" he urged to which I met his eyes in shock. I hadn't expected him to ever show me the dress, let alone ask me to try it on for him. I glanced down at the dress and swallowed hard as I nodded my head once, sharply.

I placed the gown on the bed and turned to slip out of my white dress. His eyes roamed my skin when I bent to slip the ivory material off my legs. I reached for Mary's dress and undid the delicate lacing, tugging my hair over one shoulder while I worked, sneaking a glance back at Caleb. His gaze moved from my back to my rear, to my legs and arms.

When he noticed that I'd caught him staring, he cleared his throat and quickly looked away. I bent to step into the dress, first with one leg then the other until I could tug the material up, along my legs and over my hips. I held the bodice close to my chest with one arm and reached behind me with the other to tie the corset but it was no use.

Two hands interrupted mine when Caleb stepped closer, his fingers expertly wrapping around the silk strands. I let my hand drop to my side and nervously picked at the fabric as I bit my bottom lip. I hoped I could do the dress justice. He pulled on the strings and I gasped. I wasn't used to the restrictive clothing that noblewomen wore.

I released a breath in a long drawl as he finished tying off the corset. The warmth of his body left me when he took a large step back as if to indicate that he was done.

I squeezed my eyes shut as I slowly turned around, preparing myself for whatever insult he would throw at me but it never came. There was no insult, no words, not even an uttered sound.

I opened my eyes to look at Caleb. He was taking me in, all of me, from my facial features to the tops of my breasts, my narrow waist and round hips.

"Caleb?" I asked, my voice as low as that of a whisper. He blinked, snapping out of his daze when his eyes returned to my face. He turned so that his shoulder was to me and shook his head.

"Take it off" it was a mutter at first, one that I thought I'd misheard. I stepped towards him with my hands gripping the skirt of the dress.

"What?" I asked again, not sure if I'd heard him right. He seemed distraught, confused and agitated as he glanced from me to the floor. He raised his hand to motion towards the dress that I was wearing.

"Take it off!" he snapped, louder, clearer this time. I shot upright. The calming atmosphere from earlier was instantly ruined. My narrowed eyes searched the bedsheets beside me as my chest rose and fell. Anger shot through me, starting at my chest then vibrating out towards my fingers and toes.

"Fine" I turned, my hands moving to untie the corset that he'd tied. When it was almost undone, Caleb's hand shot out to grab hold of my wrist, clamping down on it.

I turned to look up at him, nostrils flaring and eyes filled with fury but he cut me off before I could speak.

My eyes widened when he pulled me closer, one arm wrapped around my waist while the other tangled in my hair, tilting my head back to hungrily press his lips against mine. I wanted to fight him, to fight the feelings that circled in my chest but I couldn't. I melted into him, my eyes closing and hands moving to caress his chest and shoulders.

Sparks igniting my skin, trailing up and down my spine. My hands cupped the sides of his face, holding him in place as our tongues fought for dominance, our ragged and rushed breaths mingling. I could feel his heart hammering in his chest as his hand moved to further untie the back of the dress. He was desperate to feel me, to touch me.

I broke away from him, gasping when he continued to trail kisses along my neck. He pushed me back into the nightside table, causing the book and locket to clutter to the floor. My fingers ran through his hair, pulling at the strands when he bit my neck, sucking and tasting me.

I closed my eyes. Never before had I been so sure of wanting someone as I'd been in that moment. I wanted him.

I was half perched on top of the nightside table with him positioned in between my legs. He continued to kiss the side of my neck as I clung to him, desperate for all of him.

"Mary" he groaned and my eyes shot open as I froze. My muscles tensed at the sound of her name on his lips.

I pushed him away from me, sending him staggering a few steps back so that I could stand up straight. My arm wound themselves around my torso to prevent the bodice from slipping since it was fully undone. At first, he looked confused, his eyebrows furrowed up as he glanced at me then realization filled the golden depths of his eyes which was followed by instant regret.

"Evangeline, I-." I cut him off, my feet moving on their own accord as I pushed my way past him. He reached for my arm, trying to stop me in my hasty retreat to the bathroom but I tore my arm away from him. My eyes glazed over with unwanted tears as they met his.

"Don't touch me" I whispered, my voice breaking and my bottom lip quivering. He looked at me, his eyes growing dull as they searched my features. His outstretched hand returned to his side as if telling me to go, as if to say that he wouldn't follow me.

I turned to head for the bathroom and slammed the door shut behind me. As soon as it was closed, my hand moved to cup my lips as the realization that all I would ever be to him was Mary's replacement struck me.

I tore the dress from my body, suddenly despising it.

My eyes locked onto my own reflection in the mirror that hung on the wall to find Mary's face staring back at me.

Her mismatched eyes, her small button nose and her plum pink lips.

I crumbled to my knees, too afraid to look at my own reflection. I hated it, the sight of my face that looked so much like hers. I hated my eyes, my nose, my mouth. I wasn't me, I wasn't Evangeline, to everyone else I was simply Mary, the Mary they were trying to replace.

I curled in on myself, pressing my forehead to my knees as I wept, staying there until the late morning hours, naked and broken.

To think that I was going to give him all of me, my maiden head, my heart. I trembled, furious with myself for ever thinking that he could be the man worthy of such a precious gift.

He was a pirate Captain and I was merely the reincarnation of a noblewoman.

Chapter Twenty
Two Years Ago
Evangeline

I was busy making the many beds at the orphanage, pulling the pale gray sheets tight before brushing out the wrinkles.

Tessa watched me, hugging her brown teddy bear to her chest as she wiggled with her toes. Her blond curls were a wild mess and had yet to be combed. She was telling me about how she'd seen a fairy, about how it floated up to her window and told her magical things. I listened intently, moving from one bed to the next while humming in response to her story every now and then. It wasn't until she fell completely silent that I looked at her.

"Tessa?" I questioned, standing upright. She was dressed in a simple frock. Her big blue eyes, filled with curiosity and wonder stared at one of the beds.

"Big sister, look" she said, pointing at the bed. I turned to find that she was referring to my bed that was just like all the others, small with a white iron frame and covered in gray sheets. At first, I didn't understand what she was referring to.

"The bed?" I asked. Tessa shook her head furiously and scurried across the old floorboards, causing them to groan. Using her elbows and knees she climbed up onto the bed and sat down in front of something yellow.

"It's a flower" she leaned forward to get a closer look at it, her eyes big with awe since she'd probably never seen a flower up close before. My eyebrows furrowed up as I moved to see what she was marveling at. A yellow rose had been placed on my bed. I found it odd that such a valuable flower would be there. It was the kind of flower that only the wealthy could afford.

"It's a rose" I explained, picking it up by its stem and being careful not to prick my fingers on the thorns.

I inspected it, noticing the water droplets on its soft petals along with how they so delicately folded outward like puckering lips.

My eyes landed on the open window above my bed, the white curtains dancing in the breeze with the shoreline in the background.

"It's really pretty" Tessa muttered. Her wide eyes were glued onto the blossom. I smiled down at her as I pressed the rose's petals to my nose so that I could smell its fragrance. It was an oddly sweet smell that I wasn't familiar with.

I held it out for Tessa to do the same and she quickly imitating what she'd seen. She pressed her nose into the flower and breathed in.

"It smells sweet" she announced, her face clouded in confusion. I laughed lightly and eased down onto the edge of the bed, tucking the material of my old, gray dress beneath my legs.

"Most flowers are sweet" I said, thinking back to the rare occasions when I would get to smell some at the market. Even just passing by the baskets was enough to catch my attention. The scents were often overwhelming.

"Why?" she tilted her head to the side, causing her messy mane of hair to tumble down one shoulder. She was around six or seven and naturally curious. She'd once had an entire conversation with one of the women who ran the orphanage about why birds can fly, and humans can't. I smiled at her.

"Because they need to attract bees" explaining how pollination worked and so on would be too much for her to comprehend so I decided to stick to the basics.

She only seemed to grow more confused, her arms tightening around her stuffed animal that I had to stitch up a few times in the past due to how old it was.

"Bees?" I hummed in response, tapping her nose with the rose before I stood and set it down on the table beside the bed so that I could start tugging at the sheets again, patting them down.

Tessa scurried off the mattress and stood, waiting expectantly for me to continue as I worked.

"Yes, bees. They make honey from flowers" it wasn't entirely true, but she didn't need to know that. Her imagination was as wild an unruly as her hair and I could see the gears starting to turn behind her bright blue eyes. I continued to make the remaining two beds as she followed me around.

"What's honey?" I contemplated her question for a moment. She'd never had honey before and I'd only ever had it once when Lady Harlow, the owner of the orphanage, brought some honey suckle home for the kids to eat. I bent to pick her up, placing her down on the mattress that I'd just finished making with her back to me.

"It's only the sweetest syrup in the world" I replied, reaching for a brush that sat nearby on one of the nightside tables. She looked up at me with wonder in her innocent eyes. She was so precious, like most of the children at the orphanage and would most likely get adopted within a few weeks.

"Really? I want some honey!" she declared with determination swirling in her glassy gaze. I couldn't help the small smile that tugged at my lips as I turned her head so that she was staring straight ahead.

I began to section off her hair, being careful not to hurt her when I pulled the knots apart.

"I'm sure you'll get to try it someday" I reassured her, using the brush to detangle her golden locks.

She barely made a sound as I worked, years of combing through knots having paid off, making me somewhat of an expert.

Two boys came barreling into the room, one older than the other and holding onto an old toy boat. I recognized them as being Andrew and Henry, the younger of course being the latter.

Henry was a short eight-year-old boy with dark hair and deep dimples while Andrew was an older, taller boy around twelve with red hair and freckles. He was the troublemaker of the lot.

"Henry! Andrew! No running inside the house!" I scolded as Tessa scowled at the pair, annoyed by their loud bickering and laughter. Andrew held the toy boat above his head and out of Henry's reach. The smaller boy tried jumping to reach it. Eventually Henry gave up, turning to look at me with tears in his eyes.

"He won't give me back my toy, big sister!" I stopped brushing Tessa's and moved over to where Andrew was still snickering at the younger boy. He stopped laughing when I came to a stand-still in front of him, his face clouded with worry like he knew he'd done something wrong.

"Give it to me" I instructed, holding the hand that wasn't wrapped around the brush out for him to place the boat onto my palm. He huffed but did as he was told.

I handed the toy back to Henry and turned to address Andrew when the dark-haired boy ran off to go play, cheering up almost instantly.

"It's not nice to take other people's things" I stated to which he clasped his hands together behind his back and hung his head in shame.

To the children I was their older sister, but I was also someone who had authority because I was much older than then. They would listen to me like they listened to Lady Harlow.

"We have so little as it is" with him I could be more open, more honest about our current situation, about where we lived and why we were there to begin with. He understood what it meant to be an orphan and that things were harder for us, that we didn't get toys and gifts like normal children would. Andrew nodded.

"Yes, big sister, I'm sorry" he looked at the floor but when I ran my fingers through his hair, he looked up at me with confusion in his eyes. *Why was I petting his head when I was supposed to be mad at him?* I smiled a loving smile, one that always seemed to calm the children no matter what the circumstances.

"Good, now why don't you and Angus go fetch some firewood for the stove?" I suggested.

His eyes began to glisten, adventure hidden in them at the mention of collecting firewood. He loved exploring and it would be the perfect opportunity for him to do just that.

"Alright!" he exclaimed and quickly scurried off to go find Angus so that they could go wondering around in the nearby forest and fields.

I returned to Tessa, running my fingers through her still somewhat messy hair as she huffed.

"Boys" she muttered, drawing a light laugh from my lips as I continued to brush then braid her hair, tying it off with a blue ribbon.

The days had turned into weeks that spilled into months of me receiving a mysterious yellow rose every seventh day. It would always appear on my bed or near a window where I was working. It made me feel somewhat excited, having a secret admirer who left flowers for me to find.

I was busy hanging the clothes out to dry when I heard a twig snap. I turned and could see the top of a boy's head, sticking out from in between the bushes.

The blond hair gave him away. At first, I thought it was just one of the boys from the orphanage trying to sneak up on me, so I decided to play along, going back to my work and pretending like I hadn't noticed them.

165

I bent down to grab a shirt from the basket, shaking it out a few times before I pinned it onto the line.

The boy slowly crawled his way around me, in the process allowing me to see that he was too finely dressed to be an orphan. He wore a white button up shirt and brown trousers with brown shoes.

In his hand he held a yellow rose that he quickly dropped onto the grass near the laundry basket before scurrying off. I turned to stare after him, my eyebrows furrowed up in confusion. My wet hands dangled at my sides and small silver scales started forming on my fingers. The silver anchor necklace bit into the skin at the base of my neck.

The boy's name was Douglas. He was the son of a nobleman and was around sixteen years of age. He'd formed some sort of fascination with me.

The roses became more and more frequent until I could clump them together in a vase that sat in the middle of the large dining room table.

Tessa told everyone of my admirer, including Lady Harlow and the rest of the women who would constantly tease me about it.

I was about to head to the docks where the fisherman often had their catches on display when Lady Harlow caught me.

"I hear herring has been quite common lately-." she eyed the paper, her gaze narrowing as if to focus in on the small handwritten words. She always looked for a good price to save money since we didn't have much of it to begin with. Our money came from public donations and odd jobs that I or some of the older kids would do for the town's people.

"That means the price would've gone down" my hand was braced against the doorframe as I looked back at her. She was sat at the dining table, her glasses perched on the tip of her nose.

"Do try and buy some herring, dear" I could tell that she wasn't just after the good price but that she also had a craving for it. I gave a forced smile and nodded.

"I'll do my best" with that I was gone, making my way down the busy streets where people hurried past me to get to their jobs or go about their shopping.

It wasn't that I didn't like Lady Harlow, it was just that I felt trapped in that stuffy orphanage and wanted to get out more often. I wanted to see the world but even I knew that was just a farfetched dream.

166

The docks were lined with crates that were filled with iced fish as the fisherman sat on nearby barrels waiting for the towns people to stop by while running their errands.

I walked along the docks, eyes moving from one crate to the next. Lady Harlow was right, there was a lot of herring for sale.

Near the edge of the docks, I stopped to talk to one of the men regarding their herring. I shot him a brilliant smile in hopes that he would lower the price even more. He was telling me about the growing numbers of herring in the area when my eyes caught sight of a golden-haired boy that stood not too far from where I was. His green eyes were examining a white boat with a mix of excitement and wonder.

"I'll take two" I interrupted, my head turning to once again address the fisherman. He went silent, nodding as he moved to wrap the fish in paper. He placed them in my basket then took the coins from my hand.

"Thank you, have a lovely day" I said before grabbing my basket, hoisting it up onto my arm as I began making my way towards the boy in question. I froze when I noticed the finely dressed gentleman that stood near Douglas, speaking to one of the dock workers about the white boat. His hair was chestnut brown, and he had the same green eyes as Douglas with freckles littering his nose.

My mouth gaped at the sight of him, he was so handsome and looked older. I decided to talk to Douglas as a means of catching the older man's attention. The younger of the two didn't notice me until I stood beside him and cleared my throat.

"Hello. I want to thank you for all of the roses" Douglas stared at me with wide eyes as if my gentle touch to his shoulder had entranced him.

He was about to attempt to speak when the older man noticed me, handing the documents he'd been going over back to the worker as he excused himself. He approached us.

"So that's where mother's roses have been disappearing too?" I stiffened at the sound of his voice. It was deep and charming like you would expect from such a finely dressed man.

I hoped that my hair wasn't as much a mess as it usually was or that my breath didn't smell. Such irrational thoughts.

The man turned to face me, a smile on his lips that caused my heart to flutter at the sight of it.

"Not that I blame you, she is rather pretty" he took me in, his eyes trailing from my face, down to my body and shoes. I stood there, awkwardly fiddling with the skirt of my dress as he looked me over, not sure how to react in the company of such a fine man.

"Deacon Daughvis, Douglas's older brother" he introduced himself. He held his hand out for me to shake in a rather professional way. I nervously tucked a stray strand of hair behind my ear before taking his hand.

"Evangeline" I said while he shook my hand. He let go to motion to the boat Douglas had been eyeing. I looked at it, studying the white painted wood with the word 'Daughvis' painted across the boat's side in bright blue letters.

"Well, I would offer to take you out on our family boat but it would seem that you have some place to be?" Deacon questioned, motioning to the basket that I held close to my side. I glanced at the herring, contemplating whether it was as important as spending time with such a handsome man.

Tessa's smiling face popped up in the back of my mind. She was most likely hungry from not having eaten anything in a while. Preparing the herring for dinner would be a tedious task.

"Yes, unfortunately I must prepare dinner" I politely declined, suppressing the sigh that wanted to escape me. Deacon nodded, folding his hands neatly behind his back as he looked at me with all the charm in the world.

"In that case, would you perhaps like to join me for lunch sometime?" Douglas glared up at his older sibling as if he was oddly protective of me.

I was taken aback by his sudden request, asking me out on a date after only seconds of meeting me. I cleared my throat.

"It would be an honor, Mr. Daughvis" I tried to keep my composure, to not seem as though I was filled with a sudden burst of joy at the thought of something interesting finally happening. Deacon smiled.

"Then I shall come fetch you throughout the course of the week?" he suggested. I made a mental note not to make anything too laboring for dinner for the rest of the week and agreed.

He excused himself to tend to the boat. He made sure that it was ready to be taken out onto the water while Douglas sulked at his side.

I turned to leave and waited until I was well out of sight to grin. My heart was pounding in my chest at the thought of a nobleman actually taking a liking to me.

Chapter Twenty-One
1749-1751
Evangeline

I'd known Deacon for around a month or so, he'd taken me on many extravagant dates to fancy restaurants and the theater to witness a retelling of William Shakespeare's Romeo and Juliet. He bought me gifts that consisted of jewelry, clothing and bouquets of flowers that I could show Tessa to fuel her newfound love of flora.

He'd suggested that I go to get fitted for a ball gown since his family would be hosting their annual banquet and I was to be his date.

I stood in front of the full-length mirror, eyeing the green material of the dress. It wasn't something I'd normally choose to wear.

Deacon stood behind me, conversing with the tailor on what he wanted the gown to look like and exactly how it was supposed to fit me. I turned this way and that, eyeing the emerald silk that made my already pale skin seem that much paler. Eventually I turned to address the two men.

"I don't like it" I stated. It wasn't that I was being ungrateful since such a dress would cost a fortune but if I had a say I would've bought the most inexpensive article of clothing and simply worn that instead. I didn't like the over-the-top extremes that most women would go to just to look attractive. Deacon looked up at me.

"What's not to like?" I made a mental list of the things, starting with the giant puffs on the sleeves, the too tight corset, the large skirt that would knock someone out cold if I moved too abruptly. I huffed and decided to take a more-subtle approach.

"The color, it makes me look dead" I replied, looking at myself in the mirror again. The dark green would look beautiful on someone with a darker skin tone and hair color, however it made me look like I was getting dressed for my own funeral. The tailor seemed to agree with me.

"Well, it does draw the eyes away from her" he agreed, noting that if I were to walk into a room wearing such a dress that everyone would notice the gown and not the person wearing it.

Deacon looked at the tailor then gave the same smile he always did.

"Nonsense. Emerald is the color that symbolizes success in love" he argued and moved to stand behind me. His hands gripping my shoulders, giving them a firm squeeze.

Deacon was quiet the romantic, a man who enjoyed spoiling women, making them feel special but what I'd failed to realize was that he used his charm to mislead and manipulate them.

"What does the color of the dress matter when it's me you'll be introducing?" I questioned, my eyes locking onto his in the mirror's reflection. We'd shared a few light kisses, nothing too extreme since it went against his morals as a nobleman. He sighed heavily.

"I want you to leave a good impression on them" he admitted, his eyes filling with a sense of fear as he glanced off to the side.

The tailor retracted from the conversation. He went to roll up his tape measure and put it away.

"And I will, by being myself" I said, turning to face him with my hands gripping the skirt of the dress to ensure that I didn't knock something over in the process. Deacon looked at me, the adoration in his eyes turning to annoyance.

"Evangeline-." he began but I cut him off. I never was one to bite my tongue when I felt like I had to speak. If he cared for me or loved me like he said, then he wouldn't be ashamed of who I was.

"Are you embarrassed to have me, Deacon Daughvis?" I asked. The tailor went still, his muscles stiffening at my abrupt question, a question that was coming from the mouth of an orphan, directed at a nobleman. He'd most likely never heard anyone speak like that to a person of status before.

"Of course not, it's just, my parents-." he gave a small, sad smile at the mention of them. In the few weeks that I'd known him, I'd determined that he didn't really get along with his parents. I decided to give him a chance to speak, wanting to hear what he had to say.

"They don't approve of you, of us-." it was like a sting, a burn that scorched me as I just stood there. The tailor awkwardly tried to busy himself while I accepted what I'd been expecting. I nodded my head.

"So, all of this is for them?" I questioned, raising my arms and motioning to the dress.

Deacon placed that same old smile on his face, brushing off the importance of the issue at hand as he turned me around so that I was looking at myself in the mirror.

171

"That, and you look stunning in green" there it was, the flirtatious breath that lingered on the shell of my ear, the sly grin with his smiling green eyes. It was all an act to get me to give into his charm. When I only stared at him, he decided to nuzzle the side of my neck.

"You'll make a perfect noblewoman" his words struck me, the kiss he placed on my jaw went unnoticed as I processed his words.

There I was, standing in a tailor's shop, wearing a fancy dress with a nobleman showering me with affection. I wasn't made for that world, the world of expensive gifts and status. I moved away from Deacon and shook my head.

"I'm not a noblewoman" I tore the dress from my body and tossed it aside. I was left standing in pantaloons and a nude corset. The tailor nearly jumped out of his skin at the sight of me. I turned to meet Deacon gaze with my head held high and my shoulders squared.

"I'm an orphan girl-." I motioned to the many dresses that hung on the walls around us then to the racks of materials and expensive thread.

"And all of this isn't me" with that I stormed past him, heading in the direction of the door, opening it and causing the bell to chime. I paused, looking back at Deacon, my eyes darting between the two men.

"I want no part of this world" I declared then left.

Gasps and insults rang as I made my way back to the orphanage, the people staring at the sight of the girl in only her undergarments.

Deacon didn't bother to follow me. He didn't care to stop me as I retracted myself from him and the world, he'd grown up in. I found myself feeling all alone as I stood in the room that had beds made with gray sheets lining either side.

It'd been only a few months since I'd walked out on Deacon, choosing to be myself instead of becoming someone else.

Tessa, Andrew and Henry had all been adopted but there I remained in that sad place.

It was late at night and I was stood in my white night gown, staring down at the palms of my hands in the moonlight. I turned them over, examining their flawless, pale skin.

My eyes landed on the ocean beyond the window, the waters that called out to me, beaconing me ever closer.

I dropped my hands to my sides and moved towards the pane of glass, reaching out to caress its cold surface with my fingertips. The pull became stronger, like a tug on my heart telling me that I needed to go there, I needed to be somewhere other than that gray room where nothing ever happened.

I slid the window open, being careful not to wake Lady Harlow or any of the children as I climbed out. My feet met with grass simultaneously. My eyes were directed towards the water, starting to glow a bright silver-sapphire.

'A heart of the sea' the wind and crashing waves seemed to whisper in my ears as I began walking towards the shore. I didn't have control over my actions or thoughts as I moved, my mind almost blank, consumed by something far beyond my control.

The grass turned to cobblestone roads that faded into grains of sand when I reached the shoreline, having passed by a tavern on my way to the water.

I navigated the rocks with little fear, going as deep as they would allow. I came to a sudden halt at the edge of the boulders, my eyes returning to normal as I gripped the sides of my head, blinking rapidly to clear the fog that clouded it.

Why am I here? Why can't I remember anything?

My eyes focused on the water, on my reflection in the moonlight and they began to glow vibrantly. I was once again taken over by the unknown force.

'Return to me' it whispered. I stumbled and was thrown back against the rocks when my hand slipped and my back collided with a solid surface. My breathing came in short, ragged breaths, my hands gripping the wall of rocks behind me as I stared out onto the water with wide eyes.

I slid down the rock until I was sat with my knees pressed firmly against my chest.

I couldn't remember anything, not the words that had been whispered to me, not the tempting lure of the ocean or how I'd gotten there to begin with.

Time seemed to tick on as I sat there, eventually gaining the courage to dip my toes into the water, watching as silver scales began to form upon my milky skin. I studied them, running my fingers along their pattern as I hummed a tune to myself.

A drunken man stumbled out onto the docks, holding a bottle of alcohol. At the edge of the peer, he narrowed his eyes to stare out onto the sea.

173

My head shot up when his bottle shattered at his feet and he frantically yelled.

"Pirates!" I slowly stood at the sight of the ship with black sails nearing the docks, the drunken man hurrying off to alert the rest of the town's people.

My eyes locked onto a set of golden ones that seemed so familiar yet so foreign to me. They were the gold eyes of a pirate Captain.

Whatever led me to the water that night had led me directly into Caleb Campbell's grasp. It led me there with a purpose, a role that I had to play yet I had no idea that meeting Caleb wasn't just a cruel trick life decided to play on me but rather that it was my destiny.

It was fate, dragging me into something I'd long since then been deemed a part of.

Chapter Twenty-Two
Present Day
Evangeline

I'd fallen asleep on the bathroom floor with my hands gripping the fabric of the dress. My body was naked and stood out against the gold canvass beneath me.

I pushed myself onto my knees, glancing around at the tub carved from wood, the matching wooden basin and the mirror that hung above it.

My hands helped me onto my feet so that I could look at my reflection in the old, rusty mirror but instead of myself, I was met with the sight of Mary.

She had her blond curls in a delicate up do and she wore the same gold and yellow dress that I'd worn the night before. Her cheekbones, lips and eyes were highlighted with makeup that made her seem even prettier than she'd previously been.

I looked down at myself to confirm that I was still me, that I was still Evangeline but the dress that was discarded on the floor now hugged my figure, blond curls bouncing in my line of sight.

My eyes shot back to the mirror, hand moving to touch my face and hair. The reflection mimicked my movements almost exactly. I reached out to touch the surface of the mirror and she did the same, placing her palm flat against mine before the glass turned to a window and I was staring out onto the ocean beyond. The sky was painted crimson.

Movement in the window caught my attention and I turned to find Mary standing behind me wearing an emerald, green dress that looked frumpy and like the one I'd worn when Deacon tried to drag me into a life of nobility.

Behind her was a stained-glass mural of a Mermaid that seemed to glow in the scarlet light. I could see myself in it, my hair once again white, skin pale but I still wore the gold and yellow dress.

She began moving towards me 'Remember' she said, her eyes beginning to glow vibrantly.

I took a step back and away from her. My back didn't collide with the window like I'd been expecting it to but instead I stepped out onto a balcony that overlooked the ocean.

My own eyes were glowing *'You must remember'* I glanced around frantically, in search of a way out but before I could find one a sharp stinging sensation pierced my skull. I cried out, both hands grabbing hold of either side of my head as I stumbled back.

Instead of feeling my legs collide with the balcony's railing, I began to fall. I stared up at the balcony that had turned into the edge of a cliff on which Mary stood, looking down at me as I reached out for her. It was my plea for help.

My back connected with freezing water and I was dragged down into the dark depths, my dress tangling around my legs, my arms sputtering as I tried to reach the surface but no matter how much I struggled, I continued to sink until I was aimlessly drifting through the murky water.

I twisted and turned, both my hair and the dress making it harder for me to see.

A figure appeared in front of me, a woman with glowing sapphire eyes and a body made entirely of water. A tail swished behind her as she locked eyes with me.

'Remember' she said in a foreign language, her lips moving and causing bubbles to float up between us. I wanted to scream, to yell to both the Nymph and Mary *'Remember what?'* but I couldn't speak in the water, I couldn't breathe because of the necklace that hung from my neck. I reached for it but before I could remove it, I was pulled further down, gasping at the sudden force which filled my lungs with liquid.

My body collapsed onto the shore, coughing violently as I crawled onto my knees. My hands curled into the sand beneath me as small waves crashed around me.

I was on the shore at night, a familiar beach that I recognized from my many years spent at the orphanage. It was the same shoreline I'd been on when Caleb and I first met.

My body was soaked, the dress crumbling around me like dust to form a simple blue gown that hugged my form and stuck to my curves like a second skin.

A set of feet appeared in front of me. They were bare and looked like they belonged to a woman.

I looked up at her. She was more beautiful than even the Nymph. Her eyes were as white as my hair and pupilless. Her hair was as black as a raven's wings and she wore a black cloak with the hood pulled up, hiding the black crescent moon marking that sat in the center of her forehead.

She held her hand out to me, the anchor necklace dangling from her fingertips as her black claws pointed towards me.

I glanced down at my body, to find that my legs were wound together in a single fin with the necklace that had previously been around my throat now hanging from her index finger.

'Forget-.' she began, her voice like a dangerous spell as she knelt onto one knee in front of me, holding the necklace out for me to take. When her scarlet red lips moved, they spoke in an array of voices that filled my head, all saying different things at once.

'Everything' my webbed hand shot out to grasp the necklace. It sent a jolt through my body when I took it.

I froze when the images were erased from my mind. Mary, the Nymph and the black-haired woman were all erased. I cried out, my hands clawing at the sand beneath me as my mouth gaped. Saliva dripped down from the pain that coursed through my body, tightening the muscles in my jaw and skull, preventing me from swallowing or from breathing.

My eyes shot open to stare down at the gold and yellow dress beneath me on the bathroom floor as I scratched at the wooden floorboards.

When the pain finally subsided, I positioned myself on my knees, my head falling back as I gasped and wheezed. My hand gripping at my throat and the necklace that could be found there.

I managed to calm down and glanced at the dress, at my naked figure with furrowed eyebrows.

What was I dreaming?

I tried to think back but when I did it was like something kept pushing me away, forcing me to stop by sending sharp pains through my head.

I used the wall to ease myself onto my feet, washing my face with the fresh water in the basin before I stepped out of the bathroom. I tossed the dress onto the empty bed and searched the drawers for something to wear, settling for Caleb's oversized, long sleeve shirt. I

177

tugged my boots onto my feet and placed the First mate's hat on my head.

Noise came from above deck as the men set about their duties, manning the sails and watching the tides. I stepped into the morning light, glancing around at the crew, at Nolan, Ben and Snaggletooth.

Rebecca was seated near the figurehead with her dress skirt tucked in between her legs. Her head was tilted back with a hand placed over her eyes, shielding them from the sun's glare.

I made my way onto the stern, knowing fairly well that Caleb would be there like he always was. The night before come back to me in a rush of memories. The dress, the kiss, his voice groaning Mary's name.

My hand tightened on the step's railing as I shoved the thoughts to the back of my mind, preferring to not think about them. When I reached the top of the steps the ship jerked and I had to grab hold of the railing when I stumbled and fell onto my knees a few paces away.

The ship stopped moving and the crew ran around, yelling at each other, crying out in the direction of the wheel where Caleb was stood peering over the side at the water below.

Rebecca came rushing up the steps, her eyes moving from me as I hoisted myself back onto my feet, to a fuming Caleb.

"What just happened?" she asked the Captain while I tried recovering from the impact. My chest ached and my arms were trembling. Caleb glared at Rebecca, his nostrils flaring when his eyes found me. The moment I looked at him I knew that all his pent-up anger was about to come rushing out of him and onto me.

"Ye" the single word was like a growl, a low rumble that came from the center of his chest as he stomped across the stern towards me. I shrank back in response to the speed and force behind his movements.

"We. Struck. Rocks" he bit out causing me to flinch. I didn't understand why he was so mad. The ship wasn't taking on any water and we were navigating around the rocks with Rebecca manning the helm. I could hear Ben shouting for her to turn so that the ship wouldn't sustain any more injury.

"Because of ye directions me ship has been damaged!" the accusation rang through the air, echoing in the ears of the crewman, catching the attention of both Ben and Rebecca.

I contemplated staying silent and allowing him to scream at me but that wasn't who I was, that wasn't the women I was raised to be. I could never bite my tongue for a man or anyone else for that matter.

"My directions? You mean that stupid book's directions!" the world around us fell silent, the crew were staring up at us, Rebecca gaping at the sight while Ben sat watching high above on the sails.

How was I supposed to know that there would be jagged rocks that far South from Gigas? The book didn't give any specifics, only vague directions and metaphoric descriptions of what we were supposed to look out for. Nothing at all about rocks.

"Don't blame the book for ye mistakes!" at his words I stood upright, my face inches away from his when I glared at him, fire in both our eyes. His was hot and blazing while mine was cold and stung like frost bite.

"I don't blame the book; I blame the author!" Nolan, Rebecca and Ben were glancing between us, their heads moving from me to Caleb whenever we would take turns yelling.

Caleb gritted his teeth and spoke through them, his fists balling at his sides.

"Well, I blame ye reading" I felt like throwing something at him but there was nothing to throw. A hat or a boot just wouldn't hit him hard enough. I stood up on my toes, my own nostrils flaring, eyes narrowed in a mixture of anger and distaste.

"I can't read what hasn't been written!"

Nolan's words from the night before came back to me, his words about my heated, glaring gaze that seemed to peak Caleb's interest but not even that could calm the storm raging inside of me. If he thought that I was being attractive in that moment, then there was truly something wrong with him. His eyes flickered down to my lips, into the neckline of my shirt before he tore himself away and turned to stalk his way towards the helm.

"Then use ye eyes to look rather than read!" he snapped, motioning to the water with his palm facing upward. Rebecca moved away from the helm when he grabbed hold of it, his knuckles turning white from the force of his grip.

Was he being serious? I couldn't believe how much of an idiot he was as I strutted over to the table in front of the wheel, slapping my palms onto its surface.

"How about you use yours instead? All you do is stand behind the helm all day pretending to look where we're going!" everyone was in shock. We'd argued before but it had never been this heated and all because of something so petty.

The real reason we were arguing was hidden from those around us but was clear to the two of us. He was upset because I was mad at him for mistaking me for Mary.

"Be that all I do? Well, why don't ye man the ship then?" he suggested, moving away from the helm. I stayed rooted in place, my jaw muscles tightening when the thought of throwing the compass at his head came to mind.

"Excuse me? You're the one who's after these treasures, not me!" there was movement on the deck below that caught Ben's attention from up above.

His eyes landed on a sea of red sand in the distance that crept ever closer.

"Land ho!" Nolan yelled but even his announcement, the fact that we'd reached the location of the next gem, wasn't enough to draw us out of our argument.

In fact, I moved around the table to shove my index finger into Caleb's chest "So it doesn't bother me whether we find them or not!" a long stretch of silence followed my announcement.

Caleb only stared down at me, his lips frowning, his eyes deadly and filled with warning. Eventually Rebecca broke the silence, looking between us with wide, knowing eyes.

"Why is there such a strong sexual tension between you two?" I shot her a look then turned my attention to the crew. I glanced at Nolan and finally looked up at Ben.

The ship sailed onto the shore and I shot a final glare in Caleb's direction before retreating. I hurried down the steps and climbed over the ship's side. I landed in the sand below with my boots.

I began walking in the direction that I knew the gem was located, ignoring the calls from both Nolan and Rebecca. The look on Ben's face had been one of confusion and pain when Rebecca spoke. I'd been clear to all of them that there was something deeper going on between Caleb and I.

I shook my head, deciding that I just wanted to get away from it all for a moment. I just needed to breathe. That was the only reason I'd gone in search of the gem to begin with, not that I cared for it but because I needed to distance myself from Caleb.

From everyone.

Chapter Twenty-Three

All four of them eventually caught up to me in that hot, red desert terrain, climbing dunes in order to follow me.

I ignored them until Rebecca casually asked.

"So, what exactly are we looking for?" she didn't bring up the previous conversation or the fact that there was still an obvious tension between Caleb and I. I stopped walking when a strong gust of wind came blowing past us, causing the grains of sand to pelt against my legs. I held onto my hat. It was the only thing shielding my face from the harsh rays of the Southern sun. Becca held down her skirt to keep it from blowing up as Ben shielded his face. Both Caleb and Nolan didn't seem effected by the burning sensation that the sand caused against their skin.

"A green gem" I replied once the wind settled. I skidded my way down the side of a dune then kept moving, eyes narrowed onto the horizon, scanning it for any trace of a green glimmer.

No one felt the need to say or ask anything else as we ventured on, our feet leaving trails of footprints behind us.

Rebecca twisted her ankle, falling to her knees in the sand, hand gripping for the nearest thing to catch herself with which just so happened to be Nolan. She grabbed hold of his arm and nearly dragged him down on top of her as she cried out in pain. I stopped, turning to glance back at her.

"Fuck sakes, lass" Nolan complained, half bent over with his arm still in her hold. Ben rushed to her side, always a kind and caring young man who always worried about and respected women regardless of who or what they were.

"Are you alright?" Ben asked when my eyes caught sight of a green shimmer in the distance. I rushed to get to it, moving as fast as I could in the heat and dirt. When I reached the jewel, I bent to pick it up, unaware of the fact that Caleb was right there beside me.

I held it up towards the sky. The sun's rays reflected off its surface, casting green beams of light upon our faces. There was a loud rumble as the ground beneath us began to shake. I stumbled, barely able to hold onto the gem when the sand gave way beneath us, seeping down into a hidden cavern below.

I fell, my legs slipping out from under me causing me to gasp and making it impossible for me to scream before my back collided with the floor. The air was knocked out of me, the gem slipping away and cluttering across the stone floor.

"Caleb!" Rebecca's voice cried out overhead. I turned onto my side, blurry eyes blinking at the sight before me.

Caleb was standing nearby, also having fallen into the cavern. He moved towards the gem, bending to scoop it up from in between the stone and sand.

"Evangeline!" Ben called down into the cavern. I didn't move, my world dancing in slow motion as my breathing echoed in my ears. I blinked. Caleb stuffed the jewel into his pocket and raised his head to look at me.

"Lassie!" Nolan added when he realized that I'd gotten hurt. My eyes began to droop, my hand fisting around the sand that lay beside my head. My body, legs and arms were covered in the red substance.

There was a heavy thudding as the image of Mary's face flickered past my closed eyelids. They shot open, my mouth gaping as I gasped, pushing myself onto all fours when her blank expression surfaced like a thundering heartbeat in my mind. I began coughing, wheezing with my hands balling into fists against the stone tiles.

Caleb stopped dead in his tracks a few paces away, he didn't want to come near me unless it was absolutely necessary, but he stayed where he was in case things went South and he needed to reach me in time.

I leaned back onto my knees, my hands sliding along the ground to fall limp at my sides when I looked up to the gaping hole above.

Nolan had Rebecca's arm slung around his shoulder, the leg of her sprained ankle lifted to prevent her from stepping on it while Ben was on his hands and knees. He was positioned much closer to the hole to peer down at me.

"I'm fine" I reassured them, my head falling forward, hair shielding my face from their view as I leaned onto my palms. I breathed in, taking a moment to assess the damage.

For once I was grateful for Mary's endless torment, for her sudden appearances in my mind and dreams. If it hadn't been for her, I would've most likely passed out cold.

There wasn't a warm liquid at the back of my head which meant that I hadn't hit it. My arms and legs could move without too much pain and though my neck was stiff, it didn't hurt.

"Rope" I breathed out, leaning in Caleb's direction with my hand patting the stone. His eyes searching my form and face before he turned to address the three crewmembers overhead.

"Fetch me a rope!" he called up, his voice echoing which led me to believe that the room we were in was vast and empty. I could hear sand falling into the hole when Ben moved to address both Nolan and Rebecca. The trickling of water nearby caught my attention and my eyes shot open to glance at its origin for fear of me getting wet with Caleb so close by.

"Take Rebecca back to the ship, treat her ankle and bring a rope" Ben's voice instructed. I blinked at the crystal pool of water that sat off to the side. The room was gigantic and the pool was deep with statues of a bearded man, holding a triton lining the walls.

Is this some sort of temple that was built in honor of the sea god, Neptune?

"I'll stay here as a lookout" Ben declared. I knew of the threats surrounding the desert climate. Sandstorms could pop up out of nowhere and burry us alive in the cavern, the ceiling could cave in at any moment but beyond that I had something else to fear equally as much. I was starting to dehydrate, having ventured so far away from the damp ocean air and with Caleb around I wouldn't be able to get into the water.

"Right-." Nolan began and Rebecca's heavy breathing reaching my ears. The Irishman turned to start the journey back to the ship but paused to glance down to where I was gripping my forehead with my right hand.

"Ye best take care of the lass" he warned Ben. My eyes widened in response to his threat, my gaze going up to look at Nolan, however he'd already started guiding a limping Rebecca back to the ship.

Did the same man who enjoyed tormenting me so much really care about me getting hurt?

I shook my head and sat down near a wall in the shade. Ben took a seat with his back to the cavern, his eyes staring out onto the open planes and dunes of crimson dust.

184

I closed my eyes and leaned my head back against the wall with my lips slightly parted. My hands trembled from the shock of the fall.

It started getting hotter as the sun rose ever higher into the sky. At some point I kicked off my boots and rolled up the sleeves of my shirt to help combat the heat. My hat lay discarded a few feet away, covered in dust and sand.

Caleb had stripped down to his pants, pacing from one end of the room to the other like a restless, caged animal.

My head was pounding and my breathing came in dry pants.

"How long does it take to fetch a damn rope?" Caleb complained, his eyes darting towards the surface as he moved, sweat coating his chest and muscles in a glossy layer. I sighed heavily, letting the breath escape. His loud volume only sent a sharp pain coursing through my skull.

"Stop yelling" my voice rasped, catching Caleb's attention. He turned to glare at me, eyes blazing over. He was still irritated due to the prior night's events and arguments.

"I'll do whatever the hell I want!" he snapped, louder this time. I flinched when his words struck me like a blow to the head. My tired eyes blinked up at him when he stormed towards me, stopping a few feet away. He was breathing hard with his nostrils flaring as they always did when he got mad.

"Don't start" I warned, my voice faint but amplified by the echoes that the room created. Ben turned to glance down at us from over his shoulder, his elbows resting on his propped knees. I wasn't in the mood to argue with Caleb.

"Who do ye think ye-?" I cut him off when he began yelling again, my head raising to send a glare in his direction. My voice rose higher, growing like that of a lioness's roar. It was a threatening snarl.

"You want to start? Then let's start!" I gripped the wall behind me, using it to drag myself onto my feet. His hands balled at his sides when he moved to snarl something in my face but I interrupted him.

"I'm done playing games" the words brought an end to his confident burst of fury, instead leaving him silent. We both knew what I was getting at. I reached for the back of a collapsed statue, using it to steady myself as I moved closer to him. My legs trembled beneath me.

"I may look like her-." I began, bringing up the true reason behind our heated words, deadly glares and sexual tension.

185

"I may sound like her-." my hand slid along the side of the statue, helping me step closer to him until I was stood directly in front of him. The pain in my head intensified when I stood. I was too weak, too drained to yell so I spoke calmly.

"But I'm not Mary-." my eyes were rimmed with red. They burned from the lack of water when I locked gazes with his golden glare.

"And if she's what you want then I won't stand in the way of that" his body tensed at the sound of her name, his facial expression growing colder but I was done fighting, done yelling and arguing.

I glanced at the floor, at my feet in between the red dirt and gray stone tiles.

I breathed in, my chest rising and falling with a loud wheezing sound coming from my lips when I looked up at him.

"If you want to love a ghost then by all means, go right ahead but I refuse to love a man who'd rather stay in the past than move on" Ben turned to listen in on our conversation. His brown eyes grew sad as he listened to my words. A part of me felt something strong and intense for Caleb but he only felt the way he did towards me because of Mary. I stumbled back and shook my head.

"I'm not Mary and I won't pretend to be her" I finished, watching the anger start to fade from Caleb's features almost like he understood what I was getting at yet the irritation still lingered.

He breathed out through his nostrils, stray strands of hair dangling in front of his eyes while others framed his face.

"Ye're nothing like her" I wasn't sure if his words were supposed to sting or comfort me, so I remained silent. My hand tightened on the statue, so much so that it started turning white. I could feel the skin on my arms and legs starting to itch from the lack of moisture.

"Ye're feisty, fearless, reckless, stubborn and a pain in the ass to deal with-." I winced, my eyes closing as I took in his harsh words.

Yes, they were the things that separated me from Mary but they weren't necessarily good.

Caleb moved closer to me, drawing my attention up to him when he peered down at me. His eyes had softened.

"But most importantly ye're Evangeline" it was a good thing. His list of differences between Mary and I were a good thing.

My cracked lips parted with a need to speak but before I could, I choked on my own breath. My legs gave way beneath me as my hand lost its grip on the statue. Caleb moved to catch me, falling to one knee to lighten my fall. I began violently coughing, wheezing and struggling to breathe.

"Evangeline!" he cried out, his arms wrapping securely around my waist in order to support me. My hand reached for the pool of water in desperation. I knew that I wouldn't survive if I tried to hold out any longer in the scorching heat.

"Get her to the water!" Ben's frantic voice yelled down into the cavern. He knew exactly what was happening to me. Caleb glanced up at the younger man then looked at me. I moved my arm to grip at my necklace, my chest rising and falling rapidly but the air didn't seem to reach my lungs. My body fell limp, slumped against his chest, causing him to take action and snapping him out of his confused, frozen state.

There was genuine worry in his eyes when he picked me up, one arm wrapped around my shoulders, the other tucked underneath my knees. I didn't know if it was concern for him not being able to find the remaining few treasures if I was to die or whether he really cared for me.

My eyes were shut as he carried me, the swaying motion of his movements causing nausea to set in.

I mentally prepared myself for how he would react to me being a Mermaid when the sound of his feet stepping into the water touched my ears.

I gasped, eyes shooting open when the cool liquid met my back and soaked my bare legs, removing the red dust that once stuck to them. I tore the necklace from my throat, clutching it in the palm of my hand when my head fell back into the water.

My legs kicked, tangling into one silver fin that reflected violet. My hair became a silvery gray, my pupils slitting and my eyes began to glow. My canines extended to form fangs. Webbing formed on the shells of my ears and fingers as scales littered my arms, chest and face. Gills formed on either side of my neck.

I stared up at Caleb, his eyes locked onto mine before they slowly roamed over my body, most of which was still concealed by the shirt I was wearing.

I was weak and unable to move, completely at Caleb's mercy.

187

My body shot forward, pulling my face out of the water as my hands grabbed for his shoulders, holding the top half of my figure out of the water. Caleb was oddly calm, his form stiff from the feel of my scaled arms wrapped around him but he quickly relaxed, easing into it.

His hand slid up along my back and to my neck where he ran his fingers across my gills, across my scales, admiring them. His tender, curious touch sent chills down my spine, causing my mouth to gape near his neck. I could hear the blood pumping through the main artery there.

I gasped when his thumb traced my jaw, pulling me out of my trance. My instincts kicked in when I realized where I was and who I was with. The threat of a pirate Captain registered in my mind and I became frantic at the thought of him wanting to hurt me, to cut off my scales to sell on the black market.

I began thrashing against him, shoving him away from me as I dove into the water, into the shallow end of the pool where we were stood. My hands moved quickly, fastening the necklace back around my neck as my eyes locked onto a rusty, old knife in the water nearby.

I reached for it out of fear and desperation, my fin separating into two limbs. I stood in the water, my body trembling as I held the knife up in self-defense, pointing the tip of the blade at him with my pupils still slit, my mouth parting to bare my fangs with at Caleb with a threatening hiss.

Caleb had raised his arm to shield his face from the splash of water and lowered it when he locked eyes with me. His sense of curiosity faded, replaced by the reality of the situation.

He knew that I was scared, that I saw him as a threat and that made him grow cold, as if he'd been expecting me to trust him.

"I don't want ye scales" he declared, his shoulders rising and falling with every breath he took. I slowly began to lower the knife, my face returning to normal. My eyes were no longer glowing, my hair its usual ivory color and my canines retracting. I was starting to regain my composure, the fear from before having been replaced by the realization that by not trusting him, I'd hurt him.

"Caleb-." I began, taking a step towards him in the water. He turned his back to me when he spoke again, words that cut through me like the rusty knife I let slip from my hand.

"All I want is them treasures" was it his way of saying that as long as I led him to the treasures, he wouldn't hurt me or was it him saying that the treasures mattered more to him than any amount of money?

I found myself watching him as he climbed out of the pool, walking to the opposite end of the room with his back reflecting the light that shone in through the hole in the ceiling. Questions that I'd been keeping inside all this time rushed to the forefront of my mind.

Why were those treasures so important to him? What did they mean to him? Why was he so determined to find them to begin with? Why was I willing to put myself in harm's way just to find them? Why was I so desperate to get to those gems without even knowing what the purpose of them was?

Ben remained silent, studying my features. My eyes stung due to feeling so vulnerable, so exposed. I'd hurt Caleb and the thought of him hurting because of me, caused me agonizing pain.

Nolan.

I grew up surrounded by powerful, independent women. The most memorable of which being my mother who used to have vivid visions of the future.

She often sleep-walked and hardly ever got enough sleep which made her a cranky and irritated old broad. She usually took all her frustration out on either me or my younger sister, Hannah.

Hannah feared nothing so growing up, she never really stuck to the rules. My mother passed away shortly after my sister fell pregnant, the father of the baby wanted nothing to do with them, and I?

Well I ended up on the Sunken Soul scrubbing floorboards till my fingers bled.

Rebecca reminded me of my sister, as stubborn as a mule and as outspoken as a drunken sailor. She never bit her tongue.

"Do ye need me to carry ye?" I offered when she stopped hobbling to keep up with me. She breathed hard, her nostrils flaring and her hand digging into my shoulder. She was holding on for dear life. When I asked the question, it was as though she only then realized that I was there.

"No" was her simple, short reply, her hand falling away from me when she tried to hobble along on her own, not wanting my help. Her ankle was starting to turn blue and had begun to swell so after taking a few steps she crumbled to her knees in the sand, one hand holding the single boot she'd removed while the other balled into a fist in the burning sand.

I stayed where I was, watching her when she forced herself back up, limping a few feet only to fall again. She grunted in frustration and threw her boot without bothering to aim. I'd never seen a woman so determined yet so helpless at the same time. I shook my head and muttered,

"Women" under my breath before going to bend down in front of her so that I could wrap her arms around my neck and hoist her onto my back. I stood and began walking.

"Ye're stubborn, I give ye that" I said but got no reply when I bent to scoop up her boot, handing it to her. She took it and tightened her hold on me, her thighs constricting around my torso.

My own hands gripped those same thighs to keep her from sliding down or falling. She hid her face in my neck, the sweat that had formed on her forehead feeling cool against my hot skin.

"Me mum used to say that a woman is just a much prettier man with tits and a hole instead of a rod-." I paused and thought back to the old lady standing over me with a wooden spoon in hand, flicking it in every direction when she would repeat the words that I'd probably heard a thousand times before.

She had gray hair and wrinkles around her eyes and she always wore the color black. She often said that it kept her visions at bay.

"She believed that women could be just as independent as men-." I glanced up at the sky overhead and hummed in thought, feeling the weight of another person swaying along with my steps.

"Guess that's why she was so stubborn" at that point I wasn't really talking to Rebecca anymore, I was just mumbling to myself and remembering things from a long time ago. I rooted my foot in the sand and began climbing the next dune, each step taking longer than normal for fear of us falling.

"I like your mother" Rebecca's voice muttered beside my ear causing me to pause and glance back at her. There was a light frown on her lips and her eyes were hard as if she was struggling to accept the fact that she had to be carried. I breathed a laugh and started walking again.

"Trust me lass, that be one-woman ye be lucky not to meet" not that she ever will since the old bird was dead.

190

There were times, although very few when I missed her constant nagging or her cooking. I hoisted Rebecca higher on my back, noting just how light she actually was.

Nothing else was said until we reached the ship. I guided Rebecca to the navigation room and eased her down into one of the chairs. I then went in search of some bandages, a cloth and cold water.

She tugged her skirt up to her thighs in order to get a better look at her injured ankle. Her appearance caused me to still in the doorway that led to the small kitchen area.

Her shirt clung to her body due to the sweat that coated her skin. Her exposed chest, arms and legs glistened while her crimson hair framed her features. Her cheeks were tinted red and her lips were parted as she panted.

She was beautiful even when she was dirty and covered in sweat.

"It hurts" she announced, snapping me out of my thoughts. Her fingers probed at the sensitive skin, being careful not to press down too hard or cause herself anymore discomfort.

I shook my head and moved towards her, setting the supplies down on the table and reaching for a second chair. I rinsed a cloth in a bucket of cold water then reached for her foot, wrapping the cloth around her ankle to help ease the swelling.

"It's supposed to hurt" came my reply. She slumped back in her chair with a huff, throwing her forearm over her eyes. Why she hadn't insisted on tending to her sprain herself was beyond me.

I never really cared for women. I'd slept with a few on drunken nights but because of my mother and sister I'd grown to believe that women were nothing but trouble.

Rebecca was that kind of trouble, the trouble I hoped to avoid but something about her called to me. *Maybe it was her fearlessness or maybe it was her stubbornness?* Whatever it was, it intrigued me.

"I won't be able to dance" she uttered. Her eyes were still concealed by her arm. She loved dancing, it was clear from how she'd get lost in the music and sway in time with the beat. It was her love just like mine was the sea.

"Not for some time, lass" I agreed, nodding my head to show that dancing would be the last thing she'd be doing. She removed her arm from her eyes and peered down at me then glanced at the foot. She attempted to move her ankle but flinched.

"It's not that bad" she tried making excuses. I breathed a laugh, picturing her trying to dance without putting any weight on her injured foot. I looked up at her, my laughter dying down in my throat when our eyes met.

She was close enough for me to feel her breath fanning my face. I could make out the smallest of freckles on her cheeks, the delicate curls in her hair, the sharpness of the cupid's bow on her upper lip.

"Then this shouldn't hurt" I shrugged, tightening my hold on her foot. She gasped and fell forward in her chair, listening to the sound of my chuckling when I eased the pressure on her injury.

Her eyes glared at me, her teeth gritting when her hand shot out to harshly shove my shoulder.

"Asshole" she muttered, slumping back in her seat with her head turned to the side, attempting to hide the scowl on her lips. I laughed, being much more careful while removing the cloth. I tossed it into the bucket of water beside me and reached for the bandages.

Her feet were small and delicate. They were the tools she used to create her art like a painter's fingers or a singer's voice. I tied off the bandage then stood and placed her foot on the chair I'd been seated on, elevating it.

"Don't move" I warned as I began to put everything away. She rolled her eyes like the threat didn't bother her and tried to stand as soon as my back was turned. She cried out in pain when she placed her bodyweight on her injured foot and reached for the table for support.

"Told ye not to move" I said in a breath of laughter with my back turned to her. She grunted in frustration and bent to reach for her discarded boot. She chucked it at the back of my head. I ducked and it hit the wall in front of me with a loud thud. I turned to grin back at her. I still had the bucket of water in hand.

"Now that wasn't very nice" her eyes were blazing with irritation. I loved seeing the annoyance on a woman's face when I would taunt them. It didn't matter whether it was Rebecca's face or Evangeline's. The fuming redhead took a deep breath then began to storm her way towards the deck however she didn't get far.

"Ye're gonna hurt ye-." before I could finish my sentence, Rebecca knocked her injured foot against the legs of the chair I'd been seated on and fell onto it. She gritted her teeth and reached down to caress her ankle.

"Self" I finished in a low mutter but she still heard me. Her eyes were like balls of blazing hell fire when she looked up at me. I sighed and discarded the bucket in the kitchen, making my way back to where she was sat.

"Calm down, red" I said, her nostrils flaring in response to my calm tone. She wasn't just irritated but she was also frustrated with herself for not being able to do anything on her own.

The throbbing pain that radiated up from her ankle only acted as fuel for the fire in her eyes. She lashed out when I neared her, getting up and raising her hands to strike me in the chest.

I gripped one of her wrists and dodged her second blow, forcing her back down in the seat. I leaned down so that we were at eye level, our noses almost touching.

"Accepting me help doesn't make ye weak" I declared, watching as the rage began to leave her eyes. I knew what she'd been thinking, I knew why she was reacting the way she was. She'd grown up as an independent woman, never having to ask for help because she was always capable of doing things herself.

The situation was forcing her out of her comfort zone and like all animals, we tend to snap when we're forced to leave our dens. She turned her head, her eyes staring out onto the deck through the open double doors then released a long sigh of defeat.

"I want to sit on the deck" it was a statement on the surface but beneath that it was a request for help, she just refused to word it in a way that made her seem weak.

I grinned and let go of her wrist, standing to reach for a separate chair. I moved the chair to the deck then helped her limp over to it. She said nothing but eventually took the drink that I offered her.

"It distracts from the pain" I explained. She only nodded, refusing to meet my eyes. She was embarrassed, her pride hurting from having to ask for my help, so I only laughed, shaking my head. I retrieved a rope to start the long journey back to the cavern where Evangeline and the Captain were both trapped.

Chapter Twenty-Four

I sat across from Caleb on the fallen statue, my first mate's hat perched on top of my head with my boots placed neatly beside me.

My hair was starting to dry however my shirt still clung to my body, leaving little room for the imagination as it hugged my curves and stuck to me like a second skin.

I glanced up at the statue looming over Caleb. It was of a bearded man holding a triton, his lower half made up entirely of tentacles while his ears and hands were webbed. His gills were carved into the sides of his neck with scales littering his naked torso. His eyes were incrusted with sapphires that seemed to glow as the cavern was slowly cast into darkness, the sun having started to set.

Neptune was the god of the seven seas. He controlled the tides and ruled over the sea folk. He held power over Mermaids, Sirens, sea Nymphs, the ocean's Guardians such as Gigas and whoever dared to sail across his domain. I could remember reading stories about the god, how he'd come to rule over the ocean.

He was born a mortal man who had many children with many women. It was said that he fell in love with the sea which led him to crafting the first boat. He rowed out onto the ocean but his boat was capsized. It's said that Neptune drowned, however because his heart belonged to the ocean, it decided to give him new life, granting him the ability to breathe under water. The sea gifted Neptune with tentacles, scales and abilities.

The ocean chose him to be its ruler, the man that had such a vast hunger for the sea. His obsession was what granted him his title as god with his descendants all carrying the same eternal love for the water.

I sat there, my eyes staring up at the statue.

My thoughts were interrupted by Ben, standing up from the sand, his back to us as he called out to someone on the horizon. I locked gazes with Caleb and slid off the statue, reaching for my boots to tug them onto my feet while the Captain stood, moving closer to the hole in the ceiling.

Nolan appeared, carrying a rope that was draped over his shoulder, letting it go so that one end fell down into the cavern. It slapped the ground as he tied the other end of it around his torso.

"Come on, lass!" Nolan called down into the hole, his voice echoing out around us.

Caleb redressed himself in his hat, boots, shirt and coat before he knelt in front of the rope with his back towards it, propping one knee up as he held his hand out for me to take. I was afraid of touching him, terrified of feeling his skin against mine but I did as he wanted. I took his hand and stepping onto his knee then onto his shoulder.

He stood, hoisting me higher, as close to the ceiling as possible before he moved away from me.

I wound the rope around my hands and feet to keep from falling while Nolan and Ben worked together to heave me upward. I glanced down at the Captain. His eyes were locked onto my form.

I had no words to speak, no way of asking him not to tell the rest of the crew of what I was so I could only pray that he would keep my secret just as Ben had.

When I reached the opening in the cavern's ceiling, I began to hoist myself out but a hand grabbed hold of mine and pulled me into a tight embrace. Ben buried his face in the side of my neck, his arms wrapped around me.

"I won't let anyone hurt you" he reassured me, whispering the words into my ear. I blinked at the world of red sand and orange light behind him as I returned his embrace, my hands gripping the material of his shirt.

He was referring to Caleb, to what the pirate Captain had discovered. If Caleb decided to tell his crew, then it could potentially place me in harm's way. It could put my life at risk.

I hid my face in Ben's shoulder and breathed in, knowing that despite the pain I'd caused him through having formed feelings for Caleb, he still cared for me and would fight for me no matter what.

Caleb managed to scale the rope on his own, effortlessly pulling himself onto his feet when he reached the top. His eyes landing on Ben and I when I pulled away from the curly haired blond.

There was a moment of tension when Caleb's gaze flickered from me to Ben before he started heading in the direction of the ship.

His shoulder collided with that of Nolan's, causing the Captain to pause and address the Irishman "Return to the ship-." his golden eyes appeared red like fire in the fading sunlight.

"We've got gems to find" with that, Caleb was gone, his figure disappearing into the distance with his hands clenched at his sides. His red coat blended into the sand around us.

Nolan rolled up the rope, tossing it onto his shoulder and started following Caleb. My hands moved to grasp onto Ben's arm, hugging it firmly to my chest, the fabric of my shirt still damp from the water. He glanced down at me with a sadness that filled his brown eyes. I was worried, terrified that Caleb would announce what I was to the crew once we were to reach the ship. Ben brought me comfort, just being able to touch him was enough to calm the raging storm inside my heart.

We followed Nolan. I allowed Ben to guide me for what felt like hours.

I was worried about Rebecca's ankle but also about the pain that I'd caused Caleb in the cavern by assuming he'd hurt me.

When we reached the ship, Caleb climbed onboard along with Nolan while Ben took his time to guide me onto the ship. He stayed behind to make sure I didn't lose my grip and fall.

"Up we go, lass" Nolan said, reaching down with his palm held out for me to take. I grabbed onto it and he hoisted me onboard the Sunken Soul with Ben close behind.

Rebecca sat in a chair nearby, her ankle bandaged and elevated on a small wooden table as she clutched a cup of wine in hand. She was laughing at a few of the crewmembers.

My eyes locked onto Caleb's retreating back as Ben perched himself onto the railing beside me. Nolan approached Rebecca and took a swig of her drink. Ben moved to wrap his arm around my shoulder but before he could, I was already making my way to the Captain's quarters in pursuit of Caleb.

I rushed down the steps, pausing halfway to grab hold of his wrist.

"Caleb!" the name came out in a rush, almost frantic when he turned to glare up at me. My hair dangled down in between us, my face looming overhead with my free hand gripping the wall to steady myself.

There were so many emotions swirling around in my chest, so many things that I wanted to say but all I could do was stare down at him, my lips slightly parted as I panted.

"Don't ye call me that" he bit out, tearing his arm away from me to storm further into the room, tugging his coat from his shoulders but pausing midway when his eyes locked onto the dress I'd abandoned on the bed. He brushed it off, removing his coat and tossing the red dirt-stained piece of clothing onto the dress he'd been so protective of. He'd kept it in pristine condition for so long yet in that moment he didn't seem to care.

I followed him, my boots thudding against the floor as I removed my hat, placing it on the desk.

"What do ye want, Evangeline?" he bluntly questioned when he turned to the nightside table. His eyes landed on the heart shaped locket that he'd picked up off the floor.

I sat down on the chair in the corner of the room, my fingers undoing my boots' laces. I then kicked them off so that I was left in only my shirt. My hands nervously gripped the arms of the chair.

"A-Are you going to-?" I trailed off. Caleb's eyes darted in my direction, his dangerous golden gaze almost seeming to glow beneath the brim of his hat. He knew exactly what I was asking and reached out to trace the leather of the book that had been placed beside Mary's locket.

"Tell me crew that ye're a Mermaid?" he finished for me, lifting his head to lock gazes with me. My heart was pounding and I could hear it drumming in my ears as I anxiously waited for his reply.

"They may be me crew but that doesn't mean that I trust any of 'em" he removed his hat and tossed it onto the bed. Most of his hair that was dangling down his shoulders with only a few sections of it still up in its usual bun. The thickening stubble on his chin and the crow's feet at the corners of his eyes made him look much older than what he really was.

"They be like hungry dogs, as soon as they get a whiff of gold, they stop at nothing to get their grimy hands on it" he turned to face me with his jaw clenching and releasing. This caused his cheekbones to rise and fall with the motion of his tensing muscles.

I could feel my bottom lip trembling as I stared at him, not sure how to respond. Caleb held the book out between us.

197

"And because of this, I can't have them killing ye just yet" I breathed in a sharp gust of air. My eyes were unable to blink, unable to focus on the image of him moving towards me. His last two words echoed in the back of my mind *just yet* like a warning, a threat that if I didn't do my job properly, he'd let the entire crew know of what I was and set them on me like hungry hounds.

"So, love-." he began, approaching me and placing his hands on the arms of the chair. He trapped me in place with his arms like a bird in a cage. His lips pulled back in a sinister grin.

"I trust ye'll keep doing ye job?" he asked, his face inches away from mine. I searched his features and my fear faded away when I realized what he was doing. I'd been afraid of him in the cavern which hurt him, so there he was trying to purposefully scare me, threatening me in order to get the reaction he wanted. He expected me to shrink back in fear like I'd been doing.

"I will" I whispered. My hands moved to grip the arms of the chair as I moved to sit up, forcing him back. He still had the book in his hand, holding onto the seat while I continued.

"Not because of your threat" I took the book. My hand caressing the back of his when I did so. I then held the book up between us.

I wasn't afraid of him; I wasn't scared of what he could do. The only reason I'd felt threatened was because of the feral instinct inside of me that I couldn't control. It was because of the part of me that categorized humans as enemy and prey.

"But because I want to know why these gems are so important to you" his face darkened, a predatory glint surfacing in his eyes. He was hiding something, something that made the usually annoyed and irritated Campbell lion turn into a monster that was capable of murder.

"Why is Caleb Campbell trying so hard to gather the seven treasures?" I asked, seeing the metaphorical line drawn directly before me and choosing to overstep it anyway.

His darker side, his more animalistic and murderous side made my stomach flip upside down at how vulnerable it made me feel.

His gaze studied me, glancing down my body and up to my mismatched blue and gray eyes.

"Some questions are better left unanswered" he said as he stood upright. His hands slipped away from the arms of the chair when he glared at me. If I didn't look so much like the woman he loved and if

198

I wasn't his only means of finding the treasures then he would've most likely killed me.

"Start reading" he ordered, nodding his head towards the book.

He growled lowly then turned to leave, his back muscles rippling through the material of his shirt as he went above deck, leaving me there with my breath still caught in my throat. My eyes were locked onto the stairs and my heart was racing with adrenaline from having been so close to a man as sinister and deadly as Caleb. He was the man Mary had fallen in love with, the man whom I was starting to fall for.

Chapter Twenty-Five

I read until I reached the final page of the book, until every location had been engraved into the back of my mind in the hopes that the answer to why these treasures even existed were written among the pages but all I could find was a familiar town's name scribbled across the very last page like a guiding message for those who've managed to find all seven treasures.

I shut the book and tossed it across the room.

I felt frustrated and confused with so many questions left unanswered.

Why was Port Alice written on the last page? Why was the place where I'd grown up as an orphan mentioned in the book of the seven treasures? Why was Caleb so desperate to find the jewels? What was their purpose? Questions upon endless questions.

If it was all for money then Caleb would've insisted on selling the jewels the as soon as he got his hands on them but instead, he held onto them. He was keeping them safe for when he would retrieve the very last gem. *Then what would he use them for?*

I could hear the crew cheering above deck, dancing, laughing and drinking like they would whenever we'd find a gem.

They were celebrating but why were they celebrating? What were they celebrating for?

I shot up from the armchair. If Caleb wouldn't tell me and the book only gave me cryptic messages; then surely someone onboard the ship had to have the answers.

I stepped onto the deck, having left my boots and hat behind. We were still anchored near the desert since I'd yet to announce our next course.

I glanced over the crew, from the man with one eye, to the brute who was missing an ear.

My gaze landed on the group of four to my left, a laughing Rebecca with her foot still propped up while Nolan leaned against the railing beside her, a bottle of rum moving to and from his lips.

He was so close to her, chatting and occasionally touching her. He'd lightly touch her shoulder, her arm, her face and hair. My eyes moved to her bandaged ankle, and I realized why it'd taken Nolan so long to retrieve a rope.

He'd taken the time to bandage her foot before returning to the cavern which meant that he cared for her.

Caleb sat on the steps that led to the stern with a cup in hand and a sour look on his face. Ben was perched on a nearby barrel, watching the Captain intently with his knees parted and his back to me. I decided that I'd approach Nolan with my questions but that I first needed to distract Caleb by giving him the next location.

I approached the Captain, stopping beside Ben who looked up at me with furrowed brows and worry hidden in his brown gaze.

"The Aztin jungle" I announced, catching everyone's attention and interrupting Rebecca's conversation with Nolan. Her smile faded and her eyes locked onto me. Caleb's back muscles stiffened at the mention of the jungle.

Even I knew of the name and the history tied to it. I knew that retrieving the next gem wasn't going to be easy.

"As in Red Pirate territory?" Rebecca questioned, her voice lowering due to the fact that she didn't want the rest of the crew to overhear.

Nolan crossed his arms over his chest with the neck of his bottle gripped between two fingers.

"What be this about the jungle, lassie?" he asked, hoping that it wasn't what we all already knew it was. I shot a look in Caleb's direction to find that he was listening but that his eyes were locked onto the deck.

"It's the next location" I responded, meeting Nolan's dark gaze. Ben breathed in deeply, his shoulders rising only to fall when he sharply exhaled through his nose.

"The fifth treasure" he muttered, coming to terms with the danger that lay ahead.

Rebecca leaned forward in her seat. She abandoned her cup and gripped the arms of her chair in order to steady herself. Nolan moved to help but the redhead barely acknowledged him. She was too focused on glaring at Caleb.

"Are you sure you want to keep doing this?" she surprised me by asking him. A chill trailed its way down my spine when I realized that she knew. She'd known all along what the purpose of those gems were and neither she nor Caleb had felt the need to say anything about it to me.

The Captain ran his tongue across his bottom lip as he slowly raised his hand to take another sip of wine.

"Why stop now?" he asked to which Rebecca's nostrils flared. The sarcastic, free spirited dancer went cold, her eyes blazing and her knuckles turning white as she stared at her old childhood friend.

Ben, Nolan and I remained silent. We didn't dare interrupt them.

"Because this is where it starts to get dangerous, Caleb" she was right, I could ward off Sirens, I could dive down into endless pools, I could survive a crumbling mountain of solid rock or being trapped in a scorching hot desert but I couldn't control the actions of enemy pirates which just so happened to be the most feared pirates of them all.

"It's just another location" Caleb argued, slamming his cup down onto the step beside him. For the first time his eyes moved over each of us until it came to rest on the fuming redhead.

Whatever those gems meant, it was clear to see that she didn't think it was worth the danger.

"We'll go, find the gem and be gone before they even know we're there" Caleb continued. I swallowed hard, taking a swift step forward. I had to decide what I was going to do. *Was I going to side with a man who was hiding so much from me or with Rebecca who only wanted to protect the man she cared so deeply for?*

"The Red Pirates know that jungle inside out-." I began, my mind knowing that what I was about to say was a fact and not just simple logic. I locked gazes with Caleb and felt my heart rate start to pick up at the sight of him.

"It's more than likely that they've already found the gem and that-." my eyes fell to Rebecca, waiting for her to realize what I was getting at. She slowly sat back in her chair.

"Their Captain has it" she breathed out, her lungs emptying their air into the damp, dry atmosphere around us. It was caused by both the water and the desert but despite the warmth, the temperature was starting to drop since night had already fallen. It would only get colder as the night matured.

"Then we'll strike a deal" my head shot up in Caleb's direction. My chest tightened when I remembered Rebecca's tale of how Caleb became a pirate Captain.

He'd struck a deadly deal with a pirate that ended up costing hundreds their lives including the lives of his mother and sister. Rebecca was thinking the exact same thing. She shot up from her chair, ignoring the pain that shot through her leg due to her injured ankle.

"Did you forget what happened the last time you struck a deal with a pirate Captain?" she demanded. Nolan rushed to catch her in case she fell but she wasn't going to go down that quickly and stayed balanced with her heated gaze locked onto Caleb. He was the man she'd once loved similar to how he loved Mary. He was the man who'd caused the death of her parents yet she still cared for him.

My lips parted when I acknowledged something about her character. She was the most loyal, selfless person you would ever meet.

"That was a long time ago" Caleb shot back, his face stern and emotionless as if her sudden outburst didn't affect him at all. Ben noticed the conflict in my eyes when I looked from the Captain to Rebecca, not sure what to do.

I felt his hand reaching out to take hold of mine, drawing my attention onto him.

Maybe it was the emotions that Mary left behind for me to feel, maybe it was the memories of the two of them or maybe it was because I wanted to know why those gems were so important to Caleb but I moved away from Ben to stand beside Caleb. It was a message, one that said that I would stand by Caleb whether Rebecca did so or not.

Her eyes shot to me then back to the Captain.

She hobbled towards him, her hand raising to jab a finger in his direction.

"She's not worth all of us dying" she snapped, her eyes glazing over with unshed tears. Her retreat was swift as she limped in the direction of the trap door where she disappeared below deck with Nolan rushing after her.

Ben glanced at me with a mixture of pain and understanding in those brown depths. He wasn't expecting me to side with Caleb but there I was, showing my loyalty for the Captain.

The rest of the crew had gone silent during the argument, watching us and once they saw me standing there, beside their leader, they began to cheer as though I'd finally decided to be a pirate, as though I'd finally sworn my loyalty to the Captain.

My head turned so that I could meet Caleb's golden gaze. He was watching me, his hands clasped together and his figure still. Eventually he picked up his cup and held it out for me to take.

"May we always drink from the same cup" his words were fierce, cutting. *For a moment I mentally asked myself what I'd done? Whether I made the right choice or not?*

It all happened as if in slow motion. I took the cup from him. Ben looked away as if it pained him to see me give myself to such a monster of a man. The crew erupted into laughter, some whistling, some cheering as if it was a type of victory for them.

Snaggletooth poured wine into the cup from his bottle and I threw my head back, drinking every last drop with my eyes staring up at the moon overhead.

I felt like crying but I also felt more alive than I'd ever been.

It felt like I belonged somewhere for the first time in what could most accurately be described as forever.

Chapter Twenty-Six

They'd been drinking well into the night. Their breaths condensed due to the biting cold as Caleb sat in silence, drowning himself in wine and rum until the early hours of the morning.

His eyes held so many troubling emotions that I couldn't quite decipher. I sat with Ben near the figurehead, explaining to him why Caleb didn't tell the crew about me being a Mermaid.

My eyes darted towards the steps that led to the stern when Caleb stood, his cup cluttering down to the deck as he stumbled, his hand gripping the railing in an attempt to catch himself. I could tell that he was drunk. I shot up, ignoring Ben as I hurried to catch Caleb, feeling his weight slump into me when he staggered down the steps.

"I've got you" I whispered, ducking underneath his arm so that it was slung over my shoulder. I wrapped my arm around his waist to help support his weight. He was heavy, so much so that I stumbled a bit when I tried guiding him in the direction of the Captain's quarters.

My gaze locked onto Ben's from across the deck. There was a lingering look of sadness in his eyes as he followed our movements. He had feelings for me, emotions that were genuine yet there I was so consumed by the thoughts of a man who didn't even care for me. Caleb only cared about Mary Sillvan, who'd given him a reason to live. He didn't care about Evangeline.

I tore my eyes away from Ben as we staggered down the stairs and into the Captain's quarters. Caleb tripped over his feet and nearly dragged me down onto the floor but I regained my balance and managed to get him to the bed. I pushed the dress, coat and hat aside so that he could slump down onto the edge of the mattress.

I went down on my knees, my hands moving to untie the buckles of his boots, tugging them off his feet so that he could sleep. He stared at me, his eyes clouded and eyebrows knitted together.

"Ye pledged yeself to me" he stated as if I didn't already know what I'd done. I tossed one boot aside and paused to look up at him. I was so used to seeing him drunk that the smell of alcohol and his slurred words no longer bothered me. I chose to ignore him, moving on to the second boot and fiddling with the buckles.

"After I threatened ye" my body tensed, my hands stilling for the briefest of moment before they continued to unbuckle the boot as if nothing happened.

Caleb leaned down once I'd tugged the boot from his foot so that his face was only inches away from mine. I could see the brown and green specks that littered his irises and the black rims that surrounded them. I could make out the faint scars that ran along his lips, chin, nose and cheekbones.

"Ye're definitely not Mary" my eyes roamed over his features. My mind went back to our kiss, to the taste that haunted me, the taste of him. I could still feel his hands on me, caressing me, guiding me ever so gently despite his rugged nature.

He leaned back, slowly until he was sat upright again, gazing down at me like a king would gaze at his subjects from atop his throne.

Why did I feel so submissive towards him but at the same time why wasn't I afraid of him?

"She would've turned tail and run by now" I had no idea what he was mumbling on about but I figured that it was nothing and set the boot aside, standing so that I could remove the clothing from the bed, giving him more room to sleep. I scooped the dress into my arms, holding it tightly to my chest as I gazed down at its material.

"But ye, ye don't fear me" his words snapped me out of my trance, forcing me to look at him. At the cavern he'd mistaken my primal instincts for fear when in reality I was ready to kill him if need be. There is a difference between self-defense and fear.

Was that why he tried threatening me? Was that why he wanted to make me fear him? Because it would've made Mary fear him if he threatened her?

I reached for the coat and slung it over my arm as I picked up the hat.

"Ye challenge me, ye anger me, ye-." he paused to find the right word as I moved across the room, placing the articles of clothing onto the desk.

"Excite me" I froze, my back to him, too afraid that if I turned around, I wouldn't be able to control my emotions.

He was drunk. I reminded myself when I glanced back at him from over my shoulder. He didn't know what he was talking about. He stood and my stomach began to flutter.

I squeezed my eyes shut, trapped in that same position with my back to him and my hands gripping the back of the desk's chair.

"Mary was brave but even she had her limits-." He stood behind me. He was so close that I could feel the heat radiating from his body. My bottom lip trembled when his one hand caressed my waist, the other moving to tug my shirt down, exposing my shoulder.

"But ye're fearless" he breathed, his warm breath tickling my skin, causing goosebumps to rise on my arms and neck. This man was toying with me and I was at his mercy. I was unable to move, unable to protest or do anything other than expose my neck when he nuzzled his nose into the side of it, running it up and along my skin until he reached my ear where his lips grazed its shell.

"Ye're mine now" he whispered, causing a tingle to shoot through my core when he nipped at my ear. I couldn't stop the moan that escaped my lips at the feel of his tongue flicking over its shell.

He knew exactly how to manipulate me. He was dangerous and unpredictable yet something about him could capture the interest of any woman. He pulled away from me, quickly and abruptly causing me to let out the breath I didn't know I'd been holding.

"Which is why ye'll always have a place here" he informed, stumbling when he made his way back to the bed. I turned swiftly in response to his words, my eyes widening when the threat of being killed after I'd located the last gem faded away, being replaced with a sense of belonging and security.

I had a home, a place to return to. The Sunken Soul would be my safe haven, where I could live and be as free as I needed to be. Caleb would let me swim, let me wonder wherever I wished to go. Just knowing that I would always have a place to return to, a home to call my own was comforting to me.

Was that what pledging myself to him meant?

He laid down on the bed with his back to me.

The silence eventually filled with his light snoring when he fell asleep, leaving me alone with my thoughts. My eyes searched the room until they landed on the leather bound book that still lay abandoned on the floor. I looked to the steps with my mind filled with questions.

I glanced in Caleb's direction then reached for his red, dusty coat, pulling it onto my shoulders. I laced up my boots and grabbed my first mate's hat, placing it firmly on the top of my head like a sign that I was of higher ranking.

My feet carried me above deck and to the trap door that I creaked open. My boots thudded against the steps when I ducked down into the maze of bunk beds and hammocks.

Ben was fast asleep in one of them, no longer in his secluded room at the very back of the ship. I assumed that Rebecca, the only woman to sleep alongside the crew was staying in that room and since the door was closed, I figured it had to be locked.

Lamps hung from the support beams and a thin layer of water coated the floor. I hardly noticed it as I made my way past the snoring, sleeping figures of drunken men. One man clung to his bottle and another only made it halfway onto his bed. His arm dangled off the side of the bed with his hand in the water.

There was no fear inside of me, no hesitation. I stopped just short of Rebecca's door where an Irishman sat outside of it. He was wide awake and perched on a crate as if he was her guard dog.

He had a knife in hand and a sword strapped to his belt. He looked tired but even more so he looked like a force to be reckoned with.

He eyes looked up at me when I came to a stop in front of him. That same gaze roamed over my figure that was dressed in pirate's clothing including a hat that symbolized my higher rank.

"The coat suits ye" he complimented. The coat made me feel powerful in a sense and made my aura seem that much more dangerous. He knew I was there for a reason. He just didn't know what that reason was.

"It used to belong to Captain Solstice who led the Black Pirates long before Caleb" Rebecca's story came to mind of the Captain that Caleb murdered in order to take control of the Sunken Soul. I glanced down at the coat that was littered in blood stains. It was covered in red dust and smelt strongly of sea salt.

Nolan lowered his knife.

"Ye see, Solstice tore that coat from the corpse of a Red Pirate Captain after he murdered him" once I was done inspecting the velvety material of Caleb's coat, I locked gazes with Nolan.

His face was stern and there was a willingness to help me hidden behind his words.

"He is the reason why the Red and Black Pirates detest each other" I wasn't sure if he was telling me all of that because he was drunk and trying to keep himself awake or because he was worried about me. I thought back to the way he acted earlier in the desert, warning Ben to let nothing happen to me, it made me believe that he cared for me like a father cared for his daughter.

"Ye have no idea what ye've gotten yeself into by pledging yer loyalty to him" there it was, the fatherly concern that I'd been expecting. Nolan enjoyed scaring me, he enjoyed seeing me squirm and despite the anger he'd felt towards me in the beginning when Caleb demoted him and give his rank to me, he still developed some type of connection to me.

I kicked a crate closer to where I was stood and took a seat on it, leaning forward so that my elbows were propped up onto my knees.

"So, tell me-." I began, my eyes searching his with lifted eyebrows. It was both a plea and a demand which he understood from the way he let out a long sigh.

"What does it mean to be loyal to Caleb Campbell?" my question hung in the air between us as Nolan glanced down at the floor. His hand tightened around the hilt of his knife as if he was contemplating whether to tell me or not.

There were so many things that I didn't know about Caleb and the Black Pirate crew. I had so many questions about the seven treasures and I was willing to go to any lengths to find some answers.

Chapter Twenty-Seven

"He killed off his entire crew" I wasn't unaware of this. Rebecca told me about Caleb slaughtering off the old crew of the Sunken Soul in order to replace them. The reason behind this was because they'd murdered his mother and Rebecca's parents. There was fear in Nolan's eyes.

His jaw clenched and his lips trembled, not from the cold but from something else entirely.

"I be the last remaining member of the original crew" I sat back on the crate as I studied Nolan.

His words meant that he was there when Captain Solstice and his crew attacked Caleb's hometown, burning it to the ground and flooding the streets with the blood of the innocent. He was one of them, one of the people who'd caused so much pain and destruction.

"Back then, I was just a scullery rat" an image of Nolan cleaning, cooking and washing dishes surfaced in the back of my mind.

I couldn't imagine him, a tough pirate doing those things, in fact it sounded more like a joke to me than reality but I remained silent, listening to his story as he told it.

"The night everything happened, I was below deck. I heard yelling and when I went to see what all the commotion was about, I found-." he paused, his eyes filling with fear as he stared down at the ground. His hands trembled at the memory, going back to that moment in time when he'd crept above deck to find a sight more gruesome than anything he'd ever seen before.

"A woman gutted and tied to the mass. Captain Solstice with his throat slit-." my chest ached at the mention of her, of Claudia, Caleb's younger half-sister who'd been killed by Captain Solstice.

It was all a tragic tale that left me wondering how it made Caleb feel when he realized that Claudia was his sister, when he realized that he'd sacrificed his own flesh and blood to pirates.

"And Caleb who sat there, dressed in that very coat and drenched in blood-." Nolan motioned towards me, to the coat that hugged from my body. Again, I glanced at it, my mind raging with questions. *Did the blood on it belong to Captain Solstice or Claudia?*

"He was just a boy but I've never seen death cling to someone the way it clung to him that night" I met Nolan's eyes, there was terror hidden in them, a fear that I couldn't possibly describe. He was terrified of Caleb even when he pretended not to be, even when he tried acting normal around the Captain.

"After that he proceeded to kill off the crew, one by one. He stabbed them, drowned them, forced them to fight to the death-." I felt my blood run cold.

Was Caleb really capable of torture? Was the same man who was capable of loving Mary, capable of committing such cruel acts of violence?

"Watching him was like-." Nolan paused, his eyes flickering up to me before it darted towards the men around us as if to make sure that no one was listening in on our conversation.

"Like watching the angel of death reap his vengeance" the light from the lamp above me danced across his features as he sat back on his crate. Nolan had seen many gruesome and wicked things in his lifetime, that much was evident but what exactly he'd seen only he knew. All I knew was that his fear for what he saw was real, what he was telling me was the truth.

"What ye did tonight, lassie, ye didn't just pledge ye loyalty to him-." the corner of his lips tugged up in a faint, nervous smile as he stared down at the blade of his knife, at his own reflection in the polished steel. The hair on the back of my neck stood on end when he looked up at me.

"Ye sealed ye fate-." the old ship creaked around us while men snored and the lamps swung on their hooks, causing a squeaking sound that reached my ears.

"Ye either die by the sea or by his hands" the air left me as if someone had struck me hard in the chest. My eyes searched his, desperate to find some form of a lie hidden in them but there was nothing. All I found was truth.

He wasn't lying and the weight of my decision came crashing down onto me like a ton of bricks.

"Wherever he goes, death follows" his next words enraged me, made me feel like I was capable of murder.

"Take Mary for instance-." my hands began to shake, yes staring at the flooring below where my boots rested in the water. Her name echoed in my ears like a haunting song from my past and his accusation was enough to cause my ears to ring.

"She killed herself because of him" my head shot up so that my glare was locked onto him and he leaned back, able to feel the anger

211

starting to boil inside of me. My eyes sent him a message that I couldn't bring myself to say.

'*Shut your mouth*' was what they screamed and he knew to keep quiet.

My hands clenched as I decided to change the subject, not really sure why his accusation offended me so much. *Maybe it was because of Mary's letter explaining why she'd killed herself or maybe it was because of how close I felt to her?*

"Why-?" I paused not sure if asking was such a good idea but I had to know everything he knew about the gems.

"Why are the seven treasures so important to Caleb?" it was the real reason why I was there, below deck in the early hours of the morning, sitting on a dusty old crate with my boots soaked through with water. The cold causing the skin on my feet to burn despite my body not being able to feel the cold.

Nolan reached behind his crate for a bottle, pressing it to his lips to take a swig as if to prepare himself for the conversation ahead.

"Many reasons-." he began, shrugging his shoulders as he set the bottle aside and stuck his knife back into the pocket of his trousers.

"There are tales of when all seven jewels are gathered in one place, they can give ye beyond human abilities, others say that they will grant ye one wish" *A wish? What wish could Caleb possibly have in order to go to such extreme lengths just to gather all of the jewels? Could his wish be to go back in time to stop Mary from drowning?*

Caleb wasn't someone who desired more power. Inhuman speed or strength just wasn't worth all the effort. He was fierce enough, strong enough so what was the driving force behind finding all of the gems?

"But these are just stories, told at taverns and brothels" I could feel frustration setting in at the realization that Nolan didn't know much and that either Rebecca or Caleb would be my only way of finding out what the true purposes is behind the jewels.

"We're all being drug around after these gems without really knowing why" he breathed a laugh at his own statement and took another swig of his rum, leaning his head back against the wall beside Rebecca's locked door.

I shot up from my place on the crate, about to storm off when I paused to glance back at Nolan.

"One more thing-." I insisted, my eyes glowing beneath the brim of my hat. One a stark white and the other a crystal clear blue. Nolan blinked up at me as if trying to clear his vision. The water at my feet was what caused my eyes to glow and my pupils to narrow into slits. The drunken man tried to make sense of what he was seeing.

"Who are you exactly?" I asked, the question acting as a distraction as he shook his head and squeeze his eyes shut, trying to convince himself that what he saw was the alcohol or the light and not reality.

He knocked his head back against the wall and chuckled, the liquid in his bottle swishing with the sudden motion.

"Me?" he questioned, taking another swig of rum and opening his eyes to meet my illuminated ones.

"I told ye lassie, I'm just a scullery rat-." I nodded, about to leave but as soon as my back was to him, he pointed a finger at me. His eyes were red and glazed over from his lack of sleep and excessive drinking.

"The real question be-." my back muscles stiffened and my head turned to glance back at him from over my shoulder.

I could feel my fangs starting to extend and if I remained there any longer then my secret wouldn't just be an image created by the mind of a drunken man.

"Who are ye?" he shot back, forcing me to stop and think for a moment.

After my pause I left without a word, boots splashing in the water and thudding up the stairs. The sun was starting to rise, casting an orange hue onto the ship's deck.

Caleb awoke a few hours later along with most of the crew. I didn't sleep and instead sat on the figure head, staring out onto the horizon.

The sky was a dreary gray, rumbling with thunder as harsh winds swept over the ship, whipping my hair back and out of my face. I still wore Caleb's red coat. I could feel the numerous sets of eyes staring at me because of it.

Caleb was one of them and despite his anger at the sight of me wearing his coat, proceeded to address his crew.

"Set sail for the Pirate's Nest!" my head whipped around to look at him as he climbed the steps to the stern. He wore his boots and

213

Captain's hat but instead of his usual red coat he wore a brown one. A thick stubble coated his jaw and his hair was a mess. Black bags hung underneath his eyes.

The crew scrambled to lower the sails and raise the anchor. Once we were back out on the open ocean, Ben hopped up onto the railing beside me.

"Why aren't we sailing for the Aztin jungle?" I asked, tearing my eyes from away from Caleb to look at the younger man who was perched beside me. Ben was also staring at the Captain.

He shrugged his shoulders and looked at me.

"Probably to gather as much information on the Red Pirates as possible" I gazed down at the water as Ben took in the sight of the coat that I was wearing.

Rebecca emerged from below deck, wearing a dress that went down to her ankles with her hair tied up and out of her face. She hobbled along the deck, heading towards the stern when Nolan stopped her, his hand reaching out to grip her arm. They locked eyes and for a moment there was a silent flow of communication between them that forced a frustrated scream from her lips as she instead disappeared into the navigation room.

"It's better to know what we're going up against instead of just blindly rushing into things" Ben's words snapped me out of my daze, drawing my attention back onto him. I nodded, seeing the logic but finding it surprising that Caleb would have the sense to do such a thing.

Despite his temper and reckless behavior, the Captain at his core was an intelligent, cunning thief. He wasn't just capable of stealing gold or jewels but he could steal hearts as well.

"Guess we're sailing for the Pirate's Nest then" I muttered while shrugging my shoulders.

The conversation from the night before replayed itself in my mind when Nolan and I locked gazes from across the deck. He brushed it off and quickly followed Rebecca into the navigation room like a worried lover.

"They make an odd pair" I commented with a breath of laughter. Ben smiled playfully when he realized what I was referring to and leaned towards me to whisper his words as if he was afraid of someone overhearing us.

"I thought I was the only one who noticed" Ben sat back, studying me expectantly. I decided that I was in need of a distraction.

"The redhead and the Irishman" I echoed my thoughts, grinning up at the sky as I thought about the titles.

Ben hummed, his eyes glancing at Caleb who was manning the helm, his golden gaze staring straight past us as if we didn't exist. His soul focus was reaching the Pirate's Nest as soon as possible.

"It's almost as bad as the Mermaid and the pirate Captain" my back muscles stiffened, the words ringing in my ears like a mocking reminder of the weight that I carried around wherever I went. Our casual banter turned into something dangerous.

"You can't just pretend like nothing happened, Evangeline" I turned my head, searching the deck in an attempt to forget that Ben was even there. He leaned towards me, his head bending as he tried to meet my eyes but I refused to acknowledge him. My hands tightened on the railing beside me like a python would constrict around its prey, crushing it to death.

"You care about him" his words were a statement and I knew that they were true.

I swallowed hard, thinking back to the day before, the conversation between Caleb and I that Ben had overheard. I thought back to the feeling of the Captain's warm breath against my skin and the way his touch sent chills down my spine. It was clear, even to me that I harbored feelings for Caleb even when I tried desperately to deny it.

"And that's a dangerous game to play" Ben, much like Nolan was trying to warn me about Caleb but there was no reason to fear him. He'd tried threatening me numerous times before, tried to scare me off but none of it worked, in fact it had the opposite effect, instead of pushing me away, it only drew me closer to him. He was as mysterious as he was dangerous.

My eyes found Caleb. I could make out his muscles beneath the material of his clothing along with the black ink that painted his skin.

"Ben-." I began as I moved to stand directly in front of him. My hands clenched and unclenched at my sides when I tried to control my temper.

"My loyalty lies with Caleb-." I was so tired of people trying to tell me to stay away from Caleb when everything inside of me, every last piece of my soul drew me closer to him.

Rebecca had turned her back on Caleb but I wasn't going to abandon him whether he was a monster or not.

215

"If you want to see something dangerous then try and get in between us" it was a threat, blatant and deadly as I raised my head to lock eyes with him.

He stiffened at the sight of me, my fierce expression, my gaze that cut deep into him. I began to back away from him, my body turning to head in the direction of the stern where Caleb was stationed.

"Evangeline!" Ben called out after me but I ignored him, turning my back on him like Rebecca had turned her back on Caleb.

There was a method to this madness, something that I had to do and it involved Caleb, it involved Mary, I just wasn't sure what it was yet.

I was meant to be on that ship, meant to get close to Caleb, to try and find out why I was having such strange visions.

I knew the gems had something to do with it and I was going to find out what. I was going to figure out what I had to do and why fate had led me to that exact moment in time.

Chapter Twenty-Eight

The Pirate's Nest was busy when we reached it close to dusk. Men were dealing in illegal goods while women who were dressed in their undergarments, desperately tried to attract a suitor for the night. Their necks were littered in pearls and their lips were stained red.

That color reminded me of everything bad, the coat I was wearing, the blood that stained it, a fire blazing over a town, the seduction of young men.

We docked the ship and the crew leaped from its sides, getting lost in the foot traffic of the Nest, marveling at the sight of precious stones and antique items that were being sold such as swords and axes.

'A pirate with an axe' I thought feeling a chill go down my spine. My eyes found the water then the horizon. There was just something about how the light fell on the ocean's surface that called out to me.

I had to go for a swim.

My eyes searched the ship to find that Ben was drinking on its deck. He sat on a barrel with a cup of wine in hand.

Rebecca and Nolan had long since left in search of a tavern, meaning that Ben and I were the last two individuals on the ship.

I glanced in the direction of the docks and headed towards Ben, shrugging the red coat from my shoulders and tossing it onto his lap. He looked up at me with furrowed brows, his eyes clouded in confusion as I placed my hat on his head and began untying the laces to my boots.

"Evangeline?" he questioned. He most likely assumed that I was mad at him because of my earlier threat but there was no reason for me to be angry. All he was trying to do was protect me from something dangerous like he promised he would. I kicked off my boots and turned to him, my hands gripping the hem of my shirt.

"I understand that you were just trying to protect me-." I said, my chest rising and falling as my tongue shot out to wet my bottom lip.

We hadn't spoken a single word to each other throughout the day and it just didn't feel right.

Yes, I was starting to fall for Caleb but Ben held a special place in my heart without the help of Mary's emotions. My feelings towards Ben were strictly mine and mine alone.

"And I want to thank you for always looking out for me" he was a safe place where I felt like the horrors of the world couldn't reach me. He made me feel comfortable and free by just simply breathing the same air as him. I gave a sad smile.

"But I can't stay away from Caleb, not now, not when-." I could feel myself starting to tear up when the words died down out in the back of my throat and I looked out onto the sea. Smoke filled the sky of painted oranges and purples.

I pushed my thoughts aside and tore the shirt over my head, letting it fall to the ground by my feet. Ben's jaw dropped along with his cup of wine that spilled all over his boots.

I reached for his hand, pulling him up from the chair and guiding him towards the ship's stern. He kicked his own boots off in the process, letting go of my hand to remove his shirt.

Our clothes were scattered across the deck. My back collided with the ship's railing causing Ben to crashed into me. I removed my necklace and clasped it around his neck, my eyes boring into his when my fangs began to protrude and my pupils turned into slits.

I stepped up onto the railing, my hands gripping his shoulders as my breath fanned his face and he took in the sight of me, naked.

I stood upright, letting go of his shoulders when a smile touched my lips and I extended my arms out on either side of me. I let myself fall backwards until I was flying through the air, towards the deep, murky waters below.

Ben shot forward to stare down at me with fear and worry in his eyes, glancing towards the docks where no one had seemed to notice our little show.

He looked to the necklace that hung around his neck then climbed onto the railing, diving down after me.

My back collided with the water and it engulf me until I was completely submerged in it. Ben crashed into the water shortly after me, his feet breaking the surface on impact. He opened his eyes to look at me.

My legs twisted together, tangling to form a single fin of silvery white. My hair drifted around me, dancing past my line of sight as it changed color, becoming a light gray. A light of white and blue was created by my glowing eyes in the dark water. My hands moved through the water, fingers webbing as my nails extended to form claws. Scales littered my chest, torso, arms, neck and face as gills appeared on either side of my neck.

I looked to Ben and found him staring at me, forgetting to breathe as he floated through the water, my necklace lifting away from his chest to dangle in between us.

I swam closer to him, hands reaching out to caress his cheeks in the palms of my hands. The last of his air escaped him in the form of bubbles that danced towards the surface as he continued to stare at me, mesmerized by my appearance.

I spoke into the water, my voice sounding like a whale's song. It was a single word that echoed through the back of his mind 'Breathe' before I grabbed hold of his upper arms to push him towards the surface so that he could breathe. His hands slipped away from me as he let the water guide him ever upward.

I turned to delve deeper into the water, allowing my tail to trash against it in order to propel me further down at a much faster pace. I swam as deep as my body allowed me to, reaching out into the darkness where fish gathered and sharks lurked.

I twisted and turned, listening to the sound of sea turtles swimming to their designated breading grounds, hearing the current as it swept past me. I closed my eyes when I stopped moving and stayed there, existing in that single moment with my body floating in place. It was so quiet beneath the waves where not even humans could reach, there was nothing there but the beauty that the sea had to offer.

That's when I heard it, the familiar voice of a woman.

'A heart of the sea' my eyes shot open, casting light downward where a female figure danced among the waves, moving upward towards me.

Her body was made entirely of water and her sapphire eyes shone bright like lamps in the darkened depths.

'A Nymph' I thought as an image of one floating in front of a drowning Mary came to me. The Nymph had whispered those exact words to her.

The images, the dream from the night Caleb and I'd kissed came back to me. Mary, the Nymph and the raven haired woman all flickered before my eyes.

The images were telling me to remember but what was I supposed to remember? What did Mary want me to remember?

The Nymph grabbed hold of my shoulders, moving closer until her face was only inches away from mine. She was beautiful and enchanting as she gazed into the depths of my soul. Her tail swayed back and forth in the water behind her.

'Remember' she said, clicks and songs coming from her parted lips when the word entered my mind. I tried moving, tried responding but I couldn't, I was frozen as if I'd seen a ghost.

She pushed down on my shoulders and began swimming towards the surface. I followed her movements with my eyes and watched her disintegrate into sea foam above me, being carried away by the current.

I tried thinking back, I tried to remember but the more I tried the sharper the pain in my head would become, leaving me crying out in agony.

My past.

There was something about my past, something about it that I had to remember. I had to remember. What was I supposed to remember?

I screamed, the high pitched sound vibrating through the water and forcing every sea creature to scatter away from me. It swept the area clean, warding off anything that might dare to venture closer.

I couldn't think properly anymore, I couldn't comprehend anything and impulsively began swimming towards the surface, moving as fast as I could until I broke through with a gasp, breaching onto the shore near the docks where pirates were doing business.

"Eva!" I heard someone call out to me and turned my head to see Ben running along the shoreline towards me with Caleb's red coat in hand.

When he reached me, he threw the coat onto my body and clasp the necklace back around my neck, forcing my fin to fade into limbs and my eyes to stop their glowing.

Soon I was back to my human self, standing among the crashing waves with the coat buttoned all the way up in order to conceal my naked form from the hungry eyes of nearby pirates.

If it hadn't been for the dead of night they might've spotted me, might've captured and butchered me for my scales.

I stumbled but Ben managed to catch me, wrapping his arms around me with the lantern in the sand by our feet. He'd used it to help him find me in the dark. I gripped his shirt and noticed that he was completely dry. My eyebrows furrowed up in confusion when I noticed that he was wearing his boots. *How long was I down there for?*

Ben's hand caressed my hair as he wrapped his arm tightly around my waist. I took a moment to breathe then pushed away from him to stagger my way towards the clusters of flickering flames that littered the shoreline. I followed the sound of laughing men and moaning women.

"Evangeline, wait!" Ben called after me but I didn't stop not even when I reached the docks. He grabbed the lantern and began following me.

"Where are you going?" Ben questioned when he managed to catch up. I my hands rubbed at my arms to try and warm them.

My eyes were frantic, searching desperately for one thing and one thing only but he was nowhere to be found. I stopped in the middle of a cobble stone courtyard that was littered in straw. I wanting nothing more than to find him.

"Evangeline?" Ben gripped my arm, holding the lantern up to get a good look at my face. He knew there was something wrong but I couldn't bring myself to explain it, all I could do was say the five words that made him retract from me.

"I have to find Caleb" with that I disappeared into the night, leaving Ben behind as my feet slapped against the stone and my hands traced the walls of buildings in search of him. I had no idea how long I'd been searching for or how long it had been since I last saw Ben but when I passed by a purple tent my ears heightened at the sound of Caleb's voice.

I paused, about to enter the small space in order to ask him what he had to do with my past but my hand stilled on the tent's curtain when his words reached my ears.

"I've collected four of the gems" I stilled at the mention of the treasures and quickly hid myself behind the tent as I listened in on his conversation.

"Ye be serious about this spell now, boy?" a female voice questioned, not expecting any answer since her words were more of a statement.

I peered into the tent through a gap in its material to find a woman with stark white eyes. Her eyes seemed so familiar to me.

The breath caught in my throat when the woman from my dream came to mind. The image of her with my anchor necklace dangling from her fingertips as she peered down at me flickered past my line of sight.

221

"It be a deadly thing ye be getting yeself caught up in, child" the woman in the tent's hair wasn't black like the woman from my dreams but instead it was green, dread-locked and tied up on the top of her head. Golden hoops dangling from her ebony ears. She wore a green robe, similar to the one from my dream with her nails, like black claws stretching out beyond the golden rings that decorated her fingers. She gave of the same aura, a dangerous and fierce one that surrounded her. It frightened people into staying away from her yet there Caleb was, lounging back in his seat across from her and as relaxed as ever.

"She be worth the risk" Caleb's words made my heart squeeze as I contemplated who 'she' was.

Was it Rebecca, Mary or despite knowing better, was he referring to me?

The woman's fingers laced together on the desk in front of her, the rings that adorned her fingers cluttering as her hollow eyes studied him.

"I don't think ye know the full extent of what ye be attempting to do" her voice was laced with a thick, ancient accent making her sound much older than she looked. She looked to be around Rebecca's age yet she called Caleb things like 'boy' or 'child' which made me wonder just how old she really was.

"When ye play with death, the cost will always be death" Caleb's legs were parted, his elbow propped up on the arm of his chair as he leaned his head against his fist, eyes narrowing onto the woman like he didn't care for her opinion.

I glanced towards the street where lamps lit the cobble stone roads, eyes searching the area, afraid that someone might notice me snooping.

"I have me sacrifice" Caleb argued. The woman breathed in, her hands tightening as she tilted her head back to gaze down at him.

I tried summarizing what I'd heard in order for it to make more sense.

The gems could be used in a spell, the spell had something to do with death.

"Someone close to Mary I presume?" my back muscles stiffened at the mention of her and my head turned so that I could watch the woman rise from behind the desk and slowly stalking her way around it.

Caleb stayed where he was, hardly effected by her form towering over him like a force to be reckoned with.

"A sister? A mother? A-." she questioned, leaning against the desk with her hands gripping its edges. The emerald material of her cloak fell to the sides, exposing her long ebony legs and short dress.

"A reincarnation" the woman stilled, her empty eyes looking up at him.

The words caused my heart to stop and my stomach to drop.

Was he planning to kill me? Was that why he took me to begin with? To act as a sacrifice for whatever spell the treasures enabled him to cast?

My hand shot up to conceal my mouth, trying to hide my rapid breathing as my eyes began to sting with tears and fear started to set in.

"They be rare-." the woman stated, her eyebrows lifting and her forehead creasing.

It was like she was talking about an object and not a human as if all she cared about was how rare reincarnations were and nothing else.

She raised her hand to motion towards Caleb, those long slender appendages dancing like a charmed snake.

"She might just be ye only hope of resurrecting Mary" it felt like my world came crashing down around me as I stared at the pair, the knowledge that I'd been digging around for finally out in the open and yet I so wished with all my might that I could forget what I'd heard. I wished to have never known what I knew then.

I didn't bother to stay any longer, moving away from the tent to run in the direction of the docks where the ship was waiting for me. A place I called my home yet it'd never been nor will it ever be my home.

The gems were so important to Caleb because if he gathered all of them in the same exact spot and sacrificed the life of Mary's twin flame then he could resurrect her, he could bring her back.

From the very start I was just a pawn meant to be used in order to bring Mary back to life.

I fell to my knees when I reached the docks with my hands clutching at my mouth and tears streaming down my face. I was nothing to him, I meant nothing to him. I gripped at my chest, wheezing from the lack of air in my lungs, a sound that was followed by a series of sobs and cries of agony.

"Evangeline!" the familiar voice called out to me like it had so many times before and I looked up to see Ben rushing towards me. The light from the lamps around us danced across my teary face as he fell to his knees in front of me. He reached out to cup my cheeks in his large hands.

My hand raised to grab his, clinging to it as if it was my lifeline, my only hope of surviving the dangers that lay ahead.

I shook my head and continued to weep when he asked me what had happened. He was a safe haven, a comfort and the only person who seemed to truly care about me.

I swallowed my sobs and stared at him.

Rebecca knew about the jewels from the start. She knew what they were meant to be used for. Her arguments with Caleb came back to me. She knew yet she still pretended to be my ally, my friend instead of telling me the truth. Caleb hadn't kidnapped me for my eyes or voice or my striking similarities to Mary. He'd kidnapped me because I was a crucial part in his spell.

It was a dark form of magic that could bring the dead back to life.

Ben pulled me close and held me tightly.

His actions promised something, they swore that he would never let go and that he would protect me no matter what.

Chapter Twenty-Nine

Ben and I sat below deck as the night rolled on. We were seated on the top bunk of one of the many bunk beds. He'd scooped me up onto it as if I was nothing more than a feather.

I stood in front of him as he bent to lock his arms behind my knees, lifting me onto the bed. I gripped his shoulders, gazing down at him when he placed me on the top bunk, his hands moving to caress my thighs.

I let my hands drop away from his shoulders to hold onto the thin mattress beneath me. My eyes searched his features in the faint glow of the lamps, the silence surrounding us was deafening. We were the only two onboard the Sunken Soul that night.

"You need to rest" he muttered, his brown gaze falling to his hands that gently caressed my skin. I didn't want to be alone after what happened and since spending the night in the Captain's quarters with me would only anger Caleb, both of us decided that it would be better for me to sleep in Ben's bed, below deck where he could keep a close eye on me.

"I…can't" the words came out as a light whisper, spread far apart by a long pause. Ben reached up to tenderly cup the side of my face, running the pad of his thumb along my cheekbone.

"You haven't been sleeping well" he noted, his finger moving to press down on the black bags that hung beneath my eyes. The night before I hadn't slept and the one before that was haunted by images of strange women, sea Nymphs and Mary.

"Whatever you saw or heard-." my eyes shot up to meet his, his were words soft as if he was afraid of scaring me. My bottom lip trembled at the thought of Caleb and the woman in the tent. Ben squeezed my thigh almost reassuringly.

"Evangeline, I promise no one will hurt you" he knew I was scared. He could see it on my face.

I leaned into him when he pressed his lips to the center of my forehead as if to seal the promise he'd made. When he pulled away, I felt cold.

I blinked when tears stung my eyes and began to fiddle with my fingers in my lap. My head was bent in an attempt to hide the unshed tears.

"Ben?" my voice cracked when his name rolled from my lips. He let his hand slip down my neck, my shoulder and arm to take both of my hands in his, holding them like a prince would hold the hand of his fair princess.

There was a war raging inside of me, a constant pushing and pulling like the waves that crashed onto the shore. It was a war that I couldn't fight on my own.

"What is it?" he asked when I fell silent. I raised my head to glance at the room around us, at the lamps, the empty beds and hammocks that swayed when the ship rocked ever so slightly. I swallowed back the tears in order to ask the one question that kept repeating itself in the back of my mind.

"Have you ever loved someone so much that no matter how they feel, you would still do anything to see them happy?" he froze when our eyes met, knowing exactly who I was referring to.

My words caused him to pull away from me and climb up onto the bunk bed, easing himself onto the mattress beside me. He began removing his boots and tossed them into the water below.

"Once, a long time ago" came his reply with a sharp nod. His boot splashed onto the ground with a thud. He then gripped his thighs and began rubbing them like the conversation was one that he didn't particularly want to have.

"You don't-." I went to protest, my hand reaching out to caress his as an attempt to stop him from continuing but he cut me off, choosing to go on.

"She was a-." he breathed in, his hand moving to hold mine, causing my heart to stop at the feel of him there with me. I wasn't alone, I could never be alone as long as Ben was still alive.

"Pirate" that single word made my stomach drop. I could feel myself getting absorbed into his story when he began to tell it, lost in the memories of a young man who fell in love with the wrong person and got caught up in a web of lies.

"Alluring and wild as they usually are but to a fisherman's grandson, she was exactly the type of adventure he was looking for" a woman who was fearless and daring came to mind, one who wouldn't bite her tongue even for the most frightening of men, a woman more like Rebecca than myself.

Yes, I could be reckless and yes, I didn't fear the man who was plotting to kill me but I still had my fears, I still had my limits and I knew when to walk away.

"I dreamed about leaving that town almost all my life. I wanted to do something more than just haul in fish everyday" it explained why he could navigate but not read. As a fisherman he would need to be able to navigate, read the currents and track the patterns of fish, although as a fisherman his family couldn't possibly afford a teacher to teach him how to read and write.

"And when I met Sonja, I found just that, a way out" her name sounded majestic, like that of a beautiful mare, bred to be free and wild similar to the blood that ran in her veins.

I'd heard Rebecca and Caleb's story and even a small portion of Nolan's but Ben was unknown to me even though I was closest to him.

"They branded me as one of theirs-." he pulled his hand away from mine to roll up the sleeve of his shirt, exposing the scarred mark of a knife on his wrist. I'd caught glimpses of it before but never thought anything of it.

"The mark of a Red Pirate" my breath caught in the back of my throat as my eyes stared down at the raised scar tissue. *Could the young man that I thought I knew possibly turn out to be more dangerous than all the others?* He was a form of comfort to me yet he'd been branded with the park of the deadliest pirates to ever sail the seven seas.

"Things ended horribly because of her and if it hadn't been for Caleb, I would've still been trapped on that ship under Captain Darkheart's command" despite the good that Caleb had done for him, Ben still warned me about the Captain, telling me that he was dangerous. I'd experienced that danger myself, felt it, seen it but I knew that somewhere beneath it all there was a heart capable of love and a man capable of doing good.

Ben rolled his sleeve back down and looked at me, his eyes meeting mine with a serious gleam in their depths.

"So to answer your question, yes, I've loved someone to that extent-." he reached for my hand, taking it in his by wrapping his fingers around mine. I looked at our joined hands as he continued.

"But that doesn't mean you should destroy yourself just to make them happy" I could feel my chest tightening and my lip trembling as I stared blankly at our hands. I was lost in my own thoughts and memories of what Mary experienced.

227

I could see her laying with her head on Caleb's chest, listening to his heartbeat the night after they'd made love in the Captain's quarters. I could see her smiling face the first time he told her he loved her and hear her voice whispering it back. It was true love, something I could never have but Caleb, he had it and he was doing everything in his power to get that love back.

I did care for the Black Pirate Captain but he didn't care for me and if I could give him back the love that I felt, the feelings that I felt then there was nothing that could stop me from doing so.

"Thank you" I breathed, knowing what I was going to do. I knew why I'd been kidnapped and why I found myself onboard the Sunken Soul.

It was my destiny. It was my fate to die so that two lovers could find the happiness they so deserved. In that moment with Ben, surrounded by the orange glow from the lamps, was the moment I knew what I had to do.

It was the moment that changed everything.

Chapter Thirty
One Years Ago

I was out late, hauling in the nets and by the time I reached the shore, the sun had already set. The lamps that lined the streets gleamed bright in the darkness.

The heavy crate filled with fish thudded down onto the pier as I turned to reach for a second one. I was about to start packing the fish in ice when a figure appeared in my line of sight, a woman wearing heeled boots that clicked with every step she took.

I paused, setting the second crate down on top of the first when she stepped into the light of the lanterns that lined the pier.

Her hair was the color of chocolate and her eyes were a dark shade of sapphire. They were piercing and could see straight through you. She had dark tan skin and was dressed in red from head to toe.

She looked angry as she approached me like I'd done something wrong just by merely existing. One side of her head was shaven, the other half had formed dreadlocks. A cross earring dangled from one of her earlobes and she had a tattoo on the side of her face. It was a tattoo of a knife, done in black ink.

"Screw that damned pirate" she gritted out when she neared me, her words like venom before her lips came crashing down onto mine and I was forced to stumble back.

I stared at her with wide, confused eyes but eventually gave into her and returned the kiss. My hands roamed over her body, underneath her red coat, along the lining of her black trousers and into her red blouse.

She gripped the collar of my shirt and pulled away to look at me, breathing hard when her hungry gaze traveled down my body.

"I need a distraction" she said, her breath fanning my face as she licked her bottom lip. That dangerous stare of hers met my brown gaze and a cunning, sly smile spread across her lips.

"And you'll just have to do" she tugged me towards the boat I'd been unloading and shoved me into it. I fell, unable to stop myself before I tripped over my feet and landed on a pile of netting.

Her hands moved quickly, tearing her jacket from her shoulders and dropping it onto the pier before she stepped into the boat and sat down on my lap. Her hands snaked their way underneath the material of my shirt as I tasted her lips. I fell back into the netting, listening to the sound of her laughter echoing into the night when I allowed her to have her way with me.

I gave her all of me and she gave me all of her in that boat which rocked in time with the motion of our bodies, dancing in the glow of the lanterns and moonlight.

It became a nightly occurrence, every night I would dock my boat later than usual and she would come stumbling down the pier, sometimes drunk, sometimes looking for a distraction and in the morning when I'd wake, she'd be gone. It made me wonder whether I was losing my mind or just helpless to her enchanting spell.

We didn't have a decent conversation until our fourth night together when she started getting dressed instead of falling asleep in my arms like she usually did.

"I have to get back to the ship" she explained while pulling her blouse over her head and tugging it onto her body.

I pushed myself onto my elbows and looked up at her, the blanket I kept in the boat for the occasion strewn across my lower half.

"The ship?" I questioned, my voice sounding hoarse as I watched her slip into her trousers, the material gliding across her smooth skin in a similar to how my hands would. It made me jealous of the fabric that got to caress her while I was left lying there, deprived of her warmth.

"The Gray Ghost" she replied as if it was obvious. I could feel my body stiffen when her words registered in the back of my mind. The Gray Ghost was a pirate ship that'd been spotted in the waters around the coast.

I sat up straight, my hand moving to grip the blanket to prevent it from slipping.

"The pirate ship?" I asked, watching as she reached for one of her boots, slipping it onto her foot and up her calve until she could start tying them. She paused after the first boot and let out an exasperated sigh.

"That's the one" her eyes scanned the mess of blankets and netting in search of her other boot, her eyes narrowing in concentration. She eventually found it and reached for it.

I searched her features to find no trace of mock or humor hidden in them.

"You're a pirate" I declared when the realization struck me. She finished tying her laces then looked at me with a raised brow, her elbows resting on her parted knees with her gloved hands dangling in between them.

"Gee what gave me away? Was it the hair, the tattoos, the clothes?" she sarcastically quizzed as she picked up her red, long sleeved jacket that she always wore. It was her way of emphasizing her mocking questions. She then tugged the jacket onto her arms and shoulders.

"You're a Red Pirate" I stated, my eyes moving from my body to hers. I took in the sight of the boat, the mess of blankets and netting.

She stood and tugged her hair out from the collar of her jacket. I hadn't given it much thought but her choice of clothing truly was odd since most women only wore dresses and their best polished heels with their hair up in fancy twists and knots. They wore makeup but not as much as the thick black circles that were painted around her eyes.

"And, you're repeating yourself" she shot back, turning to look down at me with a playful smirk. I gaped up at her, not sure what to say or even how to respond. She stepped out of the boat and into the pier.

"I have to go" she repeated, about to leave when I called out to her. She froze, her hands stuffed into her jacket's pockets when she turned to fully face me in the orange light of the lanterns.

"What?" she demanded, seeming annoyed as her eyes roamed over my naked torso. I wasn't entirely sure what I wanted to say and resorted to asking the first thing that came to mind, blurting it out without thinking.

"What's your name?" she smiled, her head tilting to the side when her tongue flicked out across her bottom lip like it would whenever she found something amusing.

She removed her hand from her pocket to run her fingers through her hair and called back to me.

"Sonja" with that she disappeared into the night, leaving me alone and awestruck. I searched of my clothes, got dressed and iced the fish before headed back to the cabin. It was located in the woods near the shoreline, away from all the bustling commotion of the towns people.

It was well past midnight when I reached the cabin with a bucket of fish in hand and rope thrown over my shoulder.

The lamp on the porch was still lit and a man sat beneath it, waiting with his feet kicked up on an old table and a tired look in his aged brown eyes.

"Where have you been?" he questioned, his voice deeper and hoarser than mine. He was older than I was, much older by a few decades or so.

I set the bucket down with a clutter and turned my head to glance over the trees surrounding us with a sigh.

"Fishing" I explained, motioning to the bucket by my feet. The old man got up from his chair and approached me. He looked at the fish in the bucket with knowing eyes before he scratched at his white beard and met my gaze.

"Fishing? Fishing for what exactly?" his forehead creased as he waited for my response. I opened my mouth to explain but before I could he beat me to it.

"Because Jones stopped by a few hours ago, said he'd seen you with some pirate gal down by the pier" the air left my lungs and my eyes closed when I realized what was happening. He wasn't trying to make conversation, he was there to confront me, to make sure that I stayed away from Sonja.

"Grandpa-." I tried to argue but he cut me off. He raised his hand, causing my words to die down in the back of my throat.

"She's a pirate!" he snapped, his hand dropping back to his side. He was a hard and cruel man who to me was just as frightening as the Red Pirates.

"A pirate! Do you have any idea what their kind does to people like us?" he asked, jabbing his index finger into my chest a few times and pointing to the sea out on the horizon.

I tightened my grip on the rope that hung from my shoulder and stared silently at him when he continued "They use us, they manipulate us and destroy our lives, Ben"

My name coming from him forced me to meet his deadly gaze, the same gaze my father used to have before he left when I was just a little boy. That gaze left me feeling angry, frustrated and tired of always obeying it, of doing the same boring things day in and day out. I'd get up, go fishing, come home, eat, sleep then repeat it all the very next day and the next and the next.

"These people are dangerous-." I knew about the rumors, about the stories that mothers told their children at night to frighten them into behaving since they'd be afraid of the Red Pirates coming to take them away if they misbehaved. I knew it all and it frightened me but Sonja, she didn't scare me, she fascinated me.

"Promise me-." my grandfather began, his fists trembling at his sides. He sighed heavily and met my eyes with a defeated look.

He wasn't the abusive man that my father was, no matter how angry he got but that didn't stop me from fearing him like I feared the man who'd beaten my own mother in front of me. My father drove her away all those years ago.

"Promise me that you'll stay away from her" I swallowed hard, Sonja's face flickering past my eyes. Her dark blue eyes, her long brown hair and the way she smirked so devilishly. She was the only thing keeping me from leaving that town, the only thing that still managed to excite me. I wasn't going to let her go.

"Okay" the word slipped out before I could stop it, a defeated sound that was followed by my grandfather pulling me into a tight hug. That night would give rise to a series of events that I'd never forget.

If only I'd listened to my grandfather and stayed away then maybe things would've ended differently.

Chapter Thirty-One
Ben

We were drinking together, down by the local bar. There was a constant fear of someone seeing us in the back of my mind but I pushed it aside when I downed the rest of my drink.

Sonja clung to my arm, laughing and grinning as she whispered sinful things into my ear. Music played in the background as people danced and cheered.

"Come join the pirates" Sonja suddenly suggested, her smile fading as she stroked my arm with a look of hope and longing hidden in the depths of her eyes. I laughed at first, thinking that it was a joke then stiffened when I realized that she was serious.

"Sonja-." I began to protest but she interrupted me by leaning closer so that her lips were only inches away from mine. Her breath fanned my face as she tightened her hold on my arm in desperation. She wanted me to give into her and seducing me was the only way she knew how to achieve that.

"Please" her bottom lip jotted out in a mock pout that made her seem that much more alluring and playful. I played it off, breathing a laugh and turned my head, shaking it.

"You almost had me there" I admitted, my eyes scanning the bar in search of the waitress who'd assisted us earlier. When I found her among the crowd, I motioned for her to bring me another round of rum. Sonja stilled beside me, her grip on my arm loosening. There was something wrong and I was just about to ask her what it was when she beat me to it.

"We're setting sail at sunrise" it was like a cold, hard slap in the face. It knocked me out of my drunken buzz and back to reality. A frown made its way onto my face.

"What, why?" I questioned, my hand moving to take hold of hers. She kept staring at the table with her head hung in order to hide the grim look on her face. She shook her head from side to side and shrugged her shoulders.

"Darkheart is after some gem in the Aztin Jungle" she spat out like she couldn't care less about the jewel or what her Captain wanted.

The waitress returned, placing a newly filled cup of rum in front of me before tending to a separate table.

"So why not stay here, with me?" my hand constricted around hers, drawing her attention back to me.

Her earring swayed in sync with the motion of her head turning to meet my eyes with a sad glint in her gaze.

"I can't, wherever he goes, I follow" I didn't fully understand what she'd meant at the time. Her shoulders hunched and her lips tugged into a frown.

"Then don't follow" I shrugged, feeling as though she didn't want to stay with me and that it was just an excuse to run off with her Captain. I was worried that she'd grown tired of me after our time spent together.

"It's not that simple, Ben, I pledged my loyalty to him-." my eyebrows knitted together in confusion. The words didn't make sense to me. *The words 'pledge' and 'loyalty'. What did they have to do with her free will?* When she noticed the look on my face she sighed and proceeded to explain.

"To pledge your loyalty means to give your life to your Captain-." her hand raised so that her fingers could lightly trace the black mark of a knife that'd been tattooed on the side of her face. I'd heard of such a mark, the mark of the Red Pirates that they wore for all the world to see.

"I am his, therefore I can only do what he permits me to do" a chill went down my spine when she spoke the words *'I am his'*. I felt oddly protective of her, like she was mine but I was too blind to see that she was her own.

"We set sail for the Aztin Jungle at sunrise" there were a lot of things about pirates that I didn't understand such as the contract that bounded them through loyalty until death. The marks they wore to identify themselves, the deep rivalry between the Black and the Red Pirates that went back generations before I was even born.

Sonja, slipped her hand away from mine and gripped my thigh, looking at me with pleading eyes.

"But we don't have to say goodbye if-." she paused, glancing around at the bar and the people around us, her voice lowering when she spoke "You join the Red Pirates"

If I had any sanity left then I would've declined her offer and left the bar but the Ben who'd come to love her over the few weeks that had passed, couldn't resist her temptation.

If only I hadn't said yes. I found myself onboard the Gray Ghost later that night, facing the Captain in his quarters. He was slumped back in a chair across from me.

He had a long black beard, sunken in eyes and hair that was starting to form knots. His Captain's hat sat atop his head and his fingers were decorated in a number of rings. I watched them as they combed through his beard.

"Sonja tells me that ye wish to join me crew" he spoke, his voice lashing out at me like a viper. He wore a red coat, similar to Sonja's but his was worn through.

"Be there any reasoning behind ye request, boy?" he questioned as he narrowed his black gaze onto me causing the creases around his eyes to deepen.

He was a much older man who'd lived to see far more than I ever could living as a fisherman.

"I-." I began, my eyes searching for Sonja. She stood, examining a jeweled skull that'd been placed on one of the many desks. She shook her head as if to tell me not to mention her or us.

"I'm tired of this life, of doing the same things over and over again-." I placed my gaze back onto the Captain and waited for his reaction. He tilted his head back, listening intently to my words.

"I wish to see the world, to travel to places I could only dream of-." Sonja stilled, her head turning to look at me when she realized that what I was saying was the truth.

The Captain raised his hand to cut me off, the cluttering of metals echoing out around me when his rings grazed across each other.

"And what do ye have to offer me?" there it was, the cunning negotiation. He wouldn't let anyone join his crew unless they were beneficial to him.

I swallowed hard. *Pirates sailed the waters of the world as did fisherman and what did any pirate need in order to find treasure? A navigator.*

"I can navigate" his ears perked up and he raised his hand, his fingers pointing upward. He hummed then rubbed the pads of his thumb and middle finger together ever so gently only to snap his fingers once, forcefully.

The two men who'd been standing guard near the door moved towards me in the blink of an eye, grabbing hold of my arms to pin me in place.

"What're you doing?" I demanded while looking from one man to the next. A third crew member approached the fire that burnt in the fireplace. Captain Darkheart ignored me, turning his attention onto Sonja.

"Well done my dear, ye've brought me yet another fitting slave to sell" he held his hand out to her and she giggled as she moved towards him. She took his outstretched hand and plant herself firmly in his lap with a grin plastered across her scarlet lips. I stilled at the sight, a sense of betrayal filling me when she planted a sweet kiss to his lips.

"Sonja?" I breathed in disbelief when the third man grabbed a glowing rod from the fire with a gloved hand and began making his way towards me. I was too dumbstruck to react until the sleeve of my shirt was pulled back and my wrist held firmly in place for the crewman to press the searing hot image of a knife onto my flesh.

I cried out, pain shooting up my arm and my head thrown back with my muscles tensing. The man pulled the rod away and dumped it into a bucket of water, causing steam to rise around us. My head fell forward as I gasped for air.

"Toss him in the brig" the Captain ordered with a flick of his wrist but he wasn't the focus of my deadly glare, no, the brunette with blue eyes was my target and she met my gaze with a smile before they dragged me below deck to a cell where five other men all sat, laughing at me for falling for the same tricks they did.

I was just a prisoner onboard the ship. I was forced to work, to cook, to slave away until someone would come along and decide that I was worth spending their money on.

I'd been onboard the Gray Ghost for more than a month. I was on my hands and knees, scrubbing the deck while Sonja leaned back against the ship's railing watching me.

She was the Captain's toy, both in and out of bed. She was his means of tricking unsuspecting men onboard the ship where he could brand them and sell them off like cattle.

I heard her boots approaching long before she knelt in front of me with a cup of wine in hand. I met her eyes, able to see the darkness that resided within them. I could make out the monster that'd wrapped its claws around my throat and laughed in my face.

"You missed a spot" she said, raising the cup to pour its contents onto the deck in front of me. She then stood, tossing the cup aside with a sinister laugh before she disappeared into the Captain's quarters.

I'd just about abandoned all hope of ever being saved from that rat invested cell until the day Caleb Campbell set foot on the Gray Ghost. His footsteps made the floorboards above my cell rattle, dust crumbling onto me when I heard them speak, two Captain's from different corners of the ocean.

"Easy boys, I'm only here to buy me a rat" the opposing pirate Captain said, using the code I'd heard many times before. He was looking for a slave to purchase like most men did whenever they set foot on the Gray Ghost.

Me and my two remaining companions perked up at the thought of being saved but really there was no telling what awaited us once we'd be sold. For all we knew it could be a life worse than the one we were living.

"Fetch 'em" Captain Darkheart's voice commanded from above which was followed by the sound of approaching footsteps and a set of cluttering keys. They unlocked the door to our cell and bent down to grab our chains.

"Good news rats, one of ye be getting out of here today" one of the crewmen announced, a crazed look in his one eye since the other looked to have been sown shut.

The men tugged on our chains, forcing us to our feet and up the stairs, to the deck where the light burnt our eyes.

"Take ye pick, Campbell" Darkheart said, stepping aside with his hand motioning towards us. I squinted in the sunlight, a figure approaching us until it came to a stop a few feet away.

He was big, dressed in leather and wore a red coat similar to the ones the Red Pirates wore. His Captain's hat sat atop his head and an Irishman stood beside him with his arms crossed over his chest.

"How much for the blond?" I realized he was enquiring about me but remained silent as I watched the golden eyes of the tattooed man lock onto Darkheart's blackened ones.

"Ten shillings" Darkheart replied, grinning down at Sonja who clung to him like a dog in heat. I wanted to spit in their direction.

"For a rat?" Captain Campbell questioned, his eyebrows knitting together while the rest of his crew behind him burst out laughing like the thought of paying that much for a slave was something they'd never heard of. Darkheart raised his hand when he spoke.

"For a navigator" he corrected, causing Captain Campbell to study me before he turned to address his first mate while jerking his head in the opposing Captain's direction.

"Pay him" the Irishman tossed a bag of coins to Darkheart, who caught it with little effort. He weighed it in the palm of his hand before handing it over to Sonja to be counted.

She nodded once she was done and one of the men holding our chains unlocked my cuffs, giving me a hard shove towards Captain Campbell who was already stepping down from the plank that acted as a bridge between the two ships. The Gray Ghost and the Sunken Soul.

"I trust we will meet again, Campbell?" Darkheart called out after us when I was forced from one ship to the other. The younger Captain, turned to glance back at the ship with red sails from beneath the brim of his hat.

"Aye, that we will" he agreed then ordered his crew to set sail. They worked as one unit, scaling the netting, climbing up to untie the sails and raising the anchor.

That was the day Caleb Campbell set me free and gave me a choice to either leave or pledge my loyalty to him.

I did the latter, deciding that it was the safest place to be. On the opposite end of an endless battle between Red and Black but little did I know that less than a year later a woman would be forced onboard the ship. A woman more beautiful than any I'd ever seen before.

With hair as white as snow and eyes of gray and blue. She was the very opposite of Sonja. Evangeline would be the light and Sonja the darkness.

Chapter Thirty-Two
Evangeline

I awoke wrapped in Ben's arms with his chest pressed up against my back and his face buried in the side of my neck. He was still fast asleep. His shallow breathing tickled my skin while I lay there, staring at the wall in front of me.

The bustling of people outside the ship and seagulls crying out overhead indicated that it was morning. I could hear the crew moving about above deck causing me to stir. I twisted my body so that I was facing the groggy man beside me. He groaned in protest as a result of my movements.

Ben rolled onto his back, his head falling to the side when the light shining through the cracks in the floorboards above began to irritate him.

I took the time to observe his features. His relaxed face, closed eyes, messy hair and parted lips.

He groaned and turned his head to look at me past squinting eyes, his hand reaching out to caress my face. I allowed his fingers to get lost in the mess of white hair.

There was a loud thud, heavy footsteps and a familiar voice that came from above deck.

"Tie him down!" I pushed myself onto my knees and gazed up at the floorboards as Ben sat up next to me. He threw his legs over the side of the bed while rubbing at his tired eyes. There was a struggle on deck followed by an annoyed,

"Fetch me, me first mate!" I quickly climbed down from the top bunk and lowered my feet into the layer of cold water below. The world around me began to dance with silver and purple specks which reflected from the scales starting to form on my skin. I moved in the direction of the stairs that headed above deck, ignoring the display.

One of the crew members appeared at the top of the stairs, rushing down but flying past me and falling face first in the water below. He was clearly still drunk from his night of drinking and could barely walk without tripping. I glanced at him then stepped onto the deck where I was met with the light of day. The crew were gathered in the middle of the ship's deck.

"Captain" I greeted, catching Caleb's attention. He turned his golden glare onto me which caused his words from the night before to echo in my mind but I chose to ignore them having already made my choice with little regard for my own life.

Ben appeared behind me, groaning and rubbing at the side of his head. Caleb glanced at us, his nostrils flaring when the thought of us having shared a bed enraged him.

"Question the man" he ordered, motioning to a skinny, gray haired man who was slumped over and tied to a chair. A stream of blood trickled from his parted lips. Caleb moved towards me and came to a stop when his face was only inches away from mine.

"Find out what he knows about the Red Pirates" with that he left, not giving me much of a chance to protest. He made his way towards the ship's stern, pausing on the steps to snap at his gathered crew below.

"Raise the anchor! Ready the sails! Set course for the Aztin Jungle!" the crew did as they were told, scaling the ropes and raising the anchor. They were no longer examining the unknown man. Ben began climbing up to the crow's nest where he untied the bindings that secured the sails.

"Oh, the Jungle, the Jungle, they say only the dead reside there, that women lie with the bones of past pirates and give birth to soulless children" the man said, laughing madly as he looked up at me. His pupils were dilated and his chin was dripping in blood. He coughed violently, spitting blood in every direction. Nolan appeared beside me.

"He's gone mad" he declared, voicing what I was thinking. The Irishman shook his head and moved to grab hold of the back of the chair, dragging it across the deck and into the navigation room.

Rebecca followed us, shutting and locking the doors behind us to prevent anyone from entering.

"Ye be making a grave mistake, turn around, turn around!" I wasn't sure what the madman was talking about but I knew it had something to do with us setting sail for the Aztin Jungle.

Nolan took a stand in front of him, binding his hand and knuckles in some scrap material that he'd found.

"Ye better stop ye babbling and start making some sense, old man" Rebecca poured some wine into two cups, one of which she held out for me to take. I furrowed my eyebrows in confusion.

"You're going to need it" she insisted followed by the sound of Nolan's fist connecting with the side of the man's face. Blood splattered and the man went still, his ramblings had been abruptly silenced.

I nodded to Rebecca and took the cup that she offered, taking a long swig of its contents.

"Tell me ye name" Nolan ordered, gripping the wrist of his bound hand. Rebecca's eyes widened at me before she turned, drinking from her own cup. The man began laughing maniacally, the sound bouncing off the walls around us.

"I be Malcolm Watts, but ye-." Malcolm's hungry eyes flickered over Nolan. They had a rabid look in their depths which made him resemble a starved and depraved animal.

"Milord may call me Al" Nolan laughed in response to the title that he was given as if it was some sort of joke to call a pirate 'lord'. Rebecca snorted into her cup, placing her hand on her hip as she nursed her drink.

"Well then Al, what connection do ye have to the Red Pirates?" the grin that stretched across Al's face faltered at the mention of the 'Red Pirates'.

The same fear from before returned to his eyes and they began darting around in every direction, moving from me to the wall to the blood on the floor.

"Pirates, pirates! What of pirates?" he began to ramble again, looking at us with a mixture of fear and confusion. I'd never seen a man as mad as him, never seen insanity take hold of someone like it had Al. Nolan flexed his fingers.

"They be myth, nothing but tall tales and-." Al was cut off by a fist striking his cheek, his head snapping to the side. Rebecca took a sip of her wine when more blood splatters decorated the floorboards.

"Let's try that again, shall we?" Nolan proposed as he leaned forward to place his hands on each of the chair's arms so that his face was only inches away from Malcolm's.

"What ties do ye have to the Red Pirates?" when Al raised his head, his eyes were clear to an extent, that same fog that'd previously clouded them was gone. I glanced down at my cup, I wasn't in the mood for the drink anymore and placed the cup on the table near me.

"I used to be a member of the crew" Al explained, jerking his head in the direction of his right arm. Nolan reached for his sleeve and ripped it to reveal a tattoo of a knife on his upper arm. It was the mark of a Red Pirate.

"Used to be?" Nolan echoed, standing upright. I leaned back against the table, placing a hand on either side of me to brace myself. I felt sick from the smell of filthy flesh and iron.

"I was, was? Yes, I was there. I saw them-." Rebecca rolled her eyes in the background, irritated by Al's constant blubbering. You could only make sense of what he was saying every once in a while. Nolan balled his fist.

"I saw the red, the red sails, the red. Red!" there was a loud impact of bone against bone, flesh against flesh and I squeezed my eyes shut, flinching as I turned my head away from the sight.

Al spat blood. He was laughing like a crazed man when I opened my eyes to look back at him. He was smiling up at Nolan with excitement in his gaze. It was sickening sight to see.

"You better start elaborating or he might just hit you again" Rebecca warned, her finger motioning towards Nolan despite her hand being wrapped around her cup. Al looked at her, his yellow teeth stained red and dripping blood due to him having bitten his cheek or tongue a few times. His lips were split in various places.

"Oh will he? Please say he will" Rebecca eyed Malcolm, thinking the same thing I was. He was beyond saving, something made him into what he was and we wanted to know what. She slammed her cup down on the table and leaned towards him with gritted teeth.

"If you don't explain what you just said then I'll make sure that he'll never hit you again" it was an annoyed threat, a mixture of her anger towards Caleb and her frustration for having to be dragged along to the Aztin Jungle against her will.

Al's eyes widened in response to her words.

"No, no! Al'll speak, he'll speak!" his own words were rushed and frantic when he looked at Nolan in fear. The Irishman laughed, shaking his head as he tightened the fabric around his knuckles that were already stained red with blood.

"Ye're one mad bastard" Nolan muttered before he lowered himself until he was at eye level with Al. There was a hitch in the madman's breathing and he began to grow even more excited. I placed a hand over my mouth and stared straight ahead, unable to look at the sight of the groveling man soaked in his own blood, just begging to be beaten.

"Now tell me what I want to know" I silently cursed Caleb for putting me in that situation where it felt like my stomach was doing flips and its contents were about to come bubbling up.

"They sell slaves! They be making money off men they trick into boarding the ship. I found 'em out ye see, I planned to set the rats free but got caught and was tortured. They cut off me toes, branded me, sold me to a rich bloke who made me wipe his ass with a golden cloth-." he laughed so loud that he began coughing causing even more blood to splatter across the floor that Nolan had to dodge.

"I got away, wound up at the Nest and now here we are, all good mates" the Irishman's eyes flickered to Rebecca. It didn't seem like news to her as she slumped down onto one of the chairs when her injured foot started hurting. I watched her reach for her cup and take a long swig before setting it back down.

"Good boy" Nolan said as if Al was a dog, then struck him once more as a reward for his cooperation to which Al began giggling like a little girl. I couldn't take it anymore.

I darted forward, unlocked the doors and pushed past them so that I could reach the ship's side in time to vomit. I coughed and ran the back of my trembling hand over my lips once I was done, hand gripping the railing as if my life depended on it.

"Evangeline?" Ben questioned, appearing at my side, his hand rubbing my back while the other pressed itself to my forehead, testing to see if I had a fever. I had a fever but it was due to my anger towards Caleb. I met his eyes, knowing that he'd forced me to be present while Rebecca and Nolan questioned the man. It was his way of getting revenge for me having spent the night with Ben.

I shook my head and sat down on a nearby barrel, leaning forward as I tried to catch my breath. Nolan locked the doors to the navigation room to continue their interrogation.

Chapter Thirty-Three

Rebecca cleaned Al after interrogating him. She dressed and fed him then set him loose on the rest of the crew. The crew seemed to enjoy his madness and laughed whenever he'd start rambling.

I bathed myself and dressed in Caleb's red coat. Afterwards, I sat on a chair near the Captain's quarters as I watched the sky grow darker as we neared the Aztin Jungle.

The Red Pirates were slave traders. They placed money above all else and had little care for human life. To enter the jungle would not only place me at risk but the rest of the crew as well.

I stood from my chair when a landmass came into view on the horizon. Lamps could be seen dangling from the trees, lighting a pathway that led deeper into the jungle when we reached the shore.

Caleb ordered for the ship's anchor to be lowered and its sails to be risen, allowing for the ship to come to a stop. I gazed out at the mysterious jungle as Caleb addressed the crew.

"Man the ship!" he ordered then moved past me to jump overboard, landing in the shallow waters below. Nolan followed, assisting Rebecca down the side of the ship while being careful of her injured ankle.

I moved closer to the ship's railing and peered down at the waters below. Ben scaled down the side of the ship and landed with a splash in the water. He looked up at me with his arms extended.

"Care to jump?" he asked, shooting me a kind smile. I stepped onto the railing with my hand wrapped tightly around the ropes in order to steady myself before I jumped.

Ben caught me, his arms winding themselves around my waist to hold me in place, pressed firmly up against his chest. I steadied myself by gripping his shoulders with my feet dangling beneath me, just a few inches above the water.

My lips parting when he gently placed me on my feet. I noticed Caleb watching us from the shore and stepped away from Ben.

"Thank you" I muttered, my shins pushing through the water as I made my way to the beach where I followed the three crew members ahead of me deeper into the jungle.

Human skulls hung from the trees with lit candles stuffed inside them. It was as though they were trying to warn us, telling us to turn back because if we did follow their trail then only death would await us. Ben stayed close behind me, his eyes roaming from one fleshless face to the next.

I climbed over a risen tree root, leaping down onto a mess of leaves and mud as snakes slithered along the jungle floor and spiders spun webs that were larger than Caleb.

The path narrowed, becoming almost impossible to navigate until we broke through into a clearing where a wooden structure had been built. It was held up by pillars with red fabric that hung in front of the windows and doorways. Skulls were mounted on stakes and lined the path that led up to the structure's steps. The bony faces smiled at us as if to welcome us to a place that smelt like moss but felt like death.

Two men stood guard outside the doorway with their faces painted white to resemble skulls as they patiently awaited our arrival. Caleb looked almost fearless when he approached them, his boots thudding heavily onto each step before he came to a stop directly in front of the men.

"Gentlemen" Caleb greeted and they shared a look, their dark almost black eyes darting in our direction and taking in our appearance before coming to a rest on my form. I followed Caleb up the steps, the only, apart from Caleb to dare venture closer. They took in my red coat then stepped aside, reaching up to pull back the material that hung over the doorway, allowing us through.

Members of the Red Pirate crew sat scattered around the room, some drinking, others gambling while a few took in the sight of a dancing, drunk woman in the center of the room. Among the few who watched her was their Captain with a long beard and dark eyes. He was dressed in a red coat similar to the one the woman was wearing.

Her dancing was nothing like Rebecca's. It wasn't enchanting or compelling but instead it was fierce and demanding. It was quick and precise not free and wild.

Ben came to a halt beside me when he saw her, his breathing catching in the back of his throat. I glanced from him to the woman with a knowing gaze then turned to address the Captain when he forcefully raised his hand. The motion caused his men to stop playing music and drew the woman out of her strong, empowering and sexual daze.

"Why if it isn't Caleb Campbell" the Captain announced and his crew turned their eyes to the five of us, including those of the brunette who'd previously been dancing. Her sharp blue gaze roaming over our faces but coming to a stop when she noticed Ben.

"And the rat we sold him" I could feel my anger start to surge in response to the Captain's comment that was directed towards Ben. The Red Pirate woman began to make her way over to the navigator but I moved to block her.

"Benjamin" the woman greeted when she come to a sudden halt, her chest nearly bumping into mine due to my abrupt movements. Ben turned his attention to her, his jaw tensed, confirming my suspicions.

"Sonja" the way he said her name made the hair on the back of my neck stand on end. I knew she was the woman Ben had told me about and the thought of her having taken advantage of him, having manipulated him enraged me.

"And who might you be?" Sonja questioned, her eyes falling onto me with a glare in their depths and a grin plastered across her lips. I moved towards her, stilling when a hand shot out to grab hold of mine to stop me.

"Evangeline" Ben breathed. It was his way of telling me not to do anything too reckless. I calmed down, feeling my fingers intertwine with his behind me. Sonja's eyes gleamed in realization.

"I see-." she uttered, her grin widening when she crossed her arms over her partially exposed chest.

"She's your lover" she declared, laughing. She was taller than I was but that didn't intimidate me. Her mocking words caused Caleb to stiffen as he observed the scene. I looked at him, his golden eyes dimming when he turned to look away from me.

"And you're his pirate whore" the room fell completely silent as Sonja's laughter died down in the back of her throat. She locked her narrow eyes and dangerous gaze onto me. I met it with the same intensity, teeth clenching and nostrils flaring when Ben's hand restricting around mine.

Sonja took me in, from the coat that I was wore to the color of my hair. Captain Darkheart laughed almost as loudly as she had.

"The girl bites" he mused, glancing at his crew members. They too began to laugh along with their Captain but fell silent when Sonja spoke.

"That coat tricks you into thinking you're brave" I stood my ground, knowing that I was dressed in the coat of their former Captain

247

who'd been murdered by the previous Black Pirate Captain. It stood as a symbol, a warning that if they tried anything, their coats would be torn from their lifeless bodies as well.

"But you're just a scared little girl surrounded by monsters" she raised her arms, her hands motioning towards the men around her. They looked at me like I was their next meal. I could feel my eyes start to glow and my fangs nip at my bottom lip when I tore myself away from Ben to stalk forward.

"I *am* the monster" I whispered with my face just inches away from Sonja's. I felt a hand grab hold of my arm to pull me away from her. The hand was much stronger than the one I'd been holding and belonged to a much bigger man. Caleb pressed his lips to my ear and forced the words out between gritted teeth.

"That's enough" he then let and shoved me in Ben's direction. I stumbled but regained my balance. My eyes narrowed onto Caleb. He was still bitter because of the fact that Ben and I had slept in the same bed. He was jealous when he really had no reason to me. I loved him with the same intensity and passion that Mary had loved him, he just didn't know it yet.

Sonja smirked at me as if to announce that she'd won and it irritated me. I focused my gaze onto the ground as my hands balled into fists at my sides.

"He did it for you" Ben whispered low enough for only me to hear, drawing my eyes up to meet his. I only then realized what Caleb had done for me. I looked at the Black Pirate Captain. The brim of his hat managed to cast a dark shadow over his eyes.

He'd stopped me from exposing what I was, a Mermaid. I was so enraged that I didn't noticed what was happening. I was starting to change in front of everyone, regardless of my necklace or the fact that so many people stood watching.

"What business have ye here?" Darkheart asked when he stopped chuckling at the sight of Sonja and I. She shot me a sinister glare then turned to head in the direction of her Captain, sitting down on his lap with her arms wrapped around his neck.

"Ye have something I want" Caleb announced. He wasn't beating around the bush. Darkheart met Sonja's eyes and breathed a laugh when she pressed her forehead to his and chuckled as if it was all a joke.

"Ye hear that, boys? The great Caleb Campbell, the overnight Captain wants something of mine" the men around us laughed but Caleb was unbothered. He looked like he was used to their reaction as if he'd experienced it a thousand times before.

"What is it ye seek?" Darkheart questioned after his men settled down. He turned away from the brunette who was throwing herself at him and propped his chin up on his fist. Caleb glanced at me as if prompting me to speak.

"A black gem" the words escaped me and Caleb returned his gaze to Darkheart. The enemy Captain went silent, his tongue sucking at his top front teeth as he rubbed his fingertips together in thought.

"I may have that of which ye speak" Rebecca had her arms crossed over her chest, leaning up against the far wall with Nolan seated on a nearby chair. She looked as though she was trying to hide herself by keeping her head down and biting her tongue. Nolan picked up on her sudden change in demeanor.

"But what makes ye think that I'd just give it to ye?" I knew what Darkheart's words meant, that Caleb was to make a deal like he had all those years ago with Solstice. The deal could be for anything. It could be something brutal or dangerous.

"That's why I'm here, to strike a deal" it was like signing the devil's contract, bargaining your life away or selling your soul. I shifted my weight from one leg to the other. I wasn't planning on letting Caleb get himself into trouble even if it meant risking my life. Rebecca's head shot up to look at Caleb as if to tell him not to do anything stupid. It was then that Sonja noticed the redhead, her gaze narrowing in recognition.

"A deal?" Darkheart prompted, leaning forward with an irritated Sonja in his lap. She was more worried about getting Darkheart's attention than she was about Rebecca.

"The jewel in exchange for anything ye wish" my head spun around to look at Caleb when he spoke those words. The Red Pirate Captain slumped back in his seat. He tilted his head with intrigue.

"Anything, ye say?" the light from the candles danced across the faces of men and woman alike as we anxiously waited for Darkheart to name his price. He stroked his beard, his eyes gazing up at the ceiling.

"Five-." he announced, holding his hand up with all five fingers spread apart as if to emphasize the amount.

"Mermaid scales" my blood ran cold and the muscles in my body stiffened. Ben shot a glance in my direction, making sure that I was alright. Caleb was about to protest when I cut him off.

"Deal!" it was an impossible price for anyone other than myself. Mermaid scales were rare and costly but they could be found on the black market.

They give human's the ability to glimpse into their futures if the scales are ground up into a powder and consumed. It was most likely why the Captain wanted them.

Caleb's head turned abruptly and his eyes narrowed onto my frame as if to silence me but it was too late.

"We accept your price and will pay it in full come morning" I was pulled out of the room, down the steps and along the winding jungle path until we were well out of earshot.

"What do ye think ye're doing?" Caleb demanded in a low whisper. His eyes kept glancing in the direction of the structure every now and then to make sure that we weren't being followed.

"He wants Mermaid scales and we have a Mermaid" I announced, motioning to myself when I spoke. He shook his head, letting go of my arm to start pacing back and forth as if it would help him think.

"And what am I to tell me crew?" his hand flicked in the direction of the sea where the Sunken Soul awaited us with Snaggletooth, Al and the rest of the crew still onboard.

"Where exactly did I get five Mermaid scales?" only Ben and Caleb knew my secret. Rebecca knew nothing thought she would be suspicious. *Where did he get enough money from to purchase the scales? Where did he even find a seller for the scales?* I ran a hand through my hair.

"You stole them when we stopped at the Pirate's Nest" I muttered and he stopped pacing, turning to snap at me for suggesting that he portray himself as a thief. My mind went to his past, to him being a thief and I subconsciously assumed that it was a decent suggestion. He was about to snarl his reply when Rebecca, Nolan and Ben approached us.

"He will accept no less than five scales for the jewel" Rebecca announced, stopping to glance between the two of us before she shook her head and sighed as if to express how idiotic Caleb was for being willing to go to such lengths for the treasures, for Mary.

"Good luck" she said then began making her way through the trees and along the narrow path back to the ship. Nolan followed her to make sure that she didn't hurt herself on the way back. Ben, Caleb and I were left behind.

"We have no choice" I said, being the first to break the silence. Ben shook his head and grabbed hold of my hand.

"I won't let you hurt yourself for some useless gem" his eyes locked onto Caleb near the end of his sentence. I tore my hand away from Ben's and stepped away from him to show my disagreement. The Captain's eyes followed my movements.

"It's not useless-." I looked at Caleb when I spoke. His golden eyes clouded over in a question, wondering why I was defending the jewels when I'd previously asked him about what they meant to him. He was wondering if I knew about him wanting to resurrect Mary.

"I want to do this-." I argued. Ben's parted lips pressed together in a thin line. I backed away from the two men.

"I *will* do this" with that said I turned and began following the path back to the ship, leaving the two of them behind. I listening to the sound of my thundering heart in my chest.

I was nervous, scared and confused but I knew that I had to tell Caleb about my decision, my choice to willingly sacrifice myself so that he could be with the woman he loved.

I had to tell him that I loved him, that it was all for him, not Ben but for him and only him.

Rebecca

I don't know why I went with them to meet with Darkheart after everything he and Sonja had put me through but their attention was largely placed on Evangeline and Ben.

I thought that I'd gotten away with it but I was proved wrong when Nolan and I stumbled upon Sonja while we were on our way back to the ship. She was leaned back against a nearby tree and she had her arms crossed over her chest as she sneered at me.

"Long time no see" she greeted as I stopped dead in my tracks. Nolan paused alongside me but he remained silent. He looked at me with a quirked brow as if to ask 'Ye *know each other?*'

251

"I didn't think you'd survive the storm" she added when I didn't respond. She pushed off the tree and blocked our path. My hands gripped the material of my skirt as I cautiously watched her.

"What do you want, Sonja?" I demanded. I was tired of her games and her sinister way of manipulating people's mind like she'd done with Ben and I. Sonja breathed a laugh while she glanced in Nolan's direction. She scrutinized him then moved closer to me until she was almost on top of me.

"I'm going to say this in a way that you'll understand" her arms fell to her sides when she leaned closer so that her nose was almost brushing up against mine. I wasn't bothered by her close proximity and instead met her glare with one of my own.

"If I so much as mention you to the Captain, he'll imprison you again so I suggest that you stay the hell away from here" jealousy coated her threat. I knew that Darkheart preferred me to her and that it infuriated her. She just didn't want me to take her place among the Red Pirates. I laughed and pushed past her so that my shoulder collided with hers.

"You don't have to tell me twice" I said before turning my back to her. Nolan shot her a confused look then started following me but her words reached out to him. Her voice stopped him dead in his tracks.

"She didn't tell you, did she?" he looked at me expectantly to which I sighed and decided that there was no time like the present. He was bound to start prying into my past if I didn't tell him and it was better that I tell him rather than Sonja. She had a way of making things sound worse than they actually were.

"Darkheart forced me to be his mistress" Nolan's eyes darkened at the thought of me being forced to have sex with the enemy pirate Captain. Before he could react, I continued "But I managed to escape and that's why you found me on that island"

Nolan could see the pleading in my eyes. I was begging him to let it go so that I could distance myself from Sonja, from Darkheart and my past. Sonja hummed in amusement then crossed her arms back over her chest as she shifted her weight from one leg to the other.

"You can't give Darkheart all of the credit-." My teeth gritted behind my lips. I wanted to lash out at her and it took everything inside of me to restrain myself. Nolan was also trying his best to stay calm.

"I did some pretty terrible things to you too" in order to brush off the situation I rolled my eyes and turned my back to her. I started heading towards the ship with Nolan trailing behind.

"You wish" I called out to her which caused a sickening smile to spread across her lips as she watched us retreat.

Some people are just born bad while others are made into the monsters that they become. I wasn't exactly sure what type of bad Sonja was or what horrors she'd experienced in the past but one thing was for sure.

She was a bad person.

Chapter Thirty-Four

I reached the ship before Caleb did and headed to the Captain's quarters where I began pacing the length of the room, replaying my thoughts over and over in the back of my mind. I hoped that Caleb wouldn't follow me so that I could avoid having to confront him, having to tell him how I felt.

I paused when I heard Rebecca yelling.

"The dead should stay dead!" she didn't care if the rest of the crew could overhead her. I gazed in the direction of the steps, the door that stood open and the flickering orange light that seeped in from the deck. Caleb didn't respond, his boots thudding closer to his quarters.

"You're a fool!" her voice screeched and I could feel her fear mixed with grief and anger. She was desperately trying to protect him, trying to save the man she'd once loved from getting himself killed in the process of trying to resurrect Mary.

I admired her for her devotion to Caleb.

"A damned fool!" Nolan grabbed hold of Rebecca's arm and pulled her flush against him when she tried to follow the Captain. She started to calm down as Caleb made his way below deck, having little to no reaction in response to her outburst.

His eyes met mine and my hand fell away from where it'd subconsciously wrapped its fingers around my necklace's anchor pendant. He paused at the bottom of the steps with his hand gripping the railing.

"Evangeline-." He began, his voice low. He was going to argue, I knew it from the way his gaze seemed to bore into me. He wouldn't give me the chance to say what I wanted to say if I allowed him to speak so I beat him to it.

"There's something I have to tell you" I wasn't sure where to start or whether I wanted to just blurt it out. His words fell silent when I took a few steps towards him.

"Ever since we met, I've been having dreams and visions about-." I searched his features then looked at the wall behind him. My gaze fell onto the bed where I'd seen him make love to her. I closed my eyes.

"Mary" her name came out in a whisper. I dreaded mentioning her. I hated the fact that I was connected to her in a way that made it almost impossible for me to be simply just be myself but most of all, I despised the way he loved her more than he could ever love me.

His hand dropped away from the railing when I opened my eyes to look at him.

"I've seen her memories of you-." I saw an image of them dancing on the Sunken Soul's deck with her head resting on his shoulder, her hand clutched gently in his as she listened to his thundering heartbeat.

"I-." I tried speaking but my words fell short as when Caleb spun her around causing the skirt of her expensive gown to flare out. She was enchanting when she smiled up at the pirate who caught her in his arms.

"I can-." she laughed at something he said, a smile making its way onto his lips when he looked at her with all the love in the world. The moonlight reflected off their skin as waves crashed in the background.

"I can feel what she felt-." I said and the image disappeared as soon as I blinked. It was replaced by Caleb's emotionless face. I felt tears streaming down my cheeks, overwhelmed by Mary's feelings.

"The love she had for you, the sadness she felt for not being able to be with you, the burning in her lungs when she drowned-." my hand moved to grip my chest. My bottom lip trembled when I paused to savor the burning sensation, allowing the grief and agony to wash over me.

"My hands feel what it felt like for her to trace your skin on the night you made love to her" I held my hand up between us, my fingers shaking. Caleb's gaze flickered from my swollen and teary eyes to my fingertips.

I lowered my hand and forced myself to regain my composure, swallowing back the next round of tears but I refrained from wiping away those that'd already been shed. They ran down the length of my nose to dangle from my chin or drip onto my chest.

"I know what the treasures mean to you-." his face grew dark, a foot moving to block the stairs as if to stop me in case I tried to run. I breathed in and clenched my fists.

"I overheard your conversation with that woman at the Pirate's Nest" I declared and my feet began to move, slowly, carefully. I wasn't moving towards Caleb or the exit. I was taking a step back as if to convey to him that I wasn't going to run.

255

"The Witch" Caleb muttered under his breath. I froze, realizing that if the woman from the tent was indeed a Witch, then the one from my dreams and visions was one as well.

Why was I dreaming of a Witch? Why was she telling me to forget and why did she have my necklace with her? I pushed the thoughts aside and nodded.

"I'm not going to run-." I reassured him, receiving a look of confusion. I could see the questions echoing through his mind. *Why would she sacrifice herself? Why did she want to die?*

"Mary's emotions are mine-." I pressed my fingertips to the center of my chest and gazed down at the carpet, too afraid to look at him as I continued.

"And her love for you is also mine" my eyes slowly began to rise from the embroidered carpet to meet his gaze. I knew he didn't feel the same way about me as I did about him but at least I could tell him, at least I could free myself from the constant burden of desire, need and adoration.

"I love you" I uttered. The tears had stopped but the trembling continued. My heartbeat thundered in my chest like a thousand beating drums that rang through my ears. Caleb simply looked at me, his hands clenching and unclenching at his sides.

"But I want you to be happy-." I took a step forward, not sure if he felt the same way or if he felt disgusted by me harboring such feelings for him.

"And if Mary makes you happy then I will do anything in my power to bring her back to you-." his eyes widened at my words. I heard footsteps approaching but I couldn't stop, I couldn't hold back anymore as tears began to well up in my eyes, blurring my vision.

"Even if it means giving my life so that she can have hers" Ben came down the steps, causing Caleb to move aside while I hurriedly wiped my tears away. Ben looked from me to the Captain when I sniffled. I took a deep breath and straightened out my shoulders to addressed Caleb.

"A few scales are nothing in comparison" his jaw tightened, causing the muscles in his face to tense when he nodded. Caleb then looked at Ben who was worried and confused.

"Fetch me some water, a knife and a jar" Caleb ordered the younger man whom I had to smile at before he reluctantly agreed and disappeared above deck.

256

I wrapped my arms around my torso, feeling vulnerable for emotionally exposing myself to the man standing just a few feet away from me. He didn't say a word and neither did I as we waited for Ben to fill the tub in the Captain's quarters. Once the tub was filled, Ben appeared in the bathroom doorway.

"It's ready" Caleb nodded and closed the door to his quarters, locking it, He stuffed the key into the pocket of his brown coat to ensure our privacy.

I took a deep breath with my eyes closed then started undoing the buttons of the red coat that I was wearing. I undid them one by one until the article of clothing fell to the floor, leaving me completely naked.

Ben quickly averted his eyes but Caleb stared at me as I headed towards the bathroom. Ben stepped aside, allowing Caleb and I through. The Captain shut the door and both men looked at my bare back expectantly as if waiting for me to change.

I glanced back at them from over my shoulder then reached up to unclasp my necklace, holding it out for Caleb to take.

He held his hand out and I let the chain bunch together in his palm. His fingers curled around it when gills started forming on the sides of my neck making it harder for me to breathe.

Ben rushed to my side, offering me his hand as I stepped into the cold water, feeling it caress my skin like the touch of a fierce and passionate lover. I sank down into it, leaning back against the metal tub with my legs extended in front of me.

I gasped in response to the cold, my eyes widening and my mouth gaping to expose my fangs. The skin on my legs began to lace together to form a tail, the fin of which was too big to fit into the tub causing it to peel over its edges. My hands grabbed onto the sides of the tub and my claws began to dig into the steel.

Ben knelt beside the tub and reached for the knife, raising it with dread in his eyes.

"I'll be gentle" he reassured me then brought the knife closer to my tail to start cutting away the scales like he'd done a million times before as a fisherman. I raised my head and felt my tail flinch.

"I want Caleb to do it" Ben froze when I held my hand out to him as if asking for the knife. He met my glowing gaze then glanced in Caleb's direction. The pirate Captain stood silent, watching as Ben handed me the knife and stepped away from the tub. I turned to face Caleb and held the knife to him.

He looked as though he was contemplating taking it then stuffed my necklace into his coat pocket and took the knife.

I laid back down and looked up at the ceiling. My eyes refused to blink as I listened to the sound of his boots thudding closer. He then knelt beside my tail.

My hands gripped the sides of the tub and I exhaled loudly, giving away how tense and anxious I was but despite that, I still didn't stop him from digging the tip of the knife underneath one of my scales. I bit my bottom lip, trying to stop myself from crying out for fear of the rest of the crew overhearing. I closed my eyes when the pain of him attempting to cut away one of my scales shot through me. I stopped breathing and I only opened my eyes when his voice pierced the air.

"The jar" Ben rushed to retrieve it, unscrewing the top and holding it out so that Caleb could drop the scale into it. The jar was filled with salt water to help preserve the scales. I watched it drop, shimmering violet in the candle light.

He still had to remove four more scales and I wasn't entirely sure if I could handle the pain.

Caleb looked at me then started cutting away another scale. My muscles tensed, the breath catching in the back of my throat along with the scream that threatened to escape. My eyes went wide, pupils dilating in response to the pain as I stared at the floorboards above. When the second scale was removed, I fell limp and my breathing came out in pants as I watched the two men through hooded eyes.

"Evangeline-." Ben whispered while inching closer to me. He reached his hand out to touch my cheek when intense pain suddenly shot through me and I sat up. My hand reached for Ben's pressing his palm over my mouth to help stifle my screams. I squeezed my eyes shut, praying for it to be over soon. Tears streamed down the sides of my face and dripped into the bloody water.

"Stop this!" Ben snapped once Caleb finished removing the third scale. I let go of Ben's hand and he moved towards the Captain with glaring eyes and flared nostrils.

"No!" I protested, looking up at Ben who peered down at me when I spoke. I was exhausted and my vision was starting to blur but I was determined to see it through.

"No" I repeated, meeting Caleb's eyes as if to tell him to continue. He ignored Ben and continued, knowing that I would endure it for him, that I would suffer through such immense pain for him. He dug the tip of the knife into my flesh and I lurched forward. My lips parted to expose pointed fangs when a shriek escaped me.

"A cloth!" Caleb ordered, stilling his movements to look at Ben. He motioned towards the sink where a cloth was dangling from it and the former fisherman grabbed it. Ben handed it to Caleb who then addressed me.

"Bite down on this" he instructed, holding the rag out for me to take. I took it with a trembling hand then stuck it into my mouth. He was trying to mask my cries which I was grateful for. I didn't want the crew to overhear and become suspicious.

I nodded when I felt like I could take the pain and Caleb continued. I screamed into the fabric, my knuckles turning white from my grip and the veins starting to stand out against my skin.

My eyes shot open, my chest rising and falling as the fourth scale was dropped into the jar. I fell back against the tub and reminded myself of why I was enduring the pain.

I loved Caleb, I loved him as much as Mary did but he loved her and could never love me which was why I had to give him the scales. He needed them in order to find all seven treasures and finally be with her again. All I wanted was for him to be happy.

I hardly felt the last scale. I was too busy crying and I was too overwhelmed by sadness to feel the pain. My mind was clouded. I was numb and too weak to react.

Once it was finally done, Ben screwed the jar's lid back on and held onto it as if he was afraid of losing it.

Caleb set the knife aside and stood to fish my necklace out of his pocket so that he could clasp it back around my neck. My tail split into two and the webbing on my hands and ears started to fade. My eyes continued to glow and my fangs remained due to me being submerged in the water.

I felt his arms scoop me out of the bloody tub to drape a cloth over me and conceal my nude form while carrying me out of the bathroom. He laid me down on the bed, not caring if my blood stained the sheets.

When he made to leave, I reached for his hand, grabbing onto it as if it was the only thing keeping me alive.

"Rest" he said, pulling away from me to head above deck. I watched him go, trying to push myself onto my hands and knees. Ben rushed to my side, placing the jar on the nightside table to help ease me back down and prevent me from following Caleb.

I began sobbing. My hand gripped the material of the pillow beneath me as Ben ran his fingers through my hair. He sat on the edge of the bed, comforting me like he'd done so many times before despite not really knowing why he was comforting me to begin with.

Chapter Thirty-Five

I woke up close to dawn. It was still dark outside when I sat up on the bed. My skin was streaked with blood and my hair appeared almost pink due to the blood's pigment.

I was alone. There was no sign of Ben or Caleb in the Captain's quarters. I decided to rid myself of the smell of iron that clung to my body. I sat on my knees on the bathroom floor, running a wet cloth over my skin repeatedly until the bucket in front of me was as red as the water in the tub. I combed my wet fingers through my hair and looked down at my reflection in the bucket.

Mary stared back at me, with pinkish hair and tired eyes that hid the urge to cry. I wrung out the cloth, using it to scrub my hair until it was white again.

I tossed the cloth into the bucket and stood before tugging an oversized gray shirt onto my small frame.

I headed above deck. It was eerily quiet with no one in sight as the ship rocked in the gentle waves that were caused by the moon's pull and the light breeze that swept over the sea.

I decided to go for a walk and scaled down the ship's side. I was no longer in any pain nor could I feel the stinging that I'd previously experienced. I walked along the shoreline, humming a simple tune at first and feeling the water lap at my bare feet as I looked up at the night sky.

"How I grinned like a fool when they said to beware of the curve in her lips and the hunger in her stare-." I sang, hearing the haunting tune of my own voice echo around me.

My lips parted to continue my song when a nearby voice from reached my ears, causing the words to catch in the back of my throat. My feet stilled their movements and eyes searched the tree line.

The voice belonged to a woman; one I knew all too well. My gaze fell onto a flickering light in the jungle where two figures danced like shadows around it.

"You have the letter?" the woman questioned, holding onto a torch which was the source of the light. I turned and started inching closer, being careful not to be seen.

"Aye, Lady Bethany will arrive back in Martin's Port two moons from now" a man replied, finishing a piece of paper out of his pocket and holding it out for Sonja to take. She quickly snatched it from his hand and unfolded it. Her blue eyes scanned the words while she held the torch closer to the letter.

"Make sure the Captain gets word of this" she ordered, handing the piece of paper back to the man. He was tall and had long black hair and orange brown eyes that were rimmed with black paint. There was an X shaped scar underneath his left eye and he was dressed in black from head to toe. He looked fierce and unpredictable.

"He'll want to see her" Sonja added and the man nodded in agreement. She turned her back to me and began pacing, thinking things over.

"He'll set sail for Port Knot and we'll have our chance, away from the crew" I pressed my back against a tree, trying to stay hidden while silently observing and listening in on their conversation. The man spoke while stuffing the letter back into his pocket.

His rings clanged together and the metal on his heavy boots made a noise when he shifted his weight.

"We'll finally be rid of him and we'll tell the crew that he was caught in bed with the lady" Sonja turned to look at the man, a brilliant smile plastered across her lips. She moved towards him, excitement clouding her sapphire gaze.

"It'll all work out in our favor" she decided to add, the deception and sinister nature of her soul beginning to show through. The man chuckled as though the thought of her madness made him lust after her like a deprived fool.

"And you, my love, will be named Captain of the Gray Ghost" she reached out to caress his cheek. Her thumb danced across it like I imagined it once had with Ben. She was a snake and a manipulator. She was always plotting, always searching for ways to get what she wanted no matter the costs.

"All we have to do is make sure that he gets to her-." I could tell from the way she spoke that Captain Darkheart and Lady Bethany had a past. I knew they either loved each other or cared deeply for one another, so much so that the Captain would set sail the moment he discovered her location just to be able to see her.

"And the guards will do the rest-." she laughed, a sadistic sound that caused the hair on the back of my neck to stand on end.

262

"Once we alert them, of course" the man tilted her chin up to capture her lips in a kiss.

I glanced at the ocean then slipped away, back in the direction of the Sunken Soul, being careful not to be seen or heard. Their laughter followed me, acting as a reminder that despite how cruel and dangerous the Red Pirate Captain was, he was still a man and all men deserved to live.

I came to a stop beside the ship. The sun was starting to rise over the horizon, casting a blue hue over the world. I was deep in thought as I stared down at the shallow waters that lapped at my ankles.

The scales would warn Darkheart, they would show him his death and the circumstances leading up to it but if I were to tell him myself, then maybe it would prompt him to hand over the gem. Perhaps my actions would show loyalty and earn Caleb his trust. I decided that the best option was for us to gain Darkheart's favor.

"Evangeline" I looked up at the man looming overhead. Caleb stood near the ship's railing examining me with golden eyes that seemed to glow beneath the brim of his hat. In his hands he held the jar of scales that he collected a few hours prior. Ben moved to stand at his side and I nodded, knowing what it meant. It was time to meet with Darkheart. I turned to head in the direction of the tree line.

I could hear boots splashing in the water, trudging through the waves to catch up with me. There were only two sets of footsteps which meant that Rebecca and Nolan had deciding to stay behind. I assumed that it was because she didn't want anything to do with Caleb's affairs anymore but I thought back to the way Sonja had looked at her in recognition and contemplated whether that had something to do with it.

The two men appeared at my sides. Caleb's eyes were glued on the pathway ahead but Ben's brown eyes were locked onto me as thoughts continued to plague my mind.

The world around us started turning a bright orange the deeper we ventured into Red Pirate territory. Once the familiar structure came into view, I stopped, causing Ben to look at me I confusion and Caleb to halt his movements. I held my palm out, eyes darting towards the jar that Caleb held in his hand.

He glanced at the jar, noticing how the scales changed color in the light and illuminated the jungle in various shades of purple. He studied me then placed the jar in my palm, deciding that because they were my scales that I should be the one to hand them over to Darkheart. I took in the colors and forms of the scales before glancing in the direction of the structure where two men stood guarding the doorway.

"Let's get that gem" I declared. My feet began carrying me up the pathway, digging into the fallen leaves, crunching twigs and stepping on small rocks. I barely noticed them as I approached the bottom of the steps, reaching out to take hold of the railing to ascend them.

The men whose faces were painted to look like the skulls pulled back the material in front of the doorway to allow me through. I stepped into the dimly lit room where men still sat drinking.

Sonja leaned up against the far wall wearing her first mate's hat. She glared at me with her arms crossed over her chest. Her sapphire eyes turned to Ben when he entered the room behind me along with Caleb.

Darkheart narrowed his gaze, glancing from one to the other until his darkening eyes came to rest on the Black Pirate Captain.

"I figured ye be long gone by now" from the way he spoke and the words he used; it was clear that he hadn't expected us to be able to find five Mermaid scales in only a single night. I held the jar up for him to see.

His eyes widened at the sight of its contents and his hands moved to grip the arms of his chair when he leaned forward.

"Five Mermaid scales" I said, causing his gaze to lock onto mine. He took a few deep breaths then sat back as if to remind himself that they could've been fake. I could sense his doubt.

"The jar" he commanded, holding his hand out towards me. I looked at Caleb. My eyes flickered from him to Sonja before my feet carried me forward. When I approached the Captain there was no fear in my eyes or heart. I was about to hand over the jar but paused.

"A fair warning-." I began. All eyes were either staring at me or the jar that I was holding which was worth more gold than all of Paris.

"There are those among your crew that conspire against you" my eyes glanced at Sonja then looked at the man she was plotting with. Darkheart followed my gaze, aware of who I was referring to without me having to mention any names.

"Me crew has proven their loyalty" he declared, refusing to believe what I was telling him like I'd expected.

Ben swallowed hard. He was anxious because of my fearless. The corner of my lips tugged upward.

"Mermaid scales allow for you to see your imminent future-." I reminded as I handed him the jar. I staying rooted in place with my mismatched eyes boring into his.

"Tell me what you see" I said then slowly began backing away, my feet taking one step at a time. Suspense filled the air around us when I came to a stop in between Ben and Caleb.

Darkheart frowned, eyeing Sonja and the man she'd been conspiring with before he held the jar out to a nearby crew member.

"Grind one up and bring me its powder" the man hurried to do as his Captain ordered. He ground one of the scales into a white powder that he then presented to Darkheart on a piece of cloth along with some wine. Sonja's arms fell to her sides when she pushed off the wall, worriedly observing from afar.

"What be this?" Caleb demanded from beside me in a whispered snarl that only Ben and I could hear. I kept my eyes on Darkheart when I replied to Caleb's question.

"Wait and see" he muttered something under his breath in annoyance as the enemy Captain poured the powder into his mouth then took a large gulp of the wine. He swished the liquid around in his mouth before swallowing loudly and handing the cup back to the man who stood waiting beside his chair.

There was a pause, a moment where nothing happened to which Darkheart looked at me with narrowed and angry eyes before they rolled back into his skull and his body stiffened. His hands gripped the arms of his chair with his head thrown back and mouth gaping.

He was gone, trapped in the vision that the scales wanted him to see.

Sonja gaped at the sight, the rest of the men watching, frightened and weary as if it was some type of witchcraft and I was the Witch.

The room was silent, not a soul dared to move or speak until the Captain would awake from his vision and convey what he'd seen.

The Vision.

Darkheart stepped into a room with white marble floors and golden curtains. A woman dressed in pink silks stood near one of the stained glass windows with her blond curls cascading down her shoulders and back.

She had an aura of power about her, the way her eyes gazed out over the ocean were like those of a queen overlooking her kingdom.

'Bethany' he breathed as if the mere sight of her knocked the air from his lungs. She turned in the direction of the familiar voice and a faint smile touched her lips when she realized that it was him after years apart.

Her hands were clasped together over her stomach and her beautiful blue eyes, as clear as the Southern sky softened.

'Alcott' she said in a gentle and kind voice. To Darkheart it was the most comforting and mesmerizing sound he'd ever heard especially when it whispered his name.

He moved towards her, took her into his arms and pressed her to his chest.

'It's been far too long' Alcott declared, leaning down to capture her lips with his.

The pirate Captain and the noblewoman had been caught in a web of lies and lust for many years. Lady Bethany was a married woman and a mother. Darkheart was a ruthless pirate who had a girl warming his bed on the many nights he spent away from his one true love. It was a love so forbidden that it would end up being the death of him.

The image shifted from the mansion room to the streets of Port Knot where Sonja was prowling the alleyways. Her chest was mostly exposed due to her scandalous attire to draw attention to herself.

She was looking for a guard, one assigned to protecting the noble family and found one stationed near the mansion's back door.

She stood in front of him, her hands placed flat against the wall on either side of him.

'Be gone wench!' the guard snapped, placing his hand firm against her chest to push her away from him. She stayed where she was, leaning up so that her lips were inches away from his beneath the iron of his helmet.

'*I come baring news*' she said, her tongue rolling seductively as she snaked one hand, up along his chest plate. His hand remained on her chest, eyes studying her with caution as if she were tiger about to lash out.

'*I hear a pirate Captain is keeping the Lady company*' she whispered, leaning closer to his ear after she finished glancing at the streets around them to ensure that no one could overhear.

'*You best see that she's kept safe*' she stepped back, her hand moving from his shoulder to tuck her hair behind her ear in order to expose the mark of a Red Pirate that'd been tattooed on the side of her face. He shoved her away from him, knowing what the symbol meant. He then entered the mansion, yelling for the guards to find the Lady.

Sonja grinned at the shut door as she listened to the sound of bells being rung in order to alert the rest of the guards before she slowly backed away and slipped into the crowd, disappearing among the people like a shadow in the night.

The white and gold room came back into view where guards poured in from every doorway, catching Lady Bethany in the pirate's embrace. The armored men tore them apart and forced Darkheart to his knees as Lord Jarrett Sillvan rushed into the room.

'*Bethany?*' the Lord questioned, taking her into his arm. His gray eyes were filled with concern when they searched her for any wounds or bruises. She seemed to be fine so he pressed a kiss to her forehead.

'*Thank the gods you're alright*' he whispered against her skin, fingers knotting into her golden curls.

Darkheart watched with narrow eyes. Envy and irritation poured from him in waves. He was about to lash out as one of the guards bound his wrists but he stopped himself. Alcott thought about the life she would have if he told Jarrett about their affair.

She would be tossed onto the streets, forced to fend for herself. She'd become a victim to the men she'd stumble across.

He bit back his words and met her eyes with longing as he was dragged out of the room. He was being torn away from her and there was nothing he could do.

The hanging platform came into view with Sonja and her partner in crime stationed among the crowd. They watched as Alcott was forced onto the stage with smiles on their lips.

The noose was tied around his neck while the crowd cheered for the death of a pirate Captain.

A man spoke up over the chants to announce Darkheart's crimes for which he was to be executed then pulled the lever. The trap door fall open and Darkheart was forced to hang until dead. The air left his lungs and his Captain's hat fell to the ground. Sonja scooped it up and placed it on top of her partner's head while laughing.

'Well done, Captain' she complimented the black haired man who chuckled and captured her lips in a kiss before they left for the Gray Ghost. They were hardly bothered by Alcott's body that swung from the noose they'd tied.

His head fell forward, his entire body went limp before he blinked and looked up at me from his chair. Darkheart was breathing hard, his chest rising and falling causing his nostrils to flare. His gaze darted in Sonja's direction then glared at her accomplice.

"Take them away" he ordered to which no one moved. The crew were unsure of what to do. When there was no response, Darkheart looked at his men and snarled through gritted teeth.

"Now!" two of his men grabbed Sonja and began dragging her out of the room, past me as she kicked and screamed.

"Feed them to the fish!" the enemy Captain bellowed, his voice echoing out around us like booming thunder.

Sonja's eyes glared at me with her teeth clenched. She lunged towards me as if she wanted to tear me apart. I watched her, hardly bothered by the threats that she spat in my direction.

Once the two traitors were escorted out of the structure, Darkheart spoke "Ye gem" a black jewel was tossed into the air. Caleb caught it in the palm of his hand and gazed down at its reflective surface. I was too busy observing the gem to realize that the enemy Captain was staring me.

"Why worn me?" he questioned as he fiddled with his rings and ran his tongue along his teeth. I looked at Caleb then turned to face Darkheart.

"Nothing I say or do could ever mend the feud between the Red and Black Pirates-." I began, searching the faces of the crowd surrounding us which included Ben's confused and worried features.

"But I can at least try to restore some form of trust between them" Darkheart breathed a breath of laughter then held his hand out towards a member of his crew who'd confiscated Sonja's first mate's hat. He surrendered the hat to his Captain who then held it out towards me.

"It seems I be in the market for a new first mate" I felt Caleb tense beside me and heard Ben's breath catch in the back of his throat. Ben didn't want me to leave, Caleb didn't want to lose his sacrifice and I, I just wanted to be with the man I loved.

"I am loyal to Caleb" I stated, about to leave when Darkheart hummed and spoke the words that caught my attention. They dragged me back into his clutches. Caleb watched me closely, his golden eyes locked onto my back.

"Why is it that ye look exactly like Lady Bethany's daughter? What be her name again? Mary?" my fists clenched at my sides. *Why did that name follow me wherever I went? Why was she like a curse nailed into my soul ever since the day I met Caleb?*

"Didn't ye die two years ago?" I took a deep breath as I stared up at the ceiling.

The Lady of Port Knot was Mary's mother. It was a new piece of information that I was grateful for but it came with even more questions. *How exactly did Darkheart know Lady Bethany? What type of relationship did they have?*

"I'm not Mary-." I repeated the words I've said millionth time before. I slowly turned to face the bearded Captain with narrowed mismatched eyes.

"I'm just an orphan girl from Port Alice" Darkheart's eyebrows lifted as he looked from me to Caleb with a glimmer of amusement in his black eyes. He began laughing.

"Looks like ye Captain has a very particular taste in women" if only it were that simple. If only Caleb wanted me like I wanted him but despite how similar I was to Mary, I wasn't her and he only had eyes for Lady Bethany Sillvan's daughter.

I met Caleb's eyes then left. I descended the steps and followed the trail back to the ship.

Chapter Thirty-Six

I was on the beach, heading towards the ship where Rebecca was waiting. Her hands gripped the ship's railing as she watched the jungle, expecting Caleb to appear at any given moment.

Despite how angry and frustrated she was with Caleb, she still cared for him, more than she could ever care for Nolan.

I was knee deep in the shallow water when something cold was pressed against my neck. I was being pulled back and away from the ship.

"Evangeline!" Rebecca's frantic voice cried out. I could hear the person's ragged breathing in my ear when they forced my head back. My hands shot up to grip the person's arm as I thrashed my legs in the water to stop myself from being dragged along.

"You should've kept your mouth shut when you had the chance" the familiar voice spat into my ear, I knew who it belonged to but before I could try and reason with her, she placed her hand over my mouth.

"For years I've been plotting against that bastard-." I wanted to yell at her. I wanted to scream that even if I didn't tell Darkheart, he still would've seen what he had but Sonja was too far gone to be reasoned with. Her hand muffled my words so that not even I could understand them. Nolan rushed to Rebecca's side to see what was wrong.

"Lass!" he exclaimed, searching for any kind of weapon to use, anything that would help get me away from Sonja but there wasn't much anyone could do with a knife pressed to my throat.

"You'll pay for what you've done" she jerked my head to emphasize her words and I squeezed my eyes shut. Tears ran down the sides of my face at the thought of lying face down in the water with my throat slit and blood starting to pool around my lifeless body.

I reached up to grip the knife's blade and tried prying it away from me. I ignored the stinging pain that engulfed me when the metal dug into my palms.

Sonja struggled against me but she was distracted by Nolan who'd climbed down from the ship and landed in the water a few feet away. Her head jerked up in his direction as blood ran down my arms.

It dripped into the water and stained my shirt. I was breathing hard and starting to grow frantic.

"Stay back!" Sonja warned. Nolan held his hands up as if to signal that he was unarmed and wasn't going to hurt her. She was like a rabid animal, afraid and desperate for a way out.

My fingers curled around the blade as I kept trying to push it away despite the pain it caused.

I couldn't die yet. I still had two treasures to find, I still had to play my part in resurrecting Mary and I still had to say goodbye to Caleb.

Her fingers parted in our struggle, exposing my mouth enough for me to speak.

"I'm not going to die here" I muttered either to life or to myself. I wasn't entirely sure which.

Sonja's wild eyes shot down to glare at me, applying even more pressure on the knife and forcing my hands back against my throat. Rebecca watched on in horror as blood pooled around us and I frantically searched for a way out. My gaze fell onto her hand that was clasped over my lips and I bit down onto it hard, tasting iron as blood pooled into my mouth. Sonja shrieked and tossed me aside. I fell into the water with my hands digging into the sand. Their wounds stung from the sea salt and the small grains of sand that found their way into the cuts.

"You...filthy whore!" she snapped, her eyes blazing when they locked onto my fallen form. She shook her hand causing blood to splatter across the sand then began advancing towards me.

"Lassie!" Nolan called out to me as he rushed over to where I was. I couldn't get up, my legs felt numb and my arms were trembling from the pain. I watched her trudge closer, raising the knife above her head, ready to plunge it into my back

I closed my eyes and waited for the impact but instead I heard something heavy falling into the water. I looked up at her, looming over me with a knife pressed to her throat.

"Not so fast, love" Caleb's voice said from behind her, his eyes meeting mine just as Nolan reached me. The Irishman knelt beside me with one hand pressed against my back and the other supporting himself in the sand.

Ben shot past Caleb and Sonja to join Nolan in the water. His hands gripping the sides of my face while his brown eyes searched for any wounds. Ben's gaze fell onto my hands that he lifted out of the water to expose the torn flesh and bone.

"She's wounded" Ben informed Caleb who then set his sights on Sonja, he leaned closer to her so that his mouth was beside her ear then spoke loud enough for everyone to hear.

"An eye for an eye then" he raised the knife and dug it into the side of her face, starting at her chin. He then slid his way upward, in the direction of her ear. She screamed and struggled against him but it was no use, he wouldn't budge. She had no means of fighting back, her knife having been dropped into the water. Caleb tossed her onto the beach with a heavy thud once he was done.

"Leave!" he snarled, glancing back at her before he started heading towards me.

Sonja struggled to get back onto her feet. Her eyes landed on the knife in the water and he shot forward to scoop it up, raising the knife to plunge it into his back.

"No!" I cried out, shoving past Ben and Nolan as I shot up, suddenly able to move when the thought of losing Caleb began tormenting me

I jumped in between him and the blade, squeezing my eyes shut and waiting for the knife to dig into my shoulder but it never did. The pain never came. My eyes shot open when my ears were met with the sound of someone chocking only to find Sonja staring at me with wide eyes as blood gushed from the corner of her lips.

I was frozen in place, unable to move when her knife dropped to the bottom of the shallow water and her hand moved to cup her bloody stomach. The liquid was already starting to soak through the fabric of her coat.

There where the wound was, an arrow, an arrow has been lodged into her flesh. Its tail was made of raven feathers and its stem was carved from oak.

I felt my legs go numb when Sonja staggered backwards, her eyes darting down to her bloody hand as her breathing changed to ragged pants. Caleb gazed in the direction that the arrow had come from to find Malcolm on the ship's deck with a bow in hand.

"Sonja?" I whispered. My head started spinning when her eyes met mine and she coughed causing blood to ooze from her lips. The blood trickled down her chin and throat. A strong hand grabbed hold of my upper arm.

"We need to go, lass" Nolan urged. His voice and touch were gentle as if he knew what was going on inside my head.

I wanted to help her. I didn't want her to die. She didn't deserve to die. Ben sat on one knee in the water, his eyes locked onto Sonja who looked at me with pleading eyes. Begging for my help.

"That crazy bastard has proven himself useful after all" Caleb muttered in Al's direction while breathing a breath of laughter as if the dying woman in front of us didn't exist. I couldn't move, couldn't breathe because my mind was too busy racing with thoughts on how to help her.

"Lassie?" Nolan questioned in concern as his eyes searched my features. This caught Ben and Caleb's attention, their gazes turning to look at me.

My throbbing, stinging hands clenched and I tore my arm out of Nolan's grasp. I rushed forward to rip the arrow out of her stomach and tossed aside.

"Trust me" I whispered while searching her terrified sapphire eyes. When I had removed the arrow, even more blood gushed from her lips and splattered across my face. I'd been in the water long enough for scales to start covering my legs and feet. My eyes were brighter than what they usually were and the pupils were on the edge of slitting with my fangs poking at the inside of my mouth.

I raised my wrist and bit into it, wanting to cry out in response to the pain. I squeezed my eyes shut and focused on sucking the blood from my wound. My body began heaved, begging me to spit it out but I couldn't, not when I needed it.

I turned to Sonja, cupped her face in my hands and press my lips to hers. I slid my tongue into her mouth to part her lips long enough to force the blood from my mouth to hers. Her eyes widened, her hands moving to push me away. She shoved my shoulders to put some distance between us but I wouldn't move until she swallowed all of the blood in loud gulps.

I broke away from her, gasping for air. I wanted nothing more than to wash my mouth out with the sea water but knew better than to do that. I ran the back of my hand over my lips to rid it of the blood that remained there.

"Get the hell away from me!" Sonja screamed but she froze when she looked down at her stomach. Her hand moved to touch the torn and bloody fabric only to find that there was no wound or pain.

273

I exposed my secret to everyone just to save the life of the woman who tried to kill me. Sonja's eyes looked up at me in realization.

"You're a-." Caleb reached me before anyone else could get to me. I felt his presence behind me, his warmth as he approached.

"Mermaid" the Captain finished for her, solving the mystery on how he'd obtained five Mermaid scales and how I managed to heal Sonja just by using my blood.

Sonja trembled, not from pain or anger but from fear as she dropped to her knees in the water. Her hands dug into the sand when she bowed in my direction.

"Forgive me, Neptune" she pleaded with the god of the seven seas. I watched her with sadness in my eyes as Caleb wrapped his arm around my waist and began coaxing me in the direction of the ship.

I spared one last glance in Sonja's direction then allowed Caleb to guide me. Nolan was still in shock but Ben followed close behind, his presence reminding me that he would protect me if anyone tried to hurt me. I was comforted by them and knew that they would protect me no matter what.

We boarded the ship with Nolan not too far behind. Caleb ordered his crew to set sail which snapped them out of their thoughts and caused them to jump into action for fear of their Captain.

Rebecca rushed over to me and reached for my hands to examine the cuts that were still bleeding. Blood dripped onto the deck as Nolan stood off to the side. He was still unsure of how to react after what he'd discovered about me.

I was led into the navigation room where Rebecca sat me down on one of the chairs. She retrieved a small wooden box from the kitchen area. Ben soon joined us with a bucket of fresh water after he helped untie the sails and raise the anchor.

I stared at my hands. The pain was nothing in comparison to the fear of what the crew might think of me now that they knew my secret.

Would they fear me? Would they think of me as a monster? Would they treat me any differently?

I was pulled out of my paranoid thoughts when Rebecca knelt in front of me and started cleaning my palms. Once they were clean, she allowed her mind to wonder. Ben was on edge as he leaned back against the table beside me, watching Rebecca's every move.

"I thought Mermaid blood can heal wounds?" she randomly muttered, catching my attention. She rinsed the cloth out in the water then reached for the bottle that sat beside her on the floor. She dowsed the cloth in wine then pressed it to my wounds causing them to sting.

I gritted my teeth, my muscles tensing as I attempted to suppress the urge to cry out.

"It can, just not our own" I responded, hoping that I could distract myself from the pain by focusing more on the conversation.

"I guess that makes you human" I stiffened but when she looked up at me and smiled, I relaxed. Her eyes flickered from my mismatched pair to my hair before she finished disinfecting the wounds and tossed the cloth aside.

"Unless you take your hair and eyes into account" she joked, laughing when I kicked her knee since I couldn't hit her. Ben began letting his guard down, crossing his arms over his chest and tilting his head back to stare up at the floorboards above.

"Yes, because those are the only things that make her odd" Ben sarcastically said as a lop sided grin made its way onto his lips. I shot him a playful glare and Rebecca laughed. She struggled to push the thread through the needle that she'd retrieved from the box that was placed on the table.

"Well, there is the fact that she can read, despite being an orphan-." Rebecca added. I laughed, knowing that sooner or later Ben would say something about my poor navigation skills again. It felt so normal that it made me smile.

"And don't forget about her inability to navigate. That truly makes her special" there it was. I threw my head back laughing but the amusement was cut short when a sharp pain shot through me as the needle was dug into my skin. I wanted to snap at Rebecca for the pain that she caused me but before I could, she continued their conversation.

"We can't not mention her strange infatuation with Caleb" she dug the needle through my skin again and I hissed. My free hand gripped the wrist of the one she was working on in an attempt to try and cut off the pain. I was attempting to stop the message from reaching my brain to no avail. Ben breathed a breath of laughter.

"You've got to be unique to care about someone like *him*" I knew he was joking and so did Rebecca which was why she smiled. Ben didn't know that she cared about Caleb just as much as I did.

I flinched away from the needle, praying for it to be over but thanking the gods that it was Rebecca doing my stitches and not Caleb since she was gentler and much more considerate than he was.

"A green tail and seaweed corset are nothing in comparison" Rebecca agreed with a nod while tying off the thread and using her teeth to sever it. She then started bandaging my hand.

"Silver, and Mermaids don't wear seaweed" I corrected her. She brushed it off, pretending not to care but from the way her eyes sneaked a peak at me, I could tell that she was curious like any person would be when meeting a Mermaid.

"Going topless does seem to be in fashion among the fish folk nowadays" the bellowing laughter that escaped Ben's lips only widened her grin. I shook my head, knowing that she was teasing me in a way that she would've done even before she knew about my tail and 'seaweed corset'

"I'm not a fish" I defended when she finished tying the bandage and started stitching my other hand.

"Of course you're not, you're only part fish" I loved moments like those, moments when I didn't feel like crying, moments when Caleb was the farthest thing from my mind, when the treasures and Mary didn't exist. Those moments made me feel like I was alive and like I wasn't about to sacrifice myself. Those moments were my distraction.

"It explains how the moron managed to get his hands on five Mermaid scales" Rebecca stated, concentrating on my hand.

The moment I so treasured was gone, replaced by the reality of things. Memories from the night before came to mind. Me lying in a tub of blood and water. The pain I'd felt was far worse than even my hands being cut to the bone.

"It hurt like hell" I said, nodding to conform her suspicions. She paused, the needle and thread stilled when she processed my words.

Ben looked away from me at the thought of having seen me in such excruciating pain. I knew he hated watching me suffer.

"Did he force-?" she began to question but I interrupted her. I knew what she was going to ask. She wanted to know if Caleb had forced me to give him the scales.

"No, I wanted to" I said as she began to stitch my wound. I winched, wanting to tear my hand away but knowing that it would only cause more harm to an already severe wound. She looked to be deep in thought.

"Those gems don't serve a righteous purpose" she felt the need to say. I knew what she was trying to say. It was her way of warning me that I was to be sacrificed.

Caleb was a desperate man. He was fierce but so filled with love and longing that it made him frantic with a need for Mary. He was grieving and in constant pain. All he wanted to do was to take that pain away, was to go back and save the woman he loved. He could only attempt to do what'd been written in the book, gather the treasures and resurrect the dead through the use of powerful witchcraft. Objects were just ordinary objects until they'd been touched by a Witch. My necklace and the treasures were all examples of that.

"I know" I breathed and she paused her stitching to looked up at me.

It was then that she realized that I knew about the true purpose behind the treasures and her eyebrows began to crease. Ben didn't know about any of it which was why I couldn't go into detail about why I was helping Caleb gather the jewels. If Ben found out, he'd go out of his way to try and stop me. I couldn't have that happening.

"I want to do it, for him" to Ben my words meant helping Caleb find and collect the treasures but to Rebecca it meant that I wanted to help bring Mary back. She didn't say anything. Her expression grew cold as she finished stitching my wounds then bandaged my hand. The room was filled with an awkward silence until Rebecca finished tying the bandage and started cleaning the mess she'd made.

"Love is a dangerous thing" she muttered while she worked. She placed the needle and thread in the box then poured herself a cup of wine.

"It can persuade people to do things they might later regret" she downed the contents of the cup then slammed it down on the table. She then reached for the bucket of bloody water and exited the navigation room to go empty it into the sea.

Rebecca left me to contemplate her words.

Could someone regret something from beyond the grave? Would I simply cease to exist or would my soul live on in a world that couldn't be reached by the living?

Chapter Thirty-Seven

I cleaned myself and wiped the blood off my face. Rebecca laid one of her dresses out for me on the bed in the Captain's quarters.

It was a violet color. The material was soft and the dress had sleeves that flared out at the elbows. The dress was short but had a modest neckline.

I slipped it onto my body and put my hair up with a clip before I made my way above deck. It was hard for me to use my hands when even the soft material of the dress had irritated them. My palms were constantly pounding.

The ship's anchor had been lowered and the crew shared stories around a fire that'd been made in an iron barrel that sat in the middle of the deck.

The sky was starting to turn a bright orange, signaling that it was time to rest and celebrate.

Ben's eyes locked onto me from across the deck. His gaze followed me up the steps that led to the stern but mine were searching for one man in particular.

Caleb was sat in front of the small table with his elbows propped up onto his knees and his hand folded together over his mouth. He was staring down at the five jewels that were splayed out before him. Red, blue, green, yellow and black. They caught the light of the setting sun, causing the colors to dance across his features.

He was alone. Rebecca was seated in front of the fire with one of Nolan's coats draped over her shoulders and a cup clutched between her palms.

"She's so close-." he muttered when he sensed my presence. His gaze didn't bother to leave the stones as he spoke, but he knew it was me otherwise he wouldn't have said the things he did.

"I can feel her" I wasn't sure how to respond. A part of me wanted to smile but another part of me felt like my time with him was coming to an end.

I only knew about Mary from what I'd heard and the visions I'd seen. She was a kind woman who cared more about Caleb than she cared about her own life, just as I did.

"I'm sure she'll be happy to see you" I whispered, moving to stand with my back to the Captain. My hands gripped the ship's railing as I gazed out onto the stretch of orange water.

I wouldn't be there to see him cup her face in his hands or press his lips to hers. I wouldn't be able to hear him whisper how much he loved her.

"The sixth jewel can be found around the ivory throat of Bakewell" I announced before he could notice the sadness in my tone. I felt his eyes on my back and wondered why I was so determined to lead him to the treasures especially when they would ultimately end up costing me my life.

"Bakewell?" he questioned. I nodded and turned so that I was facing him. I leaned back against the railing with my hands clasped together in my lap.

"Lady Lillian Cunningham wears it around her neck" I explained, motioning to my neck. It was no secret that Lady Lillian's most prized possession was her amethyst necklace that was given to her by her late mother who'd passed the title of nobility onto her.

"The Amethyst of Bakewell?" Caleb muttered and although it was a rhetorical question, I still nodded in response. He leaned forward so that his elbows were propped up onto the table.

"I've stolen many things-." he began. His eyes searched the ship and the floorboards that'd been scrubbed clean by the crew a few hours prior.

The conversation I had with Rebecca came to mind, of her telling me about Caleb's thieving days that'd lead to so much pain and destruction.

"But never a necklace from a noblewoman" I tilted my head back. I had an idea on how we could accomplish such a feat. It would require travel and acting skills that I wasn't sure either of us were capable of.

"How do ye-?" I knew what he was going to ask *'How do you expect me to do such a thing?'* so I pushed off the railing and interrupted him with my eyes boring into his golden ones.

"I have a plan" I announced. His gaze narrowed onto me with caution but there was a hint of curiosity hidden beneath it.

"But you'll have to trust me" I finished, heading for the stairs and descending them until I reached the deck with Caleb trailing behind me. The jewels were once again safely tucked away into his coat pocket.

Ben and Rebecca looked up at us when we passed, heading to the Captain's quarters. I scooped Mary's golden dress into my arms and held it up between us. His eyes caught sight of the dress and he shook his head. Caleb made to leave when he caught on to what I was getting at. I grabbed onto his wrist.

"Do it for Mary" he stilled, his back muscles tensing. My plan was for us to pretend to be a noble couple from a small town that people hardly knew of. We'd be on our way to the coast and while passing through Bakewell we'd stop to meet the Cunningham's. He realized this and he hated it. He hated anything to do with nobility because of his noble blood and what happened to his half-sister.

He breathed out through his nose and turned to look at me. He didn't say anything but nodded as he wrenched his arm away from me and slumped down on the edge of the bed. He ran a hand through his messy brown hair that was starting to come undone from its bun.

"We should start acting like nobility if we want to fool them" I announced, rolling my shoulders back and holding my chin high as if I was a lady of status.

Surely Caleb and I had enough experience with nobility to know how to imitate them.

He groaned and fell back on the bed with his arm shielding his eyes from the orange light that filtered into the room through the porthole.

I searched the dresser drawers for some clothes for him to wear then tossed the articles of clothing at him. The polished black shoes thudded onto the floor near his feet while the white button up shirt and trousers fell across his torso.

"Get dressed" I instructed as I bent to search the drawers for a pair of heels. The heels I found were gold and I froze when I realized that they were the shoes that went with Mary's dress.

I swallowed my pride and took them along with the dress.

"And fix your hair" I added on my way to the bathroom. Caleb sat up and shot me a glare. One of his dress shoes collided with the door when I shut it behind me and breathed a laugh.

I slipped out of the lavender dress and replaced it with the golden one that held so many memories, including the memories of Caleb's lips passionately capturing mine.

I pushed the thoughts aside and stepped into the shoes before exiting the bathroom. Caleb was buttoning his shirt. His trousers and shoes were already on. I reached out to help him with the buttons since he seemed frustrated and on the verge of tearing the shirt apart.

"You look like a fine nobleman" I compliment, noticing that his hair was neatly tied back at the nape of his neck but some strands just couldn't be contained as they hung down the sides of his face and into his irritated gaze.

Once I finished buttoning his shirt, he looked down at me. I was shorter than him even when wearing heels.

"Turn around" he instructed and I did as I was told. I clumped my hair together on the top of my head so that he could fasten the corset like he'd done before. He worked faster this time as if he didn't want to pause and think about it. I gasped when he tightened the corset and turned to face him when he was done tying off the strings.

"Thank you" I breathed then headed for the stairs, turning to glance back at him.

"We must learn to waltz" I explained. Cat calls and wolf whistles erupted around me when I stepped out onto the ship's deck. My bandaged hands gripped the skirt of my dress to prevent myself from tripping over the fabric.

Ben looked at me in awe then looked at the man behind me, brooding for having to wear such *absurd clothes* and act like a *snobby nobleman*

Rebecca burst out laughing at the sight of him. She nearly spat a mouthful of wine into the fire while trying to prevent herself from choking.

"I hate to spoil ye fun Captain but what be the meaning of this?" Nolan questioned while leaning back against the ship's railing with a bottle in hand and a half drunk grin plastered across his lips. Caleb's intense gaze locked onto the Irishman, forcing him to shrink back in fear.

"The next treasure just so happens to be the Bakewell amethyst" I explained. My eyes landed on Rebecca who'd managed to calm herself. She was wiping away the tears that escaped the corners of her eyes. Al was in the crow's nest, laughing manically and conversing with himself.

"And how exactly are you going to get your hands on the Lady's prized possession?" Ben questioned. The fire that flickered between us made his eyes appear to be almost as golden as Caleb's.

Rebecca chipped in with her hand gripping her thigh through the material of her skirt.

"I assume it has something to do with those ridiculous clothes" Caleb stiffened. He didn't care about the insults towards his appearance but he did care about what was being said about the dress. It was the dress he designed for Mary. I spoke up before things got heated.

"It does, we're going to steal the amethyst by pretending to be a noble couple from Hemingford" I explained. Rebecca hummed, taking a sip of her wine to try and hide her amused smile.

Ben cocked an eyebrow at the mention of the town. It was an entirely made up town.

"Hemingford? I've never heard of such a place" I stepped towards the fire and leaned across it to smile at him with a pointed finger.

"Precisely-." I then went to stand beside Caleb and linked my arm through his with my other hand coming to rest on his forearm like I'd seen the noblewomen do before.

"May I present to you, Lady Natalia and Lord Edmond Read of Hemingford" I announced, curtsying as best I could while Caleb hardly bowed. He wasn't ready to swallow his pride just yet and to put on a decent show. Rebecca snorted.

"He may be half noble but I doubt he can speak proper English-." she took another sip of her wine as I unhooked my arm from Caleb's and once again gripped the skirt of my dress.

"Let alone pretend to be a nobleman" she added to her prior statement. The Captain rolled his eyes in response to her. It was clear that he hated her bringing it up.

"I can speak proper English, mind you, I just prefer to sound like a pirate" my eyes widened when he said the word 'you'. I was so used to him replacing it with 'ye' or 'yer' that I nearly stumbled and fell. His English accent managed to seep through as he spoke.

"Good luck with that" Rebecca said, holding her cup up as if to toast to us. Nolan watched her. His eyes longed for her touch but when they turned to look at us, they were empty and clouded by rum.

"So what can we do for ye, lass?" Nolan asked, acknowledging me for the first time since he'd discovered my secret.

I felt relieved, grateful that they didn't see me any differently despite what they'd learned. I breathed in and straightened my shoulders.

"We must learn how to waltz" I declared. Nolan, Rebecca and the rest of the rest of the crew burst out laughing at the thought of Caleb waltzing.

Ben was the only one who smiled and got up from the crate he was sitting on to stand in front of me with his right hand resting on his lower back. He held the other out for me to take with a slight bow.

"My Lady" I gave him my hand and felt him curl his fingers around mine. He then pulled me closer to him and looked at the crew. They started playing a tune that had a one-two-three beat.

Ben slowly led me. His steps were in time with the music as he guided me around in circles. The crew grew silent while watching us. Ben leaned down, his lips brushing across the shell of my ear when he spoke.

"Follow me" then he began turning faster, making three small circular motions before he held me at arms-length. He then turned me a few more times only to press my chest firmly up against his. He let go, bending to hook his arms beneath my rear and turn us.

It was a dance of circles, a dance between lovers as it showed the intimacy between them. He slowly set me down with his lips just inches away from mine.

He led us towards the fire where he caught me in his arms, my torso bent and my leg lifting into the air. The skirt of my dress had crept up to my thigh and revealed my ivory, smooth skin.

The song came to an end and he pressed me to him one last time. His nose brushed over mine while his hands gripped my hips.

"Who knew the fisherman could dance?" Rebecca teased when we were left breathing hard. I glanced at Caleb, noticing the jealousy in his eyes, most likely because of the fact that I looked so much like Mary. I put some distance between Ben and I, stepping back with my hands falling to my sides.

"My grandfather taught me" Ben explained, his eyes moving from me to the redhead that sat near the fire. My fingers curled into my palms, the pain barely registering in the back of my mind as I watched Caleb shift uncomfortably. His index finger tugged at the collar of his shirt, exposing the tattoos that lay underneath.

"Will you teach us?" I randomly asked before Rebecca could reply. Ben glanced from me to Caleb then nodded, a breath of laughter leaving his lips when he decided to poke fun at me.

"Considering that you're better at dancing than navigating, yes" my eyes narrowed onto him. My hand twitched with the urge to strike his shoulder but I suppressed it, instead I walked up to Caleb and took his hand in mine.

I then led him closer to the fire where Ben and I had started our dance. I placed my left hand on his shoulder blade, finding that I had to stand on the tips of my toes to be able to reach.

He growled low in his throat then mimicked my actions, copying what he'd seen previously.

"Gentlemen" Ben said, looking at the man with the drum and the one sat beside him with an old violin. They started playing the same tune and Ben came closer. He pressed his hand against my lower back so that I stood up straighter and my chest pressed firmly against Caleb's.

"Your hands should be higher" he instructed, taking our clasped hands and raising them ever so slightly. Once our postures were corrected, Ben took a large step back and said,

"Guide her-." Caleb started moving but he was off beat. He was clumsy and nearly caused us to fall. I threw my head back laughing, the stars that loomed overhead seemed as though they were smiling down at us. They blinked in amusement.

"Again, one-two-three" Ben counted and it seemed to help at first but when it came to the spinning, Caleb stumbled again. His hand slipped down to grip my hip in order to stop himself from tripping.

Nolan chuckled and Rebecca snorted, trying her best to cover up the laugh that threatened to escape. I imagined that it was like watching an elephant trying to tip toe.

"From the start" the music began again and we managed to get through most of it. It was messy but there were few errors which meant we were getting somewhere. Ben called out over the music and the crackling of the fire.

"Look at her!" Caleb's eyes shot up from his feet to meet my eyes. His golden orbs were so comforting, so familiar and warm despite his personality.

He was generally a cold, fierce man with his guard up but those eyes depicted so much more. He was frustrated, confused and worried about whether he was doing alright.

"Not like that! Look at her like she's the love of your life, like you're a newly-wed couple!" I felt my cheeks grow a shade pinker than what they usually were.

For me it was easy to look at Caleb with that type of love since I already loved him. It would be the only time that I would be able to freely look at him in such a way.

Caleb's gaze softened and his eyes filled with something I'd yet to see. It was like he was truly in love with me but I knew better than to believe that. He was picturing Mary, looking at her instead of me.

"They make the perfect couple" a member of the crew commented to which Snaggletooth snapped his teeth and fiercely nodded his head in agreement.

When the song ended and we were left pressed up against each other, I could feel my heart hammering in my chest from the intense passion that I felt. I looked at the floor because I was too afraid to meet his gaze. I felt his stubble scratching my forehead, his breath tickling my ear and his hand holding mine.

Rebecca turned her back to us in the middle of our dance and looked out onto the ocean.

"Now all ye have to do is learn how to act properly" Nolan said. He raised his bottle with his pinky finger in the air to emphasize what he meant.

I pulled away from Caleb with my chest rising and falling. My hand gripped the necklace that dangled from my throat.

The Captain stared at me. He had a hard look in his eyes and his jaw tightened before he stormed off, heading towards his chambers. I was left standing there, feeling as though I wanted to cry.

"Evangeline?" Ben questioned, reaching out to touch my shoulder. I turned away from him and headed for the ship's bow. I wanted to be left alone. I was too distraught and the crew were too busy drinking to hear Rebecca's words that were directed at the sea.

"You see that, Mary? Our Captain's falling in love"

My eyes were clouded, foggy but there were no tears. I refused to cry over a man who couldn't love me like I loved him.

Chapter Thirty-Eight

I sat on the steps that led to the helm with the heels placed neatly beside my feet and the dress splayed out around me like a golden halo.

I rested my chin on top of my crossed arms as the crew slowly disappeared, one by one they headed below deck to rest for the day ahead but I remained. I was unable to sleep, too afraid to go below deck for fear of what Caleb might say.

I eventually stood, daring to head below deck to strip out of the uncomfortable dress that felt like a python constricting around my rib cage.

Caleb was lying on the bed with his back towards me so I figured that he was fast asleep. My hands moved to untie the dress's strings as I turned so that my back was to the bed. The dress dropped to the floor, leaving me naked while I reached for the lavender dress that was draped over the back of the desk chair.

Caleb stirred, causing my body to freeze when I turned to glance back at him. He was on his back but his head was turned towards me, blinking at me with sleep filled eyes. My nude form was only concealed only by the purple material that I tightly pressed to my chest.

"Sing to me" he groggily muttered. It was something that he hadn't asked of me in what felt like years when in truth I hadn't even known him for that long. I turned my back to him and started singing the first song that came to mind while tugging the dress onto my body.

"*Upon the raging ocean I absently did stare down by the water's shoreline where I saw a pirate lay-.*" my hand reached for the clip in my hair, undoing it so that the messy curls could dangle down my shoulders.

Caleb blinked up at the ceiling with his chest exposed and riddled with black ink from his neck down to the deep V that dipped into the black trousers that hung low on his hips. His arms were folded behind his head and his legs were crossed.

My fingers twitched when I turned to look at him, a desire to run my fingertips across his skin, over the images of anchors and swallows, of numbers, lions and roses. None of the images were in color.

I made my way over to the bed, moving slowly and cautiously. I only dared to sit down on the mattress beside him when he closed his eyes.

"My heart's been touched by Eros, I distain all number of coin; nothing can content me but my pirate Captain's joy" I finished, the notes echoing out around us like a haunting melody.

My hand reached out to run the back of my fingers along his jawline when his breathing softened. His chest began to rise and fall in time with the soft suctions of air through his parted lips. The stubble that could be found there scratched at my skin as my fingers wondered down the side of his neck until they reached his chest. The detailed artwork gave the illusion that they were real until I touched them and could feel the skin that lay underneath.

My hand lay flat against his chest, the steady beating of his heart drumming beneath my palm. It was the heart of a human not a monster.

I smiled when the memory of our first encounter came back to me. How he'd terrified me in the inn at Port Alice, how he'd asked me to sing to him and how we'd fallen asleep in the same bed.

My smile faltered as my hand slipped away from his chest to grip the sheets that I'd changed earlier that day, replacing the stained ones with new white ones.

I'd finished reading the book of the seven treasures and I knew that once we would retrieve the amethyst that the final gem would come easy and after that it would only be a short while before we would reach Port Alice.

My time with him was coming to an end and I knew it. It was like a sad love story, something that could've been written by Shakespeare himself. The orphan girl fell in love with a man who loved another then she died just so that they could be together, always putting others before herself.

My eyes landed on the heart shaped locket that sat on the nightside table beside the bed and the book beneath it. My hand reached out to retrieve the leather bound diary.

It was a fitting end for an orphan, I thought when I stood and deciding that if I was going to die then I would do whatever it took to find the gems.

I left the Captain's quarters with the book. I stepped out onto the deck and tugged the heels back onto my feet as I took a stand on the far side of the deck where I placed the book on the top of my head.

My shoulders straightened and I raised my chin with my arms extended at my sides. I took a few steps, one foot in front of the other before the book tumbled onto the deck. I bent to pick it up and returned to my starting position to repeat the action.

The world around me began to shift as I walked. It was replaced by the scene of an empty ballroom where sunlight poured in through open windows as a pompous old bird stood nearby. She watched me walk with a sneer on her face.

'Straighten those shoulders!' she barked. I jump and stood up straighter, attempting to keep the books on top of my head while I recovered from her loud outburst.

I wanted to glare at her but I decided against it since it was unladylike. I took a few more steps then stumbled in my heels, causing the books to clutter onto the marble floor.

'Focus Mary Grace!' I flinched in response to my full name coming from her lips. When she spoke, spit flew and when she walked it was like watching a wooden puppet try to move.

I huffed and knelt to pick up all five books so that I could start again.

I despised the woman but my mother had insisted that she teach me how to keep a proper posture. I stood up straight with the books balanced on top of my head as my eyes stared ahead at a wall of mirrors and my reflection that looked back at me.

I was around ten or so, dressed in a puffy blue gown with my golden curls twisting down my shoulders. They had been curled in preparation for my ballet classes that were soon to follow my current lessons.

'Begin' the woman instructed and I did as I was told. My reflection began to shift as I walked until a young woman in dark navy stood before me. She moved with the books stacked high on top of her head as if it was second nature. She could probably dance with them and not let a single one drop.

I blinked, the book falling onto the Sunken Soul's floorboards. I knew that it was one of Mary's memories but the fact that it felt so real, as if I'd been there myself was what left me breathless and trembling.

I looked at my feet and kicked the heels aside so that I could start dancing. I moved as though I'd done it a million before but I only had her memories to go off of.

I was in the same ballroom. A young man with glasses stood watching me as I spun around on one foot a few times. I began spinning faster, my foot bobbing up and down while I raised my arms high above my head. I eventually came to a stop with one leg raised high into the air and my toes pointed. I spun again until I was upright then ran and jumped, pulling my legs apart in mid-air before landing. I was amazed by how flexible my body was.

Allegro, batterie, cambré, pirouette were all terms that suddenly made sense to me as a seven year old girl who was forced to take ballet classes. My mentor applauded my routine once the pianist stopped playing and I was left standing on the tips of my toes, frozen like a concrete statue.

I in turn was left standing on the ship's deck in the exact same position.

Mary's memories merged with mine. They helped me as if she was trying to teach me how to be as noble as possible in order to retrieve the jewels so that she could be revived.

I took a seat on the steps that led to the helm and raised my hands. My fingers began beating down onto air but I could see her, a young girl with golden curls and mismatched eyes who sat behind a grand piano. Her small fingers moved in time with mine as our beautiful song filled my ears.

We were one, the noblewoman and the orphan girl. My eyes were shut as I listened to the song that only I could hear.

'Don't rush the notes' a voice so comforting scolded and my eyes shot open both in the ballroom and on the ship.

Mary stopped playing. Her big, curious eyes looked up at the most beautiful woman she'd ever seen, her mother, Lady Bethany Sillvan. My own eyes only met with an empty deck and the waters beyond it that were dark and bleak.

The Lady of Martin's Port was said to be the most skilled pianist in all of England which was why she'd taken it upon herself to teach her daughter how to play.

By the age of twelve, Mary could play anything from Bach to Beethoven and even Mozart. She was a truly talented girl.

I crossed my arms on my knees when leaned forward to rest my chin on top of them.

Mary was such a wonderful young woman. She was able to do things that I could only dream of. She could sow, dance five different

289

styles, speak three different languages that included French and Latin. She knew all the capital cities of the world and had performed in numerous plays.

I sat there with a warmth in my heart, a confirmation that sacrificing myself was the right thing to do. I was just an orphan girl, just a Mermaid who preferred the land to the sea but Mary, she was so much more. She was capable of making the world her playground and capture the hearts of men from far and wide.

She deserved to live more than I did. She could make everything around her beautiful and bless Caleb with the most beautiful and talented children.

I smiled sadly as the sky began to grow lighter. I had no recollection of how long I'd been sitting there but I knew that it had to be at least a few hours.

Chapter Thirty-Nine

By morning, the crew set sail for Killian's Coast, heading North towards England.

Ben was attempting to teach me how to waltz on the ship's deck while Caleb loomed overhead, behind the helm. He wore his old boots and red coat with his black Captain's hat shielding his eyes from the sun.

Rebecca sat on the stern's railing as she observed the two of us, turning and spinning below.

"You're robbing her of a future" Rebecca muttered. She was unaware of the fact that I could overhear her conversation with the Captain. Her narrowed gaze locked onto him as if scolding him like she did when they were younger. Caleb's grip on the helm tightened.

"What she does with her life is her choice" came his low response. I tried focusing on the steps that my feet took in an attempt to keep up with Ben but accidentally tripped. Luckily, I managed to recover before I could fall or step on Ben's toes.

"But would she have had a choice if she didn't know about your plans?" Rebecca shot back. I knew she was referring to the jewels, to me being a sacrifice in order to resurrect Mary.

Caleb growled, his eyes staring straight ahead at the water beyond the ship.

"She does know and is eager to find the treasures" he jerked his head in my direction. I'd been up all night practicing and the first thing I asked Ben when he woke up was for him to help me waltz.

Rebecca turned and hopped off the railing so that her eyes could glare up at Caleb.

"But if she didn't. Would you have forced her onto that platform, slit her throat and left her to bleed out just so you could bring Mary back?" I mistook a step, causing my ankle to twist. I yelped and grabbed onto Ben for dear life. Caleb's eyes were on me within seconds but his worry was for nothing. Ben eased me down onto a barrel and removed my shoe to examine my foot closely.

"It's not that badly injured but it might be best to take a break" I nodded. Ben's attention was stolen from me by Nolan yelling for him to help replace the empty barrels on the deck with full ones. He shot me a smile.

"When I'm done, we'll pick up where we left off" I watched Ben go then looked at my ankle. My fingers pressed at the skin to feel for any pain other than the sharp one I'd felt while spraining it. It wasn't hurt too badly and I knew I'd be able to walk again within a quarter hour or so.

As I watched the crew members lift heavy barrels and carry them below deck, I found myself recalling Rebecca's words about Caleb murdering me for Mary's.

"I would never force her" My ears perked up in response to Caleb's voice. He was irritated. My head turned to glance up at them. Rebecca hummed while her hands gripped the railing on either side of her.

"Because you fell for her-." My eyes shot down to the Sunken Soul's deck. I was afraid that they'd catch me watching and stop having their conversation.

Was she teasing him? Was she making things up? He only loved Mary and I was just a tool for him to get to her.

"She's not Mary-." Rebecca cut him off with a sly smile plastered across her lips. She knew him better than he knew himself and he was well aware of that.

"But you didn't fall for Mary this time, you fell for Evangeline-." she paused to look at me. I pretended to be smiling at Ben who was struggling with a particularly heavy barrel. The former fisherman shot me a grin before he breathed a laugh and shook his head.

"You just can't admit it for fear of what Mary might think" if what she was saying was true then it only gave me more reason to die so that Mary may live. Living a life constantly worrying over what the dead might say or think was not a life anyone deserved.

"Well Mary's dead and Evangeline is here. She's willing to give her life for you-." my body stiffened.

Why would she say such things? Did she want him to forget about Mary? Did she think he could actually be happy with just me?

I clenched my teeth and reminded myself that he could never truly be happy without her.

"But you're so obsessed with the dead that you can't see what is right in front of you" I wanted to tell her to stop, that it was no use. I knew he could only ever love Mary and something inside of me was alright with that. I'd come to terms with my fate. Caleb struck the helm with his hands and leaned closer to the redhead.

"Ye best leave" he warned her and she smiled before turning to leave. It was then that she paused to glance back at him from over her shoulder.

"You better start talking like a nobleman if you're going to have any shot at retrieving the jewel" with that she descended the steps, leaving him brooding and uttering things to himself under his breath.

When she reached the deck, our eyes met and I realized that she was aware of me listening in on their conversation. Ben approached me.

"Lady Read" he mockingly addressed me with a slight bow. He was requesting a dance from me.

I slipped the heels back onto my feet and stood when I took his hand. I allowed him to lead me around the deck in circles, moving in time with a tune that he hummed off by heart.

"Dock the ship!" Caleb bellowed when we approached a small town a few miles out from Killian's Coast.

The place looked almost deserted. It only had a bar, an inn and some street markets. Everyone else seemed puzzled as to why we were docking there but Rebecca had a knowing look in her eyes. Once the anchor was lowered, Caleb made his way to his quarters but paused to address Rebecca.

"Dress her" he instructed, his head jerking in my direction before his golden gaze met mine for a split second.

My eyebrows were furrowed up in confusion when Rebecca grabbed hold of my upper arm and led me below deck to her room. She escorted me inside the room and shut the door behind us to start rummaging through her closet.

"Something provocative, short and eye catching" she muttered mostly to herself as she compiled an outfit on the bed beside me.

There was a brown corset with no under shirt, a short skirt compiled of many different colored fabrics along with a pair of brown boots.

She instructed me to strip and I took my time to peal the lavender material from my body until it fell into the thin layer of water by my feet.

Becca inspected the skirt before tossing it to me. I caught it, the messy cluster of rags slipping through my fingers.

293

"Put it on" I stepped into it and tugged the band up to my hips.

She took the corset and moved towards me, tugging it over my head and onto my torso when I instinctively raised my arms. Rebecca started pulling on the strings and I gasped with my hand pressed firmly against my stomach.

I hated wearing tight and constrictive clothing but knew that Caleb had a plan and I trusted him enough to go through with it.

She finished tying the strings and when I looked down all I could see were two mounds of white flesh. The amount of cleavage that stared back at me made me feel dizzy or maybe it was the corset that was designed to stop a woman from breathing? I wasn't sure.

"Why do I have to dress like this?" I asked when she place my foot inside one of the boots. She tied its laces then moved to do the other foot. Her fingers worked skillfully as if they'd tied and untied the knots a thousand times before.

"When we were younger, I used to help him steal coinage from the tavern where I worked-." I sucked in a breath, knowing that it had something to do with why I was dressed so provocatively. The shirts and coats that I usually wore weren't any less concealing but at least my breasts didn't threaten to burst through the seams like they were at that moment.

"He would have me dress like this to distract men so that he could make off with the money before anyone even knew he was there" she returned to the closet to pick up a piece of cream material and wound it around her hands. It seemed soft, like silk and when she slung it around my waist, I could confirm that it was indeed made of silk.

"He wants me to help him steal money?" I questioned while she played with my hair. She made sure that the curls fell just right. I felt like a bird trying to attract a mate by placing myself on display.

"He needs money if he is to buy Lady Read some expensive dresses" she explained. I sighed heavily when she reached for the makeup that sat on the desk in the corner. She began to pat my lips with ground up cherries and used some on my cheeks to make it seem like I was blushing.

"Why can't you be the one to help him?" I questioned. She had more experience. Rebecca glanced at me with smiling eyes and a grin plastered across her lips.

"Because-." she began while applying white powder to my face. I scrunched up my nose in response to the feeling of my face being covered in something.

"Men enjoy something a bit more innocent" it was true. The thought of a virgin girl with no experience when it came to men was appealing to them but I would only make a fool of myself by acting like I knew what I was doing.

"It's light out-." she began to explain while putting away her makeup. She picked up a fake red flower that she stuck into my hair after brushing the strands back with her fingers.

"Which means that less men will be at the bar and they'll most likely still be sober-." I tugged at the bottom of the skirt, wanting it to conceal my private parts more effectively. I felt like a harlot about to go out and sell herself off to the highest bidder.

"It'll take more than just a fiery redhead to distract them" she was anything but *just a fiery redhead*

Rebecca was beautiful. She was a woman who could hold her own and she wasn't afraid to speak her mind. She was so much more than what I could ever hope to be but I was going to try my best.

"Caleb needs a sweet, innocent little girl who blushes and gets easily embarrassed" she laughed then turned to exit the room with my hand in hers.

He most certainly got what he wanted. I was more embarrassed than I'd ever been before, especially when we stepped out onto the deck and all eyes were on me. Wolf whistles and cat calls sounded as I tried my best to conceal myself. I wrapped my arms around my chest, trying to hide my breasts that were on display.

Ben refused to look at me. He stared at the floor with a slight tint across his cheeks whereas Nolan began to snap at the rest of the crew.

"Get ye hungry eyes off the lass, ye filthy dogs!" he yelled and tossed a cup at one of their heads. Al appeared in front of me, dangling upside down from the ropes. His eyes locked onto mine.

"Hello trollop" he said with an upside down grin which made it seem as though he was frowning.

I jumped and took a step back when he began to cackle sadistically. The word he used registered in the back of my mind *'trollop'* meaning a woman who slept with men for payment but before I could respond, he was gone. He crawled back into his crow's nest to yell at the sky.

"She's ready and waiting, my lord" Rebecca announced when Caleb approached. He was dressed in a pair of trousers, his old boots and a loose fitted shirt. His hat and coat were gone and for a moment it felt like I was staring at the younger version of Caleb, the seventeen-year-old boy who tried to steal from a pirate but failed.

Rebecca curtsied low, gripping the long skirt of her dress in mocking humor.

"Stop playing games" he bit out. Caleb's words were directed at the redhead. She grinned but stood upright to enlighten him. He stepped towards me and took in my attire. I wanted to jump out of my skin at how belittling it was to have the one you love see you in such a state.

"You'll enter the bar, pretend to do business then I'll buy you and we will leave" his instructions were in proper English that I hadn't heard him use before.

I swallowed hard but nodded. He locked eyes with Rebecca.

"Send her in after a few minutes" with that he was gone. He leaped down the side of the ship and headed in the direction of the bar that sat on the other side of the beach.

I was afraid and unsure of what was to come but I knew that as long as Caleb was there that I would be safe. He would protect me even if it was just to use me as a sacrifice later on.

Chapter Forty

A few minutes passed before Rebecca instructed me to enter the bar. She was stationed outside as an extra set of eyes in case something went wrong.

She explained to me how women usually conveyed that they were harlots looking for money and how to move in order to seduce men.

It was all too much for me to comprehend but I swallowed my fear and stepped into the tavern. Three men sat off to the side as a man worked behind the bar and Caleb sat in front of him.

The Captain's eyes barely glanced in my direction while pressing the edge of his cup to his lips with his head down and shoulders hunched. I brushed out my skirt's wrinkles and started in the direction of the three men.

They were dirty and smelt strongly of sweat. They laughed among themselves and were drunk which played to my advantage. I cleared my throat and leaned over the table, making sure to shove my breasts in their faces like Rebecca suggested.

"Hello boys" I purred. They picked up on my uncertainty and grew silent to watch me. One narrowed his eyes while another took a swig of his drink "What do you want doll?" he asked.

I glanced around the bar, acting as though I was about to tell them a secret that I couldn't bare anyone else overhearing.

"I'm in need of money" I replied and locked eyes with the man who was glaring at me. Rebecca said to single one out and use him to get to the others. Jealousy, she said, was like a wild fire. It spread quickly.

"We don't pity beggars" the glaring man with a long gray beard and a scar that ran across one eye snapped. He downed the rest of his drink and slammed the cup onto the table. It shook and I flinch in response to the loud bang.

"I'm no beggar, sir. I intend to work for my money" I reached across the table to comb my fingers through his beard while my chest. The hairs felt like wire and a layer of grease started coating my fingers. I ignored it and licked my lips.

The man I'd signaled out seemed to be the most annoyed. He grabbed hold of my wrist to stop me from combing his beard. I yelped.

The small squeak drew a rumble of laughter from him as he tightened his grip on my wrist. The constriction caused my wounded palm to throb.

"Well would you look at that-." he began as he stood and walked me over to the wall that was opposite the bar. My eyes searched for Caleb in a panic but he wasn't looking at me.

"A virgin desperate to sell herself off" *he could tell that I was one just by my reaction to him grabbing me?* I winced when he shoved me up against the wall. My hand started going numb from lack of blood flow.

"I bet you've never even been touched by a man like this before-." he said. His face was so close that I could smell the rum in his breath.

"Have you, sweetheart?" he was taunting me, trying to get a reaction out of me. My eyes locked onto Caleb from over the man's shoulder. The man tightened his grip on my wrist which caused me to cry out.

"I asked you a question!" my knees began to buckle and my body sank closer to the floor when he pulled my hand high above my head. I was like a puppet being held up by a single limb, a thread. I was terrified.

"N-No!" I managed to get out which made his smile grow wider as his friends got up from the table to join him. They stood with their backs to Caleb as they pressed me further into the wall. The force knocked the air from my lungs.

"You must be desperate if you're willing to stoop so low as to spread those pretty white legs of yours" he was pressing himself against me. His leg moved to part mine and his knee rubbed against my core. I felt like crying but I looked away when my eyes starting clouding over. I couldn't look at him. Just feeling him was painful enough but seeing the hungry look in his eyes would be too much for me to bare.

"No raping in my bar!" the bartender announced. His gaze was hard and he was annoyed as he dried a glass that he'd finished washing. He didn't care about the girl being pinned up against the wall or the men threatening to rape her, he just didn't want it happening in his place of business.

"Take it outside!" he added. I began to struggle and wiggle against the man pinning me in place. His beard tickled the side of my face when he chuckled and leaned closer so that his lips brushed against the shell of my ear. Bile rising in the back of my throat when I choked out a cry.

"Isn't this what you wanted?" he whispered in a tone that caused tears to stream down the sides of my face. This seemed to only amuse him more.

"I promise to pay you for your efforts" with that I heard his free hand fumbling with the buckle of his belt. I struggled harder, wanting to free my wrist from his forceful grip.

"No, no please!" I begged. I looked at Caleb's back. I wanted to call out to him, to beg for help but my voice was cut off when the man on top of me let go of my wrist. He grabbed onto my throat and shoved my head back into the wall. I was gagging and my hands were clawing at his. I was desperate and afraid.

"I said, no raping in my bar!" the bartender slammed the glass down on the counter in front of Caleb and approach us. I couldn't speak, couldn't scream, all I could do was make gurgling sounds. The wheezing and gasping mixed together in my ears. My eyes widened as they stared up at the ceiling.

'Caleb' I thought. My inner voice was soft and almost nonexistent.

The bartender was bigger than the rest. He gripped the shoulder of the man who had me pinned to the wall and tore him away from me. I crumbled to the floor with my hand gripping at my throat and gasped as my vision began to blur.

"You know the rules, Mack" the bartender was saying as my eyes searched for Caleb. He was leaning over the bar to grab two bags of coins and stuffed them into a much larger leather one that he'd most likely stolen on his way to the bar.

He rose from his seat with the bag slung over his shoulder and made his way towards us. I felt like running to him, like throwing my arms around his neck and burying my face in his shoulder while I sobbed but I didn't move. Tears dripped onto my bandaged hands and the wooden flooring beneath them.

"I'll rightfully purchase her maidenhead" Caleb declared. He interrupted the argument between 'Mack' and the bartender. He looked at the owner of the establishment then added with a smirk.

"And take it elsewhere" the bartender seemed to agree with that and stepped away. He nodded and he returned to his place behind the bar. Mack glared at me and snorted through his nose like a bull.

"Name your price, whore" I flinched. The last time I'd heard the word was when it came from Caleb's drunken lips. I could feel myself starting to lose my restraint. My eyes were starting to glow and my fangs were probing at the inside of my mouth. My hands balled against the wood to hide the claws that were starting to form.

"Three-." I panted "Gold coins" I knew it was a price that no ordinary man could pay but Caleb must've had that much money if he'd just robbed the bar. I could see him glancing at the bar. He was signaling to me that we needed to leave before the bartender realized his money was gone.

The three men burst out laughing.

"What type of man would pay such a price, even for a virgin?" I gripped the table beside me and started pulling myself onto my feet. My legs trembled beneath me while Caleb reached into his bag and held up three gold coins.

"I would" he declared to which the men looked at him like he was insane. That much money could buy someone enough booze to last a year. I looked at Caleb. My eyes weren't glowing anymore and my fangs were starting to disappear.

"You can have the wench and her golden twat" Mack snapped. He then turned and sat back down at their table. I reached for Caleb's arm and slumped into him. I felt as though I was going to pass out at any given moment.

We left the bar and Rebecca rushing to help steady me on our way back to the ship. My wrist was a dark purple and my throat had lighter green and yellow bruises that were already starting to form.

"Raise the anchor!" Caleb ordered as soon as we set foot onboard the ship.

I slumped down on a crate while Rebecca knelt at my side and the crew scurried about around us. I was shaking and my cheeks stained with previously shed tears.

Once the ship was out on the open ocean, Rebecca grabbed hold of Nolan's shirt as he passed.

"She needs water" the Irishman looked at me then nodded and disappeared. Rebecca started untying my boots.

My hand was still gripping my throat. I was unable to comprehend what was going on around me as I tried to stabilize my breathing.

Ben noticed the state I was in and approached me. At first, he looked like the man from the bar and when he reached for my wrist I pulled away. I crawled back until I was pressed up against the ship's railing. My eyes were filled with a mixture of fear and shock as I stared at him.

"Evangeline?" his voice met my ears and the image of Mack starting fading away until it was replaced by Ben who I knew would never hurt me.

I started relaxing and held my wrist out for him to see. He gently took my hand and noticed that blood was seeping through the bandages around my palm. My wrist was a deep shade of purple. It was swollen and sensitive.

"Who did this to you?" he demanded. His eyes narrowed onto Caleb who stood behind the helm with the bag and stolen money near his feet. Ben's hands gently undid the bandage to reveal that a few of my stitches had come undone due to my struggling against Mack.

"A man, h-he tried to-." I couldn't form the words without wanting to cry. Rebecca watched me carefully as my free hand moved to grip the fabrics of my skirt and I squeezed my thighs tightly together. She knew exactly what happened just from observing me and stormed her way to the stern.

"You were supposed to protect her!" she snapped at the Captain while pointing an index finger in his direction. Ben was still trying to understand what had happened but he knew that it couldn't have been good judging from Rebecca's anger. Nolan returned with a cup of water in hand and held it out for Ben to take before he hurried after the redhead. He stepped in between her and Caleb.

"She's hurt because of you!" she yelled, catching everyone else's attention. Ben passed the cup to me and I took it with my non bruised hand. I took a few small sips of the water.

"What if they'd gotten what they wanted?" I squeezed my eyes shut. I was too afraid to think about the possibility of being raped in that bar by a man who enjoyed seeing me in pain. Nolan wrapped his arms around Rebecca's torso and began dragging her away from the silent Captain.

"That's enough, lass" he tried to reason with her but she was furious and her nostrils were flaring. I felt a hand gently grip my chin between its thumb and forefinger. My eyes opened to stare up at Ben who tilted my head back so that he could take a closer look at my neck.

301

"What is done, is done" Nolan argued. Rebecca clenched her teeth. Her chest rose and fell rapidly as she stared at Caleb. Her anger made me realize that she truly did care about me as a friend.

"Ye can't change what happened" Nolan was right. It was done and there was no changing it. Ben placed his hand on my thigh and I jumped, winching as if I was in pain. He tore his hand away from my skin and met my eyes with furrowed brows.

"No-." he breathed when the realization overcame him. I wouldn't normally have reacted that way and that's how he put the pieces together. He puzzled my words together with my reactions.

"He wouldn't let you-." he muttered with his hands dangling beside him. I looked away. I couldn't look into his brown eyes that cared so much about me.

"He wouldn't-." he couldn't even manage to form the words as he stared at me. The cup of water cluttered to the floor when he stood and started making his way to the stern. I trembled, squeezed my eyes shut and pressed my injured wrist to my chest. Al cackled and Snaggletooth snapped his teeth together.

"Ben!" a loud thud rang and my eyes shot open to find Caleb's head turned to the side. Blood trickled from the corner of his lips and dripped out of his nose. Ben was stood in front of him with his knuckles red from the blow.

"You bastard!" I'd never seen Ben so angry. I didn't think, I just reacted. I shot up from the crate to rush up the stairs to the stern. Caleb didn't move, he didn't even try to glare at Ben.

"She could've been raped because of you!" Ben raised his fist to swing again but froze when I appeared in front of Caleb with trembling legs. Rebecca was stood emotionless while Nolan held her at bay but there was no one to restrain Ben.

"Evangeline-." he began in a tone that was darker than the one he normally used.

"Move" I took a wider stand and raised my arms on either side as if to shield the Caleb, the man I loved. I shook my head. My eyes were blurry with tears that threatened to escape and my lips quivered.

"I won't let you hurt him" I declared which surprised everyone apart from Caleb who hardly moved.

Ben's gaze roamed over my body, moving from the large scar on my calve to the one on my upper arm. He looked at the bleeding slash on my palm and the bruises on both my wrist and neck.

"Look at you-." he breathed. There was a sadness in his words as his clenched fists unwound themselves at his sides. He looked like he was in pain because of how pathetic and useless he felt.

"Ever since *he* brought you onboard this ship, pain has been all you've known" he placed emphasis on the word 'he' when he jerked his head towards Caleb.

My hands clenched and I squeezed my eyes shut as I listened to him speak. In a way it was true. I'd experienced more physical and emotional pain onboard the Sunken Soul than I had in my entire life but there were still things that outweighed the pain.

"That's not true-." I argued, feeling the man behind me stiffen. Rebecca looked ready to lash out like a cobra. She loved Caleb just as much as Mary and I did but I was certain that she'd try to murder him in his sleep for what he did to me.

"I've known kindness, friendship and love-." the last word came out as a low whisper that only Ben, Caleb and I could hear. I could feel my chest starting to tighten. My throat was closing up and it becoming difficult for me to speak.

"I've seen things that people can only dream of. I've met people who mean the world to me, people who scare me, people who care about me-." when I raised my eyes to look at Ben, I was crying. Tears flowed down my cheeks to my chin.

Ben's eyes widened at the sight of my glowing irises. I no longer needed to hide who I was. My pupils were slit and scales formed where my tears touched my skin.

"I am grateful for the things this ship has brought me and I wouldn't trade them for anything!" my fangs were large and protruding when I yelled those words.

Having been on the Sunken Soul gave me a story to tell, friends to remember and memories to treasure. If I were to die it would be with a smile on my face and the ship's crew standing around me. I wanted nothing more.

"Lassie" Nolan breathed out moments before I collapsed. Caleb's arms caught me and pressed me into his chest as I was dragged down into the darkness.

The shock from the bar and the conflict that followed had taken its toll on my body.

I couldn't stay awake. I couldn't keep fighting when all I wanted to do was let go. So I let go.

303

Chapter Forty-One.

I woke up in the Captain's quarters. Daylight was still pouring into the room which meant that I hadn't been unconscious for too long. My hands, wrists and throat were bandaged and I wore the lavender dress from before.

I sat up so that my feet dangled over the side of the bed as I inspected my hands. The bandages made it look like I'd been mauled by an animal. I could feel the slashes hidden beneath them, the bite mark where I'd sucked my blood to give to Sonja and the bruises that had been left by Mack.

I heard what sounded like people talking and seagulls crying out as heavy crates were being loaded onto ships.

I slipped my boots onto my feet and rose from the mattress to head above deck. I stopped when the image of a coastline in the shape of a semicircle came into view. Buildings stretched on beyond the docks that were being trafficked by men who were loading objects onto the ships. Some were even unloading the ships. They wheeled large barrels and crates into a warehouse that towered over the docks. Its large doors stood opened while fisherman prepared their crates with ice.

I looked up at the blue sky overhead to find white birds circling above. Their cries so familiar to my ears since I'd spent most of my life near the ocean. A salty breeze blew against my face and caused the material of my dress to tangle around my legs.

Killian's Coast was a well-known shipping port. It was a place that was rich in coin and work.

The crew scaled the ship's sides, readying it to be docked. The grinding of the anchor's chain reached my ears when it was lowered along with the whipping of the sails as they were raised. I could hear the thudding of heavy boots on wooden planks and the yelling of men communicating both on and off the ship.

"Man the ship!" a voice bellowed from beside me. It snapped me out of my daze and drew my attention onto the Captain that was dressed like a commoner.

He wore the same old shirt, plain trousers and boots that he had earlier that day.

"We're going shopping" he informed me while holding one of the coin bags up for me to see. It jingled when he began walking in the direction of the plank that the crew had set up for us to depart the ship. I rushed after Caleb. His bottom lip had a cut and dried blood was still visible there.

"You're hurt" I declared. I hurried down the plank and stood in front of him to block his path and prevent him from getting away. I reached out to trace the side of his face with my index finger. The finger gently caressed the wound.

"Blame that bloody lap dog of yours" he bit out and tore his face away from my hand when a sharp pain shot through his lip in response to my touch. I instantly felt guilty when I thought back to Ben hitting him.

"I'm sorry" I muttered before starting in the direction of the buildings. I kept my eyes peeled for a dress shop or a tailor. Caleb grunted then caught up to me. He gripped the bag in one hand while the other dug itself into the pocket of his trousers.

"It's not your fault" I nearly tripped when he said that. The emotionless pirate Captain spoke words of sympathy and he spoke them in proper English.

We reached a small area that seemed to be surrounded by shops. A few dressed mannequins stood outside the windows of one of them. They beckoned us in with a sign that hung above the door and had the word 'welcome' painted on it in green letters.

Caleb reached for the handle and held the door open for me to step inside like a true gentleman. I knew it was all an act and that our performance as nobility was about to begin. I straightened my shoulders and surveyed the shop as I stepped inside.

It smelt stuffy and dresses lined the far wall while suits lined the one near the door. There was a platform off to the side with a full length mirror in front of it. It was where the tailor or seamstress would take the customer's measurements.

Caleb rolled down the sleeves of his shirt to hide his tattoos since it was frowned upon by nobility. The bell chimed behind us and as if she was summoned a young woman came scurrying out from the back.

"Welcome" her bubbly voice sang. Her hands were neatly folded in her lap and a brown dress hid most of her skin. Her brown hair was tied back and covered by a piece of gray cloth that had been folded around her head. Small, square glasses sat on the tip of her nose.

"Hello" I greeted politely while nodding. My eyes scanned the wall of dresses and took in the various colors of the fabric. Some of the material appeared to shine in the light that flooded in through the windows and glass door.

"There are certainly a few lovely pieces" I said as if speaking to my husband whom I'd known for most of my life. Caleb's hand pressed against my lower back. He'd tucked the bag of coins away in his pocket.

"Feel free to try on as many as you'd like" he said while forcing a smile. I nodded and approached the dresses. I skimmed through them while Caleb took a seat in a chair near the measuring platform. The woman joined me but her eyes widened when they landed on the orange dress that I was considering.

"Oh goodness, no!" she exclaimed. She laughed as she tucked the dress away and retrieved a green dress. The green was a much lighter shade than emerald and softer in comparison.

"This will look much better with your skin tone-." she explained while holding the dress up as if imagining me in it. She handed it to me then continued searching through the many dresses.

"It's better to stay away from bright colors as they'll only drown you out" I nodded. I thought back to the emerald dress that Deacon had wanted me to wear. I remembered how pale I looked and glanced down at the dress she picked. The lighter shade of green seemed almost perfect for my complexion.

"How about maroon? Hazel? Violet? Auburn?" she rambled while handing me each of the dresses. I felt like I was drowning in a rainbow of fabrics as they weighed me down.

Once she was satisfied with her picks, she took the dresses and escorted me to a private room in the back where I could change into them. First was the violet dress that was most similar to what I was wearing. The purple was a few shades darker than lavender and even darker purple flowers decorated the skirt.

The woman helped me onto the platform and I turned to take in my reflection. The dress had short sleeves and a sweetheart neckline that gave it a modest appeal.

"The color suits you" the woman commented while Caleb examined it. Of course it suited me. It was the color of my tail when the light would hit it just right.

I turned to see the back. Dark purple strings tied off the corset and a white train split the back of the skirt in half. I liked it but it didn't matter what I thought about it. Caleb's opinion was all that matter to me. He stood and reached out to touch the mesh layer that was draped over the skirt. It had small purple and white sequins in it.

"It's beautiful-." he began while letting the material slip through his fingers until he could stand upright again. He then neatly folded his hands behind his back as he looked at the woman.

"But it doesn't do *her* justice" my breath caught in the back of my throat. It was a dress more extravagant than any I'd ever seen before. It was more detailed and eye catching than even Mary's gold dress yet there he was saying that the dress was nothing in comparison to my beauty.

'*Mary's beauty*' I mentally corrected myself.

"I see-." the woman muttered. Her lips opened and closed a few times as if she was at a loss for words.

"Well then we'll just have to find one that does" she continued. The next dress was a white one with pale pink and coral flowers that decorated the bodice. The flowers trailed down the skirt and grew less dense the closer they got to the bottom of it. It was sleeveless and less constricting than the first dress.

I smiled at the sight of it against my skin. It seem as though the dress was a part of me.

"I like this one" I declared when I took in my appearance. The woman gave a triumphant smile that was replaced by a frown when Caleb spoke. He wasn't afraid to give his honest opinion.

"If you're to clean the stables, yes" I wanted to snap at him. Those dresses were far more beautiful than any other I'd ever seen. I could only stare at myself in the mirror.

"Next" he ordered with his hand raised. It was then that I realized he only wore one of his rings as opposed to the many he would usually wear. It was a single silver band that sat on his left ring finger. It was a symbol of marriage. I pushed the thought of us being married to the back of my mind and got changed into the third dress.

Each change made me feel like I'd run at least ten miles. The heavy material weighed me down and the corset always needed to be tightened. It made me feel as if I was as stiff as a board.

I hoped Caleb would like the third one and when I stepped onto the platform, a smile grazed his lips.

"Perfect" the image that I was met with was of a dress. Its bodice and the top part of the skirt was navy blue that faded and eventually turned white near the bottom of the skirt. The neckline dipped down in between my breasts and pointed up towards my shoulders. Black vines and flowers decorated the bodice along with top of the skirt. White flowers were sown onto the bottom of the dress and a white, mesh material wrapped around my arms.

It was beautiful and made my blue eye stand out even more. I was frozen in time and lost in thought.

Was this how he saw her? Was she really that beautiful to him?

"She's breathtaking" I muttered as I stared at my reflection. Mary truly was all that he made her out to be. I smiled sadly at her. Her blond hair replaced my white strands and her slightly darker skin stood out against the dark material of the bodice.

Caleb picked up on my choice of words. His eyes studied me before the woman took hold of my hand.

"Excellent, on to the next one then!" she exclaimed excitedly and led me back to the changing room. I had to try on a few more before I was able to find a second dress that Caleb approved of.

It was sleeveless. It had a brighter blue bodice with a skirt that went from lilac to blue then to orange and finally faded into red. It looked like I was wearing a sunset, one that had black flowers, leaves and beading decorating it.

Despite my description, that certainly didn't do the piece justice, it was even more extravagant than the first dress. Caleb wanted me to find one more dress but it had to be one that outweighed the others and it proved to be rather difficult. I'd tried on nearly everything in the store and was exhausted by the time I got to the last one.

"No" was all he said to the maroon dress but then he took another look at it. He cast his eyes over the material.

"Something red" he declared. The young woman who'd stuck by me through it all perked up. She glanced in the direction of the back room then looked at the two of us.

"Wait here" with that she disappeared. I was panting with my bandaged hand pressing against my stomach. The two dresses that hung beside the mirror caught my attention and I breathed a laugh.

"You're pickier than I am" I said while smiling down at the man who sat in the chair beside the platform. He was staring at the far wall with his chin propped up onto his palm as he hummed in response.

"Only when it comes to-." he trailed off but I knew what he wanted to say *'Only when it comes to her'*

His love for her was something only the gods could fathom. The extent of which he adored her and the lengths he was willing to go for her were beyond all comprehension. I admired him for that and was jealous of Mary for having found herself such an incredible man.

"My father just finished this piece" the young woman informed us while stepping back into the room with a red and black gown. It was different and unique. It was something that I'd never seen before.

She held it up for me to inspect. The simple red bodice had material wrapped around it like my bandages were wrapped around my hands. The skirt was black and flared out lower than all the rest. It was odd because its bodice went down to past the hips.

"He calls it a Mermaid dress" she boasted causing me to stiffen as I caressed the soft, silk material. It was ironic, so much so that Caleb too was caught off guard by it.

"Because of the elongated bodice it gives the dress a fin-like appearance" she explained and I managed to calm down just enough to understand why it was called that. It had to be the first Mermaid dress ever made since no one had ever seen such a thing including Caleb and I.

"We'll take it" he announced while getting up from his seat. The woman glanced from the dress to Caleb and then to me.

"But she hasn't even tried it on yet" he waved his hand as if it was a simple matter, one that he didn't particularly care about. She nodded and began placing the dresses into a bag for us. He worked out the price behind a desk as I slipped back into the changing room. I was relieved to be free of the constricting clothing.

When I returned, Caleb was paying and placed twelve gold coins onto the desk for the woman to see. I noticed that a few suits had been thrown into the bags along with the dresses. They'd carelessly been put together without much thought.

I smiled at the thought of him not being bothered by his own appearance as long as I, as long as Mary looked perfect.

"Can you perhaps point us in the direction of the nearest shoe maker?" he asked the woman as he took the paper bags from her.

Hopefully he would be less picky when it came to shoes. Luckily, he was and an hour or so later we were sat outside a small tavern with four bags and pounding headaches from having been out all day.

The sun was going to set soon while Caleb sipped his rum and I nurtured a cup of water. I was worried that with the trip to Bakewell I would dehydrate like before.

"Evangeline?" I was drawn out of my thoughts to find Caleb holding something in the air between us. It glistened and caught the light of the sun in such a way that it appeared almost glowing. It was a silver ring that had a diamond encrusted into it.

"It was meant for Mary" he explained. I tentatively took it and slipping it onto my left ring finger.

It fit perfectly as if it had been made for me.

He went back to his rum. He wasn't at all bothered by the fact that he'd just given me a wedding ring he'd planned on giving to his lover. I left it at that. I knew that once it was all over, that it would decorate her finger not mine.

We purchased two horses later that evening and some food for our trip then set off at sunset. We rode for Bakewell through the countryside and towns.

I didn't have time to say goodbye to Ben or Rebecca but I knew that I'd see them again.

We stopped for the night to set up camp in the middle of nowhere. Open fields surrounded us on all sides and the dirt rode we were travelling along was close by.

The horses, two fine mares grazed in the field. Their ropes were fastened to a tree that seemed so lonely in such an open landscape.

Caleb got a fire going and rummaged through one of the bags in search of a gray suit jacket that he draped over my shoulders to help keep me warm. He then slumped down with his back against the base of the tree and tilted his head back to look up at the sky.

"What was she like?" I randomly asked. My voice was the only sound apart from the crickets and crackling of the fire. He knew who I was talking about without me even having to elaborate. We hadn't really talked about her or the fact that I was haunted by her memories and emotions.

"She was stubborn-." he sounded like he was complaining. I hadn't expected him to respond and when he did, I looked at him in shock.

"But kind. Reckless but considerate. Noble but she wasn't afraid to get dirty" I reached for a stick that lay nearby and started probing the fire. I watched the tip start to burn and turn into embers that I flicked off.

A smile touched my lips as he spoke. He was describing her in such a contradicting way as if he wasn't exactly sure what she was like. She had so many sides to her that he was at a loss for words.

"She used to play the piano" I muttered. He looked at me as if he wanted to ask how I knew that but he stopped himself when he remembered what I'd said about her memories.

"She was born to play just like her mother" he agreed with a nod before staring into the orange flames. I followed the tip of my stick as I lightly swung it back and forth while watching the embers write words in the air.

"What's it like, seeing her memories?" he asked. I raised the tip of the stick and blew on it to keep the ember going for as long as I could but eventually it died out and I had to relight it. One of the horses dug at the dirt with her hoof.

"It's like-." I tried searching for the right words to explain it but I hadn't really stopped to think about it before he asked.

"Being her" the words slipped past my lips before I could stop them. Of course I wasn't Mary, I'd made that clear but her emotions and her experiences were mine. I twisted the stick in my hand when Caleb didn't say anything.

"Like playing Mary Sillvan in some grand play-." I touched the tip of the stick to a fallen leaf and watched it burn a hole into it.

"Like knowing everything about her. Her emotions and deepest secrets-." I could feel him watching me. He was captivated by my words.

One of my arms were wrapped around my knees, pressing them to my chest.

"But instead of knowing her like a childhood friend-." I exhaled. I closed my eyes as I thought about how it felt, about what it was like for someone to experience another person's life in such great detail.

"It's like not knowing where she ends and I begin" it was the truest sentence I'd ever spoken. They were the words that expressed exactly what I was feeling.

Silence enveloped me in its cold embrace as I tossed the stick aside. I'd grown bored with it after playing with it for so long. I watched it fly through the air and land a few feet away.

"Are her emotions the reason why you-?" a breath of laughter escaped my lips. It was like he was too afraid to ask. It was as if he was too afraid to ever finish a sentence for fear of looking like a fool.

I wrapped both arms around my knees and pressed my lips to my arms. My eyes watched the dancing flames while they twisted and turned much like Rebecca would whenever she'd dance.

"No-." I muttered "I thought so which was why I tried to throw myself at Ben but-." the horses wondered closer to us. One mare was brown and the other was white. They held their heads down and their lips moved as they nibbled at the grass. Every now and then they would raise their heads to survey the area.

"My love for you is mine not hers" he nodded and crossed his arms behind his head to gaze up at the stars. Constellations glistened overhead and he took them in one by one until he could paint the sky that night purely from memory.

We didn't talk much after that. We ate and went to bed early to help pass the time before daybreak when we would ride for Bakewell.

Chapter Forty-Two.

Doe clad the grassy fields around us in a thin layer of white when we departed with our bags in tow. I sat atop the white mare who was named Chantilly after a type of lace for her color while Caleb rode the chestnut mare. She was named Demeter after the Greek goddess of grain and agriculture.

We slowed to a walk a few hours later. My rear throbbed from having being seated in the saddle for so long. I swayed back and forth along with Chantilly's movements.

"The town is half a day's ride from here" Caleb informed, jerking his head in the direction we were travelling. He'd rolled up the sleeves of his shirt to expose the black ink that could be found underneath. His hair had come undone from the ride. Bakewell wasn't that far inland from Killian's Coast but it felt like forever with the sun beating down on us and the endless fields of green grass ahead.

"We'll need to stop and change before then" I nodded as my hands tightening on my reigns. My eyes were glued to the dirt road below, being careful of holes and stumps that Chantilly might injure herself with.

"Wear the blue dress" Caleb instructed when I didn't respond. I found it odd that he wanted me to wear a specific dress for our meeting with the Cunningham's.

Shouldn't I wear the most extravagant dress when trying to impress people? If that'd been the case then he would've told me to wear the red one.

"I want them to watch my wife grow more beautiful by the day" my stomach churned at his words but then I reminded myself that I was just Evangeline and that Mary was the woman he acknowledged as his wife. The way Caleb spoke of how he wanted us to grow more beautiful with time as if we were a rose was ironic to me since the red rose was the Sillvan house sigil.

"Like a red rose" I added, my eyes flickering down to the ring on my left hand.

He shot me a look and the corner of his lips tugged upward but he tried to hide it as soon as he realized that he was smiling.

The Campbell family had the golden lion, the Sillvan's had the crimson rose and the Cunningham's had the silver sword.

We reached Bakewell sometime later. We stopped at an inn to rent a room for a few hours so that we could rest and prepare for our meeting with the nobility. We left the horses outside but brought our bags and money with us to the room.

I ran a bath while Caleb laid back on the bed's mattress. His hands were folded across his stomach and his eyes closed. He'd kicked his boots aside and stripped out of his shirt. Sweat coated his dark skin that was decorated in black markings which he'd collected throughout his years as a pirate.

I began to strip once the tub was filled with countless buckets of water that'd been carried in from the well outside by one of the helpers at the inn. I didn't care if Caleb could see my naked body. He'd seen it a thousand times before and made love to a woman who could've been me. She was that similar to me that she might as well have been me. Caleb hardly looked at me when I stepped into the water and sunk into it.

My feet dangled over the side of the tub, glittering violet and silver as scales began to form on them. I squeezed my eyes shut and tilted my head back so that the water wet my hair. It wasn't too hot or too cold as some of the buckets had been preheated with the use of a fireplace.

"Tomorrow we'll bathe in rosewater and sunflower seeds" Caleb mocked from his place on the bed. He was staring up at the ceiling that was no different from that of the ship. I reached for the necklace around my neck and unclasped it. I dropped it onto a trey that the helper had wheeled in earlier. It cluttered onto the metal and the sound caught Caleb's attention, urging him to sit up on the bed.

I gasped when my legs began to tangle together and my hair starting to turn silver. My eyes began glowing and my fangs extended. My webbed hands gripped the sides of the tub and my claws dug into the iron. It felt so familiar and so similar to the night he'd cut the scales from my fin.

I leaned back until I was completely submerged in the water where I was able to breathe and stay there for as long as I wanted. I stayed there for what felt like forever before Caleb approached the tub. His figure loomed overhead and appeared blurred by the water that separated us.

He took me in, my bare chest, my silver tail and my face that was so human yet so far from it. In that form I wasn't like Mary. Mary was human. She didn't have fangs or glowing eyes. In that moment I was Evangeline the Mermaid from Port Alice.

He held something out overhead, a necklace that caught the sunlight that crept in through the window. He dropped it and the anchor necklace broke through the surface of the water just in time for me to catch it in my palm.

It was his way of telling me to get dressed so that he could bathe.

I clasped the necklace around my throat and waited as my legs separated, my claws retracted and eyes stopped glowing. Bubbles escaped my lips when my gills faded and I shot up in the tub, gasping for air with my legs tucked away beneath me.

My hair stuck to the sides of my face and back. Water dripped down my face while my parted lips panted to catch my breath with my fangs still exposed.

"Why not just kill me?" he asked. The question caused my body to stiffen and my hands to tightening their grip on the sides of the tub.

Why would he ask such a thing? Why would he even think it? I abruptly stood in the tub and turned to face him.

"What are you-?" before I could finish wording my question, Caleb cut me off. His eyes were hard and his jaw was set in stone.

"You're a Mermaid" it was like I'd only realized it then. The fact that I was in fact a Mermaid who was to be feared by all. We were expected to drag the souls of drunken sailors to the darkest depths of the ocean floor where we would devour them whole and leave nothing behind, not even their souls.

"You could kill a man in a single slash, yet you-." my eyes fell to my hand. Its palm was exposed since I had to remove my bandages to bathe. The stitches that reside there showed anything but power. I knew that I was well capable of killing a man with those hands but that didn't mean that I wanted to.

"You could kill me, run away and not have to die" my hand dropped back to my side. My eyes growing sad and my shoulders slumped when I dared to look at him.

He was a fool like most men were when it came to understanding a woman.

"But instead you-." I interrupted him by reaching for the towel that hung nearby so that I could dry myself. I wrapped it around my

315

form to conceal my body from his eyes. The black fabric stood out against my pale skin.

"If you haven't realized by now that you're worth more to me than my own life, then-." I shook my head as a heartbreaking smile grazed my lips.

"You truly are a fool" I stepped out of the tub to dry myself before I began to get dressed in the blue dress like Caleb had instructed.

He didn't say anything as he stripped and submerged himself in the water.

His legs had black markings on them as well but I knew that without even having to look at him since I'd seen him bed Mary in her memories. I'd seen every inch of him. I've traced his skin with my fingertips and tasted his kiss a hundred times before but he didn't realize that.

I sat on the edge of the bed once the dress was on. I didn't bother tying the corset since I needed help tying it. I reached for the pair of heels Caleb bought specifically for that dress. They were a silver pair that seemed almost white like the bottom of the skirt. I tugged them onto my feet, one at a time.

I stood and faced the mirror to put my hair up in messy curls. I pinned them in place so that they looked intricate and detailed. Afterwards, I began tying my own bandages back in place. I couldn't leave them and expose my wounds to the nobility. They would suspect my husband of abusing me when really all Caleb had done was save me from being raped.

Ben and Rebecca saw it as him not being there in time to stop Mack from hurting me but he was there when it truly mattered. He was there to prevent anything worse from happening to me.

I moved towards the tub to retrieve the ring from the trey and slid it onto my ring finger.

He'd gotten out of the tub by then and was already halfway dressed. He buttoned up his ruffled white shirt and tugged his gray suit jacket onto his torso. I watched him as he moved on to his hair. He bit down on a piece of thread as his hands worked to gather the hair on the back of his head to fasten it with the ebony string. His shoes were polished black leather and his chin was freshly shaven.

"Would you mind?" I asked while positioning my back towards him and glancing over my shoulder. He exhaled sharply and turned to tighten the strings like he'd done with the golden dress twice before.

Once it was done up and we were both ready we took the money and left the inn. Caleb called a carriage and held the door open for me to step inside. He offered me his hand to prevent me from tripping on the steps.

I sat down on the red velvet seat and neatly tucked my feet away neatly beneath me with my hands folded in my lap. He instructed the rider on where to take us then joined me, slumping down on the seat. He spread his legs and threw his head back with his eyes closed as a whip sounded followed by the horses pulling the carriage.

"What will we tell them?" I asked while I watched the buildings and people passed by us outside the carriage window.

Caleb groaned from beside me as if he didn't want to be there. He didn't want to meet the nobles but he would do anything in his power to get his hands on the sixth gem.

"That we're travelling to France for our honeymoon and decided to stop by" I wondered for a moment if he'd been planning on taking Mary to France and decided that it was a wonderful thought.

She would love it there. The many dresses and not to mention the theater. She enjoyed watching plays and attending the opera.

"Just pretend to be the shy wife of a nobleman and do try to be nice to Lady Lillian" as if I could possibly not be nice to her. I wasn't capable of being rude accept to Caleb when he would be rude to me but that was a different matter.

I simply nodded and stayed silent when the buildings began to shift into a long, winding driveway with a garden on either side of it.

I'd never seen so many flowers in one place. All the colors of the rainbow were laid out before me from pink to deep purple and even black.

The carriage came to a stop and the driver hopped down from his perch to open the door for us but Caleb took up a more proper seating position before he did. Caleb exited before me and once again offered me his hand. I watched where I stepped while my free hand gripped the skirt of my gown until I was stood on the cobblestone. I looked up in the direction of the manor.

A man and his wife who were around Caleb's age stood on the manor's front steps. A few maids and butlers stood around them to greet the arriving couple.

I sucked in a nervous breath as Caleb paid the carriage driver then offered me his arm. I hooked mine through his and looked at anything but the man and woman awaiting us as we approached them.

"Lord Victor, Lady Lillian. Do pardon our sudden arrival-." my ears deceived me. For a moment I could've sworn that a nobleman was stood beside me but instead it was a pirate Captain. Caleb let go of my arm to bow apologetically.

"My newly-wed wife and I were passing through on our way to Paris from Hemingford and decided that it would be best to become acquainted with the town's nobility" the woman who had light brown hair, gray eyes and freckles looked at me with a fondness in her gaze. Her husband had darker brown hair and equally as dark brown eyes.

"Oh, Victor. Tell me, have you ever seen a woman more beautiful?" I felt myself become flustered by her sudden compliment. She grabbed hold of her husband's arm when she spoke and seemed genuinely excited. The man looked at me and a spark ignited in his eyes.

"She's so young, no more than nineteen" Lady Lillian added when she noticed how embarrassed I was. I noticed Caleb smirking at me in his bowed position. His lips hidden from their eyes but not mine. I ignored it and gave a kind smile.

"Pray tell, where does a man find such a jewel?" Victor questioned. He was addressing Caleb even though his eyes were staring at me.

I didn't know whether Caleb was expecting them to be shocked by my appearance but he seemed to enjoy the attention I was receiving.

"At an orphanage in Port Fay" it wasn't a lie like I was expecting it to be.

My back muscles stiffened and I had to remind myself that he knew what he was doing. He stood up straight and gazed at the couple.

"An orphanage?" Victor questioned surprisingly. It seemed that I interested the pair even more after they received such a small piece of information from Caleb.

He was a genius and knew exactly what to say to get them interested in me, in us. It was why he'd insisted on buying the most extravagant dresses and it was why he wanted me to grow more beautiful over the time we spent at Bakewell.

What better way to capture the attention of people and earn their trust by using a beautiful and innocent woman as the main reason to be invited into their manor.

Caleb's eyes glistened with mischief but only I was able to identify it in that moment.

"Victor dear, I wish to paint her. I simply must paint her" Lillian declared. She let go of her husband's arm and approached me.

There it was, what Caleb had been counting on since we left Killian's Coast. He knew that Lady Cunningham was a woman who enjoyed painting and he dressed me up like one of her models then put me on a pedestal for her to see. She was the mouse; Caleb was the trap and I was the cheese that the it so desperately craved.

"I suppose we could spare a few days" Caleb said. He was toying with her mind even more as Victor stood off to the side.

She took my hand in hers and examined the bandages before she met my gaze. She studied them like a true artist would and took in every last detail.

"I'll have to mix some oils for the gloss in her eyes and that blue-." the lady of the manor was saying, mostly rambling to herself. She looked like a lovely woman. She was a kind and friendly woman but she was a little odd when it came to her obsession with painting.

"Do come in" Victor insisted. He turned and motion towards the double doors that sat at the top of the stairs.

The maids and butlers scurried off to prepare for our stay including the study which had Lady Lillian's painting things already set up. There was a bar off to the side with only the finest of Scotch and a sitting area but what caught my eye wasn't the fireplace that was lacking a fire or the mural painted on the walls that Lillian had done herself, it was the grand piano that sat in the corner of the room. Candles were placed on top of its smooth black surface that I ran my fingers along. I felt the familiarity of it that was so welcoming.

I'd never seen a piano in person before but Mary spent most of her life in front of one. *Perhaps that was why I felt so drawn to it?*

"Do you play?" Lady Lillian questioned when she noticed how I was admiring the instrument. I examined my fingertips; the motions were imprinted into my memory but could I play like I knew Mary could?

"I dabble" I replied. I gave a stunning smile as I turned my back to the piano. A sadness overcame me at the thought of not being able to feel its keys give way beneath my fingers.

A young maid hurried into the room with a silver tray in hand. On top of it sat a single white lily and an apple.

"Do sit" Lillian instructed while motioning to the stool in front of the grand piano. It was positioned close to the large window that overlooking the gardens. I took my seat and tucked my feet away beneath me as she examined the tray.

"This'll do" she declared with the lily in hand. The servant girl curtsied then left while Victor poured some Scotch into two crystal glasses for him and Caleb to sip on.

"Hold it like this" she began to instruct me. At first, she held the flower in her hand ever so gently as if she was caressing her child. She held it close to her cheek. I took it and mimicked her actions only to have her pose me like a puppet with the elbow of the hand holding the flower pressing down on the piano's keys and my other hand was placed on top of them.

She turned my head ever so slightly so that I was looking at the garden. Daylight poured into the room and onto my features, highlighting them just right so that she could capture the image.

"There, do try to refrain from moving" she took her seat at the aisle and tucked the skirt of her dress away beneath her before she began mixing the paints.

Neither one of us spoke. Only the men conversed on the other side of the room where Victor was showcasing his collection of sculptures that he'd gathered over the years.

Caleb pretended to be interested while sipping on his Scotch. Every now and then he would comment on the 'complexity of the various curves' that could be found in the carved busts.

I risked a glance at Lady Lillia. Her eyes moved from me to the canvass with her paintbrush carelessly dancing across its white surface. She was such a wonderful woman who always saw the light in people. She was wedded to Victor at a very young age and had come to love him over the years they'd spent together.

Sadly, she couldn't bare him any children and later they decided to adopt a baby boy from the local orphanage who would grow into a charming young man.

When I met her, she and her husband were going through rough times as she'd already lost two children. She'd miscarried one early on and the other she lost during labor. It would puzzle me. I'd think back and try to recognize the sadness in her eyes but there was none.

"It is the swan of Eden" Victor explained when he noticed that Caleb was admiring the painting that hung on the wall above the piano.

I'd noticed it when we first entered the room. It was the image of a white bird with its wings extended and water beneath it. Fish swam around it while a glowing light illuminated its figure from behind similar to a halo.

"Said to inhabit the Garden and protect the tree of knowledge" it was a simple myth but a beautiful one. Caleb hummed. His golden eyes narrowed as if in search of some imperfection among the brushstrokes but there were none.

"My wife painted it some years ago" Victor added and my eyes widened at the thought of the woman painting me having created such a mesmerizing piece. I could only imagine what the final piece would look like. Caleb glanced at the canvass that she was working on and nodded.

"She does have a talent for capturing the beauty of things" he agreed as his gaze moved from the canvass to me. I looked at the garden, too afraid to meet his eyes and I held the lily slightly closer.

Lillian was too far gone to hear them. She was too captivated by what she was doing to be able to recognize their words as spoken in her native language. Victor knew this. After having spent many years with her, he knew that when she painted, she was consumed by it. She didn't care about anything around her until the piece was done.

"I believe every woman harbors a talent-." my ears perked in response to the nobleman's words. He was handsome through his way of speaking and able to manipulate words to capture the interests of women but to me no man could possibly compare to Caleb even if the pirate was far from perfect.

"It might be something as complex as painting or something as simple as understanding a man's temper-." Victor chuckled causing his glass to shake in his hand.

Caleb was silent as he usually was when he wasn't yelling orders or cursing. I often wondered what went on behind those emotionless eyes of his.

"A talent is a talent" I agreed with the man's words. Everyone, not just women harbored a talent no matter how small or how unimportant it may seem.

"Does your wife perhaps harbor any such talents, Lord Read?" the fact that Victor spoke of me without acknowledging my presence showed just how the men of nobility treated their women. It was as if women's opinions didn't matter and that they should be silent like a perfect porcelain doll.

"She has made the piano her paintbrush" Caleb was talking about Mary but Victor didn't realize that and looked at him in surprise.

"Really?" I mentally reminded myself to slap the Captain for his idiocy. *What made him think that I could play the piano?* I wanted to protest but it was far too late to turn back. Victor set his glass aside and placed a firm hand on Lillian's arm to draw her out of her trance and back to reality.

"Do play us a piece" Victor urged me while motioning towards the piano. I placed the lily on top of the instrument and turned so that I could place my feet on the pedals.

My hands were trembling when I readied them to play the piece that Mary played in my vision. I closed my eyes and asked the blond woman who had captured Caleb's heart to guide me so that I didn't make a fool of myself.

I began playing a soft tune that started off slow and simple while an image of Mary seated in front of a piano surfaced in my mind. She tried so hard to hit all the notes and added more as she played with Lady Bethany's approval.

'Calm down, darling' she whispered to her daughter with such loving blue eyes that peered down at the twelve year old girl.

She loved her daughter like only a mother could and I found myself wishing that I'd known mine but the only memories I had were of the orphanage.

The notes came naturally to me in a slow, sad symphony that held the feel of a mother's love. It surrounded me in a warmth I've never felt before.

I could hardly hear the notes over Lady Bethany's voice reading a passage from a children's book to her daughter before bed.

'And the little lamb ran to tell his mother of the adventures he had with his friends, the ducklings-.' the room was a mixture of gold and pale pinks. It was fit for a young noble girl who had all she ever wanted apart from the man she'd fall in love with.

The bed was bigger than any I'd ever slept in and the cherubs that hung from the ceiling were meant to protect her from the horrors of the world.

'Mama, mama! Yelled the little lamb. I ate a yummy apple pie and swam in the river today!' the emotions that came along with keys my fingers pressed down on were overwhelming. They were too much for me to bare and I had to bite my tongue to stop from crying.

Mary jumped up when her mother closed the old story book to say goodnight.

'Again. Please read it again mother. Please' she begged. Her white nightgown seeming almost too big for her small frame and her golden curls hung loose around her shoulders. Her mother simply laughed an angelic laugh and promised that they would have apple pie the next day if she went to bed and said her prayers. That was exactly what Mary did and the next day she had as much apple pie as she wanted.

The notes stopped, my eyes opened and I stared straight ahead at the wall beyond the piano.

Lord Victor began to applaud. It was a slow clap that drew me out of the memory and captured my gaze. Caleb had no reaction. He was studying me intensely as Lady Lillian conveyed how beautiful my song was. I wished to argue and say that it wasn't mine but I knew if we wanted the gem that I would have to lie. I silently thanked Mary for helping me.

"You simply must play at our ball tomorrow evening!" Lillian declared and Caleb agreed. I knew that he was planning to steal the jewel out from right under their noses during all the commotion and I felt guilty for having to do such a thing.

The guilt was short lived when a young Mary's giggling reached my ears and I knew that resurrecting her would be a gift greater than any other. I would steal for the girl I'd befriended in my mind and dreams. I would steal for the man I loved who could never love me just to give him the one thing he wanted above all else.

Selfless, brave and kind. I hardly saw myself as those things but in truth they were exactly what I was. I just didn't realize it.

Chapter Forty-Three.

The sun had already set by the time the Lord and Lady were told that dinner was ready. I'd been placed in the same exact position for so long that I felt like a statue. My muscles were sore and the lily was starting to droop but Lillian most likely didn't mind one dead bloom.

Her garden stretched on for miles. It was well taken care of with probably a million other white lilies waiting to be plucked for her painting purposes.

We were about to excuse ourselves and head back to the inn for the night with the promise of returning in the morning so that Lillian could finish her painting but the couple insisted on us joining them for dinner.

The dining hall had a ceiling that was at least two stories high with grand chandeliers and instead of the usual long, rectangular table there was a large round one made of black oak in the center of the room.

We took our seats and the butlers pushed them in for us while bowing in greeting.

"Still not quiet used to the noble life, I see" Lady Lillian spoke from beside me as the dishes were being set out from pork to lamb to beef and turkey. They poured champagne into a crustal glass for me to drink from. It was the odd look I was giving the butlers and maids that'd drawn her to the conclusion.

"It's odd to be served instead of being the one serving" I agreed with a nod as I looked down at the various forks, spoons and knifes that'd been placed around my plate. It all felt so familiar yet so foreign at the same time.

I picked up the appropriate utensils that Mary's memories helped me determine and notice that Caleb copied me.

"Pardon my asking but how did the two of you meet?" Lillian asked from beside me. Her eyes moved from Caleb to me after she'd delicately cut a piece of her food. I paused and stared down at the plate in front of me. My thoughts went back to that night in Port Alice.

I was seated near the water but why I was there was beyond my memory when the Sunken Soul suddenly approached the shore and a man with golden eyes gazed into my mismatched ones. I remembered how I ran from him, how I pleaded with him to set me free the next morning but it was hard to believe that I'd somehow fallen in love with that man who I'd tried so desperately to escape from.

"He left me roses at the orphanage" I said while thinking back to Deacon and Douglas Daughvis. Lillian smiled as a romantic look light up her eyes. It was Victor who spoke next while raising his glass to take a sip from it.

"Wooing a woman with roses, quiet original" it was a mocking statement that caused the hairs on the back of my neck to stand on end while Caleb cleared his throat. He swallowed before he spoke unlike how he'd normally speak with his mouth full of food.

"They were blue roses" this had Lillian on the edge of her seat. Her eyes were wide with wonder at the thought of a blue rose. Such a thing had never been seen before and she as a flower enthusiast could only listen in amazement.

"One for each day of the year that I spent longing for her" I couldn't help the blush that rose to my cheeks. It was clearly a lie but he managed to create such a beautiful story of how two people from different worlds came together.

"A blue rose? Such an oddity has yet to be heard of" Victor declared. Caleb hid his smirk by taking another bite of his steak. His eyes met mine with a sinister glint and I could only smile.

"Oh? It has been cultivated in the South for many years now" I added. Lady Lillian grew restless and her hands tightened around her utensils as she looked between the two of us. She eventually placed her gaze on her husband.

"Victor, dear. It would make a wonderful new addition to my garden" I could only image Lord Cunningham spending years of his life searching every corner of every continent for such a rose to satisfy his wife and coming up empty.

The dinner ended with him reassuring her that he would find it and Caleb giving him some fake advice on how to locate it.

We said our goodbyes and returned to the inn where I kicked off my heels and fell onto the bed with my hands resting beside my head as I stared straight up at the ceiling.

"That was exhausting" I declared. My chest was rising and falling, begging to be free of the corset and bodice that constricted it. Caleb had already shed his coat and was unbuttoning his shirt while he nodded.

"Ye're telling me" he agreed. He purposefully using his prior accent which caused the corners of my lips to tug up into a smile. I sat up on the bed and reached behind me to untie the bodice before kicking the dress aside. I stole Caleb's shirt when he shrugged it off and tugged it onto my naked body as I untied my hair, leaving it down in messy curls.

He fell back onto the bed. His shoes were discarded and only his trousers hung low on his hips. I rested my head on his stomach with my legs dangling from the side of the bed and the shirt just barely concealing my lower half. Its buttons were only done up to below my chest.

"She wasn't wearing the necklace" Caleb pointed out while he clasped his hands together behind his head with his eyes staring upward. I hadn't noticed it but he did. The Amethyst of Bakewell wasn't where we first suspected it would to be.

"She must be keeping it someplace safe" I assumed. My fingers fiddled with the bronze sheets beneath me as I pondered over it. I could feel his stomach rise and fall as he breathed.

Not even two days ago we wouldn't have been caught dead cozying up to each other so what'd changed? *Why were we suddenly so close? Was it because we were alone or maybe it was the fake bond created by the rings on our fingers? Perhaps it was because we had to trust and get to know each other if we wanted to retrieve the jewel?*

I wasn't entirely sure. All I knew was that we had a common goal. Steal the Bakewell Amethyst and resurrect Mary.

"But where?" I uttered. It was a question that was directed more to myself than the pirate Captain. Caleb remained silent as he tried to think like a thief who had the mindset of a noblewoman.

"Their bed chambers" he finally concluded. It made sense. A person's prized belongings were usually kept close. I nodded causing the back of my head to brush across his abs. My hair was splayed out over his torso like a white blanket.

"I want you to find out where that is before the ball" I turned my head slightly so that my ear was pressing against his stomach as I looked up at him. His words surprised me. He didn't move or remove his arms from behind his head. He didn't dare take his eyes off the ceiling but he could feel my movements.

"Why me?" I questioned. I knew that I was going to be placed at the piano again. I'd be trapped in the same position I was previously. I'd be glued in place, all day, with a woman who barely acknowledged the world around her while she painted.

"Women tend to share these types of things with each other" he responded while closing his eyes and tilting his head down a bit.

The candles placed on the bedside tables and around the tub provided just enough light for me to see his facial features start to relax.

"Just say you're feeling a bit lightheaded and need to lay down" he muttered. He didn't bother to fully close his lips once the words escaped them.

His breathing evened out and he was gone. His hair had come undone from its ponytail. I could hear his steady heartbeat drumming in my ear and closed my eyes to listen to it. My body curled in on itself and my hand rested against his stomach where it was able to feel the rise and fall of his shallow breathing.

I fell asleep in that position but sometime during the night I moved so that I was lying beside him with my head on his pillow and by dawn Caleb had turned onto his side. He'd wrapped his arm around me and was pressing me into him with his face buried in the side of my neck.

I awoke to the sound of a rooster crying out to the rising sun. Out on the sea there weren't any roosters to wake you like I'd grown accustomed to at the orphanage. It was a familiar sound; one that I missed.

My tired eyes stared at the far wall and the candles that were still flickering around the tub. I adjusted my legs and felt something strong wrapped around my body. That's when I noticed Caleb for the first time. His breath tickled my neck and his hand gripped the material of the shirt I wore just beneath my breasts.

I stiffened but calmed down when my hand raised to caress his arm. I felt the veins and curves of the muscles. He groaned and shifted which caused his nose to brush against the shell of my ear. His hold on me tightened before it loosened again.

I turned my head to look at his sleeping face. I took in his parted lips and messy hair. I wished to stay in that moment forever just so that I could feel him cling to me so desperately.

If I could stay there forever, I'd be happy but I knew time never stood still and I knew that it wasn't me that he saw in his but it was a blond haired woman whom I resembled.

There was a knock at the door followed by the faint voice of a girl asking for permission to enter. I sat up on the bed and tossed my legs over the side as Caleb groaned in protest. He turned so that his back was to the door.

"Enter" I called and the door cracked open. It was a helper at the inn stepped into the room. She was no older than sixteen and had a clay pot in hand that was filled with water. She curtseyed and made sure her eyes were cast downward when she did.

"Forgive the intrusion. There was a request for an early bath to be prepared" she explained. Her short curls bobbed when she moved. I glanced in the direction of the bed where Caleb was fast asleep and smiled internally at the thought of him putting in the request.

The girl followed my eyes and began to stutter nervously at the sight of his tattooed back.

"I-I um. Will it be rosemary or lavender?" my eyebrows furrowed up in confusion. They hadn't asked such a thing the day before when preparing our bath. She noticed that I was confused and motioned to the figure lying on the bed.

"Per his request" I nodded. I thought back to Caleb's earlier comment that he'd made while I was bathing 'Tomorrow we'll bathe in rose water and sunflower seeds' he hadn't been mocking the nobles. He was hinting at what he'd scheduled for us.

"Rosemary" I said. The girl nodded and poured the water into the tub before she scurried off to fetch some more. It was a tiring process to fill a tub. I studied Caleb then shook my head and started digging through our bags in search of a dress to wear for the day.

"Wear the sunset dress" his voice surprised me and pulled me out of my internal argument of which dress I should wear. They were both spread out on the foot of the bed with me studying them. I took the one he told me to wear and hung it up near the tub before folding the other one and placing it back into the bag.

"Requesting that a bath be prepared-." I began to mutter as I put the blue dress that I'd worn the day before on the bed. I'd most likely have to take it with me so that Lady Lillian could finish her painting.

"You truly are quiet the romantic, Caleb Campbell" he sighed and turned onto his back to look at me with sleepy eyes. I was teasing him and he knew it from the smirk that crept its way onto my lips.

"It was intended for me" he muttered. I laughed and shook my head. Men hardly ever bathed in fancy fragranced water.

Why would a deadly pirate Captain want to smell like rosemary?

He ignored me and stayed in the same position as the helper girl continued to fill the tub. Every now and then her eyes would go to Caleb and her cheeks would turn a few shades darker pink before she'd scurry off again. I found it adorable that she was so captivated by his exposed skin and the markings that were placed there. She's most likely never seen a man so comfortable without clothing.

I quickly bathed. I scrubbed the salt into my skin and washed my hair with scented oils while the rosemary soaked into my flesh. Once I was done, it was Caleb's turn while I got dressed and did my hair up as best I could to resemble what it'd looked like the day before. He dressed in a navy suit with a black undershirt to match the flowers on my dress then helped me tie it at the back. My heels were black and so were his shoes.

We were welcomed at the manor with open arms. A maid and a butler greeting us on the front steps. They held the doors open for us and escorted us to the study where we'd spent most of our time. Lady Lillian was already prepping her paintbrushes but her husband was nowhere to be seen.

"Lord Cunningham has requested that you accompany him on a hunting trip" Lillian explained.

I shot Caleb a look before he left with the butler. Lady Lillian was dressed in a sea foam green sundress that was simple with a light skirt and she wore her hair down.

"Should I perhaps change?" I asked while motioning towards the bag that the maid had placed off to the side on the table in the sitting area.

Lillian glanced up from her brushes and to the bag with a curious look that shifted to realization. For a moment she was silent and her eyes gazing at me in awe before she shook her head and spoke.

"No need dear. As an artist it is important to capture the things capable of change before all else" I nodded. My heels clicked against the floor when I approached the canvass.

I had yet to see what she was capable of and froze at the sight. The blue dress, my hair and even some of the sunlight that poured in through the window had been perfectly transferred onto the canvass with even a portion of the piano finished. She just had to paint my face, body, the lily and the background while adding a few finishing touches to it.

"I was under the impression that paintings took months, even years to finish" I admitted. Lillian placed her paintbrushes in a very specific order on the tray beside her. Along with them there was a cup of water to clean them with and a cloth that she used to wipe the access paint from the bristles.

"Some artists work at their own pace however most are rushed for time" she began to explain while mixing paints on her wooden palette to get the colors just right.

"It is a gift to be able to capture an image as quickly and as accurately as possible" she was passionate about painting. I could see it in the way her eyes lit up and her hands delicately worked with her as if they were her children and she was afraid of hurting them.

"I see, then let us begin" I stated. I sat down in front of the piano and took the freshly plucked white lily in my bandaged hand. I held it up like I did before and gazed out onto the garden where two horses were being prepped for riding.

Victor and Caleb were conversing nearby with crossbows. Knives and swords were being attached to the saddles. I was drawn out of my train of thought when Lillian broke the silence.

"Why do you wear so many bandages?" her question surprised me. She was working on the flower and the hand holding it which was wrapped in fresh bandages. It would be odd for a noblewoman to be covered in so many wounds that she had to bandage herself and to explain it would cause for a clever lie.

"My body is very frail and is something that's come from my years spent at the orphanage-." I began. My mind raced with ideas on how to try and justify my wounds. I tried grasping at the closest thing.

"I tend to be clumsy and often times-." I swallowed. I felt my blood rush to my cheeks and tops of my ears.

"Caleb forgets this when he beds me" to make the lie ever more believable, I raised my hand that wasn't holding the flower and touched my neck with my fingertips as if he'd choked me during a passionate night of love making. Lillian grew quiet and her eyes grew wider than they normally were.

"I assumed it was something more common like abuse or-." I smiled at her. Her big gray eyes filled with such embarrassment even though I was much younger than her.

330

"His love for me burns so passionately that he often cannot control himself" she swallowed hard but fell silent. It was the end of our conversation. I so wished it was the truth but I knew that it could never be. He'd only kissed me once before when he thought I was Mary so to think that he'd ever love me enough to bed me was foolish.

A few hours later I remembered what Caleb told me and gripped my head with my free hand.

"Are you alright?" Lillian asked when she looked up but noticed that my head wasn't in the right position for her to paint my face. I shook my head and squeezed my eyes shut. I hated lying but I had to for Mary and Caleb.

"I just feel a bit light headed" I explained while taking on the portraits pose again. Lady Lillian's chair scraped across the marble flooring. She'd abandoned her brush in the cup of water as she approached me.

"Perhaps we should take a break if you're feeling unwell?" I stood to meet her at the piano with a faint smile that made it seem as if something was wrong but was also riddled with guilt.

"No, no. I'm fine-." I cut myself off by pretending to fall but caught myself on the piano with my hand still pressed to my forehead. Lillian rushed to my side and grabbed my hand in hers. The flower had long since been discarded by our feet.

"I insist. It might be best for you to lay down. Let me escort you to one of our guest rooms" I didn't try to fight her when she eased me up from the pian's stool and started guiding me out of the room.

A maid hurried to assist me. She took the weight from Lady Lillian who continued to walk beside us, up a flight of stairs and to a room at the end of a long hallway.

"Are your chambers on this floor?" I randomly asked while my eyes searching the hallway and eventually the room that I was led into. Lilian swatted her hand as I was eased onto the bed by the maid.

"Oh, goodness no. Victor and I share the fourth floor" the worry in her eyes when she looked at me made me not want to look at her. I nodded and laid down on the mattress, resting the side of my head onto one of the feather pillows.

"Good. I didn't want to impose" Lillian laughed. It was a joyful sound that made my heart squeeze. She took a seat in a chair near the bed then turned to address the maid.

"Could you please bring us some tea and perhaps a slice of cake?" the maid curtseyed then left. She made sure to close the bedroom door behind her. I wished that Lillian would leave as well. She was such a kind and talented woman whom I regretted stealing from.

Later that day when I started 'feeling better' we continued to paint and shortly after that Caleb returned with a dear in tow. He'd shot and killed the dear himself.

"Your husband knows how to shoot" Victor declared while pouring them both a glass of Scotch. He then handed one to Caleb who took it with a grin. I smiled as Lillian cleaned one of her brushes. How she never dropped a single speck of paint on her dress was beyond me.

"He might just have me beat" Victor added to which both of the men chuckled and shared a sip of their drinks. Lillian all but finished the painting. She only left a small portion of the background untouched when it was time for both Caleb and I to go get ready for the ball that was more like an opportunity for the towns people to dress up and dance the night away.

When we reached the inn, I told him what I'd discovered.

"Their chambers are located on the top floor" I said while tugging the red dress onto my body. He buttoned his red undershirt and stared out the window at the small town.

Once the dress was on my body and tied at the back, I couldn't help but stare at myself in the mirror. The bodice hugged the curve of my hips, breasts and waist down to mid-thigh where the skirt began to flare out like the fin of a Mermaid's tail. I left my hair down and the same black heels clad my feet while I painted my lips a bright red.

Caleb was staring at me when I turned around. He was about to head to the door when he uttered something under his breath that sounded like 'You look beautiful' I wanted to make sure that I heard right but before I could he was already walking past me and heading in the direction of the carriage that awaited us.

He held the door open for me and we headed to the ball.

Chapter Forty-Four.

The manor's driveway was crowded with carriages as people lined up to make their grand entrance one at a time. They climbed the staircase and headed for the decorated ballroom where a man was stood. He'd announce their names and their arrival to those who'd already arrived.

We waited in the carriage and sat in silence as I dreaded the moment when I would have to play the piano in front of so many people. I wasn't even sure how I managed to do it before with just three let alone around a hundred or so.

I could only talk to Mary in the back of my mind and ask her to help guide my fingertips.

When it was our turn, Caleb climbed out and held his hand out for me to take but the moment I set foot outside the carriage, I heard people gossiping among themselves at the sight of my dress and the beautiful woman wearing it.

They asked questions like, *who is she? Where did she find such a dress? Is it even a dress?*

Caleb offered me his arm and I took it. I looked down at the stairs since I was too afraid to meet the eyes of those around us.

Once we were inside, I felt like I could breathe. I raised my eyes to look at the familiar interior that I'd seen twice before while a servant guided us in the direction of the ballroom. They opened the large double doors and allowed us through. It caught the attentions of everyone below.

All eyes were locked onto my dress, my unique white hair and mismatched eyes as a butler raised a piece of paper with names written onto it in black ink. He then read our names out loud.

"Now presenting, Lord Edmond and Lady Natalia Read of Hemingford" we descended the stairs with my eyes cast downward to make sure that I didn't trip and fall in my heels or step on the skirt of my dress. When we reached the bottom, I look ahead at the people studying us and noticed their scrutinizing stares.

Two of the faces stood out among the rest. A woman with light brown curls and gray eyes and a man with brown hair and darker brown eyes. Lillian approached us. She was dressed in a turquoise gown with a glass of champagne already in hand. She placed a kiss of greeting to each of my cheeks.

"Look at you" she pulled back with her hand holding onto mine so that she could take in the full image of my dress.

"Stunning as always" she smiled a genuine smile and let go of my hand to address Victor. Her eyes glistened with desire and awe. He sighed heavily at the sight and took a sip of his own champagne.

The look she gave him screamed *'I simply must have it!'* while his exasperated response might've sounded something similar to *'Anything for you, dear'* they were drawn from their silent conversation by the sound of a violin playing in the background. Lillian turned to face the platform on which a small orchestra sat then as if remembering something she perked up.

"Oh, your performance!" she exclaimed while hooking her arm through mine and dragging me towards the platform in the center of the ballroom. I looked at Caleb with pleading eyes that asked him to help me but Victor had him preoccupied. They were conversing about the various types of wines that were being cultivated in France.

We reached the small stage and the music stopped playing. This caught everyone's attention and they all looked at Lillian who began to greet everyone as I stood silently beside her. The eyes peering at us from all sides made my heart beat faster in my chest and my hands began to tremble as I hid them behind my back.

Her speech was a long one. She thanked everyone for attending then she thanked the servants for the food and of course the musicians. My eyes locked onto a golden pair among the crowd. Caleb already had a drink in his hand and was watching me with emotionless features.

"May I introduce Lady Natalia Read who will be preforming a song per my request" Lillian turned to me. She smiled as if to reassure me that everything was going to be alright.

I nodded and began making my way towards the grand piano that sat in the middle of the stage. It was surrounded by musicians and instruments on all sides along with around a hundred noble guests.

I padded down the back of my dress and sat on the stool. My eyes stared down at the familiar black and white keys that seemed welcoming like old friends.

I raised my shaking hands and allowed them to hover over the ivory keys as I closed my eyes. The silence was deafening as I prayed to

Mary and hoped that she would hear me. I hoped that she would take my hands in hers, and play through me like she did before.

I exhaled and my eyes opened as the candle light from the chandeliers above shone down onto the black piano, reflecting off its smooth surface. I began to play. My fingers moved slowly at first since the bandages that were still wrapped around my hands made it difficult for me to move as freely as I would've liked.

Once the introduction to the song came to an end, I parted my lips and words began to flow from them. The words were so unknown to me yet so familiar.

"I may be just a fool, lost and naive to fall for you" my eyes moved from my hands to the figure in the crowd that stood out among the fancy dresses and sparkling jewelry. Caleb watched me and met my gaze with a knowing look in their golden depths.

He knew that I was singing about him and he knew that I felt like a fool for loving him. I knew that I would never compare to Mary in his eyes.

Was I foolish for having given him my heart to hold and my life to take?

"I may be just a stupid girl, too young and inane to think you would-." the emphasis in my words sent shock waves throughout the room and for a moment I believed that everyone around me could feel the raw emotions swirling inside of me.

My mind went back to that first night at the inn, to his lips brushing over the shell of my ear on the balcony and his voice urging me to sing for him.

My fingers danced over the keys as I decided that I would sing for him, a song so loud that all the world would hear.

"Be the one who would take hold of this heart. It's such a shame that you keep blaming the dark" the words were so understanding and conveyed my feelings like a window to my soul. However deeply I wished he would take my heart as his, it was Mary's that he desired and only my life was of value to him. He didn't care about the thing beating in my chest even though it beat for him. He was just a form in the darkness. One that I so longed for but could never reach.

"And now the crowds, the masses are chatting. The masses are saying that you are stringing my love like a violin" it was true, he was playing my heart and toying with it. He was manipulating it to get what he wanted in order to serve his own selfish needs. He was the man

pulling the strings and I was just his puppet to control because of my adoration of him. I met his eyes and a sad smile made its way onto my lips.

"So toy on" my voice danced around me and my eyes filled with so much love as I looked at him. Yes, he was using me and playing me like an instrument but I didn't care. I would be his instrument and give him whatever would make him happy because I couldn't force him to love me like I loved him. My eyes cast themselves back down to the keys.

"I may be just a fool, tied up in visions and cursed jewels" I was pulled into the world of Pirates. It was a dangerous world filled with lies and deception. I was forced to locate seven jewels for a man who'd kidnapped me, a man whom I loved.

The memories of him asking me to sing to him and the insults that'd been passed between us along with the arguments and tears. My heart squeezed in my chest and the words continuing to flow as I tried to fight back the fog starting to cloud my eyes.

Him holding me in the pool of the desert ruins and watching me transform. His hands working to stitch the wound on my leg and remove the scales from my tail. His rising and falling stomach the night before and his arms slung around me, pulling me closer to him.

There were so many memories swirling in the back of my mind. Finding out that I was Mary's reincarnation, discovering Caleb's past and coming to understand him over time.

The song came to an end. My fingers gradually stopped playing until they came to a still and I was left sitting there as the center of attention. My eyes were cast down with unshed tears hidden in their depths. Hidden from the peering eyes of those surrounding me.

There was a silence that seemed to stretch on forever before the crowd began to applaud and my head shot up to take them in. I saw the image of a much younger Mary stood beside a grand piano at an opera house while bowing to a cheering crowd as roses were being thrown onto the stage in light of her grand performance.

I blinked and I was back in the ballroom. Lillian stood a few feet away with the same kind smile on her lips that she always wore. She raised her hands and began applauding along with the audience.

"Beautiful, simply mesmerizing" she complimented but it didn't feel like it was directed at me, instead it was directed at the woman who'd lent me her talent for that single performance. I pushed it aside

336

and stood to curtsey before I politely excused myself and headed for the two men who stood near the back of the room.

"A truly remarkable performance, Lady Read" Victor said when I reached them. I bowed my head to show respect then dared to look at Caleb.

He watched the musicians as they played and sipped on his glass of fine wine. The nobleman noticed a few people off to the side.

"Oh, if you'll excuse me. I have some matters that need tending to" with that he was gone. I was left standing beside Caleb and looking out onto the room. I glanced at the people, the buffet and dancefloor.

The pirate Captain had his free hand stuffed into the pocket of his trousers. I could feel the tension rolling off him in waves. He didn't know how to react to me so I reached for his hand and pulled it from his pocket. I then began tugging him in the direction of the dancefloor. At first, he stayed rooted in place with a questioning look plastered across his features.

"Dance with me?" I asked, my voice low and uncertain. He could deny me and storm off. He could abandon me to those around us so I mentally prepared myself for the worst and awaited his rejection despite having practiced with Ben as our teacher.

He said nothing and set his glass down on a nearby table then began walking in the direction of the dancefloor. He pulled me along behind him until he swiftly turned and drew me closer. I was caught off guard but instinctively placed one hand in his and the other on his shoulder blade.

His hand slipped around my waist to press against the small of my back as he began to move us in time with the music. We waltzed around the rest of the guests.

"I hope this be ye last request" my back straightened more at the sound of his familiar accent talking into my ear. His voice was low enough for only us to hear.

He was irritated from the way his voice growled like it hadn't done ever since we reached the town of Bakewell.

He spun us around a few times and I had to concentrate on how to move my feet to prevent from falling.

He'd most likely meant that he hoped it would be the last thing I'd ask of him for the night but to me it was like implying that he hoped it was my last request before I died. I smiled sadly and burying my face in his neck.

"It's a fitting last request" my hand slipped over his shoulder to come to a rest on his chest when he stumbled and stopped dancing. His muscles tensed beneath me and his heartbeat thundered in my ear. I gripped the black material of his jacket and took in the familiar scent of his skin.

"Evangeline" his voice was low and serious which concerned me. *Was he upset because of what I said?* If so, it hadn't been my intention to upset him.

I hummed while stepping back a pace to look up at him with my hand still resting on his chest. I was about to speak and ask him what was wrong but before I could he began to lead me towards the double doors and out of the ballroom.

I nearly tripped over my own two feet from the speed at which he was moving, turning corners and heading up the grand staircase until we came to the third floor and I managed to wrench my wrist free from his grasp.

"You're hurting me" I declared. My hand rubbed at my wrist that he'd been holding and I winched from the pain that shot through it. The bruising was still tender. He turned to look back at me and his jaw clenched when I flinched from the pain.

I watched him as he approached the nearest door, tested it so see if it was unlocked then threw it open and left me standing in the hallway.

"Caleb?" I questioned while dropping my hands back to my sides and following after him. My head turned to glance in every direction to make sure that there was no one there to catch us.

I assumed that he was looking for the gem but found it odd that he would stop on the third floor to look for it when we'd already established that it was located somewhere on the fourth floor.

I stepped into the empty bedroom that was dark apart from a single lit candle that sat on the other side of the room. I gasped when strong hands shoved me back against the wooden door, slamming it shut in the process.

It was dark and images from the tavern came flooding back. Mack pressing himself against me as the one in front of me hooked his arm underneath my left leg and lifted it up so that my knee was near my head. I cried out when his other hand gripped my rear and shoved me harder into his groin.

My eyes were squeezed shut and my teeth dug into my bottom lip to suppress a cry when a familiar voice whispered into my ear.

"Relax" my eyes shot open at the sound of Caleb's voice and I was met with his golden gaze peering into my mismatched one.

The fear left me. It was replaced by an intense heat that was accompanied by a great sense of longing and need.

He leaned down to trail kisses along my chest and shoulder. He was being careful of my bandaged throat when he kissed it. I felt my breathing become ragged as my arms snaked up above my head. My hands balled as I threw my head to the side, offering all of me to him. If he wanted me then I wouldn't deny him, after all, I was in love with him.

He ran his tongue along my jaw as his hand that was cupping my rear forced me into him harder before he forced me back. He repeated the process a few times.

I gasped and a small moan escaped my lips that brought back memories from the night he asked me to wear Mary's dress. My eyes shot open and I reached down to place my hands on his chest. I forced him back a few steps causing my leg to drop down to the ground instead of being pinned up beside me.

We were both breathing hard with his hands braced against the door on either side of me.

"I'm not-." I began to say in between pants only to be cut short by a breath of laughter that escaped him. He hid his face in the side of my neck and spoke.

"I know who you are, Evangeline" my body tensed in response to his words. He'd known that I was about to say that *'I'm not Mary'* and managed to cut me off before I could mention her. He pulled away from me just enough to meet my gaze. Our noses brushed as his breath tickled my lips.

"You're the irritating orphan girl from Port Alice-." he continued. He raised his hand to caress the side of my face and run the pad of his thumb over my lips. I flicked the tip of my tongue against his fingertip.

"You're the woman who called me a monster but somehow managed to fall in love with me" I didn't know what to say. He'd never spoken so openly to me before. I'd never heard so much emotion in his voice as I did that night. I was frozen and stunned like prey caught in a predator's trap.

"You're Evangeline" he leaned in so that his lips just barely brushed over mine for the briefest of moments before he captured them with his.

I threw my arms around his neck and played with the hair at the back of his head as he pulled me closer. His tongue trailed across my bottom lip asking for entry. I parted my lips and felt his tongue roam my mouth as more heat shot through me.

It felt so right, like it was meant to be but a name crossed my mind 'Mary' I broke away from him causing him to kiss my throat and shoulder instead. I panted and my hands gripped his shoulders. I was trying to snap him out of his lustful daze.

"Wait" my voice was weak and my pupils were dilating. My need for him like a starvation and my body desperate for him. I shook my head and tried again.

"The amethyst" he froze and his muscles stiffened in response to those words that captured his interest. He loved Mary; I knew he did. He stopped at the mention of her resurrection and took a few steps back.

I was panting with my body slumped back against the door. My chest rose and fell rapidly. There was an unfamiliar look clouding his features that I hadn't seen before as he watched me in silence.

I was snapped out of my daze by the sound of rasping knuckles on the door beneath me. My eyes went wide as Caleb's muscles stiffened. I moved to remove my heels and held them in my hands as I moved towards him. I leaned up to whisper into his ear with my hand gripping his upper arm.

"I started feeling ill and needed to lay down" with that I quickly moved over to the bed and set my shoes down beside it on the floor. I closed my eyes with my head resting back against the pillows.

Caleb moved towards the door when the knocking continued and opened it to reveal one of the butlers.

"Pardon the intrusion my Lord but the rooms are off limits for the remainder of the night" the butler explained while attempting to peer into the room but Caleb was too large and was obstructing the older man's view. I coughed, catching the Captain's attention and snapping him out of his train of thought.

"Yes, well my wife felt a bit ill and Lady Lillian insisted on her resting" he moved slightly out of the way to reveal the image of me splayed out among the pillows with my hand resting against my forehead. I pretended to pant with eyes half closed from the exhaustion. The butler returned his gaze to Caleb and cleared his throat before he spoke.

"I see, I will confirm this with the Lord and Lady" he nodded while turning to leave but paused to glance back at 'Lord Read' for the briefest of moments.

"Do stay put, my Lord" Caleb nodded then watched him leave as he headed down the staircase. He closed the door and turned towards me. I was already sitting up on the bed and tugging my shoes onto my feet with my hair coming undone. It dangled into my eyes and concealing my face like a curtain of white silk.

"We must hurry" he announced and I nodded. I stood as he once again opened the door and held it for me while I stepped into the hall. I quickly made my way towards the stairs.

He caught up to me with only a few strides since his legs were much longer than mine. I gripped the skirt of my dress as we ascended the stairs. The light from the chandeliers reflected off my pale skin and caught in his golden gaze like a blazing fire.

The fourth floor was like one open plan room but it was separated into various areas like a living area, a library, a dining area and art room where multiple canvasses stood in the process of being painted on.

Three rooms were closed off from the rest which most likely the bedroom, bathroom and study. I turned to glance up at Caleb who stood beside me.

"The bedroom" I muttered and he nodded while studying the floorplan. After a short pause he began heading towards the room closest to the art area. He reached for the doorknob and clicked it open to reveal a master bedroom.

He caught sight of my confused expression in the mirror that hung in the bedroom and looked back at me from over his shoulder.

"People tend to have their rooms closest to where they feel most comfortable" he motioned his hand in the direction of the table of paints and to the many brushed. He pointed at the finished works leaned up against the far wall.

"I see" I followed him into the bedroom and closed the door behind me. I locked it and took in the sight of the king size bed, the walk in closet, the vanity, sitting area and the balcony beyond that. There was a fireplace and above that hung a painted piece of Lillian on her wedding day. She was dressed in white with a large amethyst dangling from her neck.

Caleb, having been a thief for many years hardly noticed the rest of the room. His sights were locked onto the closet that he began to raid in search of the gem. He opened one of the drawers and found the necklace neatly tucked away among many others. He lifted it and examined the purple jewel until the sound of scurrying feet could be heard approaching from outside the room.

I looked towards the door as Caleb snapped out of his daze. He moved to where I was and clasped the necklace around my throat.

"Search every room, find them!" the butler's voice bellowed as panic began to set in but Caleb remained calm as he turned his eyes towards the balcony.

His hand grabbed hold of mine and he began dragging me to the balcony as the sound of doors slamming echoed throughout the manor. The glass doors of the balcony swung open to reveal the town of Bakewell beyond along with the garden.

Caleb let go of my hand to climb onto its railing. He moved along the window sill that sat beyond it then began scaling down onto a lower balcony. He landed in a graceful crouch as if he'd done it a million times before and without any fear of heights.

"Jump!" he called up to me with his arms held out to catch me. I glanced at the railing then at the balcony below. A rattling sound caught my attention and I glanced in its direction to find that someone was fiddling with the bedroom's doorknob.

"Over here!" someone yelled and I kicked off my heels to climb onto the railing with one hand gripping the jewel in its palm for fear of losing it. I breathed in deeply then squeezed my eyes shut and jumped without giving it much thought.

It felt like I was soaring, like I was falling through the sky and towards the ground with my hair whipping past me. The stars glistened overhead and I kept my eyes locked onto them when they opened.

The sound of fabric rustling when Caleb managed to catch me snapped me out of my mesmerized daze and I looked to him. His one arm was hooked beneath my knees while the other wrapped itself around my shoulders. I felt my heart start to beat faster at the sight of him, at the thought of him kissing me with such need and intensity that it made my body burn for his touch.

He set me down on my feet then began scaling the rest of the manor. He climbed down to the grass two stories below. I noticed how he moved and decided to try it myself. I used the window sills and edges in the manors design to move down onto a balcony located on the second floor.

The sound of the bedroom door being kicked open from above met my ears and I dared glance up to see shadows making their way towards the balcony.

I stepped onto the balcony's railing and met Caleb's eyes. A feeling of excitement and a rush of adrenaline coursed through me as I leaped from the edge with my arms outstretched towards him. This time I took in the sight of his features instead of the stars.

He swiftly caught me then set me down and grabbing onto my hand to lead me in the direction of the stables. We kept our backs close to the manor walls with the hope that they wouldn't spot us.

Once inside the stables, it felt like I could breathe again while Caleb worked on saddling a black stallion. He worked fast after tearing his suit jacket from his shoulders and tossing it aside.

He mounted the animal abruptly then held his hand out for me to take.

"Climb on" I took his offered hand and used the saddle to toss one leg over the back of the stallion. I wrapped one arm around his waist and pressed myself flush against him. The stallion began moving, ready to gallop.

"Hold on" Caleb warned then whipped the reigns and kicked the stallion sides causing it to take off at breakneck speed. I held onto the gem with one hand while the other tightened around the material of his shirt and I buried my face into his shoulder.

I stayed like that until we reached the streets of Bakewell then dared to look up at the buildings that passed us by. The stallion's hooves were clicking against the cobblestone. There was no one in sight, no one following us and I couldn't help but laugh in response to the rush that I felt.

I threw my head back to feel the wind whipping through my hair and smiled up at the stars. Caleb glanced back at me from over his shoulder. He was trying to hide his grin but I noticed it before he could turn his eyes back onto the road ahead.

I could understand why people stole. It was exhilarating. The feeling I felt was most likely what Caleb felt during his years of thieving as a young man.

We abandoned the horse a few blocks down from the inn and made our way there on foot. We gathered our things and left on horseback.

I had insisted that Caleb hide the jewel in his pocket once we reached the inn for fear of someone recognizing it and pointing the nobles in our direction.

The adrenaline wore off some time later and I found myself traveling along the English countryside with a feeling of shame and guilt.

Lillian was a wonderful person. She was kind and gentle. She only cared about others and yet I stole from her without so much as a second thought. I shook my head as Mary's face flickered in the back of my mind. I looked straight ahead at the dirt roads and fields of tall grass.

I did it for her and Caleb. I did it for love. I was sure that if the roles were reversed that Lillian would've done the same.

I whipped Chantilly's reigns and urged her to go faster. My sights were set on the Sunken Soul, on Rebecca, Nolan and Ben. The family I'd gained while journeying with them on their ship in search of the jewels.

There was only one left to collect. It was an orange gem located within the hump of the great blue.

My time with Caleb was coming to an end but I pushed the thought aside and replacing it with the time I'd spent alone with him on our trip to Bakewell.

Chapter Forty-Five

We reached the ship around dusk the next day. We returned the horses to the stables and bought more comfortable clothes to wear.

I was dressed in a loose black shirt that had long sleeves and a pair of brown trousers that were meant for men since women rarely ever wore anything other than dresses or skirts. A pair of black boots clad my feet and my hair was thrown up with a clip.

We abandoned everything except for the Amethyst of Bakewell that was tucked away beneath the material of my blouse.

I could see the black sails dancing in the sea breeze in the distance as we made our way along the docks. Fisherman, sailors and shippers were loading and unloading their hauls for the day.

Caleb was dressed similarly to me with the only differences being the colors and the fact that his shirt wasn't tucked into his trousers like mine was. The items also didn't sit as tightly on him as they did on me and he wore a maroon coat.

I could see Al in the crow's nest arguing with himself as we neared the ship along with a few of the crew. They were laughing and lounging around like they normally would with a bottle of rum and some music.

I began scaling the side of the ship, making use of the netting on the side to haul myself up as Caleb waited for me on the deck. He offered me his hand to help me over the railing.

"Captain" Nolan greeted with the usual green bottle pressed to his lips and Rebecca seated in between his parted legs. Her eyes studied us as I took hold of Caleb's hand and shot him a grateful smile.

"You were gone for quite a while" Rebecca muttered. She leaned her head back against Nolan's shoulder and her eyes were trained on us.

I let go of the Captain's hand and reached for the necklace that dangled around my throat. I hooked my finger through the chain to pull it out from underneath the fabric of my blouse. The purple gem glistened in the light of the setting sun. It was almost enchanting.

"Our absence wasn't in vain" I plucked the necklace from my neck causing the chain to snap then tossed it to Caleb. He caught it effortlessly and gripped the stone in the palm of his hand. He seemed to be deep in thought. The crew cheered at the sight of the jewel. Some even said things like *'I knew ye'd find it, Captain'* or *'That be our Captain'*

They were celebrating, all except for Rebecca and Nolan. Both of them knew that the punishment for being caught stealing from a noble was death and they knew that the guards were right on our heels, in search of the woman Lillian had painted in her portrait but neither of them spoke, instead a familiar voice came from the stern.

"What are your orders, Captain?" I looked up to find Ben leaning over the stern's railing. His features were set in stone when his eyes flickered down to my left hand and the ring that still resided there. It was the ring I'd gotten so used to wearing that I forgotten about it until then.

He tossed something in Caleb's direction. It was his Captain's hat that Caleb caught and positioned on the top of his head.

My mind went back to the last time I'd seen them together. To when Ben struck Caleb and when I'd to stopped him from killing the Captain out of anger. His anger was still there but it was faint as if the time apart had helped Ben calm down. Caleb turned his eyes onto me at the asked question and stuffing the jewel into the pocket of his coat.

"What'll it be, love?" his familiar pirate accent was like music to my ears. It was so warm and welcoming.

All eyes were on me as I thought back to the book, the one I'd read from start to finish with the hope of finding answers. I had my answers and I'd made my choice. It was a choice that only Caleb, Rebecca and I knew of.

My eyes turned towards the orange sea that stretched on for miles and even more miles beyond that, from one corner of the world to the next.

"The last jewel resides within the hump of the great blue-." I repeated the words from the book then gave a sad smile.

The last gem would be a simple one to retrieve and after that I would die for the sake of love. I would die for the sake of the one I loved.

"We head North towards the cold" Caleb nodded then ordered the crew to set sail. Ben climbed up to the sails to manage them while the rest of the crew worked on raising the anchor with Nolan included. Rebecca was left seated on the barrel alone with the bottle in hand. She leaned her head back and looked at the ocean behind her from an upside down perspective.

"You're either the most foolish woman I've ever met or the most reckless-." she began. Caleb was already on the stern and manning the helm while I stayed rooted in place by Rebecca's words. She raised her head to meet my eyes and took a swig of Nolan's rum.

"I can't really decide which" I knew she was referring to me sacrificing myself. Normal people would do everything in their power to continue living yet I was offering up my life as if it was nothing.

I smiled at her. The same feeling from before overcame me. It was the feeling I would get whenever the topic of Mary's resurrection was discussed.

"I can't explain it-." I began. My mismatched eyes went beyond her to the ocean that seemed to call out to me. It whispered my name and always beckoned me towards it.

"It just feels like I have to go through with it" my hand fiddled with the ring on my ring finger without me realizing it which caught Rebecca's attention. She looked away from me and at the sea as the ship started sailing North.

"You've grown closer" she decided to announce. I knew that we'd shared our moments while being alone for a few days and nights. The evening spent in the fields, the night we shared curled up in bed, picking out the dresses and working together to find the sixth gem but I hadn't expected anyone to notice it as quickly as she had.

"And despite that, Mary is still the one he desires" Rebecca hummed in response to my words and looked up at Caleb who stood on the stern. His eyes were locked onto the as Ben sat perched on the sails overhead. Nolan conversed with a few of the crew members and laughed at their jokes.

"She was the one he desired long before they even met" I knew that she was talking about herself and about her feelings towards Caleb that had started at a young age but even then, he still rejected her. Even when he didn't even know of Mary's existence, she still held a claim over his heart.

Rebecca took a long swig of the rum and ran the back of her hand over her lips before she decided to add,

"It's like fate is always dragging them towards each other" she held the bottle out for me to take with her hand wrapped around its neck as I took in the sight of it. I studied it and contemplated on whether one sip would be enough.

I took it and threw my head back, feeling the liquid sting its way down the back of my throat. I coughed from the sharp taste and handed the bottle back to her.

"And who are we to defy fate?" I questioned while shooting her a lop sided grin. She breathed a laugh and continued drinking as if my question was something a child would ask of an adult.

"Fate is vague. It's love that we can't defy" her words were deep and yet they were true.

I turned to head in the direction of the Captain's quarters when she spoke again.

"We can alter our fate but we can't choose who we fall in love with" I paused briefly as the words registered in the back of my mind.

If I hadn't been on the beach the night the Sunken Soul had sailed into Port Alice then I would've never been kidnapped and I never would've fallen in love with Caleb. I'd never have met him if I'd stayed in bed but then again whenever I would try to think back to that night and how I'd gotten to the shore, it was always a mystery. Perhaps it truly was fate that guided me to the beach that night? I shook my head.

"Fate is what leads us to those we are to love" I gazed up at the orange sky that was starting to fade to a darker purple. My eyes locked onto the swirling clouds and the seagulls that circled overhead. The breeze blew through my hair and against my cheeks which made it seem almost as if it was trying to caress me.

"If you hadn't been born to your mother, would you have met Caleb? If you hadn't been stranded on that island when we set sail for the second jewel, would you have met Nolan?" she grew silent as she thought things over. I didn't wait for her response and instead I went below deck to the Captain's quarters. I glanced at the bed. It was piece of furniture that I detested the most but yet there was something comforting about it.

If fate was what led me to Caleb, then fate would lead me to my destiny and if it was for me to die so that Mary could live then so be it.

I glanced down at my hand and at the ring that resided there. It was the ring that was meant for her. I toyed with it and the diamond glistened underneath the light of the setting sun.

"Just a little bit longer" I whispered. It wasn't directed at myself or anyone onboard the ship but I was talking to Mary as if asking her to allow me to wear the ring for just a little bit longer so that I could pretend that Caleb truly loved me for just a little bit longer.

I could feel my heart constricting in my chest as I stared at the bed. The image of her beneath him with her hands gripping his arms and head thrown back. Her cheeks were tinted pink. It was the bed that they shared and I had no right to lay in it.

The locket that sat on the nightside table caught my attention. Its silver surface danced in the light almost as if it was a small flicker of Mary's face that was smiling up at me. I could see her nodding her head in response to my request.

I felt so close to her, to the women I'd yet to meet apart from in my visions and dreams.

"Thank you" I breathed while reaching up to grip the anchor necklace that hung from my throat. Somehow, I knew that she understood exactly how I felt and that she cared for me as a loving friend like I cared for her. We shared the same love for Caleb that ran much deeper than even death.

I'd fallen asleep in the armchair that sat in the far corner. The exhaustion caught up to me from not having slept the entire journey back to the ship.

I woke up to the sight of the entire ship being engulfed in water. The room in front of me was completely submerged beneath the surface of the vast ocean.

Objects were floating in mid-air. Papers, letters, books and Mary's locket were all dancing among the current.

I parted my lips and bubbles escaped them as I realized that the necklace was still wrapped around my neck, preventing me from breathing yet there seemed to be no need for me to breathe.

I could make out a figure drifting aimlessly through the water past the bubbles. A gray dress danced around her form and surrounded her like a protective barrier. Her head was thrown back and her golden hair swayed around her delicate features.

I moved to stand but the message didn't seem to register to my limbs, leaving me trapped in place.

Her mismatched eyes stared up at the ceiling as she slowly reached out as if to grab hold of something that was too far above her to touch. Her fingertips extended and her eyes began to soften when a familiar voice yelled out over the water.

'Mary!' my eyes widened at the thought of him, of Caleb being trapped in the water along with me and unable to breathe. I had to save him. I had to get to him but no matter how hard I tried or how frantically I wanted to cry out to him, neither my body nor my lips would move.

Mary's hand began to close and fall as if she'd admitted defeat. She sank ever deeper into the water with no hope of breaching the surface.

'Forgive…me' her gentle voice whispered but it didn't come from her lips, instead it was her thoughts that I heard.

The floorboards of the Sunken Soul gave way causing both Mary and I to fall down into the endless darkness that was the ocean depths.

My clothes tore away from my skin and my necklace slipped from my neck causing me to transform in the water. My legs began to morph into a single tail as gills appeared on the sides of my neck and my eyes began to glow.

Once I shifted, I began floating in the water. I hardly moved with only the sounds of the sea reaching my ears.

Something caught my attention and I looked up to find Mary drifting in front of me. Her gray dress was replaced by the extravagant gold one, the one Caleb had made for her. She met my eyes almost as if looking into a mirror and she reached out towards me.

My body moved on its own accord and I placed my palm flat against hers. My clawed and webbed hand seeming almost alien against her delicate one.

She pulled me closer and hid her face in my chest causing her hair to tangle with mine. I wrapped my arms around her form and held her flush against me.

'A heart of the sea' she whispered, using my voice. My eyes opened to look down at her and both of our hearts began to glow a bright pale white in response to her words.

A never ending calm overcame me as her dress began to dissolve along with her skin. She turned into sea foam in my arms and evaporated among the waves. I tried reaching for her but by the time I managed to move, she was gone and the water was once again dragging me deeper beneath the surface.

I tried calling out to her. I was desperate to hold her when suddenly I shot up in the same chair that I'd fallen asleep in.

I was panting and my hand moved to grip my forehead as I tried regaining my composure. It was just a dream. I tried to remind myself of that but there was something so unsettlingly real about it. I lowered my hand once I could breathe and looked at my clothes. The trousers and blouse was replaced by an oversized shirt. It was the white one that Caleb wore before we reached the ship.

I leaned back in the chair and brought my knees up to my chest as I thought back to the moments before I fell asleep. Caleb complained about the clothes he wore. He found them irritable and restricting so he came below deck to replace them with his usual attire. I'd decided to take a nap and dressed in his discarded shirt to be more comfortable while I slept.

"Pod ahoy!" my eyes shot open in response to the voice yelling out over the ship's deck. My hand was resting against my forehead as those very words registered in the back of my mind.

A sad smile crept its way onto my lips before I managed to get up and make my way above deck. I left the ring on the desk before I went.

The crew was gathered near the front of the ship. They gazed out onto the water in awe of a pod of humpback whales that swam alongside the ship but there was one in particular that led them.

Caleb was stationed on the stern and his eyes noticing me as I paused to stare down at the ship's floorboards. The sky above had been coated in gray clouds from venturing North.

"Within the hump of the great blue" I repeated the words for what felt like the millionth time.

My feet began to move towards the ship's bow and my hands reached for the material of my shirt to tear it from my body. My actions caught both Caleb and Ben's attention.

"Evangeline!" Ben called out to me but I ignored him as the rest of the crew seemed to notice me for the first time. Rebecca's eyes widened while Nolan rushed to remove his jacket. He wanted to drape it over my shoulders to conceal my naked form. The rest of the crew gave off a few cat calls and wolf whistles. I stopped a few feet away from the figurehead to remove my necklace and began running towards the front of the ship. I leaped from it and dove head first into the freezing water.

The moment my body collided with the water, I began to change while the ship sailed overhead until I was fully transformed and

351

began swimming in pursuit of the whales. The crew looked on in awe as I darted past most of the humpbacks. I swerved in and out of them while dodging the heavy beating of their tails. I could hear them singing, the sound of it was like music to my ears.

A whale calf dared to venture closer to me and its eyes watched me as it too tried to sing a song. I could feel them, their emotions and their desires as I swam among them. The final jewel was within my grasp. The last of the seven treasures was so close that I could almost touch it and along with it came the ever nearing moment of my death.

I could dive down and disappear among the waves, never to be seen again. I could swim and never stop but my mind wouldn't allow me to. There was just something that kept me there. It entrapped me near Caleb where I would eventually meet my fate.

The whale at the front of the pod was a large bull. Its body was covered in scars from years of having to fend of predators and whalers. Its large eye flickered down to me to take in the sight of my tail and fins. It looked to the front and its song sang louder than the rest but instead of a song, I could hear its voice.

'You have come for the jewel' the whale realized. Its tail beating into the water caused a strong current that threatened to carry me away. It groaned. The sound echoed out around me and came from deep within its throat like a powerful vibration.

'Neptune will not approve of this' I stopped swimming but my tail kept beating behind me as I watched him continue to move through the water.

Neptune, the god of the seas? Why wouldn't he approve of me retrieving the seven treasures?

The whale began to dive down in front of me. Its tail slipped past me and narrowly missed striking me. The rest of the pod began to dive down around me, following the bull's lead.

'Be warned' its voice echoed through the back of my mind as the orange gem that was attached to its hump released itself and began drifting upward in the water towards me. My mind racing with thoughts concerning the whale's warning about Neptune and I contemplated why the god of the seas wouldn't want me gathering the gems.

I reached out and curled my hand around the jewel as I watched the pod disappear into the dark depths of the ocean.

Once they were gone and their song was only a faint whisper, I began swimming towards the surface. I broke through the water near the side of the ship.

Ben was leaning over the railing. He gazed down into the water in search of me and his eyes locked onto my form the moment I resurfaced.

"Evangeline!" the sound of him calling my name in either concern or fear sounded so familiar. I looked up to spot the silver anchor necklace flying through the air towards me. I caught it and felt the webbing on my hand start to dissolve when the anchor charm came in contact with my skin.

Caleb was stood beside Ben and the rest of the crew were positioned behind them. They observed me like a specimen in an experiment. They'd most likely never seen a Mermaid before. They'd never seen the glowing eyes, slit pupils, scales and fangs before.

Something inside of me welled up with fear. It was the fear of them fearing me and seeing me as a monster. I hardly cared about the rest of the crew except for Rebecca and Nolan. If they saw me as a freak of nature or a threat then it would tear me apart from the inside out.

I looked at Caleb. His eyes were hard but he didn't show any fear towards me. He'd seen my transformed state numerous times. The image of awe and amazement in his eyes from the night at the inn surfaced in the back of my mind.

I gripped the jewel tighter in my palm and felt its edges cutting into my skin like a knife where the bandages had torn away during my transformation. I tossed the jewel towards him. My determination was stronger than ever. I was going to go through with the sacrifice whether Neptune was against it or not. When it came to Caleb, I would defy the gods.

He caught it and glancing down at the last of the seven jewels, deep in thought.

I clasped the necklace back around my throat and felt my tail start to separate into two legs that began to kick in opposite directions beneath me.

Ben stripped out of his brown shirt and tossed it to me. I tugged it over my head. I was grateful and I knew that the white shirt wouldn't help to conceal my naked form once it got wet.

When I was covered, I started climbing onto the ship. I used the netting to hoist myself up onto the Sunken Soul's deck. Ben offered me his hand and pulled me up but my foot slipped on the floorboards causing me to stumble into his bare chest.

I felt his arm wrap itself around my waist and press me closer to him. I placed my palms flat against his exposed skin and could feel his heartbeat beneath his ribcage. He was warm. He was so comforting like an older brother who would always be there to fend off those who wished to harm me.

My hands balled into fists against him and for a moment I felt like crying. The thought of having to say goodbye to him, to Rebecca, Nolan and even Al was enough to cause my heart to ache in my chest.

I pressed my forehead against his chest and stared at my feet. I knew that Ben not knowing about my intentions was what made it even worse. He had no idea of how little time he had left with me. He'd come to love me and would do anything to prevent me from going through with my plans.

That's precisely why I couldn't tell him. It was why I couldn't say goodbye or tell him what he meant to me until those last moments when he would be unable to intervene.

Rebecca already knew and had been dealing with it in her own time but Ben was clueless.

"Eva?" his voice questioned and his arm dropped away from my waist when he realized that I wasn't moving.

Caleb looked on with a hard gaze. His lips came together in a narrow line across the lower portion of his face. He knew exactly what I was thinking, both he and Rebecca could sense my thoughts.

I took a deep breath and forced myself to step away from Ben. I met his worried brown gaze with a fake smile plastered across my lips.

"Set sail for Port Alice" I instructed. My words were followed by a long silence as the crew looked on with furrowed brows. Caleb stuffed the jewel into the pocket of his signature red coat then turned to snap at them.

"Ye heard the woman! Set course for Port Alice!" the crew immediately jumped into action. Their voices rang out in a chorus of "Aye, Captain!" or "Manage the sails!"

Ben stayed where he was. He studied me for a few moments longer then looked at Caleb and nodded before he too began to rush about the deck. He shot concerned glances in my direction every now and then.

Rebecca approached Caleb and I with her arms crossed over her chest.

"You know; you don't have to do this" she reminded me after having seen my inner struggle. When my hands left Ben's chest it was as though my heart had said its goodbye and I was left feeling emptier than I was before. I found Caleb's golden gaze but even though my eyes were locked onto his, my words were directed at Rebecca.

"What were we saying about fate?" she stayed quiet as her hands constricted on her arms while she watched me. I saw her jaw clench and her eyes became cold at the thought of me dying for the man I loved just so that he could finally be with the one he loved.

"That there is no defying it" I answered for her. I turned to look at her with the same sad but relaxed smile on my face.

Her head lowered as if to try and hide her gritted teeth and her body began to tremble.

"I'm ready" I said while nodding with determination. I watched her go from trembling to shaking and realized that what I had first thought were tears was anger that she was trying to suppress.

When she raised her head, her resolve broke and she began to yell loud enough for everyone to hear.

"And what about me? What about Nolan and Ben? Are we supposed to be ready?" my eyes widened when her words struck me. Ben and Nolan stopped what they were doing when they heard their names being yelled. Some of the crewmembers also paused due to the sudden yelling. They were curious as to what was happening.

"I lost my parents and I had to deal with that-." her voice was calmer but her words still cut deep.

Caleb stiffened. He was unable to speak from the paralyzing effect that her words had on him.

Rebecca's arms fell to her sides and her hands balled. She was angry with Caleb for wanting to use me as a sacrifice and in that moment, she was angry with me for being willing to be his sacrifice.

"But I'm not ready to deal with losing you" I never thought that Rebecca would think of me as family. I didn't know that she cared so much about me.

She turned on her heels and began making her way towards the trap door so she could disappear below deck.

"Becca!" Nolan called. He followed after but pausing near the steps to glance back at me with sad, confused eyes. It was the same look that Ben wore. A warm hand reached out to caress my lower back and draw me out of my thoughts.

"Ye hands" Caleb announced as he motioned to my bare hands, one of which was riddled with even more cuts than before. I glanced down at them and nodded. I allowed Caleb to lead me to the Captain's quarters as my mind raced with thoughts and my chest was consumed with emotions.

Was I doing the right thing or was I merely doing what Caleb wanted me to do like a puppet on a string?

Rebecca.

I was mad and I was confused but the emotion that took root in my chest was an overwhelming sadness. My boots thudded down the stairs and into the water. I felt the liquid soak the bottom of my skirt and my legs beneath it.

"Becca!" I knew that voice. I knew who it belonged to without even having to look. I was on my way to the room I'd been staying in and reached for the handle when a much stronger one stopped me by grabbing hold of my shoulder. My body froze.

"Why?" I found myself whispering as I stared at the door in front of me. I wasn't expecting an answer but the question had haunted me ever since Captain Solstice murdered my parents. The memory of it was as vivid as the texture in the wood of the door.

I could see them being cut down, my mother's lifeless body staring down at me and my father dragging himself across the bakery's floor towards her. There was so much blood.

My parents died together in an embrace. They were grateful that their daughter would live.

"Why does everyone I care about end up dying?" that was the question I could never finish asking but I did. I thought back to the night Caleb had returned to Martin's Port. I thought about the words he spoke after losing Mary.

I could remember him yelling at the sea and cursing it when he throw himself into the waves. His hands digging into the waves as if he could find Mary's corpse floating in the shallow waters.

356

I remember dragging him away from the water before he managed to drown himself and collapsed on the sand while I pleaded for him to stop.

He was crying and he never cried but that night he clung to me, weeping like a small child.

'She's gone, Becca' he got out in between sobs. At first, I didn't believe it. It couldn't be, he had to be lying.

'Mary's gone' he repeated as if to reassure me that he was not lying but telling the truth. Everyone always died. The people came and went but Caleb and I remained. We never died.

That was the night he abandoned me after I finally found him again. He refused to take me with him but wherever he went, I followed.

The night Mary died was the night I decided to stay with him because wherever he went death would always follow and only sadness could come from that darkness.

Now it was Evangeline's turn and like an idiot I stayed onboard the Sunken Soul. I spoke to her and started caring about her only to have her torn away from me. I hated the treasures, I hated the magic behind them but most of all, I hated death.

"What are ye talking about, las?" Nolan's voice dragged me back to reality and out of the darkness that was my mind and the thoughts that swirled within it. My eyes had grown foggy with tears and when I blinked, they fell.

"Evangeline's not-." I knew what he was going to say without him having to finish his words. They enraged me, my emotions a tornado that I couldn't control, switching from sadness to grief to anger within seconds. I turned, shoving his hand away from my shoulder to meet his eyes.

"Why do you think we've been chasing these treasures?" I rushed out. I motioned towards the ocean beyond the walls around us. He seemed to be thinking back to a conversation he'd previously had.

"All of this-." I waved my arms around as if to emphasize that I was talking about the traveling, the jewels, Evangeline and where we were currently heading.

"All of it is to resurrect Mary" he knew who Mary was from having observed Caleb and Evangeline. At that point everyone onboard the ship knew who Mary Grace Sillvan was. She was Caleb's dead lover

357

who looked exactly like the white haired Mermaid we'd all come to care for.

"And Evangeline is just a sacrifice for Caleb to get what he wants" my arms dropped limply to my sides and my eyes grew sad. My voice became smaller and harder to hear. Nolan's back muscles tensed and his hands clenched at his sides. He cared about Evangeline not in a way that a friend or a lover would but more like a father would.

"And she's willing to do whatever it takes to make him happy-." I glanced to the side as a single tear escaped my eye and trailed its way down to my chin. It was unfair. It wasn't right.

How could one person be so selfish as to take a life in exchange for another? I knew that Caleb loved Evangeline even if he wouldn't admit it himself so how could he possibly kill her if he loved her?

"Even if it means dying" I whispered to the empty room. The sound of water swishing past our feet and the lamps swaying on their hooks were the only sounds surrounding us apart from my voice.

I began to turn and reached for the door handle when Nolan pulled me into a tight embrace. He pressed my face into his chest with his arms wrapped around my shoulders.

I didn't want his comfort. I was strong enough to deal with my emotions on my own. I didn't need him or at least that's what I thought until I felt him holding me.

There was a faint aching in my heart that made me feel almost numb.

"We're all different, red" he used the nickname that he only ever used when we were alone. It was a familiar sound that calmed me.

"We've got our own minds and once they be made up, they be made up-." the way he spoke was similar to how Caleb had come to speak over his years spent as a pirate but his Irish accent was thick beneath his poor English grammar.

How did I come to care so much about an annoying, dirty and uneducated pirate? Was it the way he constantly forced me out of my comfort zone or was it his constant teasing that made me feel like I was fifteen again?

"We can't change their minds or stop them from making their own choices" I knew he was right. It didn't juts frustrate me but everyone else.

The choices people make around us are theirs and those choices could hurt us, they could hurt them but we couldn't stop those decisions from being made.

The world was full of choices being made with destructive outcomes.

"But we can deal with those choices in our own way and at our own pace" I nodded in understanding.

I found myself wondering if he'd ever been hurt by someone else's decisions before? Was that why he could so openly comfort me because he'd gone through it himself?

He was nothing like Caleb. Nolan drank too much, smelt of rum and he always taunted me but despite that, I cared for him in a way that almost felt like love.

"I don't want to lose you too" I breathed into his chest causing it to rumble with a chuckle that escaped his lips. Admitting that I didn't want to lose him was hard for me to do and he knew it which was why he was laughing. He pulled back enough to look at my face with his arms still holding me.

"I won't die that easily, lassie" I looked at the floor and nodded.

How did I go from being such a loud and independent woman to being as submissive and vulnerable as I was in that moment?

It irritated and confused me and Nolan noticed this. He pressed his lips to my forehead then pulled away, leaving my body longing for his touch.

"Ye're so cute when ye're confused" there it was. The teasing comment that I was waiting for. I shoved his shoulder and turned to open the door but he bend down and scoop me into his arms. He lifted me up so that I was cradled against his chest then he dropped me onto the bed and fell down beside me causing the mattress to bounce.

He was grinning up at the floorboards overhead and I found myself staring at him. I took in his beard, his brown hair and the small scars that littered his face.

I would never admit it, never in a million years but I loved him. He somehow made Caleb pale in comparison.

After thinking that I rolled over so that my back was to him and I hid my face in the sheets for fear of him seeing the unfamiliar red tint in my cheeks.

Chapter Forty-Six.

Caleb sat me down on the foot of the bed before he started working on disinfecting my wounds and bandaging them again.

Once he was done, he reached for my neck and gently brushed his fingertips over its black bruises. The feel of his tender touch snapped me out of my thoughts and I finally noticed Caleb who was kneeling in front of me.

His eyes filled with sadness at the sight of where Mack had wrapped his hand around my throat and tried to squeeze the life out of me. I could still feel him pressing himself up against my body and looming overhead like a monstrous giant with a sinister glint in his eyes.

I knew that only Caleb could touch me like that. Only his fingers could trace the places where Mack had once been and only Caleb could pin me down or kiss me. They were all things that I knew if any other man tried to do them, I'd struggle and scream to get away from them because of fear and the fact that they weren't Caleb.

I closed my eyes and leaned into his touch. His warm hand cupped the side of my face as he spoke.

"Ye don't have to do this" his words caused my eyes to open. I looked at him kneeling in front of me and I knew what he was referring to. He was referring to my sacrifice and I raised my bandaged hand to lace my fingers through his.

"Do you love me?" I randomly asked, surprising both him and myself. He froze causing his body to stiffen while I cast my eyes down to the floor between us. My lips parted to repeat the question.

"Do you love me like you love her?" his hand went limp in mine and the fingers that once curled around my hand loosened. I waited for his response. I was unable to look at him as a small glimmer of hope swirled inside my chest.

Seconds felt like hours and when he didn't answer I knew that I was doing the right thing. I let go of his hand and my own fell into my lap.

"I can never be her. I can never compare to Mary-." I blinked and raised my head to look at him. The space between us seemed more like miles than inches.

I felt my chest ache when I continued. It was a pain worse than the cuts and bruises I'd sustained. It was an emotional pain that cut deeper than any laceration.

"And that's why-." my bottom lip trembled and my hand constricted around the brown material of Ben's shirt.

"I would rather die than live my life trying to make you love me like you love her" his hard and emotionless gaze that had been filled with shock turned to sadness. It was almost as though he was hurt by what I'd said.

He opened his mouth and he was about to speak but there were no words that would come out so he closed it again. He draped his arm across his knee and his head turned to look at anything other than me.

I stood, stepping over the bandages and needles, the bottle of wine and thread that he used to stitch my reopened cuts.

He too stood and his eyes followed me over to the nightside table where I reached out to touch the heart locket.

Nolan once said that people who could see the past or future were known as Oracles but I knew that whatever gift I had, it didn't make me an Oracle. I didn't see the future, I saw the past not from the sidelines but as memories as if I was there, as if I'd lived through them.

My bond with Mary had grown stronger over the time I spent with Caleb. So much so that it was becoming hard to know where she began and I ended. It was like we were one person yet we were completely different souls.

"I think it's time I tell him" I muttered. The 'him' in my sentence referred to Ben.

Caleb's jaw tightened. The cut on his lip had long since faded away but he could still feel Ben's fist connecting with his jaw. He seemed to be contemplating the reaction that Ben would have towards my willing sacrifice.

"And to say goodbye" I would've wanted to postpone it for as long as possible, if not avoid it completely but Rebecca's outburst changed that. Ben and Nolan had questions. There was no avoiding it any longer.

I stared at the leather bound book lost in thought as I tried to figure out what Caleb was thinking. What was he feeling? He didn't say anything which left us engulfed in a long silence that was broken by him heading for the stairs.

I was caught off guard when he paused at the foot of the stairs to speak.

"Make it clear that this is what ye want" with that he was gone. He didn't bother to stay as I looked back at him from over my shoulder. I saw him disappear above deck.

He didn't want anyone to think that he was forcing me to be his sacrifice. That may have been the case when he kidnapped me but I no longer felt like a prisoner. Dying was my choice just like it had been Mary's. She killed herself because she couldn't be with Caleb and I was about to kill myself for the exact same reason. The only real difference was the cause.

With Mary it was her noble blood and her parents that forbade her from being with Caleb. With me it was Mary and the fact that Caleb's love for her would always surpass his love for me.

I smiled sadly as I looked to the ring on the desk that caught the light of day.

Perhaps Mary and I weren't so different after all. We both wanted to die instead of living a life without the one person we loved.

Rebecca already knew and was upset about my choice. She'd most likely have to tell Nolan when he'd try to comfort her and wanted know what was wrong which meant that I had to tell Ben.

I dreaded it. My hands became clammy and my breath caught in my throat at the mere thought of how he'd react.

I spent hours trying to find the right words to say to him, hours contemplating how to tell him in the least damaging way possible and I finally decided to just do what felt right.

I was about to head above deck when Ben came down the stairs. He ducked as he stepped into the Captain's quarters where he'd been a few times before, including when he stayed by my side while I slept for days after having injured myself. Another instance was when he carried me below deck to hide the fact that I was a Mermaid.

He paused when he noticed that I was stood in the middle of the room.

I felt a lump start to form in my throat as question after question filled my mind.

Why was he there? Had Rebecca told him? Was he mad at me? He approached me and held up a black velvet pouch.

"Caleb told me to bring this to you" I knew from the simple task of sending him to me that Caleb had grown impatient by my procrastination and decided to take matters into his own hands.

I held my palm out towards him and he dropped the pouch onto my hand with a clutter. The bag felt heavy but not too heavy. When I pealed the velvet material back, I was met with the sight of seven gems. Each jewel was a different color and I'd collected all of them. I held the seven treasures in the palm of my hand. The treasures that nobody else could've possibly obtained.

"Ben-." I breathed. My hand tightened around the jewels as if trying to snuff out the reminder of what I had to do.

I felt my hand tremble and my throat tighten with the words that didn't want to be said. I didn't realize that I was looking down until Ben reached out to grip my chin and lift my eyes up to meet his as he stepped closer.

"What's wrong?" he gently asked as his eyes searched mine. He could see past my façade. He could see the cowering child beneath the powerful woman that I pretended to be.

I closed my eyes. I was unable to look at him, unable to meet the eyes of the man who loved me but who I could never love.

"Remember that night at the Pirate's Nest?" I responded to his question with one of my own. He didn't let go of my chin. He didn't move even though I silently pleaded for him to leave so that I wouldn't have to tell him. I didn't want to break his heart for a second time.

"You were crying" he reminded me. I saw the image of me on my hands and knees while weeping on the docks as Ben rushed to my side after I discovered why Caleb kidnapped me and what his true intentions were. I pulled my chin away from him to look down at the pouch in my hand.

"Do you know why Caleb were collecting these?" I asked while shaking the bag and hearing the jewels clutter against each other. He studied the bag with his eyebrows furrowed up in confusion. He didn't know anything. He thought that they were worth a lot of gold and that was the only reason why we were collecting them.

When he didn't reply, I continued,

"These jewels give you the power to resurrect the dead" when my eyes turned to look at him, his own were wide with horror. I could tell that the thought of raising someone from beyond the grave terrified

363

him and the image of a corpse being brought back to life would frighten anyone.

"Caleb wanted them so that he could resurrect Mary" there was a flicker of familiarity across his features as he recalled the time that I told him I looked Caleb's dead lover.

"But the jewels require a sacrifice-." I didn't know why I started with that and why I didn't tell him how I truly felt about Caleb first. I decided to give into the words that escaped my lips.

"That sacrifice must be the sibling or reincarnation of the person you're trying to resurrect" his face twisted with shock and anger as he processed my words. He put two and two together and realized that I would be used as Caleb's sacrifice. Ben's nostrils flared and he began to head in the direction of the stairs.

"I won't let him touch you!" he snapped with his hands balled at his sides. I reached for him and curled my fingers around the fabric of his newfound shirt. He was about to tear free from my grasp when I blurted the words without thinking.

"I love him!" Ben froze. His entire body stiffened and his muscles tensed. I dropped the jewels causing them to clutter down to the floorboards so that I could grip the back of his shirt with both hands. I buried my face into his shoulder blade. I had to keep him there. I couldn't let him leave angry. I wouldn't let him hurt Caleb.

"He gave me the choice to run, but I-." I gasped as I tried to catch my breath. My eyes were starting to fog over and my throat tightened with the need to cry but I couldn't allow it.

He glanced back at me from over his shoulder, ready to hear my next words.

"I have to do this" my voice came out in a shaky whisper. I was afraid of how he'd react to the situation. I pressed my forehead against his back and managed to get the words out.

"I have to die so that she can live" he turned causing me to take a step back. My hands dropped back down to my sides but he reached out to catch my wrist to prevent me from backing away. His grip was gentle. He held the thought of my bruises in the back of his mind as a reminder to be careful.

"Why? Why would you want to die?" his hand tightened ever so slightly and his eyebrows furrowed up in confusion. I could tell that he wanted to yell and scream at me. He wanted to ask what he'd done wrong for me to want to take my own life but that wasn't it. I wasn't sad or depressed. I was happy, happier than I'd ever been and I was surrounded by people who truly care about me.

"Let's run away. Let's go somewhere far away and start over together" he grabbed onto my upper arms and shook me as he frantically rushed the words. I closed my eyes and felt the motion of him shaking me like the waves of the sea rocking the ship.

"Ben-." I tried to catch his attention but he was too far gone. His voice cracked when he continued his trail of thoughts. He blurted them out without much care.

"It'll just be the two of us. We could-." I reached up and grabbed hold of his wrists when I opened my eyes to look at him. He was confused and desperate. He stopped shaking me and my words finally reached him.

"I can't do that" it was like a slap in the face. His words caught in his throat. The questions that raced through his eyes reached out to me. They begged for answers. I managed to pull his hands away from my arms and held them in mine.

"I could never leave Caleb. I'd spent the rest of my life unable to love anyone else. I'd constantly be searching for him-." my hands curled around his. Pain shot through my palms and up my arms when I placed pressure on the newly stitched cuts. I cast my eyes down to the scattered jewels.

"I can't ever love you like you love me" the moment I said those words, I realized what he was going through. I understood what he must've been feeling for all that time. It was like me with Caleb and Mary. I loved Caleb more than anything but he could never love me like he loved her. It was the same with me and Ben. He loved me but I could never love him.

"I know what you must be going through-." I swallowed while gripping my chest where the pain was most agonizing.

"Feeling like you'll never be good enough for the one you love-." my hand tightened and the hand that still held his slipped away to grip the hem of the shirt that I wore. I tugged on it to express the convulsing pain that was all too familiar to me.

"It breaks you" Ben seemed to stop and think. His hands fell loosely to his sides as he watched me with the expression of agony on my face. My eyes stared down at the floor. They were glazed over with unshed tears as I gritted my teeth.

He surprised me by reaching out and pulling me against him in a tight embrace.

"I don't care if you'll never be able to love me. Just…stay with me" it was a plea. He was begging me. I stayed in his arms, unable to move and unable to hide the fact that I felt like bursting into tears at having to say goodbye.

I wished that I could pause time and just stay there with them forever.

"Please-." he began. The crack in his voice was followed by a stream of hot liquid sliding down the side of my face. At first, I thought that I'd finally given in but the tears didn't belong to me. They belonged to Ben.

"Don't leave me" I had to grit my teeth at the sound of his desperate plea. My lips trembled and my eyes wanted to close with unshed tears. I wanted to touch him but I couldn't. I couldn't move for fear of collapsing, for fear of shattering into pieces right in front of him.

"I-I'm going to miss you" I breathed into his ear which caused him to cry out and tighten his hold on me even more.

An image of him and I dancing on the deck surfaced in the back of my mind. An image of us swimming in the waters at the Pirate's Nest and of him kissing me in the rowboat after we'd retrieved the jewel from Gigas.

"Don't do this!" he fell to his knees in the center of the room and dragged me down with him. He wasn't whimpering but he was crying out of fear and desperation.

I wrapped my own arms around his neck and placed my chin on the top of his head as I ran my fingers through his hair.

"I have to" I whispered while closing my eyes and taking in his unique smell. He was trembling. His body seemed so much more fragile than it had before.

"For-." before I could finish, he moved his head and pulled away from me to meet my eyes. He spoke the name that I had yet to speak.

"For Caleb?" I shot him a sad smile that was filled with heartache as I watched the tears roll down the side of his face. I cupped his cheeks and brushed the tears away with the pads of my thumbs. His arms dropped away from me. They laid limp on the floor beside him as he looked up at me in defeat. He was broken.

"You want me to be happy, don't you? Just like I want him to be happy" he froze and his eyes filled with understanding as he looked at me.

If I'd been in Caleb's shoes and Ben in mine then he would've done the same for me not because I asked him to resurrect the love of my life but because he loved me so much that he would sacrifice anything just to see me smile.

"Please let me do this" my begging tone had caused the emotion to leave his eyes.

He couldn't deny me anything. He couldn't say no, no matter how badly the word wanted to slip past his lips.

He was betrayed by his first love and there I was breaking his heart by telling him that I loved someone else and that I was going to give my life for that person whether he approved of it or not. He didn't say anything and eventually I sat back on my knees. My hands dropped away from his face.

"Thank you" I breathed, feeling exhausted and drained after having to convince him.

I reached for the stone closest to us. It was a black stone that we'd obtained from Captain Darkheart himself when Ben's hand clamped down around my wrist. I looked up at him to find that his face was turned down and his eyes were hidden from sight.

"Ben?" I questioned when he pushed me down onto the wooden floor. His hands gripped my wrists and pinned them down on either side of my head. I felt him loom over me and my eyes widened in horror. The memories of Mack came flooding back and I began to struggle against him.

"Stop!" I yelled as I squeezed my eyes shut. I tried to kick at him but I couldn't.

"Ben, please" I tried again.

In his hurt state he wasn't thinking straight. He was confused, frustrated, heartbroken and desperate.

I tried to free my hands but he was too strong. He began kissing my bandaged neck like Caleb did before but it didn't feel the same.

"C-." the name caught in the back of my throat. My eyes were wide and my lips trembled when tears finally broke past the corner of my eye sockets. They trailed their way down my face and dripping onto the wood beneath me.

"Caleb!" the name echoed out around us and caused Ben to stiffen almost as if he was snapped out of his daze.

He lifted his weight to look at my face when heavy footsteps came thundering down the stairs.

"Eva, I-." Ben tried to explain as guilt and regret filled his eyes and Caleb neared. He was cut off by Caleb who snarling at him with glaring eyes.

"Get off her!" the Captain tore Ben off me as Rebecca rushed past them and collapsed in front of me. She embrace me and held me close to her as if she was afraid that something would happen to me.

Caleb pinned Ben up against a nearby wall.

"Ye who dared to strike me for not protecting her-!" Caleb yelled in Ben's face. He was referring to the incident at the tavern. I looked on, unable to speak or move. I couldn't even cry as Nolan stood nearby. He was ready to assist Caleb if something went wrong. My wrists ached and my heart was racing like it had before.

"Ye call this protecting someone ye care about?" I squeezed my eyes shut when Caleb tugged on Ben's shirt only to force him back into the wall again where he hit his head. Ben stared down at the floor. He wasn't able to look at anyone or anything other than the floor.

"Answer me!" I pushed away from Rebecca and got to my feet. She tried to protest however I ignored her and reached for Caleb. I wanted to feel him close to me and I wanted to touch him. I wrapped my arms around his torso and pressed my face into his back.

"That's enough. He didn't mean it" I breathed which caused Caleb to stiffen. He paused for some time before letting go of Ben and taking a step back.

"Leave" The Captain ordered and with a quick glance in my direction Ben disappeared from the room. I let go of Caleb and my arms fell to my sides as Nolan approached me. He placed his hand on my shoulder when Caleb turned to look at me.

"Are ye alright, lass?" I noticed the gems that were laying by my feet and slowly began to kneel to pick them up.

Rebecca offered to help and we managed to find all seven which we then dropped into the black pouch that I held in the palms of my hands.

"He didn't take it very well" I muttered. My eyes were dry but the sad gleam in them remained. Rebecca, who was knelt beside me noticed the look in my gaze and looked away.

"Give him some time" she said, catching my attention. She didn't look mad anymore instead she looked almost defeated much like Ben did. Nolan gazed down at my form and nodded.

"Something like this be bound to take a toll on a man" it was then that I realized she'd told him. He seemed to be handling it well in comparison to Ben and Rebecca. I looked and him and forced a smile. I sighed when I finally stood upright.

"I knew he would react badly, but I didn't expected him to-." pin me down. I thought the last part and let the sentence die out as Nolan wrapped his arm around my shoulders and brought me closer to him. He laughing like he always did in that same teasing manner of his.

"Ye best be waiting for us on the other side there, lass" I couldn't help but smile in response to his positive tone. I imagined a world beyond the dead where I would be waiting on some ship in the middle of an endless ocean. Expecting the day that they'd all join me so that we could sail through the underworld in search of new treasures or maps together.

"I'll be waiting"

Ben.

I fled below deck to where the bunk beds lined the walls and began pacing back and forth. My mind raced with thoughts of what I'd done.

Images of Evangeline being pinned underneath me flickered past my eyes. I could see the fear in her eyes and hear her voice pleading for me to stop. She'd yelled his name in her rush of fear. It wasn't me or Rebecca that she reached out to. It was Caleb.

I stopped pacing and ran a hand across my face when heavy boots came thudding down the stairs. I looked up and was met with a hand grabbing hold of my shirt's collar. I was shoved back into one of the bunk beds. My head slammed into the steel frame which caused my eyes to fill with black spots.

"If ye ever touch her like that again-." a threatening voice snarled and spit flew when my eyes began to adjust. I took in the sight of the man in front of me.

"I'll kill ye" Caleb loomed overhead. His eyes glowed golden in that dark room. His teeth were grit and the veins on his neck were protruding from his skin. I raised my hands on either side of me to show that I wasn't looking for a fight but he didn't seem to care.

"I didn't mean to hurt her" I tried to reason with him. I didn't know what came over me.

I cared about Eva and the thought of hurting her made me hate myself more than even the Captain could.

He searched my guilty features then shoved me back before letting go of me and taking a step back.

I grunted when my head hit the metal again and I slumped down onto the bottom bunk. My head hung and my hand touched at the back of it to check if there was any blood but there was none. I stared down at my fingertips and blinking to see if there was a crimson liquid staining them but they were dry.

"Know yer place, boy" I looked up at the man. His finger jabbed in my direction as my hand dropped in between my parted knees and I shook my head as an attempt to clear it. Caleb was ten years older than Evangeline and I.

"She loves you" I said causing him to stiffen and his arm to drop back down to his side. His Captain's hat cast a dark shadow over his eyes. The air between us grew thicker and the silence became almost suffocating.

"And you're about to let her die" my gaze filled with hatred when I raised my eyes to meet his. His lip twitched and his nostrils flared when he turned to fully face me. His hands balled as if he wished he could hit me.

"Don't ye think I know that?" my eyes widened in response to his words as if hearing him admit to what he was doing was the blow that made it all the more real. I felt anger surge inside of me.

How could he stand there, admit to his actions and not bat an eye when saying that he knew exactly what he was doing?

"You're one heartless bastard" I got out which only seemed to irritate him more. His eyes never left me, not even for a split second. His hands unclenched at his sides and his shoulders relaxed to an extent.

"If ye'd said that to me a year ago-." he paused and shifted his weight from one leg to the other which caused the metal on his boots to cluttering together.

"I would've agreed" his eyes moved to the wall behind me as if picturing Evangeline being seated there on some open shoreline with a smile on her and a simple white dress hugging her figure.

"But I do have a heart-." I tensed.

How could he even know what it felt like to have a heart? Was he even capable of experiencing any other emotions apart from anger, annoyance and hatred? What was he getting at by trying to pretend like he knew what it felt like to love someone?

"And her name is Evangeline" his words forced me to my feet. My hands shoved at his chest and my eyes glared at him in resentment. He hardly stumbled as he looked at me when I spat the words I'd been trying so desperately to hold back.

"Then why let her die? For your own selfish needs?" my hands gripped the fabric of his shirt and bunched it up until my knuckles turned white.

He was much bigger than I was with more muscular and could easily beat me to a pulp but in that moment, it was the last thing on my mind.

"Because it's what my heart wants-." There was a flicker of sadness in his eyes and I realized that if he could stop it from happening, he would've. If he could tell her to stay then he would but Evangeline wanted to go through with it. She was determined to be his sacrifice.

"And who am I to deny her?" my gaze searched him, his shirt, my hands, the wooden pillar behind him before I dropped my arms and started slowly backing away.

Was he not the monster I'd made him out to be? Could he actually feel for Eva like I did and if so, then what chance did I stand against him?

"Who are *we* to deny her that?" he repeated and it felt like a blow to the face. I slumped down on the bottom bunk bed and ran my hands through my hair as I listened to his footsteps retreating back above deck. He left me alone with my thoughts and realizations.

I was an idiot.

How could I ever think that he didn't love her? Who couldn't fall in love with her?

Chapter Forty-Seven.

I took a bath and soaked in the water. I felt it heal my bruised and torn flesh. The feel of the cold water caressing me made my worries fade away as my ears sank underneath its surface. I was able to hear the sound of distant waves crashing, tails swishing and whales singing.

My glowing eyes shot open to stare up at the ceiling that hung overhead as a thought crossed my mind.

I hoped the afterlife had an ocean that I could get lost in.

The necklace around my neck swayed along with the water whenever I moved and my scaled legs moved through the liquid as if it was a lover that I was brushing up against.

I stood in the tub and stepped over the side before I unplugged the drain that seeped into the sea before I used a towel to dry myself with.

The smell of cheap oils on my skin stung my nose in a way that made it feel more like home. It was a place I'd grown attached to over my time spent onboard the ship.

I dressed in the maroon coat Caleb bought and buttoned it up to hide my nude figure. The coat had long sleeves that fell over my hands since my arms were shorter than Caleb's. I traced the collar that dipped down low and my fingers followed the curve of my chest in between my breasts as I stared at my own reflection in the mirror.

I knew that Caleb had seen me naked numerous times before but he'd known exactly what I looked like even before he saw me because of his intimacy with Mary.

I could see the two of them tangled in the bed sheets. Her hands grasped for him as their bodies molded together. They were both covered in sweat and were burning hot but that type of intimacy was something I'd never known. It was something that I will never know apart from how Mary had felt in that moment.

I closed my eyes and felt her overwhelming love, her longing to stay there in that moment forever with the strong desire to feel him trace every inch of her body.

My hand dropped back to my side and eyes opened for the briefest of moment to lock eyes with the woman staring back at me. I reached for the bathroom door and headed back into the room.

Caleb was lying in bed. He wore an old pair of pants but his boots, shirt and jacket had been discarded onto the floor beside him with little care. The familiar sight of his torso covered in black ink met my gaze along with the low slung waistband of his trousers that exposed the V that dipped down into his pants.

I blew out the candle in the bathroom then began making my way towards the armchair in the corner of the room. I clutched the undone bandages in my hand.

Caleb sat up. His hand reached out to grab hold of my arm and gently brought me to a stop.

"Sit" he insisted and I couldn't refuse. I took a seat on the foot of the bed. He took the bandages from me and began to roll them up so that he could wrap them around my hands, wrist and neck again. I held my hand out to him with the palm facing up so that he could start bandaging it.

One of his legs were thrown over the side of the bed while the other was tucked away underneath him.

"What was it like?" I randomly questioned. I wanted to kick myself once I realized what I had asked. Caleb didn't bother stopping as he wound the bandage around my hand and wrist then tied it off at the end only to move on to the next. To him it was just a simple question but it made my heart beat faster and caused my cheeks to turn a shade or two pinker.

"What was what like?" I offered him my other hand. My eyes were locked onto the far wall as I tried to think of something else to say. I wanted to change the topic but there was nothing that came to mind and before I knew it, I spoke.

"Making love to her" he paused. His hands stilled but they soon began to move again. My own clutched the material of the bed sheets beneath me which he seemed to notice.

"So that's why ye've been avoiding the bed" the muscles in my back tensed and I felt my cheeks grow even hotter. The tops of my ears burned with embarrassment. I didn't think he noticed but he clearly did. I gently balled my hand once he was done wrapping it and turned so that my back was to him. I brushed my hair to one side and lifting it so that he could bandage my neck.

"I can feel what she felt but I-." I lowered my head. I was able to feel every touch, every friction that Mary felt in that very moment. I felt her emotions and her thoughts as if they were my own.

373

"I don't know what you felt" he finished tying off the bandage and moved back on the bed. I remained where I was. I was too afraid to look at him for fear of him noticing the red tint on my cheeks. He hummed.

"It felt like the right thing. It felt like two people that were meant to come together finally become one" he brushed it off and didn't give me very much to go by. I nodded while reaching for the hem of my coat. I gripped it as I got lost in the memory of that night, a memory that wasn't even mine. Caleb brushed my hair aside and leaned down to press a kiss to my neck.

"Ye're flustered. Why?" he watched me as he kept his lips pressed against my skin. He was able to see the tint in my skin and the uneasy movements such as my thighs rubbing together.

"I can feel your hands here-." I explained as my hand moved to trace the skin on my inner thigh. He looked down at my lap from over my shoulder. His expression was emotionless as he watched my hand move from my thigh to my left breast.

"And here" his hands supported his weight on the bed. The only parts of him that were actually touching me were his chin, lips and nose but I could feel him. I could feel his fingers roaming my body. I could feel every kiss along my jaw, cheek, neck and ear. I'd felt him touch me there before but never once in person. He only ever touched me like that in the memory but I always pushed it aside so that I could breathe without panting from his touch.

"Ye asked me before whether I loved ye or not" he began causing his lips to move against my skin and ignite sparks. I leaned back and threw my head onto his shoulder so that our faces were next to each other. My hands were either gripping the sheets or my own clothing. I'd asked him that question to know whether he loved me as much as he loved Mary but he didn't respond.

"I do" he turned his head to whisper those two words into my ear. They caused my eyes to widen and my lips to part when I shot upon straight. I turned to fully face him.

"I fell in love with the orphan girl from Port Alice" he was being serious. His lips were pressed together in a thin line and his eyes were hard. His chin was still covered in a layer of light stubble and his hair was tied up.

"Not because of how ye look but because of who ye are. Ye're never afraid to speak yer mind-." he reached out so that his hand could cup the side of my face as he sat up on his knees. He paused when his lips were just inches away from mine.

"Because ye're stubborn and annoying and reckless" my eyes stared at him in a mix of shock and confusion. I didn't think his attraction to me went anything beyond my looks or my connection with Mary but there he was confessing that it did.

My mind raced back to the night at the Bakewell manor when he told me exactly who I was then proceeded to kiss me. He had intended to kiss me, Evangeline not Mary. I was just too blind to notice.

"Caleb-." my words died in my throat when I noticed a figure seated behind him on the bed. It was the figure of a woman with blond curls and mismatched eyes. She was smiling sadly at me and nodded as if give me her permission.

I was about to continue speaking when she dissolved into thin air but I was cut off by Caleb who pressed his lips against mine. It was a sweet and gentle kiss that left me feeling vulnerable. I placed a hand against his chest and pushed him back into the mess of pillows as I fell on top of him.

I wanted to get lost in him. I wanted to drown in his embrace and feel him having all of me but I pulled away. I sat on top of him with my legs straddling his torso.

I was panting heavily and my face was flushed. Even though Mary gave me her permission, I just couldn't do it. I couldn't be with Caleb like that no matter how badly I wanted to. I couldn't do that to her.

He seemed to notice the discord in my eyes and reached up. He pulled me into a tight embrace and rolled onto his side so that I was lying beside him with my face buried into his chest. He held me there for what felt like forever before he spoke.

"Sing to me" I closed my eyes and listened to the sound of his thundering heartbeat. We laid there, surrounded by orange candle light and the sound of the sea outside. My lips parted and I began singing the first song that came to mind.

"*Cruel and fierce like the waves of the sea. Will you ever come seek me?*" he turned so that I held his head to my chest with my back pressed up against the pillows as I sang the tune that I'd heard a hundred times before.

"*Hear my song dance with the night. My love for you shall never die*" it was like a promise that I was making to him, a promise that even if I was to die that my love for him would continue to live and grow through Mary.

He had his arms wrapped around me as he tried to pull me closer and he buried his face in my chest. His breathing became shallow as he fell asleep.

We would reach Port Alice within a day or so and then I would die so I hardly slept that night. I sang song after song as I watched his face and studying its every detail as a way to engrave his face into my memory forever.

I didn't want to forget him. I didn't want to forget his face, his tattoos, words or sound of his voice. Not even death could keep me from thinking about him or remembering him.

"Over time and across the blue. I would give up my life for you" I sang while noticing the irony in those words that'd been written long ago. They were sung by sailors out on the open seas.

Night turned to day and minutes turned to hours that ticked by until Caleb began to stir against me. His eyes squeezing tighter shut before they opened and he blinked up at me attempting to see past the blinding light. He was about to speak when a voice from above deck called out.

"Land ho!" Caleb shot up from the bed. He tugged his clothes on and heading to the deck. I remained contemplating my death. I didn't think he knew what was coming and merely conformed to the duties of a Pirate Captain. His actions were a force of habit took over whenever a crew mate would yell those two words.

"Dock the ship!" he ordered as I got up from the bed and stretched out my stiff muscles from a night of barely moving. I'd stayed in the same position for fear of waking him.

I suddenly became very aware of what I was wearing and wonder if I wanted to die in it but then my eyes landed on his red Captain's coat that he forgot on the floor and I decided to wear that instead. I buttoned it up on my way above deck. My boots thudded against the steps as the familiar smell of Port Alice touched my nose.

To others it was like any other port town but to me there was something unique about it. Everyone's eyes turned to me once the ship was docked as if to see how I was reacting to the situation.

I stared at the shoreline and at the familiar rocks where I'd been seated the night the Sunken Soul sailed into the port.

I could see the orphanage and the tailor's shop where I'd worn that hideous emerald dress that Deacon forced me into but the place that caught my eye was the abandoned church on the top of the cliffs.

I knew that church both from my past and from the pages of the leather bound book. It would be my final resting place where I'd be sacrificed on a platform of stones with each one of the jewels embedded into the rocks around me.

"Evangeline-." Caleb began but I interrupted him. I knew that if I waited for him to continue that he might try to convince me not to go through with it.

"We head for the church ruins" Rebecca and Nolan remained silent and Ben stood a few feet away. He was too ashamed to speak. I began scaling down the side of the ship with the jewels tucked into the pocket of my coat.

I stepped onto the dock and looked up at the familiar faces that I'd come to befriend and love over the weeks that I'd spent with them. I raised the gems into the air and gave a brilliant smile.

"Mary's waiting" it felt like I was going to see my long lost sister for the first time. There was something inside of me that squeezed with a need to get to her as quickly as possible. I knew she'd be there waiting for me with open arms.

Caleb was the first to follow me as I walked in the direction of the church with Rebecca, Nolan and Ben trailing behind. I slowed my pace to match Ben's and bumped my shoulder into his. He looked at me. The guilt in his eyes was overwhelming.

"I'm not mad at you and I don't blame you" I said, referring to the night before. He'd most likely spent the night agonizing over how he'd pinned me down and questioned whether I hated him. We reached the top of the hill and I paused to face Ben with the gems cupped in the palms of my hands.

"You were just dealing with the shock of losing me in your own way" I reached out and placed my hand against his upper arm so that I could stand up on the tips of my toes and kiss his cheek. He was taken by surprise and stared down at me with large eyes when I lowered myself back onto the balls of my feet.

"Thank you for loving me" I whispered then stepped closer to the gaping doors of the abandoned church where Rebecca and Nolan were waiting. Caleb had already disappeared into the church.

"We're gonna miss ye, lassie" Nolan announced as he threw his arms around me and pulling me into a tight bear hug. He smelt of rum and smoke. I found it ironic that the same Pirate who cursed me when we first met was embracing me like a loving older brother.

"You better be there when I die" Rebecca commented with her arms crossed over her chest. She had a hard look in her eyes as an attempt to hide the tears that threatened to escape them. I pulled away from Nolan and hugged her. She wasn't expecting it but she returned the hug.

"Promise to tell Mary about me?" she had to grit her teeth when I pulled away. The question overwhelmed her to the point that she couldn't hide the tears any longer and had to turn her back to me.

"Don't say stupid stuff like that" she scolded to which I laughed and addressed Nolan. The Irishman looked at Rebecca in amusement.

"Take care of her for me" he turned his eyes onto me and gave a brilliant smile as he reached out to ruffle my hair. He nodded and agreed.

I left them and headed into the church to find Caleb. He was stood neat the small altar upon which I was supposed to die with his back to me. I walked past the empty pews and stopped beside him. My eyes fell onto the altar that had seven small stones placed around it. The jewels had to be embedded into them.

"It's time" I told him as I held the pouch out for him to take. He slowly took it while I stepped onto the altar and stood in the center of it while facing Caleb.

"Start with the red then the blue-." I instructed as I pointed at the stone directly in front of me. Rebecca, Nolan and Ben looked on from outside the church. They were too afraid to come any closer and they were too afraid to see me die.

"Yellow, green, black, purple, orange" I said the order to him which was the exact same order we'd collected the gems in. Once they were all placed into their individual rocks, Caleb took a step back to look at me. The jewels began to glow brightly. Each of them glowed their own color and drowned me in a rainbow of assorted shades.

The time had come. I was ready to die.

I wasn't scared or heartbroken like I thought I would be, instead I was excited to meet Mary and give Caleb the thing he'd fought so hard for.

He retrieved a dagger from his belt and stepped onto the platform in front of me. I could tell that he was trembling with the thought of having to slit the throat of a woman that he loved especially after having confessed his feelings to me.

"Can I ask you a favor?" I asked to which he paused. His hand tightened around the hilt of the dagger with a desire to erupt but he stayed silent. I leaned towards him with my hand gripping his shoulder and pressed my lips to his ear.

"Tell Mary that she's lucky to have met a man like you" that was his breaking point. It was the peak at which Caleb's eyes began to leak tears that dropped on the concrete platform below.

I could tell that he didn't want to do it, that he wasn't planning on sacrificing me and wanted more than anything to toss the dagger aside. He wanted to drag me away from the church and hold me for as long as he possibly could but I had to go through with it. Something had brought me there for a reason and I had to find out just what that reason was.

I reached for his hand that was holding the dagger and positioned it at my throat. I met Caleb's eyes with a reassuring smile on my lips. His hand shook but it stayed in place when I let go of it.

"I love you" I breathed and closed my eyes when a stinging pain coursed through me. I fell to my knees on the altar and my hands gripped the sides of my head as the dagger cluttered to the floor beside me. *He hadn't used it so why was I in so much pain? What was causing it?* Caleb knelt in front of me as he grabbed my shoulders.

"Evangeline!" Caleb cried out and Rebecca rushed over along with Ben and Nolan to see what happened.

There was no blood but I was screaming as my heart pounded with a pain so striking that it blocked out any further noise. I couldn't hear them speaking to me or even each other. All I heard was a constant ringing and a high pitched squeal.

My mouth gaped. I couldn't close it due to the muscles in my jaw tightening. Saliva began to pool from the corners of my mouth and my vision started to blur until the image of Caleb's worried face turned into something else entirely.

I was drifting in the middle of the ocean. My eyes were looking at Mary's figure as she aimlessly drifted through the water towards the seabed. It was the memory of her drowning.

She would reach for the surface where Caleb was desperately calling out to her and a voice from the water would say in a language we somehow understood.

'A heart of the sea'

A woman with a body made from water, glowing blue eyes and a tail that swished back and forth behind her would appear in front of Mary to finish her sentence in a haunting tone.

'Return to me' then the Nymph would place a kiss to Mary's lips and a bright light would engulf them before the image faded but this time, I saw a scene that I'd yet to see.

The Nymph dove down into the darkened depths and disappeared as Mary's blond curls began to turn white and her legs morphed into a single tail that was decorated with silver scales.

She was carried along by the current. Her dress was ripped from her body and gills started forming on her neck to allow her to breathe. She floated for what seemed like days before she washed up onto a familiar beach where I stood watching her cough violently. She was a Mermaid. Her fingers dug into the sand. Her pupils were slit and her eyes glowed brighter in the dark of night.

It was a beach in Port Alice, the one that'd called out to me the night I met Caleb.

A woman who was dressed in a black cloak with empty white eyes stepped towards the Mermaid and stopped directly in front of her. The Witch's red lips parted as she spoke,

'With this you will abandon your human self and take a new identity as a heart of the sea' my anchor necklace dropped down from the tip of her index finger. It dangled in front of the Mermaid's face, tempting her to take it and when she did thunder struck in the sky above.

'Your memories will be replaced and you will become Evangeline' I froze. The world around me came crumbling down until I was stood in a black room with no doors or windows. The realization stared me in the face.

I wasn't Mary's reincarnation and I wasn't related to her in any way. The reason why her memories and emotions felt so real as if they were my own was because they were my own.

I was Mary Sillvan. I was the woman who Caleb fell in love with and thought had drowned two years prior. I was the woman he was trying to resurrect.

My memories had been replaced with false ones of the orphanage. My memories of growing up with other orphaned children had all been a lie. I gripped the sides of my head and squeezed my eyes shut.

But why? Why would that Witch erase my memories?

The same five words kept playing over and over again in the back of my mind like a haunting melody. The same angelic voice that belonged to the sea Nymph sang out around me. It repeated.

'A heart of the sea'

Epilogue
Caleb

Her eyes rolled back into her skull and her hands were clawing at the sides of her head as if she was in excruciating pain.

I called out to her but she didn't respond. I shook her shoulders but she didn't seem to notice that I was there until she suddenly went still. Her eyes stared directly at me as her arms went limp and her hands slipped away from her head to dangle beneath her.

Her mismatched eyes suddenly became empty and the life completely drained from them as she fell forward. I rushed to catch her.

"Evangeline!" I yelled while I cradled her body in my arms and pressed her to my chest. She felt so cold and lifeless that I couldn't help but weep at the thought of losing her.

The sky above the church grew ever dark and the clouds become a gloomy gray as a single crack of thunder sounded. It struck down onto the open ocean. I looked at the stained glass window that'd been shattered and beyond it to where the thunder had struck. I noticed that a woman was stood in front of the window that hadn't been there before.

She wore a black cloak with the hood pulled up and her hair was darker than a raven's wings. Her empty white eyes stared at Evangeline. Time stopped. The thunder froze in the sky as Rebecca, Nolan and Ben went quiet as if they were stuck in time.

The woman approached me and the body that I so desperately clung to.

"Finally-." she muttered. Her crimson lips moved as she spoke in a voice that sounded almost haunting. She stopped directly in front of the altar and her pale white hands brushed back the hood of her cloak to reveal a black crescent moon marking in the center of her forehead.

"It would seem that the seal over her memories has been broken" I was lost. I had no idea what she was talking about. She stepped onto the platform and knelt in front of me causing me to tighten my hold on Evangeline. I was ready to fight to keep her there with me despite the woman being a Witch that could easily kill me. I feared nothing when it came to the Mermaid. I would face the end of the world if it meant staying by her side.

"Oh, Mary" she said as she reached out to brush the back of her fingers along Evangeline's pale cheek. Her face was paler than usual. The places where the Witch's fingers touched began to fill with life. She turned her white eyes onto me and let them bore into my soul.

"Neptune will not approve of her remembering her human life" she warned while standing. The material of her cloak resembled black smoke that danced around her.

Mary? Remembering? Human life?

I had so many questions but I knew that she wouldn't answer even if I asked.

"Protect her. The worst is yet to come" with that she turned on her heels and started heading in the direction that she'd come from. She moved towards the window with her heels crunching into the pieces of broke glass that was scattered across the floor.

"Wait!" I called out after her. She paused as the echo of my voice swirled around us and she turned to glance back at me from over her shoulder.

"You will have the answers you seek in due time" with that the lightning struck again and I had to squeeze my eyes shut against the bright light that filled the ruins. When the light faded the Witch was gone.

Rebecca and Nolan were bickering again as Ben tried to reach the altar but the gems wouldn't allow anyone else through. Their rainbow light stung anyone that dared to venture too close to the altar.

The Witch was even more powerful than Briony. The Witch I'd met at the Pirate's Nest. The black haired woman's aura was beyond that of comprehension. She radiated power and when she spoke her voice would drown you in its authority.

I could feel Evangeline grow warmer as the color returned to her cheeks when I looked down at her. Her chest rose and fell again with shallow breaths.

"Eva?" Ben called out to her. He was desperate and worried as he tried to reach through the barrier only to have it burn him. Blisters began to form on his hand causing him to cry out in pain. He clutched the wrist of his injured hand to try and cut off the pain but it was no use.

"The lass is breathing" Nolan informed while motioning to Evangeline. The announcement caused both Ben and Rebecca to calm down. The redhead sighed in relief then snapped at Ben for burning his hand.

I couldn't speak, I couldn't move as I waited for Evangeline to wake up. My eyes never looked away from her for fear that if I did that she'd stop breathing. It felt like forever before I decided to pick her up and carry her out of the circle that'd been created by the gems. Their light disappeared but the jewels were left behind. I looked at Nolan.

"Gather the treasures" he nodded and reached for the pouch that I'd been left abandoned on the church floor so that he could start gathering the gems.

"Aye, Captain" he spoke, reminding me of my title and rank. Rebecca poured some water from her canteen onto Ben's hand as the boy trembling in pain. Evangeline's head rested on my shoulder. Her arms were in her lap and her lips were parted to fill her lungs with air. She looked so peaceful as if she was sleeping.

"Sure, interrupt a powerful Witch's spell by sticking your hand through beams of light-." Rebecca was muttering. She was annoyed and irritated with Ben's stupidity. The sight of her worrying about his hand was so typical of her since she'd always been a mother figure to those around her, including myself.

"What could possibly go wrong?" she was being sarcastic as she worked. She avoided wrapping his hand in anything for fear of the blisters sticking to the material and the skin being torn off.

Nolan appeared at my side. He held the black bag up for me to see and gave it a shake so that the jewels cluttered against each other. I nodded then proceeded to make my way back to the ship with the rest of them trailing behind.

Evangeline

I woke up in the Captain's quarters. My eyes blinked up at the floorboards above. The white bed sheets covered my body and a figure was seated in a chair beside the bed. Ben had his hands clutched together with his elbows propped up onto his knees and his forehead was pressed to his fists. His eyes were tired as they stared at the floor.

Rebecca came down the stairs with a trey of food that was meant for Ben but she froze when she noticed that I was looking at him with drooped eyes.

"Evangeline-." she managed to get out, catching Ben's attention. He looked at her. Dark circles surrounded his usually bright and cheerful brown eyes that looked like they hadn't known sleep for days.

When he realized that she wasn't looking at him but instead she was staring at me, his head turned to take in my frail form. His eyes widened when he noticed that I was awake.

"Call the others" Ben insisted to which Rebecca abandoned the tray of food on the desk and rushed above deck while gripping the fabric of her skirts to prevent herself from tripping over them in her haste. Ben reached for the hand that was closest to him and held it in both of his. I noticed that one was bandaged much like mine were.

"How're you feeling?" he asked. The concern in his eyes showed. I tried curling my fingers around his but I didn't have the strength to move let alone to properly hold his hand. I could barely turn my head or open my mouth to speak.

Caleb and Nolan came rushing down the stair. They asked the same question as Rebecca followed them with a second tray of food that was most likely meant for me. I tried reaching for Caleb but I was too weak and unable to properly move my fingertips.

"I-I'm-." my voice was raspy. It sounded like I didn't have anything to drink for weeks. I coughed when the scratching in my throat grew worse when I attempted to speak. Rebecca hurried over with a cup of water. She used one arm to gently ease me upright while her free hand pressed the cup to my lips.

"Drink" she insisted and I did as I was told. I swallowed large gulps of the liquid and felt it cool my throat. Ben helped position the pillows behind me so that I sat more upright and was able to drink and eat since I was too weak to keep myself in any upright position.

"I'm fine. Thank you" I said. My voice was small. Rebecca nodded and placed the cup on the bedside table to fluff up some of the pillows.

She retrieved the tray of food that had a piece of dried bread and a broth mix of meat and vegetables on top of it. It was what we always ate as pirates.

Becca sat down in the chair Ben was seated and pulled it closer to the side of the bed. She then took the bowl in one hand and a spoon in the other. She blew on the broth like a mother would for fear of her child burning their tongue.

"You must be starving" she insisted and for the first time I felt a great hunger overcome me. I nodded as best I could and opened my mouth when she held the spoon out to me. I chewed slowly then swallowed.

"Aye, of course she is. She's been sleeping for seven days" Nolan shot back at Rebecca who sneered at him as she scooped more of the broth up with the spoon before she offered it to me. I glanced around at the familiar faces surrounding me. Each of them were tired and filled with concern. I remained silent as I ate and wondered just how many nights, they spent awake, gathered around the bed and waiting for me to finally wake up.

Did they take turns to watch me? Had they fallen into a constant routine of never leaving me alone for fear that if they did, I'd never wake up?

I could only imagine how they felt while I was trapped inside that black and empty room with the voice of the Nymph constantly yelling the same words over and over again.

'A heart of the sea!' even with the constant repetition I still didn't know what those words meant. I didn't understand what she was trying to tell me.

They took turns watching over me, feeding me and helping me to the bathroom but even so I didn't speak a single word for at least another day. When they tried to talk to me, I'd turn around and fall asleep.

I wasn't angry or mad at them. I was just confused and had to process what I'd seen inside my dreams and thoughts.

The reality of who I was, was like a slap in the face that I'd to treat before I could tell them who I really was. Late at night when Nolan sat beside the bed on the floor with his head thrown back as he snored loudly, I would lie awake. I'd stare up at the ceiling as I processed my thoughts.

This went on for another two days. My mute state and confusion never once seemed to want to let go of me even when I sat on the ship's deck in a chair while staring at Port Alice.

I never spoke or acknowledged those around me, at least not until the third day when Rebecca was dressing me in a simple cream gown that Caleb had bought for me to make it easier for me to move and get changed.

"We'll set sail soon-." Rebecca randomly said while she worked. She would talk to me whenever she was in my company. It was like she was trying to get me to respond to her and on that day I did.

"Gather everyone" her head shot up and her eyes widened in response to the sound of my voice. It was a sound that she hadn't heard for a long time and that made her tear up. She helped me onto the bed then headed above deck to call the rest of them down into the Captain's quarters.

I closed my eyes and leaned back into the pillows. The white sheets were draped across my bare legs as I thought about how I would tell them.

They could all take it differently but I hoped that they wouldn't view me in any other way than they did before. Rebecca returned with the three men in tow and they all sat around the bed. Ben sat on the floor, Rebecca in the chair, Caleb on the foot of the bed and Nolan leaned against the wall closest to me.

My eyes opened to take in the sight of their worried faces. Each one was riddled with fear and concern. I felt guilty for making them worry.

I tried to stand. I was able to toss my legs over the side of the bed and lift my own weight for the first time in what felt like an eternity. My lips parted,

"I am Mary Grace Sillvan. I am the only daughter of Lady Bethany Sillvan and Lord Jarrett Sillvan. I am the sole heir to the Sillvan bloodline" I announced as my eyes lock onto Caleb's then they moved to Becca's furrowed brow gaze. I could tell that Nolan was about to say something along the lines of 'The lass has gone mad' but I didn't give him the chance to speak.

"I apologize for worrying" I bowed with my hands clutched together in my lap and my torso slightly bent. My head was turned down and my ivory hair dangled like a curtain around my face.

When I stood upright, Rebecca's eyes narrowed and she seemed to realize that something was wrong. The manner in which I was speaking belonged to Mary yet I looked like Evangeline. I still looked like the Mermaid and orphan girl from Port Alice.

"I didn't die that night on the water but instead I was reawakened as a Mermaid and had my memories taken from me. A Witch replaced them with the false identity of Evangeline" Ben looked to be the most upset about finding out that Evangeline was just a false version of me. I couldn't stand any longer and dropped onto the edge of the bed. Rebecca shot up to help me but I raised my hand as a sign to show that I was fine.

"I don't know why my memories were sealed away but I now know that they were trying to reach out to me ever since I met Caleb as Evangeline" everyone went silent. All of them were trapped in their own thoughts apart from Nolan who merely shrugged his shoulders and pushed off the wall. He took a few steps closer to me.

"Mary or Evangeline, ye're still ye and that's all that matters, lass" I felt like crying as I looked up at the Irishman. The memory of him pulling me into a tight bear hug at the church entrance replayed in the back of my mind. Rebecca was stunned and her eyes went wide when the realization struck her.

"Mary?" she tentatively questioned and I could only smile at her. It was a weak smile that barely reached my eyes but it was a smile none the less. My mother raised me to always be kind and to look past the bad in people towards the good.

"Please Becca, call me Evangeline" the sound of her nickname that she insisted I use caused her entire body to stiffen. It was as though in that moment she knew that I was both Mary and Evangeline.

She pulled me into a tight hug and I held onto her. Once she let go, I noticed that Ben was trapped in his own world on the floor near my feet.

"Ben" I breathed and threw my body towards him to wrap my arms around his shoulders as I buried my face into his chest. He stiffened at the sudden contact.

"I'm still Evangeline" I told him. He raised his arms to return the hug. He held me tightly to him while his injured hand grabbed onto the material of my cream dress as he hid his face in my hair.

"Eva" I pulled away to find that both Rebecca and Ben had unshed tears in their eyes to which Nolan decided to tease them. Becca snapped at him but Ben was too lost in my facial features to even notice. He eventually began laughing at the bickering couple behind him and shook his head. Ben stood and scooped me into his arms.

"Up you go" I squealed. My hands grabbed onto him for fear of him dropping me. Ben placed me on the mattress and tugged the sheets back up to my thighs before he reached out to tuck a stray strand of hair behind my ear.

"Get some rest" he insisted then he began to usher Rebecca and Nolan out of the room. Ben glanced in Caleb's direction and gave a nod. I watched them go, unable to help the small smile that crept onto my lips.

I was glad that they weren't mad or felt like they had to treat me any differently.

"Caleb" I called out to him. My voice drew his eyes away from the door and onto me. I removed the sheets from my body and crawled towards him. I sat on his lap with my legs on either side and my hands caressing the sides of his face.

He froze beneath me as his eyes locked onto my tired ones. I didn't want it to be sexual. I just didn't want to be apart from him anymore.

"It looks like both of us fell in love with the same person twice" I noted. I was referring to him falling in love with Evangeline and Evangeline falling in love with him.

He looked as though he'd seen a ghost and I couldn't help but breathe a laugh as I shoved his chest causing him to fall back onto the mattress with me seated on top of him. My hands traced his torso.

"It feels like I haven't been able to touch you in so long" I muttered more to myself than to him while savoring the feel of his body beneath his clothes. His eyes followed mine as they dropped down to his shirt, his coat and finally returned to his breath-taking golden eyes.

"Mary-." he reached out to touch my cheek and I leaned into his touch. My mismatched eyes closed to savor the feel of his caress.

"Evangeline" they shot open at use of both names moments before he pulled me into a loving embrace. He held me close and I was able to hear his heartbeat ringing in my ears as I listened to it beating in his chest.

It felt like our story could end there with the two of us together and relishing in each other's company.

But what of the jewels? What about the voice that repeatedly screamed the words 'A heart of a sea' in the back of my mind? What about the warning the whale gave me? What about my mother and father in Port Knot?

My eyes shot open when I realized something. The memory of them telling me to stay away from Caleb surfaced in my mind. My mother had warned me because she knew of them, of Darkheart and the power that a pirate had over a woman's heart.

I shut my eyes again and pressed myself closer to Caleb.

If there was one thing that I knew for certain it was that fate had brought us together and that we weren't going to drift apart again. No matter what hardships lay ahead. I knew that nothing could ever come between us.

A MERMAID'S HEART

The second book in the series.

Prologue

We fell asleep sometime later after Caleb stripped out of most of his clothes apart from his trousers. I still wore the cream colored dress that he'd bought me. We were curled up under the covers with my head resting on his chest and his arms wrapped protectively around me.

I woke up to the sound of thunder rumbling overhead along with the raging winds which caused the water to strike the side of the ship, rocking it. This made the wood groan under the pressure.

I sat up causing the sheets to fall into my lap as I looked at the stairs that led to the deck. The door to the Captain's quarters was locked. I could hear the sea weeping. It sobbed as rain pelted down onto it and the ship.

Something was calling out to me. It was a desperate high-pitched sound that resembled that of a whale's song.

I threw my legs over the side of the bed and moved through the darkness towards the door that was illuminated every now by a flash of lightning in the sky above.

There was something so agonizing and tormented about the call.

My hand reached out for the key to unlock the door and I allowed it to burst open. The wind caused it to loudly bang against the wall. I raised my arms to shield my eyes from the harsh winds and pelting rain as I peered out across the deck with squinted eyes. I wanted to try and find the source of the cry.

A figure was stood in the center of the deck, facing me with milky white skin that made her long blue hair stand out against its ivory color. The hair hung over her naked breasts and down to her rear. Her fingers were webbed and a goblin shark tail swung back and forth behind her as her eyes glowed a bright blue. They stared at me in desperation. Her cold blue lips parted to reveal fangs as a screeching sound similar to that of groaning metal reached my ears.

My arms lowered down to my sides as the storm faded to the back of my mind. I was hardly bothered by it when I began walking towards her. Each step followed another as if she was controlling me.

Water flooded the deck and washed over my bare feet as the sky drenched my hair and clothes in its endless downpour of tears.

She looked so familiar. Her hands were clawing at something around her waist and throat that I couldn't see until I was stood directly in front of her. She was covered in rusty chains that kept her rooted in place. She was unable to get to me even though she reached out her hand with a desperate need to touch me. I could feel her need, her fear and pain that radiated through me like a ripple through still water.

She raised both of her hands to stare at her palms where the chains were wound. She hissed at them in disdain and wanted them gone. She was panting. Her chest rapidly rose and fell. Her legs and arms were covered in cuts and bruises as if she'd fought a battle that's almost killed her.

I met her eyes. They were so recognizable when I peered into them. My breath caught when the realization washed over me. She was the Nymph that transformed me into a Mermaid the night I tried to drown myself.

'H-Help me!' a voice yelled in my mind. The voice didn't belong to me but I knew it was the same voice that'd yelled those same five words at me for days on end.

'A Heart of the Sea!'

I raised a hand and reached out to touch her cheek. I traced the places where her porcelain skin was cut. At the contact of my flesh against hers the chains shattered into pieces and dissolved into the water at our feet as if they'd been made of seafoam.

She collapsed onto her knees in front of me and her hands clawed at the deck as she gasped for air like a pressure had been lifted off her. Standing, she was taller than me. She was almost Caleb's height but in that moment; I towered over her, watching her in both awe and fascination as the gills on the sides of her neck began to fade into her skin but the rest of her remained the same. Her tail and the webbing on her hands and feet. Even her navy blue hair stayed the same.

The glow in her eyes began to dim when lightning illuminated her hunched and naked form. Her blue gaze looked up at me with parted lips that exposed her fangs.

"Tha-nk you" she said out loud. Her voice was raspy and almost uncomprehend able as if it was her first time using it in decades. A loud rumble of thunder snapped me out of my daze to find that we were both soaked to the bone. The biting winds were causing us to shiver despite our higher tolerance of the cold.

My gaze landed on the double doors to the navigation room that rattled in the storm. I bent to grab onto each of her hands causing her to look at me in confusion.

"We have to hurry" I declared then pulled her onto her feet. She stumbled and struggled to walk properly. Every step nearly resulted in her tumbling onto the deck. I led her towards the doors, opened them and hurried inside. I quickly closed them behind us.

The second the doors clicked shut, it was like the storm had been locked out. Everything became silent and the storm faded into the background.

I stood with my forehead pressed against the doors with my hands still clutching the handles. The Nymph was placed in the middle of the room. Her eyes scanned the various maps, the furniture and the doorway that led to the small kitchen area where Ben normally prepared our food.

I began lighting candles and used the matches that were on top of the table. An orange light welcomed us inside and gave off some warmth against the biting frost. I shook the last match which caused it to go out in the kitchen's doorway before I began opening cabinets in search of bandages or wine, anything that I could use to clean her wounds with.

She watched me with curious, wide eyes while I surveyed the cabinets but found nothing other than a knife. I headed to the closet on the opposite side of the room and opening it to find a few coats and blankets. I grabbed the first articles of clothing that my eyes landed on and approached her.

"Sit" I instructed. I had to pull on her arm to get her to have a seat in one of the chairs so that I could tug one of the coats onto her thin form. Her figure was a stark contrast to my shorter and curvier shape. I had to help her stick her arms into either of the sleeves then I had to wrap a blanket around her for fear of her freezing to death.

She looked at me like fisherman would look at a newly discovered and rare fish they'd just caught. The curiosity and bewilderment shone through.

I stripped out of my dress, tossing it to the side while her eyes studied me. I then tugged a second coat onto my form. I rolled up one of the sleeves before I reached for the knife that I placed on the table. I pressed it into my palm then cut it. The blade tore through the bandages and stiches to create a new gash that instantly started bleeding.

I held my palm out to her and she examined it at first. She was unsure about whether it was alright until I nodded my head and gave her my permission. She clamped onto my arm and hand with both of hers and pressed my palm to her lips. She sucked on the wound and her tongue lapped at it which caused the crimson liquid to trickle down her chin.

Her wounds began closing and they barely left a scar behind. I pulled my hand back and tore some of the fabric from the blanket that she was wrapped in to tie it around my palm. I abandoned the knife on the table and rolled the sleeve of my coat back down. I made sure to button it up all the way instead of leaving it hanging open like I had.

'You remember' her voice announced when she studied me. She didn't move beneath the blanket and coat. For a moment I wasn't sure whether she was referring to my memories as Mary or me having remembered her from my dreams and experiences but then when I looked at her, I could tell that she wasn't talking about herself.

"I do" I agreed with a nod as I tore my eyes away from her. I gazed down at the floor while one hand rubbed the wrist of my injured one. Despite not being human, I knew that Nymphs, much like Mermaids couldn't heal themselves. It was the only thing that I knew about her kind.

"Why are you here?" I questioned as my eyes turned to look at her. I had a serious expression written across my features. If she was there, it could only mean that something bad was about to happen. Her big blue eyes blinked up at me as if she was trying to process my words then she replied through her thoughts.

'The sea is in discord-.' my head shot up and my eyes widened while I listened to the sound of the waves crashing against the side of the ship. It never crossed my mind that the ocean was weeping that night until she spoke those words.

'Neptune is enraged because your memories have been restored' his name sent chills down the back of my spine. He was the god of the seven seas. He was a being more powerful than any other and I'd angered him so much that the ocean began to wail in agony.

'We've been trying to get you to remember for some time now' my mind raced back to Gigas who'd spoken those same five words 'A heart *of the sea'*, to the whale bull that had repeated them, to my dreams where the people in them tried to convey the word and to her voice yelling them in the back of my mind.

Was it her all along? Was she trying to get me to remember who I really was? And if so, why?

'*However, Neptune received word of this and imprisoned me in order to prevent me from seeking you out*' the chains that were curled around her hands, wrists, arms, torso, neck and legs surfaced in my mind's eye. Their rusty and old texture made it seem like she was locked away for years. During that time she was only able to speak to me through the help of others or her telepathy.

'*When your memories were restored, I saw my chance to escape but not without great difficulty*' she looked at her hands

'*He will come for you, for us. We are his Hearts of the sea*' her warning was pushed to the side by a question that consumed my thoughts for some time. I took a step in her direction and my hands balled at my sides from a mix of frustration and desperation.

"What does that mean? A Heart of the sea?" her hands fell into her lap. The blanket bunched on the floor by her. Her head tilted to the side as she watched me. The coat that she wore fell to one side and exposed the crevasse between her small breasts.

'*You do not know?*' the amazement in her tone took me by surprise.

Should I have known? Had I possibly missed something among the visions, dreams and memories?

Her tail whipped behind her. It lashed out like a predator as it swung back and forth from underneath the material of her coat.

'*All deities that reside in the water were once human, born with what is known as a Heart of the sea that. Only once they enter the ocean can they be awakened-.*' she looked like she wanted to move or reach out to me but she also seemed uncomfortable as if the clothing and the less dense air were irritating her.

She wasn't able to properly walk which meant that she hasn't been on land for many years.

'*It is then that Aurella would seal off their human memories and replace them with a new identity*' Aurella? The Witch? The woman from my memory who stood in front of me on the beach in Port Alice and offered me my anchor necklace appeared for a split second before she was gone like the image had been snuffed out.

"But why seal their memories?" I found myself asking. If my memories were never sealed then I would've gone after Caleb. I wouldn't have been riddled with confusion and created something of a complex from thinking that Mary and Evangeline were two separate people. In my mind they still were to some extent. The Mermaid and the noble girl.

'Humans spend their lives living and creating memories on land. It is not within their nature to remain in the water thus they eventually return to the land and abandon the sea' the way she spoke was so formal. It was so up front and she didn't care about how I would react to anything she said. It was so, inhuman.

'Neptune desired to prevent this and found a way to do so by sealing away their memories from when they were human. This is what resulted in them remaining in the sea, until-.' she paused as her eyes drooped like she was saddened by something. There was still emotion inside of her despite being further away from human than I could ever be.

'Until one of his Hearts remembered their human self' she wasn't referring to me but instead of another 'Heart' who regained their human memories some time before I managed to restore mine.

'She tried to return to the land where her family and loved ones mourned her drowning but-.' The pain that radiated from her wasn't normal for someone talking about another person who they didn't really know.

She was talking about herself, about her past and what she'd done to bring us to where we were in that very moment.

'Neptune caught up with her and completely destroyed whatever memories she had left. He also destroyed some of the humanity that went along with them' the breath caught in my throat. The thought of my memories being completely stripped from my mind was enough to make my blood run cold. I'd just found Caleb again, I just regained everything I'd lost and yet there was a chance that a god would try and destroy it all like he'd done to her.

'I sought out Aurella shortly after that part of me was destroyed-.' she was no longer referring to herself in the third person but instead spoke openly about her story, her pain and grief. It told me that she wasn't trying to hide her shame or her sadness anymore but took it as being a part of her.

'She was tricked into being his witch many centuries before and desired to be set free from his grasp' the woman from my memories, the

Witch in the ebony cloak with black hair and empty white eyes was hundreds of years old. She was able to live forever because of the magic that ran through her veins. Her magic dated back to the beginning of time when the earth chose the first god.

'Together we plotted to put an end to his cruel ways through the help of one of his Hearts' when she locked eyes with me, I knew that I was the Heart that she was referring to. I knew that I played an important role in her tale.

'Aurella would do her duty as Neptune's sealer by sealing away their memories but she would gift them the ability to walk on land. It was a simple spell that would cut the barrier separating the Hearts from the human world' my hand shot up to grab hold of the anchor that dangled from my throat by a thin, silver chain.

'And then when the time was right, she would pass the book of treasures onto a fellow Witch with simple instructions that she had to convey to Caleb Campbell-.' it felt like my heart was being forced out of my chest, like everything inside of me was being crushed by some unseen force as she spoke.

The Witch from the Pirate's Nest came to mind. The one with green dreadlocks that lived in a purple tent.

'That his journey would begin in Port Alice where Aurella compelled you to approach the sea on the night of your meeting with the hopes that you would one day regain your memories' the color drained from my face. What I once thought was fate was simply a Witch's spell that dragged me to the water that night. It was all part of some plan, as if I was a puppet on a string. I was enraged that someone would toy with me like that. My hands began to tremble and the Nymph noticed this.

'You have every right to be furious, however all of this is much bigger than you or I. There are thousands of Hearts who live with false identities. They are unable to remember who they love or who they once were-.' it was true. She could never regain her own memories but she could save the thoughts and emotions of thousands of others. She had to make a choice between toying with one person or letting hundreds of other live in constant longing and pain. It really wasn't a difficult choice to make. I would've done the same.

'Therefor I am here to ask for your help in putting an end to Neptune's tyranny' her request was formal and it was followed by her attempting to stand. She fell back into the chair due to her feet still unable to hold up her weight. Her battered and bruised body, her agonizing cries for help and the chains that confided her for so long. It all of it came to the forefront of my mind.

'Please, Mary' my previous name coming from her was like the desperate plea of a small child that made my heart want to help.

"My name's Evangeline" I corrected her. My words were cold and deprived of all emotion. I wondered momentarily if it was something that I'd picked up from Caleb after having spent so much time with him. Her eyes lowered to the floor and sadness swirled in their striking blue depths.

'I had a name of my own once, although it could be any name for all I know' her sentence cut deep and caused her suffering to shine through. I moved towards her causing her to look up at me with furrowed eyebrows or rather it was an expression that resembled confusion.

"Blue. Your name is Blue" I declared to which her eyes widened. She was just a young woman who once had a life of her own to live. It was a life filled with love and her hopes and dreams but all of that was taken away from her. It was stolen by a righteous figure that dared call himself a god. He was meant to be a symbol of love and compassion.

"I'll help you, but I'm afraid I have no idea how" there was gratitude and hope in her eyes for the first time in many years as she gazed up at me. A smile formed on her lips though it didn't quite reach her eyes not because she wasn't happy but because she was unable to smile. She wasn't aware of what happiness or joy felt like. I made a vow to myself that night, that I would help save as many memories as I possibly could regardless of myself.

I had everything that I could possibly want. I had friends, a man who loved me, a place to call home and parents who long thought me dead but there were so many Hearts within the waves of the sea that didn't know of any of that. They didn't know about love, about compassion, kindness or joy.

All they knew was to do the bidding of a being who sat at the core of their memories and kept them locked away in a box that only he could open.

About the Author:

Shané van der Walt was born and raised in South Africa. She's an aspiring author with a passion for the English language. Ever since she can remember she's created fantasy worlds inside her head to escape from reality. That is her main goal when it comes to writing; to create worlds were people can escape to.

Printed in Great Britain
by Amazon